TELL SHOOTING THE APPLE FROM THE HEAD OF HIS OWN CHILD.

WILLIAM TELL
THE HERO OF
SWITZERLAND

T. PAINE, PUBLISHER, HOLYWELL STREET, STRAND.

WILLIAM TELL,

THE HERO OF SWITZERLAND.

AN HISTORICAL ROMANCE.

LONDON:

T. PAINE, PUBLISHER, 20, HOLYWELL STREET, STRAND.

WILLIAM TELL,

THE HERO OF SWITZERLAND.

AN HISTORICAL ROMANCE OF THE FOURTEENTH CENTURY.

CHAPTER I.

A STORM—AN ESCAPE.

> " Far along,
> From peak to peak, the rattling crags among
> Leaps the live thunder! Not from one lone cloud,
> But every mountain now hath found a tongue;
> And Jura answers, through her misty shroud,
> Back to the joyous Alps, who call to her aloud ! "

ON the 20th of September, in the year of our Lord, 1307, a party of fishermen, natives of the Canton of Uri, in Switzerland, were assembled on the banks of the Lake Lucerne. Their boats were hauled up on the beach for safety, and they were anxiously awaiting the arrival of one of their comrades, whose fragile bark, still at some distance from the shore, was impelled, with all the force of the sinewy arms of its crew, towards the spot on which the anxious group were standing. As yet the sun had not performed a third part of his downward course in the sky; but the aspect of nature plainly told the experienced eyes of the mountaineers that the winds of heaven, like greyhounds in the slip, were about to be loosened from the bonds that controlled their fury. A crackling sound run through the glaciers. The summit of the lofty Mytenstein was enveloped in mist, while sudden gusts swept over the surface of the lake, as a prelude to the coming storm. The birds and beasts of the field seemed aware of the approaching conflict of the elements; the sheep greedily cropped the pasturage, the fish gambolled in the lake, and the water-fowl gave evidence of their excited state by their increased activity.

The boats were, at length, safely moored beyond the reach of the waves, and their owners about to seek for shelter under the cover of their rude huts, when the attention of the anxious group was attracted by the hurried approach of a herdsman. His face covered with blood, still flowing in crimson streams down his pallid cheeks, his haggard eye, and tottering steps, plainly told the urgent nature of the cause of his sudden apparition; in the agony of despair he clutched the shoulder of the sturdiest of the group, and besought him, in the name of heaven, to launch his boat and convey him to the opposite shore of Schweitz.

Conrad (for such was the name of the party thus invoked) was one of the most expert fishermen upon the charming lake of Lucerne; he was far above the common stature, and excelled his comrades in games of strength and daring, to as great a degree as he surpassed them in skill in his vocation. On him the task usually devolved of conveying passengers across that arm of the Lake of the Four Cantons, which separated Uri from Schweitz. The cottage of Conrad was situated close to the shore, in a delightful vale, screened from the easterly winds by the bold and precipitous crags which rose in its neighbourhood and afforded shelter to the hardy fisher and his family. To him the stranger addressed himself in hurried accents :—

" Quick, Conrad, quick! for the sake of heaven and the blessed Virgin, unloose your boat and ferry me across!"—" The passage, comrade, can hardly be accomplished," returned Conrad, with a searching glance at the heavens; " the storm is close at hand, and will soon burst over our heads,—marked you that flash?—it almost blinded me—and hark! how loud the thunder rattles! 'Tis useless, comrade, to attempt the passage; let's seek some shelter." As Conrad uttered these words, the artillery of heaven was heard in all its sublime grandeur. Stunned by its noise, the women and children ran to seek a place of shelter; for the rain now poured down in torrents, and the wind, rising in louder gusts, seemed as if emulating the voice of the big-bellied thunder. In vain did the stranger plead; Conrad, who quailed before no trifling difficulties, was so appalled by the awful conflict of the elements, that he refused to unloose his boat, till urged by the passionate appeal of the fugitive, he demanded the cause of his haste. " Thy wounds, friend, appear to need immediate help; go to my cottage, 'tis close at hand; my wife's a skilful leech, and will tend you well; the fury of the storm will soon be over, and then we'll 'tempt the waves. Thy cause of haste is surely not so urgent as to demand the risk of almost certain death."—"'Tis certain death," returned the stranger, "to remain here; the bloodhounds of the Austrian despot are at hand; Gesler, the scourge of Uri, heaps insult upon insult on our country. But now, my father's plough was in the field, the field of his forefathers, when Gesler's agent claimed the ox that drew it; my father's feeble arm could ill resist the brutal force that strove to rob him. I was by,—what could I do? I seized the yoke as the vile knave unloosed it, and smote him. The villian died; and I fled from his fellows' rage, and scarce with life escaped." A flush of colour mantled to the brow of Conrad, at the concluding words of the stranger; as if by instinct, he flew to the fastenings by which his boat was moored, and began to unloose them; but suddenly, when about to cast off his craft, his eye fell upon his humble cottage; his wife appeared at the door. Again the little bark was safely moored, and with a look of blank despair mingled with shame, he addressed the stranger:—"'Tis useless, 'twere madness, to attempt it."—"Oh! for the sake of those I love the dearest, my wife and children's sake, attempt the passage!" exclaimed the stranger with an agonized look.—"I also have a wife and children, friend," said Conrad, and he pointed to his humble roof.

Some few of the peasants had remained as spectators of the scene we have just described, and added their supplications to those of the stranger: but Conrad was inflexible; for, although his native daring prompted him to undertake the enterprise, however desperate it might appear, yet still the love of his family, a feeling so deeply planted in the bosom of the free-born inhabitants of Switzerland, compelled him to prefer their welfare even to the safety of a countryman in distress. It was not without a look of the most intense anguish that he gave his last refusal; and the stranger was about to depart in a state of utter despair, when a new actor appeared upon the scene.

The new comer was a man in appearance about six feet in height; he was in the prime of manhood, and his frame was cast in a mould which betokened herculean strength; his shoulders were broad and muscular, while his lower limbs, although strong and well formed, were more compact in their structure, and plainly denoted the activity of their possessor. He was dressed in the rustic garb of the country; but the fineness of the material, and the neatness of its make, showed that he belonged to a richer class of society than the group he was now approaching. He carried in his hand a cross-bow, and on his shoulders was borne a quiver full of arrows.

The storm still continued, but the long conference held by Conrad with the stranger had induced many of the peasants to rejoin their companions, who had congregated round the base of a group of walnut-trees, which afforded them a partial shelter.

As the man we have described approached, the peasants, to whom he was well known, divided themselves on either side, so as to offer for his acceptance a position in the centre of their group most sheltered from the pelting of the rain.

"It is a rough day," said Tell—for so the new comer was called; "it is a rough day to leave the comforts of your firesides, and meet here in the storm, my friends! But what means this? whence comes this stranger thus disfigured?—speak—what means it all?" The stranger, who we have said was about to depart in despair, his head drooping on his breast, as much from weakness as from mental prostration, no sooner heard the first words of the last speaker, than staggering towards him, he seized him by the hand. " 'Tis I, Tell; 'tis Erni—old Melctor's son! The tyrant Gesler seeks my life; his bloodhounds are at hand, and the storm rages and I cannot cross the lake."—" Who says you cannot cross?" cried Tell. —" You, Conrad, can assist him."

The fisherman, in broken speech, declared the utter hopelessness of the attempt; nor could the persuasive voice of Tell, whose judgment was usually relied on, and whose councils were generally followed by his neighbours, prevail upon him to undertake what he considered a hopeless task.

The storm still continued; but, when partial intervals of silence occurred, giving greater effect to the succeeding peal of thunder, a distant sound was heard, resembling the heavy tread of a body of horse. Erni was the first to hear and direct the attention of Tell to it. As soon as the latter distinctly understood its meaning (it announced the approach of the troops of Gesler), his whole frame was agitated by a convulsive movement. In the next moment he hastened to unmoor the boat of Conrad, and launching it into the agitated waves, helped Erni (whose weakness was fast increasing) into its fore part, and taking his station at the helm, exclaimed, " Friends! 'tis better to trust ourselves in the hands of the Omnipotent than in those of man; the rage of heaven is chastened by mercy, and its power to save none dare dispute. The monster Gesler knows not the name of pity. Should fate be adverse, friends, protect my wife and child; but it can never be; Helvetia's wrongs cry aloud to heaven; our mountain home shall still be free."

As he spoke, a sudden gust of wind bore the little bark away from the shore, and the peril of the daring navigators became more and more imminent. The assembled crowd, to enable themselves to watch their progress better, climbed a neighbouring hill; and with many exclamations of fear, wonder, and hope, marked the various fortunes of the frail vessel. Now it was seen boldly riding on the summit of a mountain-wave, as careless as the wild-bird that, scudding by, gazed with wonder on those who seemed to dispute its dominion; at another moment it was lost to view in the trough of the waves, but again it would re-appear. Still, however, it made some progress towards its intended port, and the hope of the observers, that Tell would accomplish his task, became every minute more sanguine. At length the distance they had gained, and the hazy nature of the atmosphere, completely hid the boat from their view; and the sympathising peasants began to repair to their homes, breathing prayers for the success of the adventurous men.

CHAPTER II.

ARRIVAL OF GESLER'S TROOPS.

" Sweet smiling village, loveliest of the lawn,
Thy sports are fled, and all thy charms withdrawn ;
Amid thy bowers thy tyrant's hands are seen,
And desolation saddens all thy green."

Drenched with rain, and depressed in spirits from their anxiety for the fate of their countrymen, as well as from an undefined fear of the consequences of the escape of Erni, should the troopers of Gesler arrive and find themselves deprived of their expected prey, the hardy mountaineers returned with thoughtful steps towards their humble dwellings. The village to which they were returning was concealed from the view of a spectator on the beach by a low range of hills, at the foot of which lay the spot on which the occurrences we have related took place ; but far beyond, and towering far above, the summit of a range of glaciers were seen in the distance : between the base of these ice-clad hills and the low range we have noticed, a confined, but pleasant valley was situated, in which the village of the mountaineers was placed ; a small chapel, dedicated to the Virgin, was the only building which attracted the particular attention of the stranger. Several farm-houses were situated on the most fertile slopes of the surrounding hills, whose inhabitants, together with those of the village, had lived for years unmolested, in the performance of the duties they owed to their families,— a happy race of fishermen, hunters, or shepherds. But, alas ! the period had arrived when the peaceful repose of the little village of Burglen was doomed to experience all the evils inflicted by military despotism.

Rodolphe of Hapsburg, who had raised himself from a private station to the dignity of Duke of Austria, and, by his skilful management, had induced the electors of the German states to confer upon him the title of emperor of Germany, finding all his efforts to dominate over the hardy natives of Switzerland ineffectual, had prudently resolved to leave them in possession of their privileges, on condition of their acknowledging him as their feudal lord, leaving the administration of the laws, and the appointment of their magistrates in their own hands. At the same time, a bailiff was appointed by the emperor, to each canton, to attend to his interests. This gentle yoke the Switzers had patiently borne, satisfied with their state of liberty, which was sufficient for all useful purposes, while, at the same time, their connexion with the emperor secured to them a powerful ally in case of foreign war. At the death of Rodolphe, the choice of the empire fell upon Adolphus of Nassau, who fulfilled the conditions of his predecessor's treaty with the Swiss with fidelity. At length, Albert, the son of the last emperor, who had already aspired to the crown, overthrew his rival, and was crowned emperor on the 24th of August, 1298.

Albert of Austria is described by the historians of the period as a man of the most forbidding countenance and rustic appearance—" Homo grossus, aspectu ferox, rusticanus in persona ;" and the ferocity of his aspect was much increased by the loss of an eye, which occurred during a severe fit of illness.   He possessed all the military prowess of his father, but was greatly deficient in the prudence by which the acts of his parents were characterized.   His life was passed in constant attacks upon his neighbours; he waged war in turns with Holland, Hungary, Bohemia, and Thuringia; and, although generally defeated, his appetite for bloodshed was never satiated.   The liberty possessed by the Swiss, and particularly by the Waldstetten, the inhabitants of Uri, Underwalden, and Schweitz, so rankled in his mind, that he exerted himself by every means in his power to irritate the mountaineers into some overt act of rebellion.   To this end, he appointed the most brutal of his minions to the office of bailiff in the various cantons.   At the time we are speaking, the notorious Gesler was placed in authority in Uri, Landenberger in Underwalden, and Wolfhausen in Schweitz.   The acts of persecution and cruelty committed by these men, had so roused the feelings of the Waldstetten, that the whole country was ripe for a rebellion.

The villagers of Burglen, returning homewards, as we have already stated, had just passed through a narrow defile on the hills, which led from the beach to their rustic homes, and were about to enter their respective dwellings, when they perceived to their terror a troop of horse slowly winding its way along a circuitous path, which, gradually descending the steep sides of the mountain, led at length into their peaceful valley.

As the troopers drew near, the alarm of the inhabitants was increased, by perceiving that the band consisted of a detachment from the body-guard of Landenberger, the bailiff of Underwalden, in addition to the well-known agents of the brutal Gesler.   This combination of the forces of the oppressor plainly told the affrighted peasantry that no common act of violence was contemplated.   In what manner they should resist any inroad on their personal liberty they knew not; for those on whom they placed most reliance in the hour of danger were absent.   Erni had fled, and Tell had not yet returned.

As soon as the troops of the bailiff had defiled from the mountain-path, they formed themselves into a compact body at the extremity of the valley; they then advanced in military order until within bow-shot of the village, when one of their leaders, accompanied by four of the soldiery, advanced to the assembled crowd who were collected on the level ground in front of their dwellings.   Unwilling to provoke the aggression of their dreaded visitors, the men presented themselves unarmed; the women hanging on their arms; and the children alarmed, yet delighted, at the military spectacle, peeping with timid curiosity through the openings in the group.   As soon as the officer of the ba liff had approached sufficiently near, he addressed the foremost of the villige group :—" We've tracked a murderer here into your valley, and, in the governor's name, we claim his body."

" We know not whom you mean," returned the villager.

" Rebels, you know him well! 'tis Erni, Melctor's son: we tracked him closely to yon mountain's gorge; we saw him climb its steep and rugged side, and by some path, known only to yourselves, he reached the mountain road. Within this village now he lies concealed : give up the murderer, or dreadful vengeance falls on all your clan ; we'll spare nor age nor sex. Point out the hiding-place in which he lurks !"

" He is not here ; search every dwelling, sir."

One of the soldiers now approached his captain, and pointing to the road which led to the beach, exclaimed, " Is it not likely the culprit has escaped across the lake ? ten minutes' march will lead us to its brink."

" The lake !" exclaimed the first speaker, " in such a day as this ? The winds and waves combine together to bar the murderer's progress ; what boat could cross the troubled waves to-day ? No, he's concealed within these rebels' huts."

" Still, sir," persisted the soldier, " he knew he was pursued ; his life was forfeited, and for a stake like that, he'd risk a desperate chance. Sir, I was bred within these hills, and I well know the mountaineers ; I've seen them on as wild a day as this, for the mere object of a lover's meeting, pursue their path along the slippery glacier, enveloped in the mists which rose around, or blinded by the lightning's glare."

" Say, are there dwellings nearer to the beach ?" returned his leader. " A rude hut" exclaimed the soldier, " is near the shore, Conrad the fisherman's ; it is his task to ferry passengers across the lake."

" Then there we'll seek him ; but should he have escaped the hands of justice, we'll place our seal of vengeance on this spot with such an impress, that all who pass may read the dreadful lesson, and learn to fear the rage of Gesler worse than death itself." Having thus spoken, he turned to one of the troopers that accompanied him, and giving orders that every pass from the valley should be secured, proceeded towards the road which led to the beach, in company with the remaining three of his followers.

To describe the consternation of the villagers at this juncture, would be vain—the rage of some, the fear of others, and the despair of the women, was a cruel and heartrending sight.

At length the villager who had already spoken addressed his companions as follows :—

" Comrades, what should we do ?—submit to all these insults, and tamely crouch before our blood-stained tyrants ? We have borne with patience every heavy impost the avarice of Gesler placed upon us ; we have borne his insults, and his minions' scorn, yet we were patient, fearful to bring the dreadful scourge of war to our own firesides. What should we do ? there is a time when patience is a crime ; the very worm will turn when trod on ; the gentle hind when hunted stands at bay ; the timid chamois, when all hope is lost, rushes upon the hunter's panting chest, and hurls him from the precipice, though in the effort his own life is lost. Shall we be worse than brutes, and tamely sink beneath their cruel hands ? Alas ! I speak but what I wish ; if Tell were here he might direct us. They'll soon return from their fruitless search, goaded by disappointment ; we cannot here defend ourselves. Behind those rocks there are convenient caverns formed by nature ; they'll form a place of refuge for the women, while we, though few in numbers and badly armed, may still if need be, within the mountain's narrow gorge defend our lives. Could some one reach old Melctor's cottage? if he arrived, his age might guide our acts. Say, who will venture?"

There was a pause when he ceased to speak, for the danger of the proposed undertaking was apparent to all. At length a young woman stepped forth from the ranks, and offered to undertake the dangerous enterprise. She who had thus set an heroic example to the rest was Hildegard, the affianced bride of Ernest, a chamois-hunter.

The proposal of the mountain maiden had strengthened the resolution of the men, and she had scarcely ceased speaking, when at least twenty of the latter rushed forward simultaneously to offer their services. On this Hildegard resumed her speech. "Neighbours," she said, "I have well considered what I have undertaken; but although I do not conceal from myself the danger I shall run, I am certain that danger will be less in my case than in that of any other. The troops are busily engaged at the further end of the valley, searching for the secret passes through the mountains. You see yonder gray stone near Ulrich's cottage at the base of the hill; behind that stone there is a narrow covered pathway among the rocks, which leads to the side of the great ravine, through which the waters of our little stream flow. If I can gain that point unmolested—and that I'm sure to do—I can easily cross it by the Tenfel's bridge, and then shall soon reach old Melctor's cottage. If I am seen, no one will heed me; they will but think I seek a wandering sheep or a stray goat." Without awaiting an answer, she tripped lightly across the green sward towards the spot she had indicated, and was soon lost to the admiring eyes of her neighbours. Meantime the captain of the troops and his three companions pursued their journey towards the beach; they rode directly up to Conrad's cottage, and knocking at the entrance, rudely demanded admittance. "We seek," said the leader, when the door was opened by the fisherman, "a murderer who has fled from justice."

"I know of none," said Conrad.

"He is either concealed here, or you have conveyed him across the water," returned the inquirer.

"It needs an arm," said the fisherman, "more powerful than mine, to perform the task on such a day as this."

The storm had by this time somewhat abated its fury, but the waves still rolled high; the rain had ceased, and at intervals gleams of sunshine fell upon different parts of the landscape. The green fields and the wooded shores of Schweitz were partially disclosed to the eye of the spectator, as the oblique rays of the sun glanced upon its beautiful landscape.

The last observation of Conrad induced Gesler's party to look towards Schweitz; Conrad himself also, ascending a fragment of rock which lay near the door, looked anxiously in the same direction. A broad and brilliant blaze of sunshine suddenly passed across the waters, and, although it rested not a second upon the waves, it sufficed to show to the fisherman and the troopers a dark object on the water, and near to the opposite shore. With what different feelings did each party make the discovery! It was the boat containing the fugitive, still

safely riding on the waves! It must be it! no other would have ventured out on such a day.

"By St. George," exclaimed Gesler's minion, "he has escaped!"

"Do you see," cried Conrad, his excitement overcoming his prudence "him in yonder boat? Ride on! ride on! and if you follow hard you yet may take him."

"Villain! you have assisted the escape of the murderer. Down with him, comrades; bind him hand and foot," roared the leader of the party.

The orders of the officer were readily obeyed by his followers, and in spite of his resistance, the fisherman, overpowered by numbers, faint and bleeding from the wounds he had received, was thrown across the back of the horse of one of the troopers, and the party galloped off to the village, breathing vengeance against its inhabitants.

CHAPTER III.

THE AVALANCHE.

" Burning for blood! bony, and gaunt, and grim!
Assembled wolves in raging troops descend;
And pouring o'er the country, bear along,
Keen as the north wind sweeps the glossy snow."

INSPIRED by the courage natural to her sex when circumstances call. forth its exercise, Hildegard pursued her lonely, and from the nature of

2   B

the road, her dangerous journey, with the alacrity of one earnest in the task she had undertaken, and confident in her knowledge of the intricacies of the route. By the time she had been engaged some two hours in the performance of her solitary task, she had reached a part of the road which passed through a gloomy grove of firs, which in this spot skirted the Alpine hill, and formed a natural barrier against the threatened invasion of the overwhelming avalanche.

The last rays of the setting sun still lingered over the villages of Sweitz; but the valley of Burglen, shrouded by the lofty mountains by which it was surrounded, had for some time ceased to feel their cheering influence. As Hildegard proceeded further into the forest, the darkness became so great that objects at a few feet distance could scarcely be recognised. And now, for the first time, a feeling of terror entered the bosom of the daring girl. It was not that the dismal road through the forest alarmed her, or the rugged and dangerous nature of the path; these were dangers to which she was accustomed; but she suddenly came upon a rude cross, placed by the road side, which indicated the spot where some tragic occurrence had taken place. The fear of meeting with the prowling savages of the wood suddenly flashed across her mind, for the country was infested with wolves, and she had no means of resisting an attack, excepting a staff shod with an iron spike, which she had brought with her to render her steps more safe in the difficult parts of her journey.

Pausing for a time by the side of this rude memento of bloodshed, she breathed a fervent prayer to heaven for protection, and again with her mind re-assured, proceeded on her way. The darkness with which she was now surrounded was gradually dispelled by the moon, which, rising in silent majesty, spread her pale rays in a flood of silver over the landscape; cheered by its presence she proceeded with renewed vigour, and had already come within sight of the extremity of the grove, when her attention was suddenly attracted by a low dull sound, resembling the laboured breathing of a person in a troubled sleep; this was succeeded by a rustled noise among the underwood, and turning to the side from which it proceeded, she was terrified by the appearance of two sparkling eyes glaring upon her. "The wolf!" she exclaimed in terror, and from the first impulse of the moment, instead of taking to flight, she stood as it were fascinated, with her eyes fixed upon the shaggy brute about to make its fatal spring. In another instant she was thrown to the ground by a rude shock, expecting every moment to feel the fangs of the monster. She lay for some time in a kind of stupor, but by degrees recovered her self-possession, and looking round, perceived her enemy was gone. The iron-shod staff was still in her hand, firmly grasped, and to it she owed her preservation.

When the wolf was in the act of springing at her throat, she had instinctively held forth the staff for protection: held as it was in a direction pointed towards the object of her fear, the starving brute did not perceive the obstacle between itself and its intended victim, and springing forward, with all the eagerness of famine, his brawny chest came in contact with the pointed end of the stick. The consequence was that the maiden was thrown to the ground, as we have already seen, and the wolf, checked in its mid career, swerved from its course, and fell over the edge of the precipice down the precipitous sides of the crag.

Hildegard, having recovered from the shock occasioned by her miraculous escape, hastened forward with all the speed that fear alone can impart. Being well acquainted with the Alpine road, she was aware of the existence, at the distance of a few hundred yards, of a rude chalet, which had been erected by the mountaineers to afford protection to the wanderer, when overtaken by a storm of snow. To this place of refuge she directed her hurried steps; for she well knew that the wolf rarely made its appearance singly; nor were her anticipations of danger without foundation, for scarcely had she entered the solitary hut, and secured the doorway as well as her agitated state would allow, before a loud discordant bark announced the arrival of her fierce pursuers; the wolf, from whose fangs she had so miraculously escaped, was but the leader of a pack of those ravenous creatures.

Involved, now, in almost utter darkness, the trembling and exhausted girl had time to consider her solitary and dangerous position; she again tried the fastenings of the door, to ascertain if they were secure, and felt satisfied that the walls of the hut formed a sufficient barrier betwen herself and her enemies, who still continued to surround the building, uttering the most dreadful cries, and scrambling up its rude walls in their endeavours to reach their victim.

Hildegard, well acquainted with the nature of her pursuers, and aware that, unless driven away by force, they would not relinquish their attempt, or retire into their hiding places until the break of day, it was manifest that no means, at her command, would enable her to drive off the famished pack, and that no alternative remained to her but to wait patiently in her dismal retreat until the appearance of the morning sun.

By nature daring, and taught by habit, the necessity of self-possession in the hour of danger, and finding all idea of escape at present useless, she directed her attention to the means of rendering her solitary sojourn as little inconvenient as possible. To this end she applied herself to the task of lighting a fire with the faggots of wood which had been providentially left there for the purpose; while enjoying its cheerful blaze, and anxiously brooding over the consequence of her unexpected delay, she had almost forgotten the danger by which she was surrounded, till she was suddenly roused from her reverie by the new mode of action resorted to by her besiegers.

The hut in which she had taken refuge was built of stone; it was rude in its construction, and the upper part formed a kind of irregular dome, in the centre of which an opening was left to allow the escape of the smoke. As soon as the hungry band without perceived the light of the fire through this loop-hole, they began to scale the walls on every side; the unusual noise this occasioned attracted the attention of its inmate, who suddenly raising her eyes to the roof, perceived one of the largest of the wolves thrusting aside his competitors in the chase, and forcing his huge body through the opening we have mentioned; he appeared to the affrighted eyes of Hildegard, about to make his fatal spring; when urged by despair, she promptly seized the largest of the burning brands, and mounting the table, thrust its blazing end into the gaping mouth of the shaggy brute. Attacked in this unusual manner, and at the same time pressed upon by those which surrounded him, he fell from the roof of the chalet howling with pain; but his place was soon filled by another, and although the courageous girl stood boldly on the defensive, it was evident she would be unable long to maintain the unequal conflict. At length, when about to sink from exhaustion, a loud and crashing sound was suddenly heard; in an instant the baying of the wolves was hushed in silence, the opening in the roof was closed, and a sudden shock like an earthquake was felt. Hildegard had scarcely time to think on this sudden interposition, before the hut was filled with the dense smoke of the faggots, which unable to find an exit by the usual channel, spread its suffocating fumes through the chamber; overpowered by its effect, she rushed in an agony of despair towards the door, and endeavoured to undo the fastenings, but the care she had taken in barring the entrance against the wolves rendered the task difficult, especially in her present agitated state. At length, when nearly exhausted, she so far succeeded as to remove the heavy beams that closed the door, and lifted the latch with caution; but, oh God! what were her feelings when she found herself unable to force it open beyond a few inches! The hut was buried in an avalanche. Still, in spite of the terror of her mind, the instinct of self-preservation, caused her to apply her face close to the small opening of the door, for the purpose of inhaling the external air. It was then a ray of hope entered her mind; for, through the chink, she could discern in the distance the moon still riding through the cloudless sky. It was evident that her hiding-place was but partially buried in the snow. She listened; all was silent, and, thrusting her arm through the opening, endeavoured to feel the extent of the opposition to her escape; in doing this she suddenly withdrew it, for it fell upon the yet warm head of one of the wolves which hung across the lintel of the doorway, against which its body had been crushed by the mass of fallen snow. She soon recovered from the shock this incident occasioned, and, feeling satisfied of the fate of her enemies, directed all her efforts to the devising some means of escape. Before she could make any attempt to remove the snow, it was necessary either to destroy the door or to separate it from its hinges; but to neither of these acts was her physical power equal; at length she resorted to the desperate resolution of endeavouring to burn it, and having succeeded in setting fire to the wood work she patiently awaited, at the other extremity of the hut, the result of her stratagem. At first, from the want of a proper supply of air from within, the fire burnt but slowly, and the dripping of the melted snow seemed likely to extinguish it. Hildegard anxiously watched its progress, and thrusting the beam of wood with which she had barred the door through one of its half-burnt timbers, the air rushed freely in, and it was soon a heap of ashes. As soon as the heat of the flames would allow, she looked out of the hut, and found the obstacles to her escape less than she had expected; the heat of the fire had melted a considerable portion of the snow which had caused the obstruction, and little more remained for her to do in order to be enabled to proceed. Fervently did she raise her hands to heaven in gratitude for her deliverance, and having, with some difficulty, regained the path, she pursued her way with all the alacrity her exhausted frame would allow towards Melctor's cottage.

The time occupied by the occurrences we have related, trenched far into the night, and in less than two hours the glorious sun would again cheer the landscape with his presence. Meantime, overcome by fatigue, and trembling, from the mental excitement she had undergone, the maiden Hildegard slowly pursued her journey; although at any other time she could have accomplished the distance in half an hour, the sun had already begun to gild the summits of the glaciers, before she reached the Tenfel's-bridge. Here, exhausted nature refused its help, and she sat down upon a rock near the chasm, over which it was thrown, utterly unable to proceed.

She had not remained long in this position, when the distant sound of the Rauz-des-vaches fell upon her ear, and she could perceive upon the green slopes of the steep, on the opposite side of the chasm to that on which she was resting, the shepherds of the mountain driving forth their flocks to pasture, and solacing their labour with their favourite ditty. As they drew nearer, she could distinguish in the midst of them an old man, whose abstracted air and melancholy look, plainly showed he was a prey to some overwhelming sorrow. He appeared in the act of taking leave of those by whom he was surrounded, and giving them some parting directions. It was Melctor himself. As soon as Hildegard recognized the ancient shepherd, she rose from her seat, and by waving her hand-kerchief, soon attracted his attention. The old man, astonished at the appearance of a female in such a situation at that early hour of the morn-ing, hastened, accompanied by two younger companions, across the bridge which nature in one of her romantic freaks, had thrown over the yawning gulph. The tale of Hildegard was soon told, and she learnt from the old shepherd that the storm of the previous day had alone pre-vented his following his fugitive son, and that he now was on his road to the village of Burglen. The fatigues which Hildegard had undergone, rendered rest a matter of imperative necessity, and she was carefully con-ducted to Melctor's cottage, while he himself proceeded on his road to the ill-fated village.

CHAPTER IV.

THE SKIRMISH—CAPTURE OF MELCTOR.

" Hark !—heard you not those hoofs of dreadful note ?
  Sounds not the clang of conflict on the heath ?
Saw ye not whom the reeking sabre smote ;
  Nor saved your brethren ere they sank beneath
Tyrants and tyrants' slaves ?"

Let us now return to the party by whom the fisherman Conrad was borne captive. By the time they had again entered the valley, the dark-ness of the evening had increased to such an extent, as to render objects at a few paces distant from the spectator, indistinct. Being burdened with their prisoner, they deemed it most prudent, in the first instance, to proceed to that part of the valley where the greater number of their party were placed. Having reached their comrades they left the fisherman, bound, under the care of a guard, and the captain placing himself at the head of the combined force, rode towards the village.

Great was the surprise of the troopers as they advanced, to find the cottages deserted, and the stalls and outhouses, in which the cattle were usually placed during the night, untenanted by their usual occupiers. " They cannot all have escaped," cried the leader of the band ; " quick, light the torches, and search in every nook." As the soldiers had not calculated on a service of this description, they were unprovided with the means of obeying their leader's orders. " Light we must have," cried the captain ; " fire yonder barn, 'twill force the rebels from their place of hiding." His bidding was soon accomplished, and although at first the thatch of the building, saturated by the rain which had fallen during the day, resisted their attempts to fire it, and almost suffocated the soldiers with the smoke and steam it emitted in volumes, yet the rafters of pine being once fairly alight soon proved the power of the destructive element, and the whole building, now in flames, blazed like a thousand torches, and threw a light almost equal to that of day upon the surrounding objects.

Guided by its glare, the troops of Gesler searched every dwelling, but without success ; thus disappointed, they committed every variety of excess within their power, burning and destroying the moveables, and wastefully expending every kind of provision that came within their reach.

With bosoms filled with rage, yet fearful of showing themselves before the infuriated soldiery, the desolated inhabitants, spectators of the destruction of their property, remained still in their hiding-places. At length, foiled in their hopes of vengeance, and maddened by the intoxicating liquors of which they had partaken, the troops of the bailiff were about to proceed to the destruction of the village itself : already had brands been snatched from the blazing ruins, and they were on the point of firing the foremost buildings, when the mountaineers, no longer able to endure the sight, announced their presence by a loud shout of execration and rage, which, mingled with the screams of the women and children, burst with terrific force upon the ears of the troopers. The latter instantly dropped the blazing fragments from their hands, and, quickly springing into their saddles, were soon in full career towards the concealed peasantry.

The burning ruins of the barn were now nearly consumed, and the light shed by its embers scarcely sufficed to guide them on their path ; but the moon had now arisen, and, guided by her friendly beams, they surmounted the obstacles which the nature of the rugged path threw in their way, and found themselves close to the rocks among which the mountaineers were concealed. The leader of the troopers rode forward to survey the ground, and discover, if possible, the entrance to their place of retreat, when his attention was attracted by the appearance of a man standing upon a prominent part of the crag, which rose above his head. The villager raised his hand, as if to command attention, and, in a loud voice, thus addressed the leader :—

" Austrian ! thy master's cruelty and acts of blood will heaven in good time revenge. Oppression's tide is nearly at its height ; beware the ebb ! 'twill sweep before it all thy vaunted power. A race of quiet huntsmen would we live, shepherds or fishers, but we are mountaineers ; our hardy fathers came from the far north ; they sought a land congenial to their minds, and found the vales and lofty hills of Schweitz ; they brooked not tyranny, and handed down to their posterity their hatred of a tyrant. Rodolph of Hapsburgh, mightier far than Albert, failed to subdue us ; he in his height of power took the Switzer's hand in brotherly alliance ; he knew us not as vassals, but as brethren ? I tell thee, Austrian, the hatred of thy master is spreading wide ; 'tis firmly seated in the souls of all ; 'tis growing year by year and day by day, and long ere now it would have fallen heavy upon his head, but the Swiss like not change ; we would remain in peace upon our hills, a race of shepherds ; but you well know, in time of need, we can be warriors !"

The listener to this bold address could scarcely give a patient hearing to the mountaineer. " Rebel !" at length he exclaimed," our cup of vengeance is not yet full ; a bitter draught is now preparing for your rebellious Cantons ; the Emperor with all his power is marching hither, and Uri, Schweitz and Unterwalden shall feel his wrath, but on himself has Gesler taken the punishment of this rebellious canton.—Soldiers !" he exclaimed, dismount and seek them in their burrows, where these warriors hide like the timid coney." The soldiers spread themselves on all sides to seek for the entrance to the strongholds of the peasants ; at length a party called to their comrades that they had discovered a clue to their retreat ; thither they all proceeded, and began to climb the rugged path. Their road lay between two lofty crags, and appeared formerly to have been a water course ; it was strewed with fragments of rock, which rendered its otherwise difficult passage still more dangerous. They had not, however, proceeded far, before other obstacles, besides those which the nature of the road offered, became evident ; the mountaineers had ranged themselves on either side, on the summit of the crags above their head, each poising upon the edge of the precipice a fragment of rock ; the troopers perceived their danger, and made a precipitate retreat, indebted only to the forbearance of their opponents for their escape. It was evident that the position taken up by the peasants, was too strong from natural causes to be easily taken ; and thirsting as the leader of the troopers was for vengeance, he could perceive no means of gratifying it.

While thus contemplating the disappointment of his hopes, the soldier we have already noticed as being well acquainted with the intricate pathways of the district, informed him of the existence of a foot-path, which led along the side of the mountain, and from which the position of their opponents might be commanded (it was the road along which Hildegard had passed) ; thither a party was sent to reconnoitre, while the remainder of the troops remained in the valley,

Things had continued in this position for some time, when the captain who anxiously watched their progress, suddenly exclaimed, " Do you see that flame on the hill side ? it is a beacon !—the mountaineers are rising ; 'twas not an idle threat that rebel uttered ; quick ! let us hasten and leave the valley ere they stop the passes ; but let us mark this spot with some deep token of our vengeance. Burn all their dwellings ! they sought the rocks for shelter, there let them find it."

We need not point out to the reader that the Austrian was deceived by the burning of the hut from which Hildegard had escaped.

The concealed villagers in the meantime, hearing the threat of the chief, and perceiving the number of their enemy was reduced, resolved to make a desperate effort to save their property from destruction ; they descended from their hiding places, and armed in the best manner circumstances would allow, rushed upon the troopers, in the hopes of rendering the combat more equal by attacking them before they had time to mount their horses.   Taken thus by surprise, the Austrians fell back, but soon rallied from the shock, and having succeeded in gaining their horses, in their turn attacked the villagers.   The issue of the conflict was now no longer uncertain, although the villagers pertinaciously defended themselves until the broad light of day was spread over the scene; the superior power of the well-armed troopers prevailed, and at length the villagers endeavoured to make good their retreat to the hills.   In this, although pursued by Gesler's myrmidoms, they had nearly succeeded, when their progress was intercepted by the return of the party who had been sent to explore the road ; they carried along with them an old man, prisoner ; it was Melctor, whom they had met on his way to the valley.

As soon as the Austrian leader was made acquainted with the name of the prisoner, and the relation he bore to the fugitive, he directed his men merely to stand upon the defensive ; for, having so far gratified his vengeance, he began to calculate the danger he incurred by remaining in the valley, believing, as he did, that the mountaineers were rising.

The villagers, from the issue of the recent combat, found themselves unequal to the task of rescuing their countryman ; and as the troopers showed no signs of acting on the offensive, they stood by, mournful spectators of the passing scene.

" Countrymen !" cried Melctor, the " power of tyranny will have its limits ; grieve not for me ; my days are almost run ; no act of theirs can rob me of the happy time I've spent among these hills amid my dearest friends.   The tyrant's power, believe me, must find its limit. When he that is oppressed finds justice is denied him, the load's too great to bear, he casts it off, spurning oppression's chains, appeals to heaven, nor calls on heaven in vain, who even on the side of justice stands, and metes out power to aid the weakest arm, when crushed by the oppressor."   " Why stand you still and let that dotard preach ? mount and away, and seek the mountain road."   So saying, the chief of the troopers placed himself at their head, and directed his course towards the opposite extremity of the valley.

With desponding steps the villagers returned to their homes, to witness the destructive effects of the Austrian's vengeance ; they then assembled together to consult as to their future conduct, for they could not expect to remain long unmolested, after the threats they had received.   It was at length agreed that as the return of Tell might soon be expected, they should patienly wait for the benefit of his advice and assistance.   On this each returned with painful steps to his humble dwelling and mournful family.

CHAPTER V.

GESLER'S VENGEANCE.

" The night has been unruly : where we lay
    Our chimneys were blown down ; and, as they say,
    Lamentings heard in the air : strange screams of death,
    And prophesying, with accents terrible,
    Of dire combustion, and confused events
    New hatched to the woeful time."

The hardy natives of Helvetia reposed in sleep, though troubled
dreams disturbed the rest of those who, with minds intent upon their
country's wrongs, and burning with thoughts of vengeance, tossed
restlessly upon their humble pallets ; not so the tyrant Gesler ; seated in
the halls of the Castle of Altdorf, surrounded by all the glitter his ill-
gotten riches enabled him to display, he gazed proudly upon the assembled crowd of sycophants, while his bosom swelled with vain-glorious
thoughts of the success of his arbitrary measures.

It had been his aim to imitate, as closely as he could, the rude
splendour of the Austrian court, and to change the business-like aspect
of the high bailiff's castle to the resemblance of a viceregal palace.   To
enable himself to meet the expenses consequent upon such a mode of
living, he had strained his offensive power to the utmost, exacting
contributions, levying fines, and punishing, as we have already seen,

the inoffensive natives with the most unrelenting and cruel barbarity. There existed, at this time, many families of the ancient nobility of the land, who, possessed of considerable property, and distinguished from the other classes of their countrymen by their titles, which many still retained, flocked to the banquets of Gesler, as to a resort more suited to their taste than their own well-furnished, but unassuming, halls. Many of these were anxious for the more direct influence of the Austrian power in the government of their country, hoping by that means to be enabled to assume more of the outward appearance of nobility than they did at the present moment.

But although the inherent vanity of human nature—that desire planted in the breast of man to stand pre-eminent amidst his fellow-men, enabled Gesler to fill his halls with the ancient nobility of the land, still the desire of redressing their country's wrongs, burned not with more ardour in the breast of the oppressed peasant than it did in that of many of the lordly frequenters of the Castle of Altdorf. Among these, none more keenly felt the tyranny under which her native land was suffering than Gertrude, Baroness von Walstein, one of the richest heiresses of Switzerland, and the most celebrated beauty of her time.

Gertrude, though high born, and by early associations naturally attached to the distinctions which separated the class to which she belonged from the mere tillers of the soil, had too much of the free-born spirit of her ancestors not to sympathize deeply with the sufferings they endured. And now she sate the honoured guest at the banquet of Gesler. The Castle of Altdorf had never, on any previous occasion, exhibited so much splendour, as it did on the night we are recording, for envoys from the emperor had that day arrived, and the haughty bailiff availed himself of all his resources to do honour to his distinguished guests.

The night was far advanced, and the sounds of mirth and revelry rung through the massive roof of the ancient hall, but the small circle of the most distinguished guests, who graced the upper end of the festive board, deeply intent upon the well-understood purport of the visit of the Austrian emissaries, mixed little in the general conversation of the lighter-minded visitors, but discussed, generally in under-tones, the means of enforcing the demands of Austria.

" The authority," said Gesler, addressing the messengers from the emperor, " placed in my hands by my gracious master, I have exerted to its fullest extent, but still these stubborn churls refuse to bend ; it was but two days since, an officer of mine was slain outright when levying the state-dues upon a herdsman ; as yet, the murderer is not taken, but ample vengeance will I have on him and all his kin. To-morrow's sun shall prove these stubborn knaves. They will not yield, forsooth, to Austria's lord ! They will not stoop to his authority ! But they shall bow before my simple hat."

"Your hat !" cried Arnold, the Austrian envoy, "what mean you, bailiff ? "

" I'll have my hat placed on a pole, before the castle gates, and all who pass shall bow before the emblem ; if they refuse, I'll break their stubborn hearts. Not yield to Austria!—e'en to my vilest garment shall they stoop."

Gertrude, who had anxiously listened to the conversation Gesler held with his guests, could no longer remain silent when she heard the last threat of the tyrant.

"It ill becomes a maiden, sir, to speak on state affairs; but I have known this shepherd people long, they are my countrymen; I have heard my uncle Roland often say, he saw them at the battle of Faventium, prove well their hardihood and might. In peace I know them gentle and affectionate; they're rude, it's true, but love the land that bore them with so intense a feeling, that I'm sure, if urged to desperation, their stubborn nature would refuse the yoke, though backed with all your power."

The bailiff regarded the speaker with looks of surprise and anger, which his respect for her rank and sex could ill disguise. "I well knew, Lady Gertrude," he exclaimed, "your feeling for these haughty peasants, who say that they acknowledge Austria's power, and hold the land from him; they wish to have the Emperor for their master: that they may have no master but themselves! Why, lady, even you they do despise, and all your class: they call you peasant nobles. Let Austria's power reign amid these hills supreme, and then the nobles of this land shall hold the place which most befits them, or, under Austria's banners, gather laurels, and not pine idly here, amid the stillness of their native vallies."

"May heaven ward off those evil times," returned the Baroness, "when I shall see the men of Switzerland, reduced by idle pomp, despise the soil that bore them, and scorn the manners of their father-land—when the shrill trumpet's sound shall please them better than the rude minstrelsy of Switzer hinds!"

"'Tis well your sex protects you, lady, or you might learn to fear the Emperor's power; but tempt me not too far."

The bailiff of Uri uttered these words in rather a louder voice than the preceding part of his dialogue; this, together with the threatening tone in which they were spoken, attracted the attention of a youthful party of the native nobles, who, seated at a little distance from the speakers, had been engaged in rather a more animated or at least a more noisy discussion.

Their eyes were now directed towards the last speaker, with looks of surprise and anger, for Gertrude's high rank and beauty had rendered her the favourite of all the youth of the Canton. One of the number, suddenly rising, addressed himself to Gesler.

"The right of hospitality, Lord-governor, restrain my actions; I am your guest, but I may still demand why a noble lady is thus insulted?"

"Silence, good Arnold," exclaimed Gertrude, "'tis past; 'twas my rude speech provoked the Governor, and I deserved it."

Although no further words passed at the moment, the company were naturally much disturbed at this interruption of their harmony. Suddenly the door of the hall was opened, and a soldier in the uniform of Austria, wrapped in a large cloak and drenched with rain, entered; from the state of his garments he appeared to have ridden some distance, for he was wet and travel-soiled: it was the captain of whom we have already spoken. At the sight of his officer, Gesler descended from his seat, and approaching the captain, the latter in a low voice, explained the nature of his errand.

"Escaped!" cried Gesler, "what! crossed the lake in such a night as that! but speak—go on—what did you next? The fisherman, I think you said, is safe?"

"As safe as bonds can make him, and snugly stowed."

"'Tis well, what next? you have more to say."

"We thought to take revenge upon the peasants; but the hinds resisted, and sheltered by their rocks——"

"Speak lower," whispered Gesler, still continuing to listen to his officer; there are Swiss hearts within this hall to-night.—Ha! resisted did they, we'll raze their village to the ground." The next words that were uttered by the captain, seemed to fill the breast of the bailiff with a kind of savage joy; he clenched his hands, as if in anticipation of vengeance, and in a hurried tone gave directions to his follower, who left the room.

"Nobles and friends!" said the Governor, addressing his assembled guests, "the rights of the Emperor must be enforced with a strong hand; these rebel mountaineers have dared, not simply to resist our lawful power; their headstrong rage has led them to attack the Emperor's troops. The murderer I have mentioned has escaped; but, though the son is missing, we have the father safe. Come in."

As he spoke, the door again opened, and Melctor was brought in, bound hand and foot.

"Unloose his bonds, and place the hoary villain on his feet.—Thy name, I think, is Melctor; confess the truth, ere torture makes you speak—where is thy son?"

"I know not, sir; I went to seek him when your men secured me."

"Traitor, 'tis false. Know you not well, he who conceals a murderer shares his crime?"

"My son is not a murderer, nor have I concealed him. He raised his hand to save his father's herds, but never meant to slay."

"'Tis false! Now mark me well; though he may have escaped, I have you here. Quick, bear him out, and fling him to the ground, then with the pointed steel bore out his eyes."

At these dreadful orders a scream of horror burst from the assembled group, some of whom crowded round Gesler, entreating him to recal his words; but, lashed into the wildest rage by the disappointment of his revenge, and excited, moreover, by the intoxicating draughts of which he had partaken during the evening, he refused to retract his words, and the cries of anguish which proceeded from his victim too plainly proved the execution of his savage orders.

Disgusted, beyond measure, at the cruel and impolitic conduct of the bailiff, the assembled guests, with the exception of a few of his more immediate followers, remained unseated, in spite of the earnest entreaties of their entertainer; and, collected in groups, conversed in whispers on the dreadful scene they had just witnessed.

In the midst of this agitated assemblage, Arnold and Lady Gertrude were seen in earnest conversation. Young and enterprising, the noble blood of Arnold panted for distinction; and he longed to assume that position in the world for which his daring character was so well adapted. On this account, blind to the evils which such a state of things would bring upon his country, he desired to see the Austrian dominion established in Switzerland; and, while anxiously waiting for such a turn in the affairs of the two countries as might assist him in his ambitious projects, he was a constant visitor at the Castle of Altdorf. Another cause also rendered his visits yet more frequent than they would otherwise have been; this was the presence of Gertrude, towards whom he had long avowed an ardent attachment, but, hitherto, his suit had been unavailing. We have seen that, on political matters, at least, their opinions were diametrically opposite, yet, by some secret sympathy, they now found themselves together, and separated from the rest of the crowd.

" Is this the tyrant, Arnold, you would follow, and to his will and that of his proud master submit the fortunes of your native country ?" exclaimed Gertrude.

" To Austria do I render such honour as is due, not more; but yet, what power have we to oppose his sway ?—if it were politic, it would be useless to attempt it. Say, could the German empire interpose and save us from the power of Austria's lord ? No ; every state obeys his will. Is it not wise to seek a refuge beneath the eagle's wings ?"

" You, then, alone remain unmoved amid the general sorrow," said Gertrude ; nay, more, renounce your friends and kindred, and place thyself upon the stranger's side, scorning your humble countrymen—a purchased slave of Austria."

" Oh, do not bend those scornful looks upon me. If I seek Austria's court, 'tis but to gain the meed of glory, and lay it at thy feet—nay, do not turn away—no laurels have I now to deck my brows; I've naught to offer but a heart true to love."

" Truth and love are words that ill become him who is faithless to his country's cause."

" 'Twas thee I sought, here in proud Gesler's halls."

" And thought you, then, to gain me by a traitor's vows, Arnold ? No ! I would rather wed the man I detest—the butcher Gesler—than he who is faithless to his country's cause."

" What do I hear ? you hate me, Gertrude !"

" Perhaps 'twere better if I did, better than—as it is—to see that man contemned ; nay more, deserving of contempt—whom I might gladly love."

" Gertrude ! did I hear right ?"

" Oh ! if the generous feelings of thy heart are not extinct, but only slumbering, let me awaken them. Be what your nature destined you to be. Stand for your country and your country's right !"

" But, Gertrude, if 'gainst Austria's power I move, I bid farewell to thee and all my hopes ; removed to the Emperor's court, thy kinsmen, who beneath his banners serve, will place their stern command upon your acts."

" Here lie my lands; and is the Switzer free? so am I also. Think not through Austria's favour to possess me. But stop, we are observed; the hall is almost empty; the guests retired; farewell—remember!"

By this time the greater parts of the guests had retired, disgusted at the conduct of their host; and with short leaves-taking, repaired to their respective homes, leaving Gesler in moody silence, surrounded by a few of his most devoted followers.

CHAPTER VI.

THE SPIRIT OF THE MIST.

" Were such things here, as we do speak about?
Or have we eaten of the insane root,
That takes the reason prisoner?
. . . .
The earth hath bubbles, as the water has,
And these are them."

The sun had scarcely risen, on the morning after the escape of Erni, when the manly form of Tell might have been seen, slowly moving along a mountain-path, amid the Alpine district of the Canton of Schweitz; for, after concealing his friend in a place of safety, he deemed it a wiser course to reach home by a circuitous route than again to cross the lake, being well aware that no pains would be spared in tracking the fugitive.

Immersed in gloomy reflections on the oppressive acts he was doomed to witness in his father-land, the bosom of Tell swelled with indignation; and with panting chest and burning brow, he grasped yet more firmly the fated bow, by means of which his country's liberty was doomed to be effected.

"This Austrian bear," he exclaimed, "has threatened to invade our native hills. Are then the cruelties of his minion Gesler not sufficient, that he must strive to add unto our burthens? Let him beware! the Switzer's heart yearns kindly towards his home; but his right arm is strong, and firmly knit. The arrow from his bow sweeps on with deadly aim; bright is his battle-axe, and keen its stroke. Oh! who can wield the huge two-handed sword like our bold mountaineer. From every hill they'll rush in torrents down, when the shrill blast is heard from Uri's horn."

Soliloquizing thus, and relieving his scorching thoughts by giving vent to his feelings in words, the rising of the mountain mists had passed unheeded, until enveloped in their dense atmosphere, the neighbouring objects became so indistinct as to render it a task of danger, as well as difficulty, to proceed on his journey. When he first discovered his situation, he had nearly reached the edge of a precipice, whose perpendicular sides descending into the yawning gulf beneath almost made his experienced eye shrink with terror.

Gazing down the unfathomable abyss, "How readily," he cried, " could the weak arms of twenty mountain maidens, from such a spot as this overwhelm whole cohorts of the tyrant's legions; and then with outstretched arms, raising their voices shrill, exclaim, ' Thus perish all, who strive to conquer freemen ! ' "

As he spoke, he raised his arms as if in the attitude of imprecation, and lifting his head in exultation, beheld upon the summit of the opposite crag, a shadowy form, in an attitude resembling his own ; the figure was surrounded by mist, and of gigantic size : Tell started back, the phantom did the same ; he shouted, and he heard his call repeated—'twas not so loud indeed, but it was in keeping with his shadowy semblance, as indistinct, and as mysterious.

Tell had less of the weakness of superstition in his mind than most of his countrymen ; he had heard of the Spirit of the Mist, which was said to make its appearance in prognostication of some fearful event, about to overtake the party to whom it appeared. He had been told it was seen by the huntsman Oswald, before his fatal meeting with the ibex, which hurled him from the brow of the three-peaked crag, above the torrent, near the Austrian's dyke; old Melctor saw it once, and his wife soon after left him—a mournful widower.

These tales, at the time, had little effect upon him, but connecting them with the present apparition, and taking his present mood of mind into consideration, it is no wonder that his usual strength of nerve failed him, and his knees so trembled beneath him as to render his position still more perilous ; he staggered some steps backward, to a place where the narrow road somewhat widened, and resting on a stone, remained for some moments in contemplation. When he raised his head, the shadowy form had vanished, and the morning breeze had withdrawn the misty curtain from the face of the rising sun.

The appearance of the orb of day had the same effect upon the mind of Tell, as the removal of the mountain mist had, upon the brilliant landscape, which now burst in all its beauty upon his eye. The tone of his mind and body were both restored, and with a more elastic tread, and more cheerful anticipation, he proceeded on his journey, ruminating on the pleasure his return would occasion his wife and children.

It was not until the day was far advanced, that he reached the foot of the mountain, and began his progress through the charming fields of Schweitz, directing his course by the road to Uri, which passing through the town of Altdorf, led to his humble dwelling. As he came within sight of the lofty towers of Gesler's castle, he met three villagers, who conversing together, at times broke out into violent fits of laughter, and as frequently relapsing into a melancholy mood, sighed deeply, and shook their bushy heads.

As they drew near to Tell, they burst into a loud peal of merriment. " Well," said the first of the peasants, " this will please my old dame mightily—a hat ! who ever heard the like ?"

" Had it been, now, young Arnold's helmet, the thing might have looked well at least, but an old hat !" said one of his fellows.

The third peasant, who had not yet spoken, here put in his word. " You are merry, neighbours; but 'twere well if soon you have a head to wear a hat upon : the bailiff, friend, would care but little to place your head upon as high a pole ; he did not stand on trifles, when poor old Melctor's eyes were from their sockets scooped."

" What's that, man ?" cried Tell, gasping for breath.—Melct—Mel—what said you about Melctor? was it old Melctor, who lived behind the mill, of whom you spoke ?—well, what of him ? What more grief has he seen ?"

"Alas! master, no more grief will he see—he has lost his eyes. Gesler, the tyrant, deprived him of his sight. Oh! 'twas a piteous spectacle to see that poor old man—his grey beard spattered with blood—his vacant sockets still bleeding from his wounds, suffering from pain and blindness both at once, tottering across the bailiff's castle-yard. I never wish to see such sight again."

" When did this happen ?" eagerly demanded Tell.

" But yesternight; the Governor was midst his revels—they say he was overcome with wine—but let that pass. Oh! 'twas a cruel deed !"

" Monster !" cried Tell, " and I not by, and Erni at a distance ! How long, my country, will you bear this scourge ?"

" Ah, master, the strangest is to tell; this morning, as if to scoff at us, he placed his hat upon a lofty pole upon the village green, at Altdorf, and all who dare refuse to bow before it, are bound and cast into prison."

" Hah ! smiles he thus in mockery at our wrongs ? That shadowy form came not uncalled, I see. You have far to go, friends ?"

" Not far, but we must hasten; fare thee well. I think you had better not pass through the town." So saying, the peasants pursued their road; and Tell, fixed to the spot by emotion, raised his head to heaven, from the attitude of grief into which it had sunk, and exclaimed, in a prophetic tone—

" On every side I see Helvetia's land rising in hardy bands. The nobles with the peasants, will unite, and join the martial host. Clad in bright armour, I see the countless throng of Austria's despot move towards our hills. With naked breast, at many a pass I see the peasant rush upon the serried mass of glittering lances, and, breaking their array, dash to the ground the pride of chivalry; and far above, a glorious banner waves, inscribed in words of flame—' OUR FATHER-LAND AND LIBERTY.'"

CHAPTER VII.

THE RIVALS.

" Use me but as your spaniel, spurn me, strike me,
Neglect me, love me ; only give me leave,
Unworthy as I am, to follow you.
What worser place can I beg in your love,
(And yet a place of high respect for me),
Than to be used as you use your dog ? "

We left the maiden Hildegard under the care of the inmates of old Melctor's cottage, after her perilous adventure, there to rest herself from the fatigues of the night, previous to her return to the village. We have no wish to detract from the merit of her daring offer to undertake

her dangerous journey, which no doubt was founded upon a wish to assist her countrymen; but we are bound to say that other motives, perchance, assisted in causing her sudden and bold resolution.

There was a certain young chamois hunter, named Ernest, to whom we have already said she was betrothed, who dwelt in a cottage at no great distance from the farm of Melctor; he was the sole support of a widowed mother with whom he lived, and, on whose account, the marriage of the young folks had been postponed to an indefinite period. The affectionate feeling entertained towards her future mother-in-law was, perhaps, less ardent than it would otherwise have been, seeing that she apparently stood in the way between the lovers and their expected happiness. But if this feeling really did exist, we owe it to the Swiss maiden to declare, that she took such good pains to conceal it as effectually to screen it from the observation of the most acute observer; and never did daughter and mother-in-law appear more cordially to love each other.

The same perfect agreement existed between the two lovers, although, at times, these little impediments would occur which are said always to accompany true love, and like the pebbles over which the brook runs, serve to make the stream, either of true love or clear water, appear purer, clearer, and more sparkling than it would have done without their opposition.

Now these impediments were not of so serious a nature as to interfere materially with their happiness; there were no "fathers, with cruel hearts,"

4   D

to place their ban upon the union of the young folks; no dear plotting friend to intercept their letters, and render them miserable. There was no rival—yes, there was a rival, but he was no fierce bewhiskered hero, who carried daggers at his belt, or pistols at his holster; and although, at times, the prosecution of his suit caused unpleasant feelings, these arose rather from pity for the poor fellow, than from any more deeply seated cause.

Hans Winkelried, who dared to rival our friend Ernest in his love for the fair Hildegard, was just such a figure as an artist would select, if he wished to represent a Swiss warrior in the act of wielding one of his country's huge two-handed swords; his enormous frame seemed better fitted for the exercise of the strength required in using that clumsy, but, under certain circumstances, dangerous weapon, than for tending the flocks on the hill-side, or collecting the goats at milking time. Indeed, for the latter occupation he seemed peculiarly unfitted, the task requiring a lighter frame and a more active foot than that of Hans. He had frequently, when engaged in the task of driving one of his bearded charges from the brink of the precipice on which it had taken its station, been sadly troubled in effecting his purpose. On several of these occasions he had been indebted for his success to the light and active foot of Hildegard.

From these interviews arose that flame which, with a kind of spontaneous combustion—for certainly his will had no art or part in the business, slowly consumed the heart of our giant, whose whole soul, softened by the influence of the little archer, like that of another Cymon, reflected no other object than the image of his Swiss Iphigenia.

Hildegard having recovered from her fatigue in much less time than could have been expected, was seated at the door of Ernest's cottage, waiting, we may suppose with some degree of anxiety, for his return, when hearing the sound of footsteps she turned suddenly round to the side from which it proceeded, and felt a slight degree of vexation on perceiving the approach of her herculean lover, who no sooner caught a glimpse of her figure, than his naturally inexpressed countenance was lightened up with a kind of grim smile of pleasure.

"Well, Hans," said the maiden, "how fare the goats? have you yet learned how to induce them to leave the wolf's crag at milking time?"

"Leave the wolf's crag? a murrain take 'em! they scramble up the sides like the chamois. Persuade them, indeed! I find it as difficult to persuade them to leave the crag, as it is to induce myself to follow them."

"You're somewhat lighter than you was, Hans; you'll soon be active enough to chase them from their stations."

"Lighter, am I?" said Hans, surveying his huge limbs; "for the matter of that I have not yet fallen away to nothing. But I should not wonder if I had."

"How so?" said Hildegard, with an inquiring look.

"Why, look you; I never sleep;—I that was so difficult to rouse, that father used to kick and cuff me for an hour together, before I woke; and then I scarcely eat!"

"Why, how comes this? you used to be a pretty trencher man."

"Ah! so mother used to say; and then I dream, and yet I'm not asleep, I know I am not; and, would you think it? I always dream of you—and of the goats."

"Indeed!"

"Yes; I saw you there as plainly as I do now; there they were, jumping from crag to crag, and you a following, as nimble as themselves. Oh! how I did wish that I could follow too—as Ernest did; ah! you remember."

"What nonsense you are talking, Hans!"

"Nonsense, is it? I tell you what, I thought you would have fallen, you ran so quickly, and so you would if Ernest had not caught you; how I did tremble! and then when, he had caught you."—

"Be quiet, simpleton."

"That's what you always call me; but I'm not half so simple as I was once, but I'm not half so happy."

"How so, poor Hans?"

"I never see you now, since you have gone to the village, as Ernest does.—Oh! here he comes," said Hans, with rather a mortified look. For he began to fancy that Hildegard was becoming an interested listener, and so in sooth she was—but it was with a feeling of pity for the poor fellow.

Ernest now entered, and appeared surprised at the sight of his affianced, to whom, after nodding kindly at Hans, he approached and demanded the cause of her sudden appearance.

"Dear Hildegard," he exclaimed, "a little longer will these men be borne, a little longer will our patience last; fear not, dear Hildegard, there is a heaven above that watches over our safety—You'll not return unto the village yet?"

"I must, indeed, dear Ernest; my father's flocks want tending, and I fear Gesler's men have made sad havoc in our household stuff."

"Well, wait till the morning and I'll accompany you. It is not safe that you should go alone, I have business leads me on, which will prevent our meeting for a while."

"What business, Ernest?"

"Such as I must not tell; but the time soon will pass. How say you, Hans; can you neglect your goats and go with us?"

"Neglect my goats!" cried Hans; "I'd let every goat and sheep in Switzerland run wild upon the hills, to follow Hildegard."

"Nay, Hans, what I want is that you should follow me. I've work in hand will suit your brawny limbs."

Poor Hans, glad of any opportunity of following in the train of Hildegard, willingly agreed to the proposal of Ernest; and it was agreed upon that they should start early in the morning for the devoted valley.

CHAPTER VIII.

THE HAT.

Pity, like a naked new born babe,
Striding the blast, or heaven's cherubim, horsed
Upon the sightless couriers of the air,
Shall blow the horrid deed in every age,
That tears shall drown the wind.

The first pang of anguish, which the recital of the outrage upon his ancient friend had produced in the mind of Tell, having passed away, and his mind being relieved, to a certain extent, by the anticipation of the hour of vengeance, the hardy hunter again directed his steps towards the town of Altdorf; for, in spite of the warning of the peasant, he was too much interested in the progress of events to avoid any opportunity of ascertaining the truth, even although it might be accompanied by danger. Still he made up his mind to proceed cautiously, when he made his entry into the stronghold of the tyrant.

As he approached nearer to the town, he reached the summit of the hill which overlooked the valley in which it was built, and when he had half-way descended its slope, he perceived, seated on a stone by the road side, an old man and a boy. When he had almost reached the spot on which they rested, the boy raised his head, and, perceiving Tell, rushed into his arms exclaiming " Father! father!" It was his only son, young Walter Tell.

The words of greeting caused the old man to turn towards the spot from whence they came, and he exhibited to the agitated view of Tell his old friend Melctor deprived of sight, with a bandage across his brow, and a countenance expressive at once of mental and bodily agony. Overcome by his feelings, it was some time before Tell could utter a word of condolence or recognition, at length he fell upon his knees before him, and embracing his ancient friend, shed tears of agony upon his bosom.

" And has the monster dared to lay his parricidal hands on thee? Had he no pity for thy age? no fear lest the red bolt of heaven should fall upon him. How could his minions, Austrian though they be, hear his foul orders given, and yet not fell the monster to the earth? The vengeance of a mighty people, Melctor, is sure though it be slow. But, William, what brought you so near to Altdorf, how does your mother? did she fear for me?"

" Ernest, the hunter, father," returned the youth, " was at our cottage seeking for you; we had just heard that you had crossed the lake with Erni and we had learnt from poor old Melctor where his son had fled."

" But what of Ernest Walter?"

" Ernest said, father, that you must meet him next Tuesday night, at eight, at Rutli."

" At Rutli!—well!"—

" And so I offered to seek for you in Schweitz; he was so urgent, mother said no, I was too young, too young! she could not spare me; but I soon coaxed her and she let me go, but then she would not let me cross the lake, or go through Burglen, for fear of Gesler's troops."—

" 'T was well advised."—

" And so I came through Altdorf and there I met poor Melctor."

"I'm glad I've met you, boy," said Tell, " we must return to Altdorf; but what is this I'm told about a hat?"

" Oh, father, the bailiff's troops are on the village green, and every man that will not bow before it is sent to prison."

"We must go through the town, my boy," said Tell.

So saying, our travellers directed their course towards Altdorf, the steps of the unfortunate Melctor supported by Tell and his son.

As they came nearer to the town, instead of the bustle which generally pervades the streets of the place of government, Tell and his companions could not help remarking the unusual degree of silence, and the melancholy expression of countenance of the passers by ; they did not even assemble in groups to communicate their thoughts to each other, but communing with his own mind, every male inhabitant visible, appeared anxious to avoid his neighbour. The women and children, however, exhibited in their conduct a different mode of action ; they were huddled together in various spots, gazing vacantly on the unwonted scene, and conversing in suppressed whispers.

As Tell and his companions passed along, words of condolence, and pitying looks, greeted them from every side, until they reached the village green, across which it was necessary they should pass to gain the open country.

In the centre of the green, and near to the pathway by which it was crossed, a pole some twelve feet in height had been driven into the earth, on the top of which a hat, such as was worn by the Austrian nobles, was placed, decorated with rather an ample feather. Around the foot of this pole a guard of soldiers was stationed, whose duty it was to see the orders of Gesler obeyed.

When Tell arrived sufficiently near to perceive distinctly what we have just described, a man dressed like a hunter was crossing the green, and about to pass the spot on which the pole was placed. As he was proceeding on without noticing the hat, one of the guards stepped forward, and levelling his spear cried out to the hunter,—

" Obey the orders of the bailiff; bend before the hat."

" Before the hat! no, not before its owner," returned the peasant.

" Rebel! 'tis Austria's badge,—will you not bend before it?"

" How say you, neighbours?" said the hunter, addressing a party of his countrymen, who now appeared; "shall we bow down before it?"

Alarmed at the sight of the armed soldiers, the men appeared undecided as to their actions; but reassured by the example of their companion, they began to pass on without obeying the order of the guard. These latter seeing the obstinacy of the peasants, were about to proceed to extremities, by laying violent hands upon them, while, on the other hand, the countrymen, whose numbers were now increased, feeling themselves sufficiently strong for the purpose, although unarmed, began to make a show of resistance.

Matters were in this situation, and bloodshed seemed inevitable, when a priest, who happened at the time to be among the spectators, suddenly placed his back against the pole, and raised a crucifix above his head. At the sight of the holy symbol all fell upon their knees, and after crossing themselves and uttering a short prayer, again arose.

Although it was clear that their genuflection had no reference whatever to the proposed proof of their obedience to the orders of Gesler, the guard, unwilling to commence a conflict in which they might be worsted, and having at the same time some little repugnance for the task imposed upon them, allowed the peasants to pass on, and the space in front of the hat was again unoccupied, except by Gesler's agents.

Tell, now, along with his unhappy charge and his son, prepared to cross the green, carefully turning his head in another direction.

"See you, boy," said Tell, addressing his son, and pointing to an object in the distance, "those glaciers yonder, with a broad belt of pines along their base ?"

"I see them, father, and think I know them well."

"They are the same that rise between our home and Melctor's cottage."

"But, father, why is it they say, my mother told it me, that if you use an axe, and fell one of those trees, the tree will bleed, bleed like a living creature ?"

"'Tis said, my son, because to fell those trees would clear the way before the dreaded avalanche. Thus every tree cut down might cost a human life."

"See, father, there's the hat !"

"Well, what's the hat to us ? walk on."

"What ho !" cried one of the guards, and placing his halbert across the breast of Tell, he tried to prevent his passing. "Obey the orders of our Lord Governor ; kneel to the hat."

Tell endeavoured to avoid the soldier, and putting the spear gently on one side, was about to move on, when a comrade coming to the assistance of the guard, he was again urged to obey the order.

"Never !" exclaimed Tell ; "what ! in the presence of the monster's victim. Oh ! are ye men? and can ye serve one who could do this act ? See his gray hairs, enough to raise compassion in the breast of famished wolves ; they would not have harmed him, unless hard pressed by hunger's gnawing pains. Even then their cruelty would have been less than his."

"We must obey the Governor's orders, friend. See, here he comes," said the soldier.

As he spoke, Gesler appeared at the castle gate, at the head of a party of his retainers, and noticing the altercation which was taking place, he rode up to the group and demanded the cause.

"And who are you ?" he exclaimed "that dares to disobey my mandate. Bow down your stubborn head before the hat.——

"What ! you refuse ?" he exclaimed again, after a pause—

"Guard, seize on that rebel, and bear him to the castle. Fell him if he resists."

"Father, father ! they shall not bear you off."

"Fly, Walter, fly !" cried Tell, "and seek your safety, boy. Nay, do not stay, but fly at once, poor Melctor needs your aid."

"Melctor," exclaimed Gesler, "I thought I knew his face; that boy remains with me."

The soldiers, obeying the orders of the bailiff, bound both father and son, and conveyed them to the castle, leaving Melctor, sad and solitary, upon the green.

CHAPTER IX.

THE FATHER'S TRIAL.

Alas poor country ;
Almost afraid to know itself ! it cannot
Be called our mother, but our grave : where nothing,
But who knows nothing, is seen to smile ;
Where sighs, and groans, and shrieks that rend the air,
Are made, not marked.

The hoarse bray of the trumpet, and the loud sound of other warlike instruments, were heard at day-break within the embattled towers of Altdorf Castle. The soldiers appeared dressed in their best array, and all the inmates of the tyrant's stronghold were on the alert.

On the preceding evening, after Tell and his son had been committed to prison, the former under the sentence of death, for disobedience to the orders of Gesler, the bailiff had ascertained the name of his captive, and being well acquainted with his skill in the use of the crossbow, he had during his evening revels, stated to the assembled company his intention of pardoning the mountaineer, on condition of his exhibiting some act of consummate skill in the use of his favourite weapon.

This promised act of clemency had spread an unusual degree of hilarity and good humour among his followers, for wicked as they knew their leader to be, and little used as they themselves were to acts, or even thoughts, of pity, yet still they were pleased at this indication of a gentle feeling on the part of their brutal lord. So beautiful is the appearance of virtue even in the eyes of her greatest enemies.

Gesler himself was during the evening in unwonted spirits, and at a late hour of the night, they all separated, better satisfied with each other than they had been for many a long day.

As we have seen, the lateness of their revels, had not prevented their rising on the next morning, and accordingly at an early hour they were all accoutred and ready to attend upon their commander. The bailiff had that morning bestowed more than usual care upon his toilet; his horse was richly caparisoned, and the pleasing anticipation of the pleasure of performing a merciful action seemed to illumine his countenance.

"These men of Uri," he said, addressing Arnold, who rode by his side, "are skilled, I hear, beyond the rest of their countrymen, in the use of this formidable weapon ?"

"Your Lordship has been truly informed," replied the young Swiss. "I have seen such deeds of skill among some of my peasant countrymen, as might well astonish the most skilful archer in Europe. The fame of the English bowmen is great, but I doubt much if an equal can be found to many of our mountaineers.   Tell, as your Lordship hears, is considered the best marksman with the cross-bow of any in the Canton of Uri, and I am sure will acquit himself well in any trial of skill you may impose upon him."

"I doubt it not," said Gesler, "and I mean to put his power to no trifling proof, but as you say, I doubt not he will acquit himself well."

So saying, he gave directions to his attendants to produce the prisoners. Tell and his son being brought into the presence of the Governor, the latter, addressing the mountaineer, observed—

"Thy act of disobedience, Tell, deserves the heaviest penalty the law awards, but I have heard thou hast a wife and children."

"I have, sir."

"That boy there is thy son, or I'm mistaken. He seems to bear as bold a brow as thine."

"The boy has courage, my Lord; it has been proved upon the glacier's brow."

"And thou art famed to use the cross-bow well?"

"My father," exclaimed Walter Tell, "can strike an apple at a hundred yards."

"Is that true, Tell?" said Gesler.

"I have done so, my Lord."

"Indeed! we'll try your skill; if you succeed your life is spared. Where is the cross-bow and his sheaf of arrows?—quick, bring me an apple."

A female peasant in the crowd advanced to the bailiff and presented to him a basket of apples, from which he selected one.

"Here," he exclaimed, "this apple shalt thou strike at the first shot, or I retract my pardon."

"It is the smallest apple in the basket," cried Tell.

"Nay, take thy choice, but see you fail not."

"'Tis a hard task," said Tell, "and needs a steady hand; my arms are cramped by lodging in yon dungeon yester night; besides the bonds were tight; to-morrow I should take a steadier aim."

"Perform the task at once."

"Where shall I place the apple for the trial?"

"Upon the head of Walter Tell, thy son."

"On my boy's head!" exclaimed Tell, with a look of incredulity, mingled with horror; "what! on my own child's head? No —no—you never mean it. My own life I dare risk—but not my child's—no—no —I would sooner perish."

"Perform the task, or he falls with thee; succeed, and both are saved."

The sudden turn which this affair had taken produced a feeling of consternation among the crowd; they had assembled to witness the accomplishment of an act of mercy on the part of their Governor, instead of the present unparalleled proceeding. At length the Countess Gertrude approached and supplicated him to alter his resolution.

"You cannot be in earnest," she said; "it is but in sport; but see how pale they look—they do not understand it——"

"In sport! Lady, who said I was in sport? Quick, measure out the distance: he says, I think, that at a hundred paces he can strike the mark —give him ten paces—nay, give him twenty. I would not overtask his vaunted skill."

"Down on your knees," cried the bystanders to Walter, "down on your knees and beg for mercy."

"I'm not afraid," said the boy; "my father will not hurt me."

"What has he to complain of? I but impose a task he can perform; his fate rests with himself; why need he fear? The skilful gamester when the stake is high, but nerves his hand the more before he strikes the blow."

"I have no fear, father;" exclaimed Walter, "why, you can strike the bird upon the wing."

"Not always, boy; but then my hand is steady."

"Here, take this boy," said the bailiff, "bind him to yonder tree, and place the apple on the urchin's head: take that which Tell shall give you."

"I'll not be bound," cried Walter; "let me not be bound, I'll stand quite still, indeed I will; but if I'm bound I struggle, and shall move."

"Make room there for the trial—place the boy yonder, beneath that linden tree—there, that will do—now, measure eighty paces, give Tell the cross-bow there, and choose an arrow from his quiver for him."

5   E

On the last order being given, one of the soldiers handed his cross-bow to Tell, and at the same time gave an arrow from the sheaf. Tell having carefully examined it, returned it to the trooper, observing that the point was blunt, and requested another; this pleased him as little as the first, and he begged he might be allowed to select one himself. The mind of Gesler was at the moment occupied by an unwilling attention to the remonstrances of his suite, among whom none were more earnest than Gertrude and Arnold. During this interval, the soldier having yielded to Tell's request, the latter selected an arrow from the quiver, and while the soldier's attention was directed to his master's movements, he contrived to secrete a second arrow in his vest.

Gesler, having shaken off his importunate followers, now imperatively ordered the trial to be made. Tell was about to address himself to the task, but his eyes swam with giddiness, and, with trembling hand, he dropped the bow.

"What! is thy vaunted skill an idle boast? thy hand trembles, what ails you, man? I've given you twenty yards."

Arnold now addressed himself to the bailiff for the purpose of interceding for the prisoner, but was repulsed by the Governor with more than his usual haughtiness. Incensed at his treatment, the blood of the young Swiss nobleman boiled within his veins, and turning to Gesler, who evidently endeavoured to avoid him, he said—

"It is well, my Lord, they have witnessed now your power; your end is gained. There is a limit even in severity; if pushed too far, it overshoots its mark, and fails in its design."

"When we have need of youthful counsellors, we'll call on Arnold Attinghausen; till then silence would best become you," said Gesler.

Incensed beyond measure at the insulting language thus addressed to him, Arnold returned—

"My Lord, I will speak out. In this act the honor of the Emperor is concerned. It is not his will—I'm sure it is not. My countrymen do not deserve this usage."

"Ha! what say'st thou?"

"Oh! long have I maintained a peaceful tongue, though my heart bled within me, when I saw the cruel acts which turned within this land. If I were now to hold my peace, I should be a traitor to my countrymen's cause, and to the Emperor also.

"This to me, to your liege Lord, young man!"

"I own no Lord but one in all the land—the Emperor Albert; he is thy Lord and mine. I'm free as thee, and bear as proud a name as you, Lord Governor," returned Arnold.

While the dispute was becoming more serious between the two last speakers, the attention of the bystanders had been so much attracted by the unusual occurrence, that the proceedings of Tell, to which they had lately paid so much attention, had remained unnoticed. The disputants at length had almost proceeded to extremities, Gesler being about to order the young Swiss into the custody of his guards, when a loud shout of surprise and joy burst simultaneously from the throats of the assembled crowds. Turning round, that he might understand the cause of this sudden ebullition of feeling, he heard the cries of—"The apple has been struck!"

"The madman! has he shot?" asked Gesler.

At that moment Walter Tell came running to his father with the apple in his hand, and flinging himself into his unconscious arms, exclaimed "Father, here is the apple, I knew you would not hit me."

"Hand me that apple," cried Gesler; "by heavens he has struck the apple through the core!"

Tell, in the meantime, remained in a state of stupefaction, resting upon his knee, and staring vacantly around.

Gertrude, whose feelings had been wrought up to the highest pitch of painful intensity by the occurrences of the morning, with all the bustling eagerness of womanly feeling had approached the spot where the prisoner and his son remained, and endeavoured to restore the bewildered man to a sense of his situation by soothing words, and other little attentions, which a woman, even of the highest class, never refuses to administer in the hour of distress, although at other times the conventional habits of society oblige her to perform a part foreign to her nature. How well did our Scottish bard express this inherent quality of a woman's nature when he wrote—

Oh, woman! in our hours of ease,
Uncertain, coy, and hard to please,
When pain and sorrow wring the brow,
A ministering angel thou!

Under the kind attention of Gertrude, Tell soon recovered his self-possession, and falling on the neck of his son, he sobbed aloud. While this scene was passing, Gesler, urged by curiosity, approached the spot. Tell, at the sight of his oppressor, and bearing in mind the dreadful ordeal he had passed through, started on his feet, and was about to address the Austrian, when an arrow dropped from the breast of his vest, and fell at the feet of Gesler's horse.

"I asked but one shot of thee, what means this second arrow?" said the rider, with a look of suspicion.

Tell, confused, and fearful for the safety of his son, replied—

"It is the usual custom of a bowman, sir."

"Indeed! to make a quiver of his bosom, man, and bear a sheaf of arrows thus about? Thou hadst some other meaning for the act. Speak, what was it? Nay, answer me."

Tell, for a time, hesitated; at length raising his manly form to its full height, and directing a scorching look of pity and defiance at the Lord Bailiff, he spoke.

"It is true, my Lord, I had another meaning. If, guided by my own unsteady hand, or urged by fate, the arrow from my bow had missed its aim, and my poor boy had suffered, not twenty seconds would have passed before the second barb had pierced a tyrant's heart!"

"Ho! traitor, was it so! Now mark me well; thy life is saved; I promised that before, but for thy liberty, it is not well you should have freedom 'till thy blood is cooled. I'll be thy leech, and cure thee of this itching to shed the blood of those who rule above thee.—Here, guards, convey him to his dungeon—nay, the boy is free, he'll spread the tale, and Switzer hinds shall know, that Gesler's vengeance is quick as it is sure."

The guards of the bailiff quickly obeyed the commands of their master, and Tell, disdaining to attempt an escape where his struggles would have been useless, suffered himself to be led quietly through the castle gates; the boy, who strove hard to follow his father, was forcibly detained by the soldiery, until their comrades had safely lodged his parent in the stronghold of the tyrant.

Gesler and his troops then retired into the castle, and the peasantry remained on the green, conversing together on the events of the morning. At first they spoke in a low and subdued tone of voice, collected into groups around some single speaker, to whose words they were paying attention. In a short time the conversation became more animated, and by the frequent communication which took place between the different parties, some general feeling seemed to pervade the whole assembly. The whole mass then moved in a body towards the pole on which the hat of Gesler was suspended, and violently throwing down the staff, and breaking it in two, they hacked it into a thousand pieces with their knives, and tearing down the hat of the tyrant, carried it off in triumph.

The rapidity with which these acts were performed completely took the soldiers by surprise, and they had hardly time to collect themselves in sufficient number, to make head against the unarmed peasants, before the latter had dispersed themselves in various directions, and the troopers were left alone upon the village green.

CHAPTER X.

THE STORM UPON THE LAKE.

Remember whom thou hast aboard.—
None that I more love than myself. You are a counsellor;
If you can command these elements to silence, and work
The peace of the present, we will not hand a rope more;
Use your authority. If you cannot, give thanks you
Have lived so long, and make yourself ready for the
Mischance of the hour, if it so hap.—

A rumour of the occurrences of the eventful morning, which we have just described, spread through the land like wildfire, and added fuel to the already inflamed minds of the inhabitants of the Three Cantons; low and ominous whisperings were heard in all directions, of an intended rising of the country to resist the Austrian power; several fugitives, from the vallies more to the west of the lake, had arrived and they all agreed in their accounts of the advance of the Austrian army, under the guidance of the Emperor Albert in person.

Gesler already perceived the dangerous position in which he stood, but he had proceeded too far in his career of crime to retrace his steps, even if his disposition would have allowed him so to do.

Having possession, as we have seen, of the person of Tell, and aware of the influence he possessed over the rest of his countrymen, he determined to make the safety of his prisoner doubly sure, by conveying him to his stronghold, the Castle of Kusnacht, on the banks of the lake of the Four Cantons. This act, he was aware, was in utter violation of the privileges guaranteed to the Swiss by the Austrian government, in accordance with which no native could be conveyed beyond the bounds of his native Canton.

Regardless of the consequences of this additional outrage upon the feelings of the Waldstetten, he made preparations to put his resolution in force; but fearful that, in the present highly excited state of the country, he should not be able to hold his prisoner against any sudden attack by his countrymen, which, from the nature of the road, might take place at a time when he was least aware, he resolved to convey him to Kusnacht by water, and in order to make assurance double sure, proposed to become a fellow-passenger in the vessel that was to convey him thither.

Under a strong escort of soldiers, early on the morning of the day succeeding that upon which Tell had made his famous shot, the skilful bowman was conveyed to the place of embarkation.

Surrounded by the troopers of Gesler, whose ranks completely hid him from the view of those whom curiosity had assembled to witness his departure, bound hand and foot, and thrown across the back of a powerful horse, was William Tell, although deprived of the power of using his native weapons, his famous cross-bow and his arrows were thrown across the neck of the same horse which bore their owner; as if, by placing within his sight, though not his reach, weapons of defence, they wished to add to his humiliation; and in this degrading manner was the future hero of Switzerland borne to the vessel, in which it was purposed to convey him to the Castle of Kusnacht.

We are attributing no unmanly feeling to our hero when we say, that the hopeless condition in which he then found himself placed, had depressed his spirits to such an unusual extent, as to cause him not only to curse inwardly the author of all his miseries, but to blame himself for the part he had taken in the escape of Erni.

"Fool that I was," he said, mentally; "are not my country's wrongs and my own cares enough for me, but I must rashly meddle in the cause of a rash boy, who slays a man to save a paltry ox, and risks a fearful war for a few thalers?"

In this gloomy mood he continued until he was brought to the place of embarkation. Here the bonds by which he was confined were loosened, and massive chains having supplied their place, which although they effectually prevented his escape and impeded his motions, still enabled him to stand upright and to move slowly.

This release from his previous state of close bondage was sufficient to drive from the mind of Tell the desponding thoughts with which it was lately filled. With more buoyant spirits, and with an eye which betokened more of defiance than despondency, he, with the assistance of one of the crew, ascended the plank which conducted him on shipboard.

When he had reached the deck of the small vessel, in which he was about to take his departure, he raised his hand, as if about to address the spectators, but his intention, whatever it might have been, was frustrated by two of the crew who were already on board.   These, by the orders of Gesler, threw the captive violently down into the bottom of the boat, and the bailiff, anxious apparently to be fairly afloat, quickly leaped on board, the rope by which it was moored was cast off, the sail hoisted, and the crew, which consisted of two rowers and a helmsman, having taken their respective places, the little bark, after a few strokes of the oars, was at a short distance from the shore.

But the sail still hung sluggishly, or, from what might have been supposed some sudden impulse, and as if it possessed vitality, flapped violently against the mast, like a wounded serpent in its last agonies.   In vain did the steersman endeavour to cause the ample canvas to fill ; the baffling winds refused to perform their office, and they were at length obliged to proceed onwards in their course with the aid of their oars alone.

The impatience of Gesler, at the slow progress they were making, became every minute more apparent.   The steersman anxiously watched the eye of his master as if anticipating some dreadful act, for, with a wildness of look almost amounting to the appearance of insanity, it glanced from the flapping sail to the manly and prostrate form of his captive.

"How long," he asked the steersman, "shall we be, Hubert, before we reach the castle ?"

"With a fair wind, my lord, one hour would well suffice : but this is sluggish work—these toilsome oars."

"It is strange ! this sudden lulling of the wind," observed Gesler, as he looked into the horizon ; "but, Hubert, do you mark that cloud out yonder—there, in the east—nay, nay, more to the right—just over Altdorf's tower ?"

The steersman gazed intently in the direction which Gesler pointed, and motioning to the rowers, directed their attention, also, to the object of his scrutiny.

"We shall have wind enough, ere long, my lord."

"Enough !   I hope it will be no more than is enough," said one of the rowers.

The cloud, on which all were now intent, had no appearances which, to an inexperienced eye, would render it an object worthy of notice, but the boatmen, more versed in the signs of the heavens, became more seriously alarmed at its threatening look, for, small and insignificant as it was, still,—

> Like that cloud, in size like human hand,
> Which slowly overshadowed Israel's land,

it gradually assumed a more formidable appearance, while from various parts of the horizon, as if summoned to the meeting ; huge masses of vapour arose, and rolling together in accumulated heaps, formed a series of mimic mountains.

At the same time the rising wind was plainly heard, although, at present, it was unfelt.   Soon, however, the loosened sail flapped with more violence than before ; it then suddenly filled, and before the sailors had time to cast off the rope, the boat was scudding on nearly upon its beam ends, and shipping water at every fresh gust of wind that hurried her along.

It was not long that matters continued in this condition, the violence of the wind ceased, and, with the exception of the uneasy motion she had acquired by her sudden righting, she glided smoothly along under a gentle breeze. But the aspect of the heavens grew more threatening at every minute, and, fearful of the consequences of any increase of the wind, they thought it most prudent to shorten sail.

It was not long before the wisdom of these precautionary measures became apparent, for the gale again rose with great fury, and in spite of all the efforts of Hubert to keep her head close to the wind, the danger of driving ashore became every minute more imminent.

The shore upon their lee was a vast and confused heap of granite rocks, piled upon each other to an inaccessible height, and assuming all the fantastic forms which nature could devise. The huge tabular fragments were in some places so arranged as to resemble embattled towers; others stood, as it were, isolated from the rest, and might, when seen dimly through the mist, or in the shades of evening, be easily mistaken for the spires of some gigantic cathedral.

That portion of this romantic coast, towards which they were now so rapidly approaching, formed a bold and precipitous promontory, well known on account of the dangerous shoals and sunken rocks in its vicinity, amongst which many a goodly boat had perished, and many a hardy fisherman breathed his last prayers. The danger now became apparent to all, for if, by dint of great skill and exertion, they should be enabled to weather the cape, still their passage must be made in the midst of all the intricate mazes of the channels of the sunken rocks we have already mentioned.

The utmost skill of Hubert was unequal to the task he had to perform, and, directing his speech to the bailiff, he told him of their almost hopeless condition, for the violence of the wind had increased, and the rain, falling in torrents, was driven violently into the faces of the drenched and wearied crew.

"There is but one," said Hubert, "could bear us safely through this dangerous passage."

"Would he were here," cried Gesler; "if his skill could save us. I never saw so fierce a storm before."

"He is here, but helpless. Tell only knows the passage."

"What! Tell our prisoner here?"

"The same, my lord."

"He knows these channels well?"

"None better; he was bred near the spot, and knows each inlet in the rock, and every sunken stone about this cape, be it no bigger than your lordship's hat."

"Hat! what hat! what mean you, Hubert?"

"I crave your pardon, my lord, I only meant there's scarce a stone near to this stormy spot, no matter what its size, but is well known to Tell."

"But, dare we trust him?" said Gesler, addressing his retainer in a whisper; "he has good cause of hatred 'gainst our person,"

" That's true, my lord," returned the other speaker, " but his own life's at stake, as well as ours."

It must not be supposed that this conversation took place with as much regularity as that with which we have described it, nor was it possible to prevent the purport of their discourse reaching the ears of Tell, who, in spite of the painful and helpless condition in which he was, could hardly forbear exulting at the danger in which Gesler and his followers found themselves, or smiling at the fears which they expressed more by looks than words. He almost wished his country might be avenged by the death of the monster, even though he himself should share his fate.

But, again, the thought of home, and all its endearments crossed his troubled brain, and he conceived that other opportunities might occur to avenge the wrongs of his native land—he had worked himself into this mood of mind, when he was roused from his reverie by the words of Gesler.

" Tell," he exclaimed, " well didst thou redeem thy life by thy bold shot ; and had you not, by thy expressed intentions, aimed at my life, thy liberty had been thine own as well. You see the danger which we all now run, I am told thou art as skilful at the helm, as with bow. We need an arm like thine to save our lives—and thine own too. Save us and thou art free, I pledge my word—refuse us, and you perish as well as us ; thou hast less chance, seeing that thou art fettered."

Tell, slightly raising himself in the boat, as well as his bonds would allow him, casting a stern glance upon Gesler, replied, " Tyrant, it is not for thy sake or my own, that I now promise to use the skill that God has granted me. It is but for my children and my Charlotte's sake, and that of my poor country. For thy promise of liberty, I heed it not, if I obtain my freedom, these hands shall work it out."

So saying, he held up his manacled arms, and the boatmen soon relieved him of his chains. He then seated himself at the prow, Hubert resigning his seat to him, and grasping the tiller in his hand, he looked around in all directions, with a scrutinizing eye ; having well considered the situation in which they were placed, he appeared suddenly to have made up his mind as to the plan he intended to pursue, and then suddenly gave direction to the boatmen to shake out every inch of canvas they could find.

The men, seeing the fury of the wind, hesitated to obey his orders, and it was not until Gesler, who had now made up his mind to rely implicitly on the skill of Tell in his extremity, had reiterated his orders, that they reluctantly complied.

No sooner had they exposed the whole surface of the sail to the wind, than the little bark, staggering under its influence, flew onward with increased velocity. It was now rapidly advancing towards a shelf of rocks close to the promontory of which we have already spoken.

All now looked aghast, even Gesler himself began to quail, and fear it was the intention of Tell, to drive them upon the precipitous rocks, and whelm them all in one common destruction.

Tell now putting forth all his strength, until the muscles of his arms seemed ready to burst the seams of his dress, endeavoured to port the

helm, and by sailing as close to the wind as possible, strove to weather the promontory. But although possessed of herculean strength, he was unable to effect his object without the assistance of Hubert, the power of the gale upon the wide-extended canvas defying his control.

Sailing now, almost in the teeth of the wind, the little bark, though she bore it bravely, had the pennon that decorated her mast-head brought so low, that it tripped along the surface of the waves, hanging to the summit of each, as if by its tiny efforts it endeavoured to retard the progress of the boat itself.

Anxiously now did all on board mark their advance towards the point they had to round, for the intention of Tell was, by this time, evident to all. They now appeared to be not many hundred yards from the spot at which their destiny was to be decided. They approached it—before them lay a narrow channel, between the lofty sides of the precipice which formed the cape, and an isolated rock, whose summit far overtopped the mast-head of their frail vessel—onward they drove, and their prow was now entering the channel; in another moment they were becalmed in the lee of the detached rock, and the vessel strove to right herself.

Still she maintained her onward course with rapidity, for although no longer feeling the influence of the wind, the rapid race of the current, as it passed through the narrow strait, and the impetus they had already attained in their course, bid fair to carry them safely through;

6   G

but an unexpected obstacle suddenly arrested the progress of the little vessel. The boat, as we have already said, endeavoured to right itself as soon as it was screened from the influence of the wind, but before it could effect this movement, the top of the mast was arrested by a portion of the overhanging crag, and having already been weakened, by the straining of the canvas, during the gale, it suddenly went by the board, and the sail falling with it, Gesler and his crew were enveloped in its ample folds, and for a time unable to extricate themselves from the mass of dripping canvas.

CHAPTER XI.

THE HUNTER'S LEAP.

> Now would I give a thousand furlongs of water for an
> acre of barren ground; long heath, brown furze, any
> thing;—but I would fain die a dry death.

As soon as, by dint of great exertion, Gesler and his companions, had relieved themselves from the folds of the wet sail in which they were entangled, they perceived that the boat, after the fall of its mast, had been drifted through the strait by the force of the current, and now lay like a helpless log, beating about at the mercy of the winds and waves, which threatened every moment to cast it upon the rocky shore.

The skill of Tell was again called into action, to clear away the wreck of the mast and rigging; with which the boat was encumbered. As soon as this had been effected, as well as circumstances would allow, they were obliged again to have recourse to their oars to avoid the danger of having the boat swamped, or driven on the rocks.

The rowers pulled lustily, and Tell, again resuming his seat, took charge of the helm. Slowly indeed did they now make head against the opposition of the elements, and it needed all the skill of their helmsman, to keep their disabled bark from foundering. As they had by this time weathered the headland of which we have spoken, they found themselves in a little bay or bight of the lake, with the wind still strong against them, but with the advantage of more sea-room, if we may use the term when speaking of a mountain lake.

The rowers now, putting forth all their energies, bent to their oars, and Tell directed the course of the boat towards that part of the shore which lay midway between the cape they had recently passed, and the high land forming the opposite side of the bay. Having by dint of great exertion, neared the shore at this spot, they found themselves protected, in a great measure, from the action of the wind, by the land, and were enabled to relax their efforts, and creep slowly along the shore under its protection.

In this manner they proceeded, until they were approaching the opposite promontory, in rounding which they would again have to cope with the fury of the gale. In order to be better prepared for their conflict with the elements, they lay-to for a time in the quiet water. Having refreshed themselves by rest, the rowers again commenced their task, and when, nearing the cape, they began to feel the influence of the wind, they boldly plied the oars, more confident in their own strength, after the dangers they had already safely passed.

While the Bailiff and his crew were thus struggling with the tempest, their progress had not been unmarked from the cliffs, on which a party of fishermen were assembled, who had left their occupation on the water to escape the fury of the tempest. Two of the party, an old man and his son, had been gazing intently on the waters for some time, when the boy suddenly exclaimed.

"Hark! father did you hear that bell?"

"'Tis from the chapel of our Lady; surely, some vessel on the lake is in distress; look out upon the waters, child, and see; my sight is growing dim."

"Father, there is a skiff upon the waves."

"Say, is it near the land?"

"It's driving on, with all the tempest's force, directly to the foot of the great Axenberg."

"Heaven save the souls of all that are on board! On such a day as this they cannot escape."

"Father, father, 'tis Gesler's boat; I know it by the pendant and the red deck; it has passed the breakers now; a skillful helmsman they must surely have."

"No skill can save them, boy. Avenging Heaven stands on our country's side, the tyrant's days are numbered!"

"Father you're right; I cannot see them now. Stay—there's a dark object close amid the breakers."

"Where, boy?"

"No, 'tis a rock, the white foam made it darker."

"Come, come, let's in, it's hail;ng fast. In, in, and let us hope better days."

As the fishermen were directing their steps from the cliff, Tell suddenly sprang upon the rock, bearing his bow and arrows in his hand, and sinking on his knees, in an exhausted state, appeared to address a fervent prayer to Heaven.

"Father," cried the lad, "it is Tell, our great bowman."

"Why, how has he escaped? I thought he was confined in Altdorf's towers."

Tell, now rising from his attitude of prayer, approached the speakers. "Friends," he exclaimed, "the hand of Providence is on our side."

"Why, how have you escaped from Gesler's power?" exclaimed the fisherman.

"Did you not see a boat upon the waves?" said Tell.

"We did, it was the Bailiff's, as we thought."

"I know it was the Bailiff's, father; I know it well."

"It was the Bailiff's," said Tell; "to Kusnacht he was bearing me in chains; but when the storm arose, he asked my aid; I promised I would use my utmost skill to save the boat, if Heaven's good will were so. I thought of home, and did my duty well; but ever as we passed near to the shore, I kept my watchful eye upon the rocks, to see if I could compass my escape. Long, long it was in vain, for their bare sides were too precipitous to yield a footing e'en to the nimble chamois."

"They are the boldest cliffs on all the lake," observed the fisherman. "Your task was hopeless."

"Indeed, it almost was. At length I saw a little jutting rock, that, like a table, stood out from the cliff. I bad the rowers pull with all their might, and well did they obey me. Close to the base of the o'er-hanging cliff I steered the boat. I suddenly sprang up, and snatched my arms, which lay within my reach; a short prayer breathed to Heaven for my success, then pressed my foot against the gunwale's side, and took the desperate leap—I reached the rock, and once again am free."

"A miracle was surely wrought to save thee—what of the boat?"

"Driven from the land by the rude shock it felt, it drifted far away, at random tost o'er the abyss of waters."

"Then he may yet escape, and if he does your life's no longer safe—where do you now proceed?"

"Homewad my course is bent," said Tell; "one interview at least with Charlotte and the children I must have, ere I forget my hill-side haunts, where I so often have the chamois followed, or tracked the famished wolf; alas the day that I must turn from these, and dip my arrow in the blood of man!"

"Were it not better," said the fisherman, "to seek some safe retreat, and wait awhile, until the Bailiff's rage has passed away."

"There is no fear from him at present, friend; in the low lands the waters all are out, the bridges swept away."

"Then fare you well!" returned the fisherman, "and Heaven direct your steps; you take the mountain road!"

"Aye, I breathe more freely, and my step is firmer when my foot treads upon my native hills. But I must hasten, 'tis a long road, and I would reach my home ere nightfall; fare you well—"

So saying, William Tell, grasping his recovered arms, and with the cheering feeling of regained liberty, strode forward with a firm and elastic step, in spite of his recent trials, followed by the good wishes of the group of fishermen. With glistening eye he carefully examined his cross-bow, to see if it had been injured during his late perilous adventure, but the good bow was perfect still. "Perhaps," cried Tell, addressing his favourite weapon, as if it were endued with life, "by thee the wrongs of Switzerland shall be redressed, you never failed me yet in all my sports, fail me not now when justice needs thy aid. But why," he cried, soliloquizing, "why do I let the dreadful thought assail me of this projected murder?—murder—my country needs the sacrifice, it is no murder—it is an offering that even-handed justice loudly calls for—my country's safety demands it at my hand; nay, mercy looks with a complacent smile upon the tyrant's death, her cause will be served, and one man's fall shall save the lives of thousands."

"But let me banish all these thoughts," he continued, "I go to meet my Charlotte and my children; they must not see my clouded brow or know what I contemplate."

So saying, he passed his hand across his forehead, and arranging more carefully the eagle plume with which his cap was decorated, proceeded cheerfully upon his journey.

The mountainous path which Tell had selected to lead him to his cottage home, was beset by more difficulties than the hardy mountaineer had anticipated; the late storms had been more general and disastrous in their effects than he had been led to believe; the road in many places was much obstructed by the fall of masses of granite, which had been shaken from their ancient resting places by the violence of the wind and the disruption of avalanches.

The impediments thus produced were many of them difficult to surmount, and materially impeded the progress of our bowman, and he had not proceeded above half way on his route, before the sinking sun announced to him the rapid approach of evening,

He now found it would be impossible for him to reach his humble dwelling before the morning, and, anxious as he was to calm the fears of his family, he deemed it more prudent to seek some shelter for the night than to hazard an encounter with a sudden storm, such as that which had swept over the lake during the day, the dangers of which, great as they were in the broad light of the sun, would be much aggravated if encountered during the darkness of the night.

Being well acquainted with the mountain roads, he was aware of a small chapel or rather hermitage, at no great distance from the road, whose solitary inmates would willingly afford him the accomodation he required.

Thither therefore our hero proceeded, and having partaken of the rude fare of the monks, he laid himself down to rest his wearied limbs, determined to rise before the sun, and pursue his homeward journey.

CHAPTER XII.

THE HAPPY MEETING.

Though poor the peasant's hut, his feasts though small,
He sees his little lot the lot of all;
Sees no contiguous palace rear its head,
To shame the meanness of his humble shed;
No costly lord the sumptuous banquet deal,
To make him loathe his vegetable meal.

With anxious heart, and unquiet looks, had Charlotte waited the return of Tell; five nights had already elapsed since his departure, and as yet she was uncertain respecting his fate. Her boy, too, had not returned, and the wild rumours of passing events, that had reached her humble home, tended to add to the miserable state of her feelings. In this condition of mind, with her two younger children clinging to her side, did the wife of Tell pass the hours, wearied from long watching, and chilly and miserable although close to a blazing fire of pine timber.

From time to time she would rise from her seat, and look out from the door of her cottage, in the sickening hope of catching a glimpse of his form, as he moved along the distant mountain road. The slightest sound attracted her attention and caused her to start, and to such an extreme state of nervous susceptibility had her feelings been raised, that you might have supposed a fashionable dame stood before you, instead of a hardy Swiss matron, who had boldly faced the storms of her native country, in the severest weather, and stood fearlessly on the edge of the overhanging precipice, undaunted by the roar of the cataract.

On this her fifth morning of watching, she had not remained long in a state of suspense before she saw an old man and a boy approaching the cottage; she at once recognized the form of her son Walter, and rushed rapidly along the path to meet him. In her progress she took notice of the old man who accompanied, and seemed to bear upon, the boy, for support and guidance. His bandaged eyes bespoke his blindness, and at once the whole truth of the gloomy rumours that were abroad flashed upon her mind.

In the first transport of her feelings she strained her son in her arms, then, still retaining her grasp, she held the boy at arms' length, and gazed anxiously at him. As if still dissatisfied, and unwilling to trust her sense of sight alone, she gently passed her hand across his brow and smoothed back his hair, then again pressing him to her bosom she exclaimed, while a flood of tears came to her relief.—

" Thou art unhurt ! But could thy father do it ? had he a heart ?"

" Alas !" said Melctor, " the lives of both depended on it."

" He is no father ! none with a father's feelings could have done so ! what—draw the bow against his own child's head ?"

" Rather," replied Melctor, " thank Heaven for their deliverance."

" My father's hand is sure, dear mother, I knew he would not hit me."

" And you stood by, and heard the monster's orders, and did not rescue him."

" This is poor Melctor, mother, his eyes are out."

" Melctor ! oh monster ! monster ! and men of Switzerland stood by and saw it—Switzers alone in form, their hearts were Austrian."

" Have patience, woman, the hour has not arrived."

" But where's thy father, Walter, thy cruel father ?—nay, speak."

" It is a cruel tale," said Melctor, " but must be told.—He threatened Gesler, and was borne back to prison."

" To prison !—say not so."

" Would that were all the danger !"

" What greater can there be ? in prison, and in Gesler's power !"—

" Gesler along with Tell embarked for Kusnacht, thy husband bound —the people say the boat could never live in such a storm as swept the lake soon after—But let us trust in Heaven, it can save—and it will. Hope for the best, thy boy is safe."

With powers completely paralyzed by the shock imparted by this last news, Charlotte suffered herself to be led towards her cottage, in a state of mind bordering on distraction.

Matters were in this condition, excepting that the efforts of Walter, and the caresses of her younger children, had somewhat restored their mother to a state of consciousness, when Ernest entered, accompanied by Hans Winkelried.

Their presence, and the information brought by Ernest, that Tell had escaped, and that his return might be soon expected, succeeded in restoring Charlotte to her usual frame of mind. By him she also learned, that the Baroness von Walstein, with the kindness which characterized all her acts, had repaired to the village of Burglen, after receiving information of the outrages committed by the agents of Gesler, and by all the means at her disposal relieved the wants of the distressed villagers.

After enduring so many anxious hours of watching, this sudden accession of good news had so powerful an effect upon Charlotte, that her acts partook more of the character of one beside herself, than of the rational behaviour of the mother of a family.

She asked her visitors to partake of refreshment, arranged and re-arranged her frugal board, heaped piles of wood upon the already blazing fire, and directed and misdirected the children so frequently, that if Ernest and Walter had not put an end to the confusion arising from the highly excited state of her mind, by taking matters under their own management, it is uncertain how long this chaotic condition of things might have endured.

In the midst of this turmoil, William Tell himself entered the cottage. He was somewhat astonished at the appearance of things, and at the bustle and pleasant countenances of all assembled.

The fact was the sight was to him unexpected; his heart during his journey had been yearning after home, and he had pictured to himself the painful state of anxiety in which he should find his wife on his return, so frequently and so vividly, that, to tell the truth, he was rather disappointed, and vexed, at finding the different aspect affairs had assumed.

He was too good a husband, however, to allow this feeling to retain possession of his mind, and as soon as his presence was discovered, he returned the affectionate greetings of his family with ardour, and was soon informed of what had recently occurred to cause this unexpected rise in the spirits of his household."

"Well, Walter," he exclaimed, "you have reached home first."

"Not much before you, father, I have but just arrived; but then the way was long, and poor Melctor, so faint and wearied."

"Alas! I know it, but here he can have rest."

"Tell," said Ernest, "you had the message I sent by your son."

"I had; but come this way, it is not well that Charlotte should o'er-hear us."

"There has been a meeting," said Ernest, "at the house of Walter Furst, and it was there agreed to rouse the country to a sense of wrong, that, when the plot is ripe, they may be ready to rise at once, and break our bonds asunder."

"And by what means is this to be effected?"

"I'll tell you shortly; young Arnold Attinghausen, has left the court and now is one of us. I saw him in the valley, assisting Lady Gertrude. Furst and the rest rely upon his faith. By his advice old Melctor goes with me; his tale of grief will move the hardest heart, and stir men to revenge."

"I think it's wisely counselled."

"So they all do," said Ernest. "I'm glad I found him here, we'll start tomorrow—Tell, I think you must remember Hildegard"—

"Yes, your affianced, what of her?"

"She is with Lady Gertrude, her mother also. In troubled times like those which must ensue, their unprotected state needed some help, and in the halls of Walstein she is safe."

"It's ordered for the best;—does Hans go with you?"

"It's so intended."

"Come, wife," said Tell, "we've all been early risers and need refreshment, after the mountain air."

Before their humble meal was well discussed, young Walter had begun to practice with a cross-bow; he soon came running to his father to show him the broken string and request his aid to mend it.

"Not I," exclaimed Tell. "A skilful bowman mends his own thong always"—

"Oh, William!" said his wife, addressing Tell, "you cannot think how sad it makes me, to see how fond that boy is of the chase. He's ever out from morn till eve upon the mountain's side."

"Why should you be unhappy, Charlotte. The man who lives among these mountains should ever be an expert hunter." "The boy but follows what he has seen me do."

"I cannot be a shepherd, mother, I hate the dull and melancholy life; 'tis wearisome to sit all day and watch the silly sheep. No, mother, I'll be a hunter, another William Tell"—

"And lead your father's life of danger, boy, and leave me here a prey to grief and fear. Oh! Walter, you little know the dangers of that life; straying perhaps amid the dreary glaciers, the land-marks swept away by the last avalanche, night coming on—no food or shelter near. Perhaps the path you travelled in the morning glides from the slippery mountain's side, and leaves a horrid gulph, impassable to all. There to remain a prey to hunger and to cold, till the gaunt wolves prey on your stiffening corpse!"

"Why, mother, Hans yonder is a shepherd, and Ernest is a hunter, which would you rather see me?"

While mother and son were thus engaged, Ernest and Tell had arranged their future proceedings. Ernest accompanied by Hans, was in the first instance to proceed through Unterwalden, along with the unfortunate Melctor, while Tell and his family were to direct their course to Burglen, so that in case of danger, they might, by crossing the lake, evade the persecution of the bailiff.

CHAPTER XIII.

THE COMPACT OF BLOOD.

Can splendid robes or beds of down,
  Or costly gems to deck the hair,
Can all the glories of a crown
  Give health, or smooth the brow of care?

We left Gesler and his little crew apparently at the mercy of the waves, and beyond the reach of human aid, but heaven is above all yet, and as if it were in order that a more signal vengeance might overtake the tyrant, against all human calculation, the boat at length reached the shore and her unworthy burthen was safely landed, at the spot from which he had started in the morning.

But how different in all things, with the exception of his brutal thirst for vengeance, was the conscience-stricken and wearied Gesler as he again placed his foot on shore, to the Lord High Governor of Austria, when he seated himself in the vessel in the morning, exulting over the captivity of his victim.

Foiled in his revenge, terrified by the fear of death, drenched with rain, and all his faculties overpowered, Gesler slunk from public view, and retired to the house of one of his adherents. From thence,

7   H

having somewhat recovered from the effects of the storm, he repaired privately to the castle of Altdorf. Soon after his arrival it was publicly announced that on the following morning he would hold a High court of Justice to enquire into offences against the authority of the Emperor. Many were the surmises as to who was the intended victim, for that some sacrifice was determined upon was evident, and many were the restless pillows during the ensuing night.

At length the ominous morning arose, and Gesler, seated in his chair of state, and surrounded by his satellites, proceeded to discuss the object of their meeting. It was evident from the lowering brow of the tyrant, and the restlessness he evinced, that his mind was ill at ease.

Having recapitulated the occurrences of the preceding day, as methodically as his exasperated feelings would enable him, it was unanimously agreed upon, that a price should be set upon the head of Tell, and every exertion made for his apprehension. At length, in rather a hesitating tone the Bailiff addressed his hearers—

"The safety of the Austrian power," he said, "demands our utmost vigilance. Deeds more adverse to the Emperor's welfare, than all these petty outbreaks of the mountaineer, are acting in this land. The evils we have felt, this obstinate resistance to our will, you must suspect arises from no common source. Our firm enforcement of the Emperor's rights, is said to be the cause of this rebellion; 'tis false—more potent spirits are at work. The ancient nobles of the land it is who foster discontent among the people, to raise themselves above the Austrian rule."

" It is but as we suspected," observed one of his hearers.

" You have noticed Arnold Attinghausen," said his neighbour, " how boldly he has borne himself towards the Governor ?"

" I marked it well—before the people too !"

" You are right," said Gesler. " By him they were excited to tear down the hat; 'tis well that he were watched, but we have no law will reach his present acts, in the mean time some happy chance may rise, to rid us of his presence; but there's an agent still more great than him, who, with the cunning of her sex, has stirred the people more to discontent than any other; by her young Arnold was induced, nay urged, to raise his voice against us; he seeks her hand that he may join her lands unto his own; it is Gertrude von Walstein of whom I speak. She is within my power, under my guardianship does Gertrude stand, the proud girl shall find, that I can use my delegated power to stay her plots—call in the Lady Gertrude."

At the orders of Gesler, Gertrude entered, if not in close custody, yet evidently under the surveillance of two of the guard. She was accompanied by Hildegard, and advancing towards the table at which the Bailiff and his myrmidons were seated, boldly confronted the Austrian Governor.

The latter, on the other hand, in spite of his proud spirit, could scarcely raise his head, so as to look his intended victim in the face. Whether the injustice of the act he was about to accomplish, his wounded pride on account of the occurrences of the preceding day, or the innate power of virtue, which like Ithuriel's spear—

Naught evil can resist
But of force, returns to its own likeness—

subdued his usual haughty bearing, we know not, but there he sat more resembling the accused, than the accuser.—At length, having apparently mustered sufficient resolution, he said—

"Lady Gertrude, the safety of the Austrian power requires, that I should place a check upon your actions. The sympathy which you have shown towards those whom I have been called upon to punish, and your expressed opinions, have done more harm, aided the rebels' cause, and have produced more discontent than all the acts of justice I have done."

"My Lord," exclaimed Gertrude, "I am a free agent. My station in the country imposes on me the task of helping those who need. I never spoke yet, against the power possessed by Austria : if I have spoken on my country's side, it has been when I saw the Emperor's delegated power abused. I have done no wrong my Lord, and fear no punishment."

It is thy free speech, Lady, does the wrong—for punishment, that's not intended. But I am bound to watch o'er Uri's peace, and thy impetuous language must be checked. To Rossberg must you go ; its halls are wide, and fitted to receive a noble guest, such guest as Gertrude, Baroness von Walstein."

"Tyrant ! thy power reaches not to that. I am a free born Switzer, and cannot be imprisoned at your simple fiat."

" Remember, lady, I hold greater powers o'er thee. Here under my protection are you placed. I sit here guardian of thee, and all thy land. Thy foolish passion, maiden, for Arnold Attinghausen, is not unknown to me ; a barrier must be placed 'twixt him and you, or I shall not perform my duty well."

So saying he rose from his seat, and Gertrude disdaining a reply was, along with Hildegard, conducted from the apartment.

The bailiff's observations as to his influence over Gertrude, and her property, were not exaggerated, for ample powers had been placed in his hands by her kinsman, which he could exert when he thought fit, during their absence at the Imperial court.

Although the principal reason he had given, for his act of cruelty in immuring the Baroness in the castle of Rossberg was political necessity, yet there was another impulse, which more powerfully influenced his act, being as it was, much more personal.

The bailiff himself, then be it known, had conceived a most ardent passion for the broad lands of Gertrude, and on this account he aspired to her person. Her noble and well known political opinions deterred him from prosecuting his suit with his usual ardour, although he was aware of the affection of young Attinghausen for the noble maiden, for he conceived that their difference of opinion, as to the affairs of the country, had placed an insuperable bar to a reciprocity of feeling between the two. On the night on which Gesler's outrage upon Melctor occurred, the conversation which we recorded, as having taken place between the lovers, was partially overheard by one of his partizans, and reported to the Governor. Since then the altered conduct of Arnold had satisfied him of the truth of his follower's report, and of the certainty of the existence of a mutual passion.

His object now was to separate the lovers, and from the hint thrown out by him, during the morning, it plainly appeared he would have had no objection to the assistance of some kind friend, in relieving him ı the man he regarded as a rival, in his mercenary suit.

That such a man should be found among the followers of a leader, like the Austrian governor, is not to be wondered at, nor is it a greater matter of surprise, to find this agent, in the person of the Captain we have already noticed, as leader of the troops that went in pursuit of Erni.

This man, whose name was Friesshardt, was present in the Hall during the occurrences of the morning, and having heard the observations of his master, resolved to gratify his vengeance by an attempt upon the life of Arnold ; but as the young Swiss was more than a match for him in point of personal strength, he resolved to associate with himself in his murderous enterprise, a comrade of his named Leuthold, 'equally cruel with himself, although perhaps not possessed of the same share of animal courage.

To his rendezvous therefore he repaired, and after sounding his intended partner, with all the skill of an old tactician, and ascertaining that the depth of his villany was sufficient for his purpose, he began to develope his intended plot.

The actual commission of the crime raised no feeling of repugnance the breast of Leuthold, but the fear of the consequences of Gesler's rage, in case he should feel it good policy to declare his horror for the deed of blood, caused him to raise sundry objections to the scheme, which all the persuasion of his comrade, could not for some time overcome. At length, in the course of his arguments, he happened to lay great stress upon the liberality of the governor, towards all who served him, in his favourite schemes of cruelty.

The avarice of Leuthold, of which he possessed far more than an average share, was excited at the prospect of the additional pleasure of being well paid for an act, which, in itself, was far from being uncongenial to his soul, and without more argument he agreed to share the crime and the reward, with his worthy coadjutor.

CHAPTER XIV.

THE OATH.

Oh ! 'tis a noble, noble, gift of heaven,
The gift of light—each being lives on light,
And all creation feels its gladdening power !
The plants themsel ves turn joyful to the light :—
And he amidst thenight must groping sit
Of an eternal darkness.—

We must now repair to the retreat of Erni, where he had concealed himself from the pursuit of Gesler's emissaries, and where, ignorant of his father's unhappy fate, he remained impatiently waiting for the arrival of the day when Switzerland should be ripe for throwing off the Austrian yoke.

The friend of Tell, whose house afforded protection to Erni, was possessor of a large estate, in a highly cultivated spot, in the canton of Schweitz ; this estate he held in fief, direct from the Emperor of Germany himself. As the Emperor was elected by the general diet of the empire, it was not a necessary thing that the high office should be borne by the Duke of Austria, indeed we have already seen that ; previous, to the accession of Albert, the dignity had been conferred upon Adolphus of Nassau.

Albert of Austria, being now Emperor, endeavoured to oblige the Swiss to swear allegiance to himself, not as Emperor of Germany, but as Duke of Austria. On this account all the principal men of the country, who possessed landed property, under the tenure we have mentioned, were peculiarly obnoxious to Albert and his agents, and, as feelings of this kind are generally mutual, the great landed proprietors were foremost, among those who wished to throw off the yoke of the House of Austria.

Among these, Werner Stauffacher, in whose house Erni was now concealed, stood pre-eminent for his wealth and independence, and in his dwelling the first elements of the Swiss confederacy were formed.

Werner, as he was usually called, had been endeavouring to reason with his inmate as to the uselessness of his grief during his absence from home ; for Erni, uncertain as to the fate of his father, who had been left unprotected, and more than usually exposed to danger from Gesler's vengeance, had made strenuous attempts to induce his protector to allow him to leave his hiding place, and revisit his home, if only by stealth. To this his host objected, that he was under his roof, and that he had pledged his word for his safety. While this friendly argument was proceeding, the arrival of a stranger, an inhabitant of Uri, was announced.

" What! Walter Furst," exclaimed Werner, " my ancient friend!—a better man, or one more welcome here, ne'er crossed my threshold."

" What news from Uri, Walter ?"

" Alas! my friend, sorrow I left at home, and sorrow I find here. Where'er I turn I hear the voice of mourning. They used to call us happy ; ' the happy Swiss ' were words in every mouth. All classes feel the scourge, the noble and the peasant—all are subject to the oppression of the Austrian Bailiff."

" It is the same here in Schweitz. Wolfhausen lords it with as high a hand as Gesler does with you," replied Werner.

" I scarcely think it," returned Furst. " A deed that makes the very blood run chill, has Gesler lately done."

" Wolfhausen surely equals him in crime ; of what is it you speak ?"

" You knew old Melctor on the hill, near Burglen ?"

" Yes surely—well! but what of him ?" said Werner, scarcely able to conceal his agitation. " But come this way—speak lower, Walter.'

"Why should I so? deeds such as these cry out aloud to Heaven, and every man in Switzerland should hear them."

"Nay, but speak lower, friend; you see that youth, his modesty prevents his drawing near, but his heart throbs with anguish for your news. He is Melctor's son, fled here for safety."

"Alas, poor youth! the news that he must hear will break his heart. Hark to you, Werner;" and he communicated with his friend in a whisper.

"What!" exclaimed Werner, in a voice choked by emotion, "both his eyes?"

"I can no longer bear it," cried Erni interposing. "What news of my father? I know you spoke of him. This terrible suspense is worse than all;—what of my father?"

"The monster Gesler has torn out his eyes!"—

"His eyes! oh Heaven! my poor, poor, father.—And here I stay a miserable wretch, and meanly hide my head, to save myself, while my poor father—no longer will I stay, you shall not stop me, till I have avenged my father's wrongs upon the tyrant's head, and slaked my vengeance in his blood!"

As Erni was about to depart, he was forcibly detained by Werner and Furst.

"Nay, stay awhile," cried the former, "vengeance is nearer than you are aware. Your countryman has come with mighty tidings. Through the three Cantons every heart beats high, and every hand is ready to rebel—they want but leaders. The nobles, we have found, are on our side, and at the field of Rutli do we meet, to reason on the state of the Three Cantons. Will you join us there?"

"Wherever vengeance can be found I follow."

"On Tuesday next, at night, the meeting is; you know the spot," said Werner.

"'Tis near the lake I think, upon the left, to him who sails towards Brunnen."

"You are right; it is a meadow embosomed deep in wood, two sides by toppling crags are overhung, and it is placed directly opposite the Mytenstein. From Schweitz the passage easily is made. There we may spend the hours in secret council, secure from interference. Give me your hand—now your's;—as we three here join hands in honest truth, so may the three lands stand by one another, for freedom or destruction —life or death!"

The excitement caused by the undertaking they had entered upon had somewhat subdued the grief of the three, and they were about to retire in a more settled mood of mind, when young Walter Tell entered the apartment, he had been despatched by his father to Erni, to give him information of the fate of Melctor and of the errand on which he had gone.

The boy also brought news of the imprisonment of Gertrude, and of the open declaration of Arnold Attinghausen in their favour.

"This is great news," said Furst. "This outrage upon the baroness will rouse them all; we have naught to fear, save the three castles they have built to overawe us."

" Yes, Sarnen, Rossberg, and Gesler's den at Altdorf," returned Werner. " They must be taken—castles called you them, they are prisons rather, with dungeons deep and dark—alas my country, before these Austrians came they were unknown. The person of the Switzer then was free, as is the breeze that blows upon the hills."

" 'Tis needful they should fall," said Walter Furst; " but for the means—How can it be accomplished ?"

" At Rutli, when we meet, it shall be thought of."

" Well, be it so, meantime young Ernest has, by my advice, gone through the furthest confines of the land, to spread the knowledge of the dreadful deed : Melctor accompanies him; at sight of him, I know full well the rudest hearts owned by Helvetia's sons, will pant for vengeance, and take their rusty broadswords in their hands, and, when need be, will rush into the field."

" Well, then, we meet again at Rutli. Let each bring with him ten chosen friends to join our holy bond. Through Uri, Furst, you spread the patriot flame. In Underwalden Erni tells his tale, and here in Schwietz my friends will not be idle.—Tell meets us I suppose at Rutli, Walter ?

" I urged him to do so," said Walter, " and he answered that, 'when his arm was needed it was ready to serve his country in her sacred cause; but,' he exclaimed, 'I was not born to weigh and chuse—I am useless in your councils, but when you are once resolved to act, call upon Tell and he will answer you !" '

" It is like the daring hunter," returned Werner. " Well, fare ye well; at Rutli, next, we meet."

CHAPTER XV.

THE PRISONERS.

This castle hath a pleasant seat; the air
Nimbly and sweetly recommends itself
Unto our gentle senses.

The castle of Rossberg, to which the Lady Gertrude and her hand-maiden had been conveyed by the orders of Gesler, was seated on a lofty rock, at the extremity of an extensive and elevated valley, near the foot St. Gothard; on three sides it was perfectly inaccessible, on account of the precipitous nature of the rock on which it stood, but it was connected with the lofty hill at whose base it was placed, by a long ridge of granite, chiefly composed of huge blocks that had fallen from the sides of the mountain.

The rude surface of this mass of fragments, formed the only path-way to the castle gates; in several places it had been necessary to level the irregular causeway by filling up the holes, or, in some cases, removing the more prominent obstructions in the road, to render it passable. Between that extremity of the path-way which was nearest to the castle, and the castle itself; a deep gulf or opening occurred, across which a person about to enter the building must cross on the unstable footing of the trunk of a large tree, which had been laid across the chasm, and formed a rude bridge. Amid the fragments of rock at the bottom of this ravine, a mountain stream, one of the tributaries of the River Reuss, went roaring along, until it found a smoother channel, through which it was conducted in a serpentine direction round the foot of the rock upon which the castle rested, towards the extended plain it had to traverse during its course to the Lake Lucern.

In an earlier part of its course, this little stream formed a beautiful cascade, which at times was swelled into a magnificent cataract, adding to the grandeur of the scene, and rendering the castle on its precipitous rock, and surrounded as it otherwise was, by a dark plantation of fir, an object worthy the contemplation of an artist. To this solitary, but delightful and healthy retreat, were Gertrude and Hildegard escorted by a party of Gesler's followers.

The castle of Rossbergh had been, in earlier times than those of which we are speaking, the abode of one of the feudal chiefs of the land, under a former order of things ; it was found by the bailiff in a ruinous state, and was, under his direction, partially repaired, being at times visited by the governor on account of its romantic situation. As soon as he discovered the growing discontent of the Swiss, at his tyrannical conduct, the castle of Rossberg occurred to his mind, as a place well adapted for the confinement of those, whom, having become troublesome to his government, it was deemed fitting to confine at some distance from the capital; accordingly to render it more suitable to the new pur- pose to which it was to be applied, he added to its naturally strong position all the advantages of defence which art could supply. In this altered condition, Rossberg became a strongly fortified castle, with internal ar- rangements, which rendered it a fit abode for any guest it might be destined to receive.

The observations which the baroness had been enabled to make, on the conduct and disposition of her humble companion, during the short but eventful term of their acquaintance, had produced highly favourable impressions on her mind. The kindheartedness and the subdued but firm behaviour of Hildegard, during the trying scenes, in which she had to bear no inconsiderable a part, and which were so foreign to any of her former experiences, had won the heart of Gertrude.

On the other hand, the goodness of heart displayed by the Baroness, and the cheerful endurance with which she met her unmerited suffer- ings, claimed the respect and love of the mountain maiden; so that al- though only a few days had elapsed since their first acquaintance, both mistress and maid were delighted with each other.

The similarity also of their situations, caused them to sympathize with each other's sufferings. Both had attached lovers, from whose presence their present imprisonment separated them.

Both these lovers were actively employed in the service of their mutual country, and both were alike exposed to the danger of the Bailiff's vengeance. Happy it was for the imprisoned maidens that

they were ignorant of the extent of danger which threatened them.

In the mean time the progress of Ernest, with his blind charge, through the more distant parts of the country, produced greater results than could have been anticipated.

The sight of the victim of Gesler's cruelty overpowered every prudential motive, and promises were given, on everyhand, of assistance to the good cause, whenever the leaders of the confederacy thought it prudent to demand an open demonstration of force.

Ernest was on his return from the highland of St. Gothard, a messenger of glad tidings, to those who were now directing all their energies to the salvation of their country. In the course of his route he had to pass in the neighbourhood of Rossberg, and among the few inhabitants of that thinly peopled district, he found the imprisonment of Gertrude had created a complete fever of excitement, for she was well known throughout her native canton, for the beneficence of her disposition and the numerous charitable actions she had performed.

As soon as Hans was made acquainted with the fact of Hildegard being her fellow prisoner, the poor fellow became perfectly unmanageable, and it required all the skill of Ernest to restrain the impetuosity of his temper. Overawed by the superiority of his companion, Hans, at length, with a cunning, of which he could hardly have been thought capable, suppressed the feelings by which he was agitated, and by the assumed calmness of his behaviour completely deceived the vigilance of Ernest.

I

Unaware of the proximity of those in whose fate she was so much interested, Hildegard was seated alone, in a chamber in the castle of Rossberg, and solaced the hours of her confinement by the repetition of some favourite ditty.

HILDEGARD'S SONG.

'Tis the horn, 'tis the horn! from the mountain's brow—
The sons of Uri are rousing now;
The shepherd speeds to the green hill's side,
The herdsman seeks the pastures wide,
The fisher's boat is on the lake,
And their way to the hills do the hunters take.

'Tis the sun, 'tis the sun! its upward ray,
Gold and crimson, awakes the day.
The shepherd tends his fleecy charge;
The herdsman's kine now rove at large,
In the lake the fisher takes his prey,
But the hunter's chase is far away.

'Tis the moon, 'tis the moon! her gentle ray
Is sweeter far than the garish day;
It falls on the shepherd's humble cot:
The herdsmen's hut forgets she not;
The fisher's boat floats in her light,
And the hunter loves her beams at night.

She had just concluded her song, when Gertrude unexpectedly entered the apartment; she waited until it was ended before she addressed her attendant, to whom she then said:—

"I admire your behaviour, Hildegard, under the circumstances in which you are now placed, I am afraid, through my acts; and if I did not, on that account, lament your present situation, I should say that, like the caged bird, your song was improved by confinement. It's a pleasing ditty you have just concluded."

"It is one of Ernest's favourite songs," replied her attendant.

"I wish my heart, my good girl, was as free from anxiety as yours; but I fear a heavy responsibility is attached to me for having roused the passions of the Bailiff. But who could avoid speech, after witnessing as I did, the cruelties of Gesler?"

"Dear madam, I feel no fear, the Governor dare not proceed to greater lengths in his persecution of the Baroness von Walstein; but if farther violence should be attempted, there are those at liberty who will watch over our welfare."

"Alas! my good girl, I am fearful it will require all their ingenuity to save themselves from the tyrant's power, but let us hope better times. For ourselves, Gesler's ends would not be answered by my death; the aim of the monster is the possession of the broad lands belonging to the house of Walstein, to obtain which he would condescend to accept the hand of her whose heart he knows is fixed upon another. But come, Hildegard, though imprisoned we are not confined in a dungeon; the terrace on the rock is pleasant now, and the autumn sun shines warmly."

The terrace to which Gertrude alluded was formed close to the edge of the extremity of the rock on which the castle stood; it was laid out as a garden with great care and some degree of taste. Gesler had caused the surface of rock to be covered to a considerable depth with fertile earth; trees had been planted, flower beds laid out, an alcove and garden-seats supplied, and every care taken to render it a pleasant retreat for the inhabitants of the fortress. In addition to its own beauties, the garden afforded, from its walks, a most delightful prospect over the luxuriant valley below. To this terrace did the Baroness and her attendant repair to pass away their hours of solitude, and many a wistful look did they cast on the landscape below, and willingly did they think they could have changed situations with the toilworn labourer, who trudged wearily along, but still possessed his liberty, circumscribed only by the natural barriers of his native hills.

The part of the rock on which the garden was placed was in most parts nearly perpendicular, but in other places it stood prominently forward, heavy masses of rock standing out and overhanging the base. Some of these rocks were flat on their upper surface, and afforded resting-places to the birds of prey that inhabited this Alpine region. For want of other employment the imprisoned maidens would for hours together watch the motions of these denizens of the air, and gaze with wonder and envy upon their uncontrolled powers of flight. One of these birds, perhaps, after casting his eagle glance around, would perceive in the distance some object, invisible to all but his piercing eye; expanding then his wings to prepare for flight, the prisoners would mark his course, as sailing, rather than flying, the majestic bird would sweep through the air in circles during its flight, large at first, but gradually becoming narrower, as they were described nearer to the surface of the valley, until at length sure of its mark, it would pounce upon its prey with the rapidity of a shot; then rising slowly from the earth, would return, laden with spoil to its resting-place upon the rock.

The Baroness and Hildegard were in the act of watching the motions of a large eagle, whose depredations were well known to the shepherds of the district, when their attention was suddenly called off by a loud sound from the face of the cliff below, from whose precipitous face a large mass of rock had been detached, which bounding downwards, carried with it in its course many smaller fragments. Looking naturally to the place from which the rock had been torn, they perceived the form of a man seated on a projecting ledge, immediately above the spot; he was evidently exhausted, and panting for breath, after some recent extraordinary exertion.

Looking more intently at the daring adventurer, Hildegard could scarcely trust her eyes, when she recognised Hans Winkelried; and Hans it was, sure enough. He had eluded the vigilance of his companion after lulling his suspicions to rest, and proceeded towards the castle to endeavour to obtain an interview with Hildegard. What other motive he had for his rash enterprise, excepting that of obtaining a sight of his beloved, is unknown to all the world; even Hans himself, when questioned on the subject, was at a loss to give a probable reason for his attempt.

Having discovered the utter hopelessness of entering the fortress by the castle gates, like a skilful general he proceeded to take a general survey of the place. He wandered for some time round the base of the rocks, to endeavour to discover some spot more easily scaled than another; and had nearly given up his task in despair, when, at the foot of the precipice, at some distance from the place on which the garden was laid out, he perceived a group of stunted trees, which, deeply rooted in the crevices of the rock, extended in a slanting direction for some distance upwards, along its face. By means of the twisted limbs of these shrubs, Hans had succeeded in scrambling to a flat ledge of rock, about half way between the base and the summit.

Here for a time he sat, perched in mid air, unable to discover in what manner he should continue his course, for the friendly trees no longer offered their limbs to his grasp. Being possessed, however, of Herculean strength, he managed by a dint of violent effort to reach a species of cavern in the face of the precipice, where he again rested himself from his toil.

His further progress now seemed hopeless, unless he could succeed in reaching the ledge of rock we have already noticed as the favourite resort of the birds of prey. Midway between the cavern and the ledge a large stone projected from the smooth face of the precipice. Had he been on level ground, he could easily have placed one foot upon the stone while the other rested on the flooring of the cavern, and from that place, another step would have brought him to to the eagle's resting-place.

But to perform this feat on the bare face of a rock, nearly two-hundred feet above its base, was a task requiring a light foot and great presence of mind. In the latter qualification Hans was not deficient, but he depended more upon the strength of his arm than the active employment of his legs. Nevertheless he must endeavour to proceed, for it would be almost as hopeless a task to return as to go forward.

He looked out from his resting-place to see what further assistance nature could afford him. Above his head, but yet within his reach, several straggling roots of the mountain ash presented to his mind the chance of success. Having mustered all the resolution he could assume, and measured with his eye the distance he had to cross, he stretched forth his hand and grasped tightly one of the roots above his head; swinging himself forward, he soon found his feet upon the stepping-stone, part of his weight being supported by the tough ash root he still held in his grasp.

But in this situation it is evident he could not long remain. Stretching forward his other arm, he grasped another root of the friendly ash; but this being somewhat lower on the rock than the first support, on which he no longer depended, his whole weight rested on the stepping-stone, which, unable to bear the additional load, shook beneath him. No time was now to be lost; he grasped still more tightly the root of the tree, and trusting to its strength, sprung forward to the eagle's resting place.

With some difficulty he landed on the ledge of rock, and, with still greater, secured himself in his new position. But the stepping-stone, by means of which he had gained his present situation, was detached from the rock, as we have already seen.

Hildegard, having recovered from her surprise, hailed her forlorn lover;

she questioned him as to the cause of his appearance in that perilous spot, but obtained little information from his replies. She then warned him of the danger he ran if he was discovered by the inmates of the castle, and urged him to make good his retreat; but this advice was easier given than followed, for the stepping-stone by the aid of which he had reached his present elevated post, having fallen, his retreat was completely cut off, and he must either proceed in his course or remain where he was.

Both Gertrude and her attendant perceived the difficulty of the situation in which they were placed; it was clear that Hans could not return by the road he had come; his advance also was difficult, but still not impossible; but then, if he reached the terrace, what was to become of him? he could hardly be concealed from the eyes of Gesler's agents, and if he could, the impropriety of his presence in the part of the castle occupied by themselves was apparent.

CHAPTER XVI.

THE TRIAL OF STRENGTH.

To-morrow, Sir, I wrestle for my credit;
And he that escapes me without some broken limb
Shall acquit him well.
Yonder, sure, they are coming; let us now
Stay and see it.

While the two maidens were debating in their own minds the line of conduct they ought to pursue in their delicate position, Hans remained seated on the eagle's resting-place in a state of puzzling indecision; but he had seen Hildegard, and he almost instinctively placed himself under her guidance. Having, therefore, made up his mind to remain a passive agent in her hands, he felt himself relieved from the necessity of thinking for himself, and remained quietly awaiting the orders of his inamorata.

It was not long before it was decided by the ruling powers in the garden, that Hans should continue his ascent, which was now less dificult than it had been in any previous part of his adventure; and that, having reached the terrace, they would conceal him for the present, leaving to the chapter of chances the task of discovering some means of enabling him to escape from the castle.

Hans, having received his orders, again began his toilsome ascent— and by dint of great caution, assisted by the directions of Hildegard, he succeeded at length in reaching the summit.

A strange figure did our Swiss Hercules appear, as he stood in the presence of the Baroness and Hildegard; his clothes torn and fluttering in the wind, his hands bleeding from the injuries he had recieved in his ascent, and his brawny chest heaving and panting for breath, after his violent exertions. An awkward bashfulness, at finding himself thus suddenly in the presence of the youthful Baroness, added also materially to his uncouth appearance.

Nor were the maidens themselves much less under the influence of an uncomfortable feeling of restraint, as they gazed upon the gigantic herdsman.

With the adroitness, however, which characterises the female sex, they soon shook off the appearance of constraint, and succeeded in eliciting from Hans a narrative of those events which had occurred within his knowledge since their last interview; and the account he gave of the feelings of the people, when they were informed of the cruelties of the Bailiff, increased the hopes of all as to the ultimate success of their cause.

When these topics had been sufficiently discussed, the conversation again flagged, and the presence of Hans again became an object of solicitude; but while they were thus engaged in consultation, as to the best method of concealing their uninvited guest, the sound of approaching footsteps fell on their ears, and two of the soldiers of the castle made their appearance. They had been dispatched to ascertain, if possible, the cause of the late fall of the portion of the rock, displaced by the foot of Hans.

Great was the astonishment of the new comers at the sight of Hans Winkelried; they looked to their prisoners for an explanation of this unwonted appearance of a stranger in the castle, and more particularly in the portion occupied by them. Coupling the confusion of the Baroness and her attendant, which they were unable to conceal, with the presence of Hans, they at once conjectured it was a plot to enable them to escape from the castle, and at once advanced to the herdsman for the purpose of taking him into custody.

Hans, perceiving their intention, sprung back a few steps, and lifting up a fragment of rock, which lay on the ground, hurled it with all his force against the foremost of his assailants; the sharp edge of the stone struck the soldier on the forehead, and he measured his length on the ground.

Seeing his companion treated in this manner, the second soldier, who was armed with a spear, levelled his weapon, and rushed at the mountaineer. Hans avoided the blow, and seizing the staff with both hands, endeavoured to wrest it from his opponent.

The trial of strength which ensued would soon have ended in the discomfiture of Gesler's agent, had not the recent exertions of Hans reduced his strength; as it was, the soldier being fresh in the field, appeared likely to gain the advantage. Each maintained a firm hold of the weapon, and their struggles for its possession were fearful. This continued for some time, when at length both the combatants fell, and in the fall the spear was broken.

As if with one accord, the broken piece of which each retained possession, was flung over the precipice, and again they closed upon each other. The struggle for mastery now appeared to have a definite object; the glance each had cast upon of the precipice, as the broken spear fell into the abyss, had produced the same effect on both; clinging together, as if with the determination of maintaining his grasp until the last extremity, each tried every method that skill and strength could suggest to force his adversary towards the brink, but they were so well matched that neither could gain his end.

Now, as if by mutual consent, they rested awhile, from very exhaustion, still however, retaining a hold of each other. Again the struggle began, until, at length, the combatants, during a powerful effort for mastery, both fell on the ground together. While in this prostrate condition, their mutual efforts brought them gradually near to the edge of the rock, and a few moments longer would have seen them both precipitated into the vale below, if a party of the guard had not entered at the moment, and making Hans prisoner, relieved their companion from his grasp.

The Baroness and her fellow-prisoner had left the scene of action at the beginning of the strife, but contrived to witness its termination from their place of concealment.

While these occurrences were taking place in the castle, Ernest and his blind companion waited impatiently for the appearance of Hans. Enquiries were made in every direction, but all without avail; no tidings could be obtained of their missing friend. The urgent nature of the mission on which Ernest had been dispatched would not allow him to make a long delay; and after waiting for two nights at Rossberg, he was obliged to proceed on his journey, unable to form the most distant conjecture as to the cause of the absence of their burly friend.

Ernest and Melctor had not proceeded far upon their road, the towers of Rossberg still enveloping them in their shadows, when they became aware of the approach of a horseman. As he drew nearer they recognized the form of the youthful Arnold von Attinghausen.

Arnold having heard of the outrage upon the person of Gertrude, had ridden with all speed towards the place of her confinement, with the almost hopeless intention of rescuing her from the walls of Rossberg. Being aware of the attachment which existed between Ernest and Hildegard, he was delighted at meeting him so near to the castle, since he was well aware that no one would more earnestly assist him in his enterprise, in case it should become practicable.

With these intentions the young Swiss noble persuaded Ernest to retrace his steps; he assured him that the state of public feeling in the country through which he had passed was so satisfactory for the well-wishers of Switzerland, that the object of his mission was already fulfilled.

Convinced by these arguments, or willing to imagine himself convinced, he agreed to the proposal of Arnold; the enfeebled condition of Melctor also urged him to remain, as well as his anxiety for the fate of Hans, and though last, not least, his affection for Hildegard.

The whole party now returned towards the little village of Rossberg, with the intention of taking up their abode at the dwelling of a friend of Ernest's, named Ulrich, but had not proceeded far on their journey when two horsemen at full speed overtook them; by their dress it was clear they were not natives of Switzerland; their general bearing and mode of managing their steeds might induce an observer to suppose they were Austrian soldiers, although not attired in the costume of Gesler's followers.

When they had overtaken the returning party, they appeared inclined to stop in their course, but after reconnoitring our travellers, apparently changed their mind, and without one word of greeting, resumed their course towards the village. The slouched hats the horsemen wore, and the large cloaks in which they were enveloped, so completely concealed their features, that even if they had been well known to Arnold and his companions, they would have been unable to recognize them; as it was, they were not able to form a conjecture as to their identity, but their behaviour produced a vague feeling of fear in their bosoms.

"It is singular," remarked Arnold, "but, three times during my journey from Altdorf, I have been crossed in my course by two horsemen, much resembling those who have just passed us. I took them at first sight to be two of Gesler's men, on some errand of oppression from their tyrannical master, but they wear not his livery."

"Disguise, perhaps, may suit their purposes," returned Ernest. "If they have ill designs, they would hardly show their faces to the world. I would that Hans were here, his giant form would do good service in the hour of need."

Conversing in this manner, the little party returned to Rossberg, and took up their abode at the house of Ulrich.

CHAPTER XVII.

THE MIDNIGHT VISIT.

> Now o'er the one half world
> Nature seems dead, and wicked dreams abuse
> The curtained sleep; now witchcraft celebrates
> Pale Hecate's offerings; and withered murder,
> Alarum'd by his sentinel, the wolf,
> Whose howl's his watch, thus with his stealthy pace,
> With Tarquin's ravishing strides, towards his design
> Moves like a ghost.

The little village of Rossberg was composed of a small number of cottages, principally occupied by a few families of the mountaineers, whose occupation chiefly consisted in following the chase. The only buildings of any note which it contained were a small monastery of Carthusian monks, and the house of Ulrich the smith, under whose roof our travellers now rested.

As soon as Arnold had entered the dwelling of Ulrich, he made inquiries respecting the state of the castle, and the means of defence it had at its disposal. He ascertained that the troops by which it was garrisoned were few in number, the strong natural defences of the castle being so great as to render unnecessary the presence of many soldiers, The communication between the tenants of the fortress and the villagers was extremely limited, the former seldom leaving their stronghold, and the latter never entering the castle gates.

One inhabitant of the village alone was admitted within the precincts

of Rossberg castle, namely, Benedict, an ancient monk belonging to the monastery, who fulfilled the duties of father confessor to the savage followers of Gesler, and by the frequency of his visits his office appeared to be no sinecure. Benedict was believed to be well affected to the popular cause, although he had never openly declared himself to that effect, notwithstanding his frequent intercourse with the inmates of the castle. As it was the chief object of Arnold to ascertain the state of affairs within the castle, he determined at the recommendation of Ulrich to sound the old monk, as to his willingness to afford whatever information he possessed, or to convey a letter into the hands of Gertrude. Benedict, when the subject was mentioned, entered more cordially into the views of his interrogator than could have been expected, and it happened, luckily for their cause, that he had that instant been summoned to the castle, to grant absolution and attend to the last words of a man at the point of death. He agreed, if possible, to convey a written communication to Gertrude, and to collect whatever information might be useful to his employers, Matters being so far satisfactorily settled, Arnold inquired of his host, if there was no possibility of entering the castle from the side of the valley. Ulrich informed him that the crag upon which the fortress was built was considered perfectly impracticable. Before the late political events had closed the gates of Rossberg to the villagers, it had been a favourite amusement among their most daring spirits to attempt the difficult ascent as a trial of skill and courage, but no one had ever been able to accomplish more then half the task. It was indeed said that old

9 K

Kuoni, the hunter, had in his younger days performed the feat; but although the old man himself related the fact, his listeners shrugged their shoulders, and looked at each other with a credulous smile, when his attention was called off in another direction.

The sun had been several hours below the horizon, and the inmates of Ulrich's cottage still anxiously awaited the return of the monk. The simple fact of his prolonged absence had in itself nothing particularly alarming, since it was no uncommon occurrence for the old man to remain within the castle during the night, the rude bridge which communicated with its gates being considered a dangerous path, to one of his age; but the anxiety they felt to obtain information as to what was going on within the castle, filled their minds with a vague sensation of fear.

Midnight was now fast approaching, and Benedict still being absent, the travellers and their host considered it useless to remain longer in expectation, and accordingly they retired to partake of that rest which they so much needed.

The cold rays of the moon, which during the early part of the night had shed a silvery lustre over the landscape, had for some time ceased to bless the sight of the wanderer; the stars themselves were obscured, and night had shrouded herself in her darkest mantle. Arnold and his companions were enjoying their first deep sleep, their restless minds completely subdued by bodily fatigue, when two men wrapped in cloaks, with their hats drawn as carefully over their eyes to conceal their features as if the broad light of day was shining full upon them, might have been seen stealthily gliding, with long and silent strides, towards the dwelling of Ulrich; they conversed together in whispers,—

"You are sure he sleeps on this side of the house?" said the tallest of the two.

"Did I not learn it from Ulrich's chattering wife?" returned his companion. "Her pride was pleased; young Arnold Attinghausen slept in her cottage. She had prepared the best room in the house for his reception; I heard her tell it to her neighbour here."

"The best room—that may be true; but how know you which is the best room, Leuthold?"

"Tut! man, I know it well; when Gesler was at Rossberg, was I not here? See, in yon corner is his resting-place; his bed stands there."

"Should Ernest sleep in the same chamber! how say you?" observed his tall companion, whom the reader must now perceive was Friesshardt.

"I think he sleeps in the same room as Melctor, that's in the front; we must be quick and silent in our work."

"The window is open," cried Friesshardt; "get on my shoulders and look into the room."

His companion having done as he required, slowly put back the window, which was unfastened, and peering round the room endeavoured to ascertain the situation of the different articles of furniture; but the darkness was so profound he was unable to distinguish one object from another. His organs of sight proving of so little service, he raised himself higher upon Friesshardt's shoulders, and felt round in various directions. Suddenly he withdrew his hand, and stooping down, whispered in an undertone to his companion,—

" A well-aimed blow would end the job at once; he sleeps profoundly."

" Then why not strike ?" said Friesshardt.

" My arm will scarcely reach him from the window, and it's so dark, if I should enter I know not where to place my feet, I am sure to stumble; you are longer in the reach than I, and from this place could deal the fatal blow with certainty."

So saying, he descended from the shoulders of his comrade, and after some consultation it was agreed between the two that Friesshardt should accomplish the murder. As the casement was at too great a distance from the ground to enable him to perpetrate his crime without the aid of some means by which he might contrive to raise himself to a level with the scene of his operation, the next duty of the worthy pair was to pile together a heap of stones, so as to form a raised platform, upon which Friesshardt might stand while he accomplished the deed of blood.

They had nearly succeeded in the object of their labour, one additional stone being all that was needed to complete the structure, when, after searching for some time in the dark without success for a fragment of rock suitable to their purpose, they were obliged to make use of a piece they had already rejected on account of its size. With some difficulty they raised it from the ground, and endeavoured to place it on the summit of the pile. They had almost succeeded in their task, and were beginning to congratulate each other on the promised success of their enterprise, when the weight of the last addition to their stepping-stone to murder, caused the whole of the pile to fall to the ground: a sharp-angled fragment of granite fell with violence on the foot of Leuthold, and caused him so much pain that, forgetful of consequences, the faint-hearted villain howled with pain.

The noise occasioned by this disaster roused Arnold from his sleep, and rushing to the casement he was able to distinguish the sound of re-treating footsteps, mingled with exclamations of pain and anger: unable to account for the cause of this disturbance, he determined to remain for the remainder of the night on the alert; and thus he passed the hours until day-light, revolving in his mind the oppression under which his ill-fated country was groaning, and building scheme upon scheme for the release of Gertrude from her present state of thraldom.

The morning came at last, and with it brought all the blessings which light alone can bestow, and before the first frugal meal was served the monk Benedict entered the cottage. He had been detained until a late hour of the night, by the task of watching over the last moment of a soldier of Gesler's. The inmates of the castle, he said were in a high state of excitement; a countryman had by some means, obtained entrance into the ladies' apartment, and mortally wounded the soldier, whose death he had witnessed.

It at once occurred to Ernest that this countryman might be Hans Winkelried; but how could he account for his appearance within the walls ? he certainly could not have passed the gates, and other mode of entrance there was none.

"How had they disposed of this countryman ?" asked Ernest.

"He is confined, I understand, in one of the dungeons of the castle."

Arnold now related the occurrences of the night which had fallen under his own observation. His narrative appeared to be as great a mystery as the appearance of Hans, if it was he, in the midst of Gesler's troopers. The monk had not as yet found the means of delivering the letter to Gertrude and the whole party, busied in an endeavour to explain to their own satisfaction the mysterious circumstances which had occurred, finished their meal in silence.

CHAPTER XVIII.

THE CONFEDERACY.

Now know you, Casca, I have moved already
Some certain of the noblest-minded Romans,
To undergo, with me, an enterprise
Of honourable dangerous consequences:
And I do know, by this, they stay for me
In Pompey's porch.

The night on which that bond was sealed which insured liberty to the hardy Swiss and their posterity at length arrived.

The little field of Rutli slumbered in the moonshine, and the waters of the lake, as smooth as glass, shone like burnished silver, reflecting from their placid bosom the objects upon their margin. The spot where the confederates were about to meet was a small secluded meadow, close to the borders of the Lake of the Four Cantons; it was surrounded, on three sides, by vast barriers of rock richly clothed with wood, through which the rugged surface of the cliff was visible at intervals. The fourth side was open to the water; but even here it was concealed from all but the most curious observer, by the luxuriant herbage that fringed the banks of the lake.

The hour of meeting approached, but silence as yet reigned over the solitary spot; the moon, now at full, was in the zenith, and every object was distinctly visible in her flood of borrowed light. The hour of meeting had almost arrived, when a small group of men appeared at the summit of one of the most accessible rocks by which the meadow was surrounded; it was Walter Furst, with ten sworn friends, natives of Uri, whom he had brought to the meeting.

"We are nearly at the spot," he exclaimed; "see, the pass opens; I I know well the little cross that crowns that rock—see, here is Rutli."

As he uttered these words, he prepared to descend the rocks, by the aid of some rude steps cut in their face. His friends following in his footsteps also descended, and the whole party soon found themselves on the green sward.

"The place is empty," exclaimed one of the party, "we are the first upon the grouud. Hark! did you hear that bell?"

"It sounds from Schweitz," said Furst; " 'tis from the forest chapel. It strikes the hour we all should meet."

"Since we are first upon the spot," said Furst, "let us prepare the place of meeting, friends: pile up these faggots, and let a cheerful blaze await their coming."

The followers of Furst immediately busied themselves in making a large fire with the fragments of broken timber that lay scattered about. The green wood hissed and sent forth volumes of smoke and steam, when it first felt the effects of the fiery element; but soon yielding to the devouring flame, the pile, at which a hecatomb might have been sacrificed, burst forth into a blaze, and tinged all the surrounding objects with a blood red hue.

"See, what object is it on the water yonder?"

"It is a boat, it comes from Schweitz; it is Werner Stauffacher and his brave band, I knew he would not delay."

"How smoothly do they glide along! They will soon be here."

"The Underwaldners have not yet arrived."

"They have a long tedious round to take, quick! hail the boat," cried Furst.

"Say—who goes there? The word."

"Friends of the land," returned Stauffacher and his followers, as they stepped on shore.

"You are welcome, Werner," said Furst, addressing Stauffacher. "Erni cannot be long: but Gesler's blood hounds are quick and cunning, and it is not easy to avoid their path. See! here they come."

As he said this, the men of Underwalden began to descend the rocks. Erni was the first to reach the ground, then followed Tell, and after them Ernest and the rest of the party.

"Tell," exclaimed Werner, "I feared you would not come; without thee our meeting had not been complete."

"I am more for action, Werner, than for council," said Tell; "but Erni knew not the road among these fastnesses so well as I, and Gesler's troopers covered all the country."

"And must we thus," said Furst, "meet here in darkness, stealing from our homes, here in our native land, as if our cause were one that shunned the light?"

"The time will come, when in the face of day, the deeds we plan to-night shall be made clear—but here is young Ernest; what news has he brought to the meeting?"

"With my blind charge" said Ernest, "I sought the Alpine pastures, were the men of Engelberg and Uri feed their herds in common. Even there, we found the deeds of horror of the Bailiff known. I spoke the names of those who planned this league, and they have sworn, what you think right, they are ready to perform. Where'er we went the rights of hospitality protected us, and even on the utmost verge of frozen nature, near eternal snow, the mountaineers have promised their support."

"You have well performed your task," said Werner; "but now, friends, let us consult how we had best proceed, It seems to me, few as we are, we may be said to represent a general council of the land;

let us proceed then to assert our rights, as if we were within the council chamber."

"Three tribes are here convened ; to which belongs the right to give a president to the meeting ?" said Tell.

"Uri and Schweitz together may dispute the honour," observed Furst; "we Underwaldners freely yield it up. Let Uri take the sword."

"Nay," remarked Erni, "to Schweitz belongs the honour ; from Schweitz we all may boast we are descended."

With this Erni, raising the sword, offered it to Werner.

"Have we not here," observed Werner, "our old Landamman Reding ? where can we seek a worthier man ?"

"Let him be president," cried Tell. To this the whole meeting assented, and the old man, stepping into the centre of the circle, formed by the assembly, raising his reverend face to Heaven, exclaimed,—

"The ancient books are gone, I cannot lay my hands upon them ; but by the eternal stars I swear, I will uphold the cause of justice."

Two swords were now placed before their president, and the representatives of the Three Cantons having taken their places—Schweitz in the centre, Uri on the right, and Underwalden on the left—the old Landamman opened the proceedings formally.

It was a solemn sight to behold the small assembly of patriots met together at this solitary spot, in the middle of the night, to assert their country's right. Their little court of justice assembled, with few of the ancient forms, which in former times gave dignity to their proceedings— and yet perhaps on no former occasion was it invested with so much real grandeur. The glorious dome of heaven was to them in the place of a canopy of state. The light from the blazing fire in the centre honse brightly on the venerable figure of their president, while the intensity of thought expressed in every eye gave a solemnity to the ceremony no artificial aid could have increased.

"Now tell me," cried the ancient Landamman, "what is the great occasion that brings three mountain tribes together at this dread hour of night, here on the lake's inhospitable shore ? What new bond have we to contract ?"

"It is no new bond," said Werner; "'tis but the ancient league made by our fathers in the olden time, which here we would renew. For though the mountains and the lake divide us, and each tribe has its separate laws, yet from one common root we spring. Still are we all as Swiss distinguished, and own one heart, one blood."

With this he seized the hand of Erni and Furst, and all the assembly simultaneously clasping each other by the hand, exclaimed, as if with one voice—

"One people, and will act together."

"The other nations," continued Werner, "by which we are surrounded, bow to a foreign yoke ; but we, the genuine race of good old Swiss, have ever known how to maintain our freedom ; the power of the Empire we have owned, but not the power of princes."

"Yes, truly, we are of one heart, one blood, one people, and will act in unison," exclaimed the assembled group with one accord, and each grasping his neighbour's hand, raised his head to heaven in attestation.

"See," cried Werner, "see you nought yonder?"

" 'Tis strange, indeed, a rainbow in the middle of the night."

" 'Tis formed by the reflection of the moon."

"It is a wondrous sign, and seldom known; many have lived who ne'er have seen the like."

"See; now it's doubled? there's a paler one."

"It is the bow of promise to our hopes," said Werner.

"Our cause is sacred, we freely sought the Emperor's protection; a voluntary league of mutual succour—so it is marked in the Emperor Frederick's brief."

"You are right; yet e'en the freest must not be masterless; a sovereign head must be—a judge supreme, to whom we may appeal. So, when our fathers won this land from the old wilderness, we gave that honour to the Emperor; and when his service called, gladly did we step forth to meet his foes in arms, as other freemen did. For it is a freeman's duty to defend the land that shelters him."

"But more than this," cried Tell; "were servitude. So, when the cry of war was heard, we fought beneath the banners of the Empire, and graced the Emperor's march to Italy to place the Roman crown upon his brow. At home, we free and happy, ruled ourselves by our own laws and customs."

"All you have said is true—the tyrant's law, the law of force, we never have endured."

"How did our fathers act, when the Emperor strove to strain the law? The abbot of Einsiedlen claimed the lands they pastured; he showed the Emperor's charter to our sires, when thus they spake:—'Nought is the charter worth; that which is ours, no Emperor can bestow.' So spake our fathers; and shall we endure the shame of this new yoke, and from this foreign slave bear what no emperor dared yet impose? By the possession of a thousand years the ground is ours, and shall the stranger now, the slave of princes, come to forge us chains?"

"Never," exclaimed the whole assembly, clashing their swords, "we will defend our wives and children and our native land."

As soon as the excitement the words of Werner had caused had somewhat subsided, Rosselman, the priest stepped forward, and with the cautious words of age strove to persuade his hearers that the evils of Gesler's cruelty might be redressed without the shedding of blood, by recognizing the claims of Austria.

"What says the priest?" cried Tell, with excitement; "we swear to Austria!"

"Nay, hear him," observed Werner.

"Hear him! it is the council of a traitor, an enemy to the land. Let him be put beyond the protection of the law, who speaks of concession to Austria.—Landamman," exclaimed Tell, "let me beseech thee, let this be the first law that we pass."

"Let it be so," cried Werner; "who speaks of concession to Austria shall outlawed be, his rights and honours forfeit, and no man shall receive him at his hearth."

On this the whole assembly, raising the right hand, cried out, "We will it. This be law."

After pausing for a time, the old Landamman solemnly exclaimed, "The law has passed."

Werner now again took up the word: "Friends, we have tried gentle means without avail, our messenger to Austria's court has just returned—speak, William Hun, what did the Emperor say?"

"I went to Rheinfeld, to the Emperor's court, to lay our grievances before the throne, and claim the charter of our freedom, which each new Emperor is wont to ratify. What was the answer I received? 'the Emperor had no time, but at convenient season would think of us'."

"We have heard enough," cried Tell, whose excitement had rapidly increased—"Mercy and justice we can no longer expect from the Emperor. We must help ourselves."

"We must," observed Werner. "How best may we accomplish our design? Let us wrong no man's rights."

"Let all that justice needs be done," said Tell. "The Bailiffs and their followers from the land we will expel, break down their fastnesses, and if it may be, without shedding blood."

"But," observed Werner, "let us hear how you propose to execute this scheme so boldly planned. An armed and powerful foe will not depart without a struggle."

"Yes, when they see the land in arms. We must surprise them ere they arm themselves," said Tell.

"But the three strongholds of the Austrians, Tell, which they have built to overawe the country, how may they be subdued?"

Here Ernest interposed. "For Rossberg I can speak; young Arnold Attinghausen plots its downfall; his love for Lady Gertrude will urge him on, as well as his sworn faith to our good cause".

"And I," cried Tell, "will rouse the country against the towers of Altdorf; but when shall this be done?"

"Were it not better we should defer the deed to the Lord's festival. At Altdorf, on that day, all the proprietors of land assemble and offer presents to the Bailiff; some ten or twelve might enter, secretly armed, and by their assistance the rest may be admitted."

To this proposition of Werner's the meeting readily agreed.

"When, on the appointed day," said Tell, "the castles fall, mountain to mountain shall proclaim the news with kindling beacons, and the people, assembling in the chief place of every land, shall rise in general mass."

"A heavy stand Gesler will make, fenced as he is by his bold troopers. Not without blood will he forsake the field—'tis hard, 'tis almost dangerous to spare him. But see, while we are here consuming the night in council, the gray light of the morn is fast approaching; once more, friends, let us swear that we will live as free as did our fathers—and rather die than live in slavery."

The little band of patriots repeated the asseveration, and each began to prepare for his homeward journey; the confederates from Schweitz recrossed the lake, and the Underwaldners and the men of Uri retraced their steps and scaled the precipitous sides of the rocks, by which the field of Rutli was enclosed.

CHAPTER XIX.

THE DISCOVERY.

I am a villain : yet I lie, I am not.
Fool, of thyself speak well:—Fool, do not flatter.
My conscience hath a thousand several tongues,
And every tongue brings in a several tale,
And every tale condemns me for a villain !

The unexpected appearance of Ernest and Tell at the meeting of the confederates arose from the arrangements made with Arnold ; in pursuance of which, Ernest hastened to the abode of Tell to ask his assistance in their design on the castle of Rossberg, and, at the same time, conveyed information of his progress with Melctor to the meeting at Rutli. At the close of the meeting, accordingly, Tell and the young chamois hunter proceeded on their road to that fortress, pursuing a circuitous route, to avoid the emissaries of Gesler, many of whom, they had good reason to believe, were acting as spies upon the mountaineers.

Owing to the length and intricacies of the road, the shades of evening were beginning to fall upon the landscape before they reached their destination.

By the time they found themselves in the street of the little village, and near to the dwelling of Ulrich, it was quite dark, and the inhabitants had retired to rest.

They were proceeding to the rear of the house for the purpose of

10   L

rousing Arnold, of whose place of rest they were aware, when the quick ear of Ernest was attracted by an indistinct sound ; he stooped down for the purpose of bringing his ear nearer to the ground, to enable him to hear more readily, when he distinguished the noise of approaching footsteps.

Taking Tell by the hand, he drew him towards an obscure corner of the building, from whence they would be enabled to mark the approach of an intruder without being themselves observed.

They had not remained long concealed, when two figures, apparently wrapped in cloaks, exhibited their dark outline against the gray sky.

They cautiously approached the cottage of Ulrich, conversing together in whispers ; the listeners were unable to detect the purport of their conversation ; but the result was, the intruders separated—one, the tallest of the two, proceeding towards the front of the cottage, and the other remaining near to the door by which it was entered from the rear.

Ernest stealthily followed the first, leaving Tell to watch the proceedings of his associate.

As soon as the latter was left alone, he approached the entrance to the cottage, and busily engaged himself in an endeavour to undo its fastenings. After a short time he succeeded in his object, and cautiously opened the door.

He retreated, however, as if fearful of being watched, and spoke to himself in an under tone :—

" 'Fore George ! I have no great fancy for this deed. Why did not Friesshardt act ? He has a firmer hand than I. Gesler, he says, is bounteous. His golden salve shall heal my wounded conscience. Conscience ! I talk of conscience ! I never flinched before ; but this dark job has roused an unknown feeling. Tut, man, 'tis nought but fear—I ever was a coward from a boy ; why should I fear ? he sleeps profoundly."

"Indeed !" muttered Tell to himself.

" One blow, and all is over : while I stand idling here, he may awake."

With that the speaker adjusted his cloak, and drawing a dagger from his belt, entered the cottage, followed by Tell.

In the chamber adjoining that into which the outer door opened, a light was burning with sufficient brightness to enable Tell to distinguish the dress of the assassin.

The cloak in which he was enveloped was of a dark colour, and sufficiently large to conceal his figure ; but as he partially threw it on one side, that its ample folds might not impede his motions, Tell could perceive the well known uniform of Gesler's troopers.

Before the stranger had advanced another step, one hand of the bowman was upon his throat, while with the other he seized the hand that held the dagger !

" Villain !" exclaimed Tell, " drop your weapon, and unmask yourself ! "

The detected coward dropped on his knees when discovered, and letting fall the dagger, in abject tones cried out for mercy.

" Say, who imposed this task upon you ? Was it Gesler—speak ! who was to be your victim ?"

"Ar—nold At—tinghausen," said the ruffian, his teeth chattering in his head.

"What, will the monster ne'er be satisfied? noble or peasant—every generous soul bespeaks his hatred."

The noise produced by this encounter had roused the inmates of the cottage, and the astonished group stood looking on in silence.

The cause of the present state of affairs was soon explained by Tell and the trooper being properly secured, was about to be conveyed to some place of confinement, when he beseeched his captors to listen to him, if it were only for a moment.

Having acceded to his request, the abject wretch, crouching like a fawning hound, offered to make a full disclosure if mercy was shown to him.

No decided answer being given to his request, he was placed in security, and the attention of the group was directed to the absence of Ernest.

Tell and Arnold were about to proceed in search of their fellow-countryman, when he himself appeared at the door.

He had followed, he said, the tall figure, who moved on with a quick pace, towards the Carthusian monastery, in the rear of which two saddled horses were seen; these he led back towards the cottage of Ulrich, and was about to secure them to a tree in the neighbourhood, when the outcry within the cottage reached his ears.

"Did you not secure him?" said Tell.

"I was in the act of doing so, when his eye suddenly caught mine; on the instant he leapt into the saddle, and putting spurs to his horse, was soon out of sight.

As it was not likely the companion of their captive would return to the attack, now he must be assured they were on the alert, Arnold and his friends deemed it most advisable to defer the consideration of their future plans until the morning, when they could have the assistance of the aged priest, on whose faith they found themselves obliged to rely; having therefore seen their prisoner safely secured, they again retired to rest.

Early in the morning the inmates of Ulrich's house arose from their beds, and while they awaited the arrival of Benedict, proceeded to the examination of Gesler's trooper.

Leuthold, overcome by the terrors engendered by the dreary hours he had passed in darkness and bondage, was, if possible, yet more abject in his manner than on the previous night;—he fully disclosed the plot against the life of Arnold, which had been arranged between Friesshardt and himself, in the hopes of obtaining favour and reward from their sanguinary master; at the same time, much to the satisfaction of his examiners, he exonerated Gesler from all direct participation in their scheme.

"Was it you and your companion," observed Arnold, "who passed me on the hill near Sarnen?

"It was, my lord," said Leuthold; "and had you not made such good speed upon your road, we should have overtaken you in the defile, and Friesshardt would have tried his dagger's temper."

" The hand of Providence," observed Tell, "is in all this—my life preserved in the most desperate strait, and the chief stay among our ancient nobles saved from the assassin's dagger."

" Had the captive and his companion been within Rossberg's walls?"

" They had not yet," was the reply; " but he had friends within, from whom he could obtain such information as they might require."

The arrival of Benedict being now announced, Leuthold was removed in custody, that the safety of the friendly confessor might not be compromised by Gesler's agent becoming a witness of the interest he took in their affairs.

" If the Austrian's agents within your walls," said Arnold, " are meet companions to those at large, your work of shrift, good father, must be an irksome task ; we have one here in confinement has sought my life, and one has fled.

" Their names ?" said Benedict.

" Friesshardt and Leuthold."

" I know them both," returned the monk, " for desperate ruffians; Friesshardt is Gesler's agent in his most cruel acts ; it was he conducted Lady Gertrude hither."

" But, father, touching Gertrude, and that same letter—can you convey it to her hands to-day ?"

" With heaven's assistance, son, it shall be done; rest you in peace, and do not leave the house. At noon I go to Rossberg, and ere night you shall hear of me."

" Our prisoner," observed Tell, " has offered his assistance; he has friends, he says, within the castle walls, whom he may trust; as I conveyed him hence, he mentioned one—his name was Romont."

" If we could trust him," observed the monk, " he might serve us well. Being the least rude of all the Austrian soldiers, his post is near the Baroness ; he and two others guard the gentle captives. A letter to this man from Leuthold might prove him."

" Ask him merely to place my letter in the hands of Gertrude, and if he can obtain an answer to it, you, father, can be the bearer."

" But should he be faithful to his master's orders, I fear my holy calling would not save me, and our cause might then be hopeless. But first obtain the ruffian's letter; perhaps its tenour may show if his repentance is sincere."

Arnold accordingly repaired to the captive, and soon returned with the desired communication ; it merely requested Romont, for the sake of ancient friendship, to obtain for the monk an interview with the Baroness, or, at all events, to allow him to communicate with her by letter ; it was only, he assured him, for the purpose of informing her of some matters relative to her estates, which it was fitting she should be apprised of.

The old monk, satisfied with the contents of this epistle, soon afterwards started on his errand, leaving Arnold and his friends in a state of considerable anxiety for the success of his mission.

Towards evening the good father returned, and as he entered the room, the cheerful look he wore contrasted strongly with the solicitude so powerfully depicted on the countenances of Arnold and his friends; at length he relieved them from their anticipations of evil by relating the events of the day.

After performing his professional duties, he had obtained an interview with Romont, who without much solicitation promised his assistance; for the gentle manners of the Baroness had so wrought upon the feelings of the trooper, that he was willing, by every means in his power, to testify the sense he entertained of the unworthy treatment she received.

Indeed had it not been for a relaxation of discipline on his part, the intrepid Hans would have found it a more difficult task than he did to land unobserved by the garrison on the garden terrace. By another act of insubordination, he now allowed the monk to hold a communication with his captive.

Gertrude was necessarily delighted at seeing the hand-writing of her lover, and being made acquainted with the progress of the good cause, and she satisfied the monk that Hans was the peasant by whose hands the trooper had been slain.

Hildegard, on the other hand, felt equal delight when she heard that Ernest and Arnold Attinghausen were proceeding in concert with each other; it identified, as it were, her cause with that of her mistress, and thus, by this additional tie, more closely cemented the bonds of affection, which had sprung up between them.

This auspicious commencement of their intrigue inspired all present with such feelings of hope, that Arnold himself determined to endeavour to effect an entrance into the castle, and obtain an interview with the object of his affection.

This could necessarily only be accomplished by entering the castle in disguise; and after much consultation it was decided that the dress of their prisoner should be borrowed for the occasion—that, thus attired in Gesler's uniform, Arnold should disguise himself in the cloak and cowl of the monk, and so pass the gate.

The intention of this double concealment was, that if, when within the walls, he could find means to unrobe himself, he would be less likely to be noticed in the soldier's garb.

CHAPTER XX.

THE LOVERS' MEETING.

By whose direction found you out this place?
By love, who first did prompt me to inquire;
He lent me council and I lent him eyes.
I am no pilot; yet wert thou as far
As that vast shore washed by the farthest sea,
I would adventure for such merchandise.

The morning after the interview between Father Benedict and the Baroness, Arnold Attinghausen prepared for his dangerous attempt. The clothes of the short but sturdy trooper were not calculated to set off the handsome figure of the young Swiss to advantage, and he felt considerable repugnance at being obliged to appear before his mistress in so uncouth a garb; but as her safety, perhaps, as well as his own, depended on his assuming the Austrian's uniform, he conquered his adversion to the masquerade, and adjusted his dress at all points so as to resemble one of Gesler's followers.

Being well armed in case of necessity, and enveloped in the cloak of the friendly monk, he assumed as much as possible the appearance of age and decrepitude, and he proceeded to the castle.

As he approached the dangerous bridge which led to the gateway, one of the troopers crossed to meet him, to assist his feeble steps. As it was necessary to maintain the character he had assumed, the young Swiss was obliged to acknowledge by an inclination of his body the kindness of the offer, and at the same time to accept the proffered hand.

When Arnold and his guide, had about half-way crossed the yawning chasm, the real danger of the passage caused the former to forget his assumed weakness in the reality of his danger, and placing his foot more firmly upon the rude bridge, he grasped his staff with so much vigour as to astonish his companion, whose suspicions were for the moment aroused by the unusal action.

It was but for a moment that Arnold was thrown off his guard; relapsing suddenly into his feigned state of decrepitude, the suspicions of the trooper were as quickly lulled, although a man of more acute perceptions would most likely have detected the deception.

As soon as they had safely arrived within the walls of the castle, the soldier relinquished the arm of the pretended monk.

"There, father, that danger's past; but why they allow the crazy bridge to remain in that condition, is beyond my comprehension. If I ever by chance have the good luck to partake of a bottle or two of good Rhenish, I feel some difficulty in keeping my balance on those old timbers; and, by the mass! it would be an awkward fall into the torrent below; small need would there be of shrift for the poor devil who should make the slip."

"Blundenz, Father Benedict," said one of the soldiers at the gate, "is waiting for your ghostly advice."

"Blundenz!" exclaimed another in surprise, "I thought he never troubled our holy church, or asked advice of monks."

"I know not what ails him," returned the first speaker, "but ever since his last visit to the village, he has been marvellously out of sorts; his comrades think he is possessed."

"You know the way to his quarters, father? it's near where Romont lodges. And there's another change, that Romont was the wildest dog in all the troop, but now he is gentle as a lady's page, and takes more trouble with his dress and beard than if he had a seat at the Lord Governor's table."

"You recollect," said a third, "that dagger which he wore when fighting beneath the Emperor's banners? he has exchanged it with old Munster for a feather—a feather to deck his cap."

At this observation the whole group burst into a loud fit of laughter, and Arnold having been carefully instructed by Benedict as to the course he was to pursue, made the best of his way to the quarters of Romont; he succeeded luckily in concealing his real character, from the effeminate trooper, and was by him directed to the spot where he might find Gertrude.

As Arnold Attinghausen entered the romantic garden we have already described, his heart beat within his breast with a violence which threatened suffocation; a confused train of ideas rushed through his brain—natural anxiety for the safety of his own return, suppressed rage against the author of the imprisonment of Gertrude, and an indefinable feeling of joy and timidity as he drew nearer to his mistress—all combined to produce a species of stupefaction which he found it difficult to shake off.

Seated in an arbour in one of the sunniest spots in the garden, Gertrude and her attendant were engaged in conversation on the late extraordinary events,

"Whatever opinion, Hildegard," said the Baroness, "you may have formed of your admirer Hans, he at least is the only one who has been bold enough to pay us a visit in our lofty abode."

"Alas! poor fellow," replied her companion, "I could have spared the pleasure his goodwill towards me afforded, to have enabled him to avoid his present fate."

"Let us hope for the best; the time cannot be long distant when even these walls shall resound with the voice of freedom. Meantime the Bailiff will be too much engaged, in providing for his own safety, to have time to consider the fate of your sturdy admirer."

"See, my lady," exclaimed Hildegard, "here comes the holy father once again."

Arnold slowly approached, but with a steadier step than was fitting for the character he had assumed; when he drew near, he made a low obeisance to Gertrude, and raising his cowl, disclosed to her astonished view the features of her lover.

"Arnold—you here! How did you come? you are not safe an instant. What is your object?"

"Your rescue, dear Gertrude; I would trust no eyes but mine to learn the secrets of this prison-house."

"Oh! wait with patience, Arnold; escape is hopeless now."

"I cannot think it; how did Hans reach the garden?"

"The madman! he climbed these rocks; but see how steep they are! Stay, do you see that root projecting from the precipice?—beneath it was a stone on which he stepped; that stone is gone, so not e'en Hans could again perform the feat."

"It is hopeless by the rocks," said Arnold, after having carefully examined the face of the precipice; "but might not some disguise—you see I have entered."

"Believe me it is useless, Arnold; no women are allowed within its walls: 'tis useless—wait with patience—let me beseech thee. The time will soon arrive when without risk we shall leave our prison gaily."

"But to leave you here, exposed to the insults of these reckless men!".

"Nay, Arnold, not so; although confined, we are unmolested, nor dare these men offend us in these our own possessions; within the limits of our palace here I am lady paramount."

"But still you are in the power of Gesler."

"If that is true, should I attempt to fly and fail in the attempt, what might I not expect?"

"I cannot leave you, Gertrude; and yet I know not how to help you hence."

"The time will come, believe me," said Gertrude.

"The time shall come, and Gesler's bands shall see these walls of Rossberg blazing upwards like a torch into the sky, a beacon to the mountain tribes that tyranny has fallen."

Arnold, while uttering these words, in the excitement of the moment had raised his voice to such a pitch as to attract the attention of Romont,—who suddenly making his appearance before the affrighted women, demanded the meaning of the loud voice he had heard.

Then, quickly turning towards the supposed monk, who in the hurry of the moment had not been able to conceal his features entirely with the cowl, the soldier at once perceived he had been imposed upon; he rushed upon Arnold, and endeavoured to seize him; but the latter, being more active than his opponent, succeeded in eluding his grasp, and rushing from the garden, gained the interior of the castle.

Arnold made the best of his way through the intricacies of the building, pursued by Romont, who shouted at the top of his voice as he followed close upon his heels, "Seize him! seize him!—a false monk, impostor! strike him down."

Arnold, as soon as he had distanced his pursuer sufficiently, retired into a recess in the building, and throwing off his priestly habit, appeared in the disguise of an Austrian trooper.

Mingling with the crowd of men, who had now assembled, attracted by the cries of Romont, he apparently joined in the pursuit; every part of the castle was carefully examined, but neither true or false monk could be discovered.

Vexed at being thus foiled in his search, and more so at the jeers of his comrades, Romont returned towards the part of the castle occupied by the Baroness and her attendant, in hopes of being able to elicit from them some clue to the riddle.

Meanwhile the rest of the garrison, after they had for some time amused themselves at the expense of their more polished companion, began, at the suggestion of one of their party, to remember that Benedict, as they supposed him to be, had entered the castle during the morning; but no one had seen him repass the gate.

The recollection of this fact again caused a stir among the troopers, and the subsequent discovery of the monk's dress, as it had been cast off by Arnold, proved the truth of their comrade's suspicion.

Arnold, now fearing he should be discovered, made his way towards the gates, and succeeded in effecting his escape.

When he reached the cottage of Ulrich, a consultation was held as to their future proceedings, which it was ultimately decided should be postponed until the Feast of our Lord, on which day the whole country was expected to rise against the power of the Bailiff.

In the interim, Tell was to visit his home, and take a final leave of his family, previous to the time when the freedom of Switzerland was to be accomplished.

CHAPTER XXI.

THE PARTING.

So they loved, as love in twain
Had the essence but in one;
Two distincts, division none;
Number there in love was slain.

With heart beating high with emotion did Tell address himself to his homeward journey. His secret intentions—for as yet he had made no one acquainted with his contemplated deed, the destruction of Gesler—preyed anxiously on his mind; by nature formed for kindness, the heart of our hero felt oppressed and sad, as he regarded mentally the fate of his

11   M

victim; but the wrongs he had suffered, and the apparent necessity of the act, partially reconciled his mind.

He was now proceeding to take his farewell of Charlotte and his children, perhaps for the last time; for, however cautious he might be in the execution of his deed of blood, he could not close his eyes to the evident uncertainty of the issue. But, resolved upon his object, he regarded his personal danger as a trifle, when the possibility occurred of saving his country from the rule of a tyrant.

Twilight now spread over the landscape, and the different objects within the range of his sight became clearly visible. Steadily did he pursue his journey, now along the brow of some beetling precipice, at times shrouded by the dark foliage of a cluster of pines, and frequently pursuing his winding path along the borders of some mountain lake.

In this manner, with unwearying steps, did our hero plod onwards towards the little village of Burglen, where his wife and children were anxiously awaiting his return.

It was not until the close of the day, that Tell approached the cottage under whose roof his family at present rested; as soon as it came within sight, he quickened his pace, until he reached the door, when placing his hand upon the latch, he lingered a while before he ventured to make his appearance in their presence.

When Tell entered the cottage, Charlotte and her two younger children were seated near the fire, the young ones listening with profound looks to the tales their mother told them of the hair-breadth escapes their father had endured while following his occupation as a hunter.

"Why does he seek such danger, mother? I am sure, if he knew how you cry when he's away, he would stay at home."

"Alas! my child, he has chosen the hunter's life, and seeks the chamois to bring it home as food for you; alas, I would he had been a shepherd; my mind forbodes some ill whenever he is away."

"Charlotte!" cried Tell, who had been gazing fondly upon the group, "see, I am safe; what avail these tears? there is a Providence that watches over me."

At the sight of her husband the wife of Tell suddenly rose, and uttering a scream of joy, rushed into his arms, and sobbed aloud.

"You cannot think how fearful I have been!" at length she said; "there is some dreadful act in contemplation."

"Ha! what dreadful act? how should you know?"

"I know you was at Rutli last Tuesday night."

"At Rutli, true! I thought—at Rutli, yes I was, and so were many others."

"I am sure they are plotting against the Bailiff, Tell!"

"Well, Charlotte, and what then?"

"Whate'er is done you'll in the place of danger be."

"We must risk something, Charlotte, to rid us of the tyrant; but be of good cheer; Heaven is on our side. But where is Walter?"

"Like you, he is never happy unless upon the hills; but hark, I hear his voice. He sees not the storm that threatens; he's ever merry, Tell!"

"Nay, listen, Charlotte—what song is that he sings?"

With arms entwined, the happy parents listened, with pleasure depicted in their countenances, as the cheerful boy trolled forth the following ballad :—

> While the dew is on the earth,
> Girt to chase his nimble prey,
> See the hunter sallies forth,
> Oe'r the hills by break of day.
>
> High in heaven the eagle soars,
> King of the rolling clouds is he,
> But lord of mountain and of dale,
> Roves abroad the hunter free.
>
> Strength or speed are no avail,
> Every bird that cleaves the air,
> Every beast on hill or dale,
> Victims of his arrows are.

" Ah, father !" exclaimed Walter as he drew near, " have you returned? I am so happy; see what I shot just now."

" 'Tis a bear's cub," said Tell ; " that's dangerous sport, boy ; it is well you was not followed by the dam. But come, let's in to supper, for in the morning I must rise betimes. I've a hard task before me, and need some rest."

" What ! leave me again so soon ? Nay, Tell, this restless life can never end in good. What calls you hence ?"

" Ask me not now, we'll speak of that anon; at present let's in, and let me once more see my children's happy faces ranged round our frugal board."

With this the happy family entered the cottage, and after partaking of their evening repast, and praying to Heaven that its fostering care might guard them through the night, each retired to his humble couch.

Before the first streaks of crimson in the eastern sky announced the rising of the sun, Tell, his wife, and Walter Tell were partaking of their morning meal.

Tell had already informed Charlotte that business of the highest importance required his immediate absence from home; he recommended her to place her trust in Heaven, and to have no anxious fears respecting his safety, but to rely upon the justness of the cause his countrymen had undertaken, and dream of nothing but success.

All the arguments the afflicted woman could advance were useless in dissuading him from the course he had determined upon, and after taking an affectionate farewell of his wife and giving the younger children, still wrapped in the arms of sleep, a parting kiss, he departed on his journey.

Walter was to accompany his father a part of the way he had to go, and afterwards to proceed to the house of Werner, to inform him of the progress of events at Rossberg.

As soon as Walter had left his father, Tell again began to think seriously of his intended attempt upon the life of Gesler.

" Alas !" he cried, " once I lived quiet and innocent, and never bent my bow save in the chase; but thou, tyrant, hast turned my thoughts to bloody deeds—what, shall the hand which at my own child took a steady aim, tremble or fail to strike a tyrant's bosom? It is not for myself I take this vengeance, Bailiff, but from thy bloody hand I must protect the weak and innocent. With what a devilish joy did you not urge me to draw my bow against my own child's head !— and shall my hand then tremble to draw it against thee ?—No !" he exclaimed with more vehemence, "I have sworn the oath, that the next arrow parted from my bow should pierce your heart; the debt is sacred, and it must be paid."

Again he moved onward, and presently saw two men approaching; as they approached, he saluted them—

"Friends, what news abroad ?"

"Naught but the news we are so well accustomed to."

"How say you, countrymen ?"

"Fresh cruelties of Gesler greet our ears."

"You come from Altdorf, as I take it; is the Bailiff there ?"

"He was this morning, but, as I heard, intends, with a strong escort, to pass through the mountains—on what errand is not known—doubtless some fresh oppression."

"Know you the road he takes ?" demanded Tell.

"Yes, if I am not mistaken, he passes close by here, through yonder gorge in the mountain."

"Indeed! well, fare you well."

"Farewell," replied the travellers, and proceeded on their journey.

"He is placed within my power; through that deep narrow passage must he pass; this brushwood here will form a shady covert, whence the avenging arrow well may reach him.—Bailiff, make up thy reckoning, thy hour is almost come. Here on this mossy stone I'll take my seat.— See how each traveller presses on his road, each on his business bent; they all go forth, each on a separate errand—for trade, religion, love— my errand, what is that? it is murder. Alas! my children, once when I left your cot, you joyed at my return; then I sought for you a flower, a bird perchance, a curious stone—now here I sit watching, with murderous thought, the life-blood of my foe."

While Tell was thus ruminating on his enterprise, the sound of lively music was heard in the distance, and he could plainly perceive a bridal procession move along the narrow road through which he expected Gesler to pass.

A straggler from the group approached the spot where our hero sat; regarding Tell, he observed—"Yonder is the wedding of the Convent farmer; he is rich, they say; he now brings home his wife; there will be rare doings in the town to-night: if you'll come with us, you will be welcome; every honest man is invited."

"A gloomy guest," replied Tell, "suits not a marriage feast."

"Tut! man, if you are oppressed in spirits, go with me; the times are bad, I know; it more behoves us then to seize the passing joy."

"Bad enough, friend; perhaps they soon may mend."

"Well, fare you well; you wait for some one here ?"

"I do," replied Tell.

On this the villager departed, leaving Tell wrapped in thought, and anxiously directing his attention towards the pathway by which he expected the arrival of Gesler.

CHAPTER XXII.

THE PLOT.

But such is the infection of the time,
  That for the health and physic of our right,
  We cannot deal but with the very hand
  Of stern injustice and confused wrong.

We must now return to the Castle of Altdorf, where Gesler sat, receiving, at all hands, news of the growing discontent of the people. Rumours also were abroad of an intended resistance of the power of Austria by the country at large.

To meet the exigencies of the times, Gesler had endeavoured to strengthen himself by all the means in his power; he had collected as large a body of armed men about his person as his influence and wealth could accomplish; he was busying himself also in strengthening the garrison of the Castles of Altdorf and Rossberg, and intended to proceed to the latter place himself, for the purpose of having an interview with the lady Gertrude.

While seated thus, deliberating on his future proceedings, notice was brought to him of the arrival of one of his officers, who required an immediate interview. The new comer proved to be Friesshardt.

"My lord," he exclaimed, "I have news for your private ear; may I crave an audience?"

Aware that the proceedings of his agent were not always fitted for any ear besides his own, Gesler at once acceded to his request, and having motioned for all to retire, he desired Friesshardt to unburden his mind.

"My Lord," said the trooper, "aware of your suspicions with regard to young Arnold Attinghausen, accompanied by Leuthold I have tracked him through the country, to discover if your Lordship's suspicions were founded on truth."

"It was well done, Captain."

"After many a wearisome march, we traced him to the neighbourhood of Rossberg castle."

"Of Rossberg, say you?"

"Of Rossberg, my lord, where Lady Gertrude is confined; there also is a young chamois hunter, the blind man who suffered by your orders here in Altdorf, and other turbulent spirits."

"What can they intend by meeting thus at Rossberg?"

"Young Ernest and the blind man have filled the country people with alarm, excited them against the Austrian power—"

"But why meet they at Rossberg?"

"I know not my lord; one of their party, it seems, has found the means of entering the castle—but he is secured."

"Friesshardt, I have always found you devoted to my service, will you assist me now?"

"With heart and soul; how can I serve Lord Gesler?"

"Arnold Attinghausen!" said Gesler. "He must be cared for."

Little did the Bailiff suppose that the wishes he had now expressed, as to the fate of Arnold, had been anticipated by his wily follower! The latter, although pleased to discover that he had properly interpreted the desires of his master, was too good a tactician to acknowledge the fact.

Still less was he inclined to let him know of his failure in the attempt, and of the capture of Leuthold.

Assuming, therefore, as much the appearance of virtue as he could manage to arrange on the moment, he evinced an apparent reluctance to undertake the task.

Disappointed at this backwardness on the part of his follower, Gesler was somewhat disconcerted, for it was not the first time he had imposed duties upon Friesshardt, whose accomplishments included crimes of nearly as deep a dye as that he now proposed.

Besides, he had not said in direct words that he wished for the death of Arnold, although what he had uttered might have been interpreted in that manner.

He returned, however, again to the attack, and after enumerating the many favours he had bestowed upon him, the cunning villain appeared to yield to the governor's entreaties, and agreed, for the promise of a large reward, to sacrifice Arnold to the vengeance of his rival; for whatever political reasons he might assign, his deadly hatred to the young Swiss noble arose more from jealousy of the interest he possessed in the affections of Gertrude than from any other cause.

Friesshardt, satisfied by his former failures that there was little chance of effecting his purpose while Arnold was surrounded by his friends, proposed the adoption of some measure by which he might be separated from them, and attacked single-handed, when off his guard.

How this was to be brought about was a question requiring consideration. After some consultation, it was proposed to deliver a letter to Arnold, containing a pretended desire, from one of Gertrude's relatives, to have an interview with the noble Swiss, for the purpose of consulting him with respect to the affairs of the Baroness.

As his fictitious correspondent was to pretend a hatred for the conduct of Gesler, it would be necessary that the meeting should be concerted in some solitary spot, where there might be no fear of being detected by the Governor's spies.

Their plot being thus cunningly laid, the mode of putting it into execution was to be next considered. Who was to be their messenger?

It was clear that after the late attempt upon his life, Arnold would be cautious in meeting a stranger at any secluded spot.

Friesshardt proposed to proceed at once to the village of Burglen, and having disguised himself so as to prevent his recognition by the villagers, to see if he could not induce one among them, to convey the letter to Arnold. Coming from such a quarter he was in hopes suspicion would not be excited in the breast of Gertrude's lover.

Bent upon this purpose, he accordingly directed his course towards that ill-fated village. But as the success of the scheme of assassination depended upon the celerity with which it was executed, he determined to take the mountain track, which was considered much the nearest.

Armed with a mountain staff, and disguised as an Austrian peasant, Friesshardt commenced his journey.

Our trooper was hardy and bold, and well enabled to endure fatigue and to face danger; but the labour of travelling this mountain road was, to him, a new species of toil, and he had scarcely performed one third of the distance before he was obliged to seat himself on a stone to rest.

If the path he had thus far travelled was wearisome and dangerous, that which lay before him was infinitely more so, for a portion of the glacier had to be crossed, whose sloping sides, covered with frozen snow, offered no barrier between its verge and the gulph below.

When Friesshardt approached the confines of these realms of eternal winter, his heart failed him, for he had heard that the snow concealed from view many fissures in the solid rock of ice, which formed the glaciers, through which the unfortunate traveller at times had been known to fall, and meet with a horrid death by being suffocated in the snow, or dashed to pieces in the dreadful gulph below.

Full of these horrid anticipations the assassin began to venture along the glacier's side.

He had not proceeded above a hundred yards, when he lost his footing, for the treacherous snow slipped from under his feet, and he found himself sliding down the side of the glacier, with an accelerated velocity.

All now appeared lost, and the gulph below seemed yawning ready to receive its victim. His descent had continued for some time, and he was rapidly approaching the verge of the precipice, when, by a violent effort, incited by despair, he struck his staff into the ground, and at the same time, being thrown upon the ground by the shock, his feet came in contact with a projecting mass of ice, and his further descent was arrested.

Thus miraculously preserved from expected death, the terrified trooper rested on the glacier's side, fearful to rise, and incapable of proceeding or retreating.

While he was occupying this uncomfortable and dangerous elevation, he descried a youth crossing the glacier at an elevation considerably above that which he had selected. In the agony of despair he cried aloud for help, and the youth returned his hail.

"Countryman," he exclaimed, "you should not have tried to cross the snow without a guide; it's almost certain death to make the passage at the spot you have chosen. But rest there quiet till I descend."

So saying the intrepid boy began cautiously to approach the spot where Friesshardt sat. When he reached the Austrian he told him to rise cautiously, and assisting him in his efforts, soon placed him upon his legs. Then pointing out to him the spots on which it was best to rest his staff or place his foot, in a short time they both succeeded in reaching a part of the glacier where the passage was more secure.

"You are not of this country?" said the boy, addressing the trooper.

"No," returned Friesshardt, "I am an Austrian born."

"An Austrian! you are not like Gesler's men?"

"No, my lad, Heaven forbid I should be; I am an Austrian peasant—I was on my road to Burglen."

"And so am I; and as you are unacquainted with the road, I'll show it to you."

"I shall feel bound to you; but may I ask your name, my lad?"

"My name is Walter Tell."

"Tell! your father's?"

"Why, William Tell,—every body knows his name."

"I've heard it before now—the famous bowman?"

"The same," replied Walter; "but come—this is our road."

At this moment a sudden thought appeared to strike the trooper. Who could be better for his purpose than the son of Tell? If he were the bearer of the letter, it would disarm suspicion at once.

Impressed with this idea he gradually brought the conversation to bear upon the purport of his present errand. Walter had heard of the imprisoned lady and deplored her sufferings, his young mind being so fully impressed with hatred for the cruelties of Gesler. Hearing, therefore, from Friesshardt that his object was to convey a letter to her lover, Walter readily offered to become the bearer of the communication himself.

Friesshardt, having now gained his object, felt little inclination to pursue his hazardous journey across the glaciers. He accordingly informed his companion that as he kindly offered to carry the letter for him, his intention was to return to Altdorf, instead of proceeding to Burglen, as he at first proposed.

Young Tell endeavoured to persuade him that it would be safer to continue his journey, than to return without a guide; but the trooper having so well succeeded in his plot, was anxious to report the promised success of his schemes to his employer. Walter Tell finding persuasion useless, as the stranger was determined to return, pointed out to him his best mode of proceeding, so as to avoid the dangers of the road on his return to Altdorf.

Having received these instructions with apparent gratitude, they parted company, and each addressed himself to the task of reaching the confines of the glacier.

Friesshardt had not proceeded far on his dreary road, before he began to repent of his determination to return alone, the novelty of his situation, and the danger attached to his journey, soon confused his ideas, and he forgot the directions given to him by Walter. Bewildered in his mind, he soon wandered from the direct course, and found himself, as he turned an angle of the cliff, upon the verge of a steep precipice.

Suddenly he recoiled from the sight of this unexpected danger, and endeavoured to retrace his steps, but, bewildered in the waste of snow, he only became more confused in his ideas; at length he reached a spot on the glacier, which, from certain appearances indicated by Walter, pointed out the situation of an immense chasm or fissure in the hill, hidden from view, as he had been warned, by a hardened mass of snow.

This unstable bridge, Walter had informed him, must be crossed, to reach the track in the hill side which led to Altdorf; the passage at this place was not difficult of accomplishment if proper caution was used; but before he was well aware of the proximity of the dangerous locality, he had taken one step upon the treacherous arch; the snow slightly shook beneath his tread, and at the next step its insecurity seemed more palpable.

If the trooper had proceeded with caution, he might have crossed in safety; but urged by terror, he endeavoured to spring backwards, and regain the solid snow. This attempt at escape was the cause of his destruction; the fragile bridge gave way, and disclosed to his view the fearful chasm it had covered; in his effort at retreat, Friesshardt had slipped through the opening in the snow, and now found himself suspended, supported only by the strength of his arms, over the horrid gulph beneath.

In the agony of despair he shrieked aloud for help, and Walter, who was not yet out of hearing, returned to his assistance with all the speed the nature of the road would allow.

As soon as young Tell came in sight of the trooper, a ray of hope gleamed upon his despairing soul; fresh strength seemed to have been acquired by his relaxing muscles, and he clung more firmly to the side of the rock.

12   N

Walter was now within a few paces of the Austrian, when his over-strained muscles began to lose their power : yet again despair gave him energy, and his bleeding fingers clutched the cold crag with renewed vigour. It was but for an instant; they relaxed their hold again, and at the very moment the boy had stretched out his hand to save him, the terrified wretch, with a cry of horror, loosened his hold and fell into the yawning gulph.

Overcome by terror at the dreadful occurrence, Walter gazed over the edge of the precipice to endeavour to distinguish the form of the fallen villain, but so profound was the depth, that objects near the bottom were but indistinctly visible. Once or twice he thought he could discern the fluttering of a garment, but on clear examination it proved to be the bough of a tree waving in the wind.

The boy now retraced his steps and hastened homewards with all the speed he could ; the vision of the ghostly features of the Austrian, as he gave his last look of despair and agony, haunting his fancy until he reached his father's dwelling.

CHAPTER XXIII.

THE DUNGEON.

> This is some fellow,
> Who, having been praised for bluntness, doth affect
> A saucy roughness ; and constrains the garb,
> Quite from his nature : he cannot flatter, he !—
> An honest mind and plain,—he must speak truth :
> An they will take it, so ; if not, he's plain.

The mysterious disappearance of the false monk within the walls of the castle of Rossberg, coupled with the entrance of Hans Winkelreid into the fortress, had created the highest state of excitement among its inmates.

Romont might, by the evidence he could have afforded, have assisted in some degree to clear up the mystery, but he was himself too much implicated in the transaction, to be enabled with safety to disclose all he knew on the subject. Under these circumstances, there seemed little chance of elucidating the truth.

Ravensdorf, the captain of the guard, caused every precaution to be taken against the further intrusion of strangers, by more strictly enforcing the rules of discipline, which, from the apparent security of the fortress, had been of late considerably relaxed. Their only visiter, the Carthusian, was closely questioned on his next visit, and it required all his dexterity, backed by the credit attached to his holy office, to satisfy his interrogators that he had not participated in the deception.

It now occurred to the mind of Ravensdorf that some information might be gathered from their prisoner, and, accordingly, he proceeded to the dungeon in which Hans was confined.

Partially released from his bonds, the sturdy herdsman stretched his huge limbs and chafed his stiffened joints. He seemed to pay but little attention to what was going on around him, and, when addressed by the captain, he assumed a look of sullen obstinacy. He was questioned as to his reason of entering the castle, and the mode in which he had effected it. Fearful of compromising Hildegard and the Countess, Hans for a time refused to answer the interrogatories of the Austrians; at length, after duly weighing the matter in his mind, he came to the decision, that perhaps it would be as well to speak the truth at all hazards.

Accordingly, when the question as to how he entered the castle, was again put to him, he related his perilous ascent of the precipice.

"Ruffian!" exclaimed Ravensdorf, "do you seek to impose upon us? you had better speak the truth at once, than let us force it from your stubborn tongue. We have means of torture you little dream of."

"You are so false yourselves, you Austrians, that a plain tale, told by an honest man, finds no belief. I tell you that I scaled the castle cliffs."

"'Tis false! The chamois, or the goat, have never dared to climb their rugged sides, much less a clumsy hound like thee."

"Clumsy or not," retorted Hans, "I climbed the castle rocks, and if you'll but remove these bonds, I will perform a harder task than that."

"Indeed! what mean you?"

"Give me my liberty, and I'll descend the precipice before your eyes."

"If, as you say, you did indeed climb up its rugged side, say for what purpose did you make the bold attempt?"

"If I speak truth you'll doubt me."

"Say on."

"I heard that a Swiss maiden was here confined. She belongs to the same village as myself, and I wished to see her."

"'Tis likely! what is the maiden's name?"

"Hildegard, and she waits upon the Baroness."

"Was you not sent to see her mistress upon some treasonous errand?"

"I have spoken what is true."

The plain and unabashed bearing of Hans completely baffled the endeavours of the captain to obtain farther information; and, partially satisfied that the prisoner was speaking the truth, he dismissed him for the present, assuring him of certain punishment as soon as he should receive orders from the bailiff.

Hans being removed, the captain and a party of the troopers repaired to the garden to examine into the possibility of the assertion of Hans, that he had entered the castle by ascending the rocks.

Gertrude and Hildegard were both questioned on the subject, and agreed in pointing out the spot at which the herdsman had reached the summit of the rock. They pointed out the place from whence the rock, which had yielded to the weight of Hans, had fallen, and, at length, they were constrained to admit that the difficult task had been accomplished. Ravensdorf, the captain of the guard, was busied in the useless endeavour to obtain information respecting the cause of the visit of Hans, which he could not avoid attributing to some political motive; when one of the troopers entered the garden in a breathless state, and in hurried accents informed him that Gesler himself, accompanied by a strong escort, had been seen in the distance directing their march towards the castle.

Ravensdorf was alarmed at this sudden arrival of the bailiff, after the recent occurrences, and yet at the same time gratified that the responsibility of further proceedings had been removed from his shoulders ; he left his fair captives without much ceremony, and prepared to receive his dreaded commander.

Meantime Gesler and his followers were slowly threading the steep and circuitous path which led to the castle gates. As he moved along, the conversation between the tyrant and his more immediate atttendants became animated by the discussion of the present alarming state of affairs, for the truth of the reports he had listened to at Altdolf had been fully confirmed by the observations made during his journey hither.

The result was, that in spite of former experience, the infatuated man had determined to adopt further measures of cruelty, and those among his followers who ventured to remonstrate with him on the subject, and to point out the impolicy of such a mode of proceeding, were repulsed with rudeness, and suppressing the anger they dared not exhibit, in sullen silence retired to the rear. In this manner did Gesler and his escort enter the village of Rossberg.

The escape of Gesler from the contemplated vengeance of Tell is to be attributed to one of those sudden changes in the course of events which so frequently interpose between the determination and the act, and baffle or defeat the best laid scheme.

The bailiff, it seems, had not proceeded far upon his journey, which he began soon after the departure of Friesshardt, and of which Tell had received information, as we have already seen, when fresh news from Rossberg created so much alarm in his mind, that he determined to retrace his steps, double the number of his escort, and examine the aspect of affairs with his own eyes. At the same time he despatched a messenger to the Emperor, pointing out to him the necessity of immediate assistance being afforded to himself in Uri.

Breathing vengeance as he passed through the little village, in which he had reason to believe Arnold and his companions still remained, he pursued the direct road to the castle gates, and having dismounted to be enabled to cross the rude bridge with safety, he entered the castle itself, and was received with all due honour by the captain and his band.

Having ascertained the state of affairs within its walls, he issued orders for the execution of Hans on the following morning, and having dispatched several of his men into the village to learn what they could respecting Arnold and his friends, he himself proceeded to the apartments of the Baroness.

Gertrude, although she dreaded this interview with the hated bailiff, retained full possession of her faculties, and desiring Hildegard to remain with her, patiently awaited his approach.

" Ere I left Altdorf, Lady Gertrude," said Gesler, " strange rumours reached me, in which, if I am well informed, your ladyship is much concerned."

"I, my lord Governor?"

"You, Gertrude Walstein! So strange they were, I could not rest until I knew the truth; they said that you conspired against the state; your agent was well known, a vile peasant, who, as I find, is now within these walls."

"What—Hans?" exclaimed Gertrude and her attendant, as it were, in one breath."

"Aye, some such name he has; but he is safe, and ere to-morrow's sun has two hours risen, he meets his fate."

"Alas! you are mistaken," said Gertrude vehemently; "treason and him are strangers. He came to seek an interview with Hildegard."

"'Tis true, my lord," said Hildegard.

"Indeed! your vanity deceives you, child; what! risk his life to seek a sickly girl? Yet you may save him, Lady Gertrude."

"How may that be?"

"Deliver up the papers that he brought."

"There are no papers."

"Well, as you will—I'll find a means to see them; meantime your tether must be shortened, lady. There is too much space within this garden here. You have abused my ill-placed lenity; besides, since one can scale these rocks, another may. Your safety must be seen to;—and mine also," he said in an under tone.

"I am now within your power, my lord, and it were useless to resist; as useless would it be to plead for favour, even should I deign to sue.— Come, Hildegard; poor girl, I pity thee; you might have lived as free as yonder bird. But better times will rise—come, let's in."

Hildegard and her mistress entered their apartments, and Gesler, in moody silence, stood for some time, with folded arms, gazing upon the door by which they left.

CHAPTER XXIV.

THE MESSENGER.

The stranger's form was tall and spare,
Pallid his cheek, jet black his hair;
His jaded courser's reeking side
Showed he had come a weary ride.

The sun was about to set beyond the hills of Schweitz, when a solitary horseman was seen directing his course towards the village of Rothenthurm; the distressed appearance both of horse and man bore evidence of the toil they had undergone.

The powers of the steed seemed almost exhausted, and the excitement of whip and spur appeared to have little effect in hastening its pace. At length the spire of the village church came in view, and both horse and rider were cheered at the prospect; the former, as if anticipating relief from his toil, snorted loudly, and exerting all its remaining strength, improved its speed until it reached the village market-place, where the rider, drawing bridle at the door of a house that bore some resemblance to an inn or house of entertainment, flung himself from its back and called lustily to the inmates—

"What, ho! Bernard," he exclaimed, "haste, man, haste! saddle me another horse, and send me some refreshment."

The man to whom these words were addressed had more the air of a freebooter than a publican; he seemed well acquainted with the horseman, and addressing him familiarly, inquired the reason of his great haste.

"What errand, Grisach, are you now upon; what new mischief is in the wind? Has Gesler brought the mountaineers to reason, and are you speeding to the Emperor with the pleasant news?"

"I am speeding to the court, it is true; as to my news, that's as the case may be,—perchance the Emperor may relish it; they say he only wants some good excuse to find his way among these mountaineers. The three cantons, Bernard, are almost up in arms."

"Aye, indeed."

"But come, I have no time to spare—I must be on the road—farewell." So saying, Gesler's messenger again leaped into his saddle.

"Which road do you take?" said the host.

"The pass of Morgarten."

"You're a staunch horseman, Grisach; may your success be equal to your merits!" As soon as the horseman was out of hearing, Bernard shouting loudly, summoned two sturdy countrymen to his presence. "You saw the man who parted just now?"

"Yes, father," said the elder of the two; "he rode the black horse you bought of Werner Stauffhausen."

"Well, you must prevent his passage through the hills; go the byeroads you know so well, and intercept him ere he reach the plain. If you are active you are sure to be in time; the road he goes is difficult for horsemen."

"Should he resist?"

"The safety of our country then demands his life; but spare it if you can; obtain his papers and make him prisoner."

Totally unconscious of any danger lying in his path, refreshed in body and mounted upon a good horse, Grisach proceeded on his journey with increased speed; but ere he had ridden five miles towards Morgarten, the road became more intricate, and he was obliged to slacken his speed.

As he proceeded, the difficulties of the track increased; and buried now in the deep shades of the mountains, he was at times obliged to dismount and lead his horse. In this manner, alternately riding and walking, he had proceeded so far into the pass as to be able to distinguish in the distance the waters of the little lake Egeri reflecting the form of the newly risen moon.

Suddenly two men sprung from the thicket, and he found himself rudely grasped by the arm by one, while the other seized the bridle of his horse. They desired him to stand and deliver up the letter he carried about him.

Thus violently assailed, Gesler's messenger endeavoured to shake off his personal assailant, but ineffectually, and finding opposition useless, reluctantly allowed the papers he was the bearer of to be taken from him.

The two brothers having possessed themselves of these important documents, stooped down to examine their contents by the imperfect light; and while thus engaged, the wily Austrian, putting spurs to his horse, dashed down the ravine, and was soon lost to their sight.

Onward he went, reckless of the dangers of the path along which he urged his steed, at times obliged to stoop to his horse's neck to escape the overhanging boughs, or nearly fling himself from his saddle to avoid being dashed to the ground by the angular masses of rock which projected from the sides of the mountain gorge.

His better angel seemed to protect him in the midst of all these difficulties, and he reached a more level track without meeting with any serious accident. For a few minutes he moved more gently along to allow his horse time to breathe and recover from his recent exertions. The fear, however, of being pursued would not allow him to grant his steed a long respite, and putting spurs to his sides, he again moved at a rapid pace towards the borders of the little lake.

The horse ridden by the Austrian was strong and fleet, and maintained its speed without flagging along the margin of the water, until he had borne his rider as far as the little village of Egeri, from which the lake takes its name.

Here the half-reasoning brute slackened its speed, as if in anticipation of rest after its fatiguing journey; but the haste or fear of the Austrian would allow of no respite, and again he dashed onwards through the silent streets of the village.

The road now laid between two high ranges of hills, extending on either side far beyond the traveller's ken; in traversing this long and dreary track the greater portion of the night was consumed, but when the first rays of the sun cheered the landscape, the spire of the little church of Baar was visible in the distance, glistening in its beams; thither the wearied traveller directed his course, and before the sun was far above the horizon, drew up his panting horse in a wide space in the centre of the village.

The inhabitants of the Canton of Zug, in which the village of Baar is situated, were less disaffected towards the Austrian yoke than those of the three mountain Cantons; accordingly, being now at a considerable distance from the spot whence he began his flight, Gesler's messenger determined to give rest to his horse for a few hours, before he continued his journey.

He entered the little inn of the village, and having seen proper attention paid to his horse, and partaken of the refreshments he so much needed, he flung himself upon the rude seat on which he was placed, and was soon wrapped in deep slumber.

The master of the house and a group of idlers had now assembled in the room in which the Austrian rested himself. Their conversation, attracted to the subject by his appearance, naturally turned upon the present troubled state of affairs, their proximity to the disturbed districts having made them acquainted with many of Gesler's acts of cruelty.

"We shall have troublesome times, Reich," said the landlord, addressing one of the group; these frequent messengers from the Unterwalden betoken no good."

"Ah! it would make your heart bleed to listen to the tales I have heard of the cruelties of the bailiff,"

"'Twere well if that were the end of all, but the emperor himself is marching hither, he is now near Eschenbach, about to cross the Reuss."

"Near where?" exclaimed the Austrian, suddenly rousing from his sleep.

"Near Eschenbach," repeated the speaker, "and with him comes his nephew, John of Hapsburg,"

"How soon," demanded the Austrian, "could I reach the place?"

"With moderate speed by mid day, if you take the nearest road and cross the lake. If not, your journey will at least be two hours longer."

"I cannot take my horse across the lake, I must perforce go by the longest route! Well, farewell, comrades."

So saying, Gesler's messenger prepared to recommence his journey. He was soon in his saddle, and urging his refreshed steed along the road, hastened forward to meet the emperor.

The loss of his papers now occurred to the mind of our traveller, and dreading the violent nature of Albert, some doubt arose in his mind as to the prudence of appearing before him; but aware of the nature of the communication, and the necessity there was for speed, he determined, if he found it necessary, to declare himself the bearer of merely a verbal message, and to state that the necessity for haste had induced the bailiff to depart from his usual plan of despatching a written communication.

In this mood of mind, and perfecting his excuses as he proceeded on his journey, he hastened forward on his mission. Having frequently before been the messenger of Gesler, he was well known to the emperor and those by whom he was surrounded, and, therefore, was under no fear of being immediately admitted to his presence.

Cheered by these reflections he proceeded on his journey with more alacrity, expecting rather to receive the applause of Albert for the speed with which he had accomplished his journey, than censure for being unprepared with his usual credentials. His horse, likewise, as if conscious he was approaching a place of rest, improved his pace without being urged forward by the application of either whip or spur.

CHAPTER XXV.

THE ARMY.

High minds of native pride and force
Most deeply feel thy pangs remorse;
Fear for their scourge mean villains have,
Thou art the torturer of the brave.

The peaceful inhabitants of the town of Eschenbach had been frightened out of their propriety by the arrival of the head-quarters of the Austrian army, headed by the Emperor in person, who was accompanied by his nephew, John, and the principal nobles of the empire.

The ancient castle had been prepared, as well as circumstances would allow, for the reception of its distinguished guests. At the time we are speaking of, the emperor, who had been appointed guardian to his nephew at his father's death, withheld from the former certain heritages to which he considered himself entitled.

John, now accompanying his uncle on his expedition against the Swiss, considered the time well-fitted for renewing the application for a restitution of his rights.

Goaded into rage by the repeated appeals of his nephew, whom he looked upon as an effeminate and weak-minded youth, Albert had determined to shame him into silence. Accordingly, on the repetition of his demand when they arrived at Eschenbach, he ordered garlands of various flowers to be brought, and presenting them to him with mock solemnity, observed, "These are more befitting your youth and inexperience; leave the governing of states to me."

John withdrew from the presence of his uncle with a heart deeply wounded, and brooding over some dreadful act of vengeance.

His ancient teacher, Walter of Eschenbach, to whom he was much attached, endeavoured to console him in his trouble, and promised him assistance in the endeavour to recover his rights, and be revenged upon his uncle. Three of his young associates also joined in the plot, namely, Rodolph de Wart, Rodolph de Balm, and Conrad de Tegelfeld.

In this position matters stood when Gesler's messenger reached the town. Albert, when his arrival was announced, was about to proceed, accompanied by his suite, to inspect a portion of the army, which had recently arrived at head-quarters.

When Grisach appeared in the presence of the Emperor, he sprung from his jaded horse, and kneeling before him, awaited the commands of Albert to deliver his message.

"What message bring you from the bailiff? Rise, man, and speak."

"The mountaineers are ready to be up in arms, my liege."

"But where are Gesler's letters?"

"His letters—the haste with which I was despatched, my lord, gave him no time"—

"Indeed! it is against his usual custom.—Asks he for aid?"

"He does, my liege; the plot against your rights is deeply laid."

"'Tis as I wished," said the Emperor, addressing one of the nobles; "these restless hinds have worked their own destruction; we'll push our army on without delay. They talk of separate rights—obey the emperor! but not the dukes of Austria! What may the numbers of our army be? Have the new levies yet come in?"

"We can advance with twenty thousand men."

"Then on, my lords; at daylight in the morning we advance.—Now, nephew, if you wish to win a name in arms, the time is come, is near at hand; these hardy Swiss will give your sword some practice."

"You are right, my lord; I hope, before it's long, to flesh my sword," returned his nephew.

"My lords," said the Emperor, "let all be ready for our march at day break; till then, farewell. I have matters of great moment to transact, and would, until that time, be private."

The Emperor retired; and for the remainder of the day, the town and its neighbourhood were in a state of confusion and excitement, from the arrangements, necessary to be made, on account of this sudden decision of Albert; and it was late at night before the noisy din of preparation was hushed.

The morning rose and found Albert resting upon his uneasy couch, a prey to distracting thoughts; he was on the eve of his endeavour to accomplish another deed of blood and injustice, and the memory of his former acts of violence arose, like so many spectres, before his disturbed vision. He turned restlessly on his couch, and hailed with pleasure the return of day.

The cheering rays of the rising sun fell like balm upon his wounded conscience, and the spectres of his diseased imagination fled at their approach. He was soon arrayed in his armour, and appeared at the head of his troops, inspiring confidence by his bold and warlike bearing, haughty and ungraceful as it was.

The word was given to march, and the whole army moved forward to the sound of warlike instruments, their flickering pennons glittering in the sun, while the standard of the empire floating above their heads, disclosed to its morning rays the Austrian eagle, with its two-fold head and neck.

As they approached the wooden bridge by which the river Reuss was crossed, it was necessary they should pass over in small parties, and form again in masses as they reached the level ground on the opposite bank of the river. While this manœuvre was being performed, a task which occupied several hours, the Emperor and those officers whose actual assistance was not in immediate requisition, strayed about in groups, busily engaged in conversation, on the momentous events about to take place.

John and his associates, among others, had separated themselves from the mass, and in deep consultation were devising means to accomplish their revengeful object,

"His death alone," said Rodolph de Balm, can procure the restitution of your rights; besides, our own safety requires it. If any other means were used and justice obtained, the lives of all who aided in the scheme would be as surely sacrificed as yonder water flows into the Rhine."

"And yet," said Conrad de Tegelfeld, "'tis hard to take his life; what say you, John of Hapsburg? it is your cause and we have sworn to help you; say, shall your uncle live?

"I'm in your hands, my friends, and cannot act without your help; but his base conduct towards me, and the last taunt he uttered, have crushed each bud of pity in my bosom. I know him now no longer as an uncle, but an oppressor, and could look with smiles upon his mangled corpse."

" Then it's decided, and we have but to choose a proper opportunity."

" What time more fitted for our purpose than during our march through Zug? How frequently he rides apart from all, save two or three of those he most delights in! Could we not then, on one of those occasions, detatch him from his friends, and thus despatch him?"

"Nothing would be easier," said John; "we cannot fail, if we are but true to our own cause."

"Silence!" exclaimed Walter d'Eschenbach; "the Emperor approaches."

As he spoke, the Emperor, accompanied by his principal officers, drew near; he passed the group of friends who surrounded his nephew, and casting upon him a scowl of mingled anger and suspicion, rendered more forbidding by the defect of vision to which we have already alluded, continued his course without further noticing the object of his hatred.

"By heavens," cried John, "my uncle suspects our plot! Did you observe his look as he passed by?"

"Tush! man, there's nothing in that look more than is usual; I never saw features more forbidding."

By this time the army of Austria was again ready to recommence its march; and spreading its huge masses over the plain, commenced its devastating course towards the banks of the lake of Zug.

The messenger from Gesler was summoned into the presence of Albert, and received communications for his employer, pointing out the course he was to pursue, and warning him of the approach of the Austrian army. With these he was ordered to hasten with all the speed he could to Rossberg Castle.

Meantime the army continued its march, and the conspirators watching for the expected opportunity of executing their murderous scheme, were less cautious in their movement than was consistent with safety. The consequence was, they excited the suspicion of the two eldest sons of Albert; Frederic and Leopold, who as carefully dogged their movements as they themselves did the proceedings of the Emperor.

They were now approaching that branch of the river which takes its rise in lake Zug, and preparations were making to cross the stream by means of rafts, as near to its source as possible. The task of superintending this operation resting with the two sons of the Emperor, their attention was consequently drawn for the time from John and his associates.

These latter, on the other hand, had felt uneasy at the constant intrusion, as it were, of Frederic and his brother, which occurred so frequently and unexpectedly as to render them uncomfortable as to its cause. Their present employment, consequently, caused the conspirators to be more easy in their mind, and more at liberty to pursue their machinations.

Accordingly, the Emperor was more closely watched and followed than he had previously been, and a speedy accomplishment of the intentions of the conspirators was resolved upon.

It had been ascertained that before the troops again resumed their march, the propriety of taking a more northerly road than that usually travelled was to be decided on. As this was a business on which the successful commencement of the campaign materially depended, the Emperor determined to accompany the reconnoitring party, and that with a very small escort.

This then appeared to be the auspicious moment; the plan of operations was immediately laid, and the conspirators departed for the scene of action on the previous evening, determined to take advantange of circumstances as they arose, but with the full intention of accomplishing their task.

CHAPTER XXVI.

THE ASSASSINATION.

.... Ere to black Hecate's summons,
The shard-borne beetle, with his drowsy hum,
Hath rung night's yawning peal, there shall be done
A deed of dreadful note.

With a party of six only, in order to excite less suspicion, the emperor Albert left the camp on the fated morning, disguised in the uniform of a subordinate officer, his followers being dressed as common soldiers. In this manner they passed almost unnoticed to their destination.

The road they wished to reconnoitre was separated from that usually followed, by a low copse of underwood about a quarter of a mile in width, and extended, between precipitous rocks, for a mile in length. In case it was found desirable to follow the northern road, this thicket would have to be cut through to afford a passage for the army.

To this place, also, the conspirators had directed their steps, and from their place of concealment were enabled to obtain a view of the advancing party.

As soon as they came within sight of the assassins, the latter more closely ensconced themselves amid the shadows of the wood, anxiously watching the proceedings of the Emperor and his attendants; for, in spite of his disguise, the well-known features of Albert were at once recognised by the concealed party.

As the reconnoitring band advanced further into the wood for the purpose of pursuing their survey, John and his companions, also, shifted their position. The rustling among the brushwood, caused by their stealthy movements, at times attracted the attention of the advancing party, who frequently stopped to listen; but all being again still, they attributed the sound to the movement of one of their own party, for the nature of the ground prevented their keeping close together during the advance.

Albert, in the meantime, from his greater anxiety to satisfy himself of the nature of the road, lagged behind the rest of his party, who were at length concealed from his view by the thick foliage. His nephew and Rodolph de Balm, close upon his heels, watched every movement of their victim, and the noise produced by the crackling of the bushes, as they shifted their position, impressed upon the Emperor the belief that he still was close to his own attendants.

Several hurried words spoken by Albert at length made his assassins aware of the delusion under which he laboured; of this they immediately took advantage, by drawing him still further from his own party. In this manner they gradually approached the verge of the wood, and Albert turning round as if to address his followers, at once perceived the nature of the danger into which he had run.

Before him, with uplifted dagger, stood his nephew, on whom he had heaped injustice and insult, behind whom appeared his attached friends, each with a drawn weapon, and ready to assist their youthful friend. Albert, accustomed to scenes of danger, on percieving the snare into which he had fallen, drew his sword, determined, if necessary, to sell his life dearly.

"What mean you, nephew," he exclaimed, " by this hostile attitude? Dare you to raise your hand against our life; do you not know I am the Emperor, or does this disguise deceive you?"

"It is no deception, tyrant; we know you well. Tamely till now I have borne the wrongs you have inflicted, and unrevenged I have sat down beneath your insults and your scorn. But here, away from your proud myrmidons, I rule your destiny, and with this blow I satiate my revenge."

With this, John rushed forward upon the Emperor, and plunged his dagger into his bosom. The blood flowed from the wound in torrents, but Albert, raising his sword, aimed a deadly blow at his nephew : this, in spite of the injury he had received, would have well avenged him on his assassin, but his arm was suddenly arrested by Conrad de Tegelfeld, and, at the same instant, the spear of Walter D'Eschenbach passed through his body.

The emperor fell to the ground mortally wounded, and, alarmed at the consequences of their act, his assassins fled with the utmost speed from the scene of action, leaving their victim bathed in blood, and groaning from the agony he endured from the spear wound of D'Eschenbach, who had forcibly withdrawn the weapon from his body.

Thus, in one instant, was the haughty leader of the house of Austria checked in his mid career; and, yielding up his life's blood upon the bare ground, with no one to witnsss his last sigh, or soothe his dying moments. In vain he strove to call for assistance ;—his feeble voice sunk into a plaintive moan, and, groaning as much from vexation of mind as from bodily pain, he lay extended at the foot of the tree where he had fallen.

And did the proud Emperor of Germany, the chivalric Albert, shake off his mortal coil thus lonely and unattended ? Was no one present when his spirit fied ?

A poor houseless mendicant—a beggar woman—who had repaired to the wood to collect firing from the thicket, found him lying upon the ground before life was extinct. She placed his drooping head upon her knee, and endeavoured to staunch his wounds with the rags torn from her scanty clothing. But life was fast ebbing : the blood still flowed from his lacerated wounds in spite of every effort of his unskilful nurse ;—the senseless film of death spread over his sightless eyes, and the death-bed of Austria's despot was a beggar's lap.

The followers of the Emperor discovered, after they had proceeded some distance, the absence of their leader, and carefully retraced their steps for the purpose of rejoining him ; they searched in every part of the thicket, and shouted loudly, but all in vain, till they reached the place from which they started, and after some delay discovered the corpse of Albert as it rested in the woman's arms.

Struck with horror at the sight, they wildly questioned the mendicant ; all she knew she told—she found him wounded and strove to staunch his blood.

" Who was his assassin ?"

She knew not—she had seen no one,—she saw the wounded soldier on the ground and raised him up, she knew no more.

" Woman ! it is the Emperor."

"The Emperor !" exclaimed the mendicant, in terror and astonishment.

Having ascertained that life was quite extinct, they raised the body from the ground, and placing it on one of their horses, prepared to return to the camp. The woman also was forced to accompany them ; with brain dizzy from the scene lately witnessed and from her recently acquired knowledge that she had witnessed the death of the emperor, she seemed almost unconscious of what was taking place.

At a rapid rate did the melancholy and alarmed group direct their steps towards the Austrian camp, bearing their lifeless burthen and the terrified prisoner.

They had proceeded about half way on their journey, when they perceived in the distant horizon a group of horsemen; they rapidly approached, and as soon as they perceived the returning party, urged their horses to the top of their speed until they met.

Before the advancing party had reached the disguised officers, a young man, mounted on a fiery steed, and somewhat in advance of his companions, shouted out in an agonized voice—"The Emperor!—is he safe?"

"Alas! my lord, the Emperor is murdered," was the reply.

"Say, have you taken his assassins?"

"We know not who they are; the Emperor by some mischance mistook his road, and parted company; we found him murdered, and this woman seated by him."

"Duke John of Hapsburgh and his companions have been his murderers. Woman! did you note which way they fled?" cried Leopold, the second son of Albert."

"I saw no one," cried the terrified vagrant,

"My friends," said Leopold, "ride off in all directions, our steeds are chosen the fleetest in all the camp; you cannot surely fail to overtake them. You know them well. Besides my assassin cousin, see you seize D'Eschenbach, De Wart, De Balm, De Tegelfeld; they left the camp in company; I was long aware they had some murderous plot in contemplation, but never dreamt it was so near its issue."

The friends of Leopold now departed in all directions in search of the fugitives, and the remainder of the party returned to the camp, bearing the body of the Emperor.

The consternation spread throughout the Austrian army when the murder of the Emperor was known, can be better conceived than described. Among some his frequent cruelties were freely canvassed, and his miserable end attributed to the just resentment of heaven. The mercenaries were eagerly discussing the probability of a dispute as to the succession to the crown, in which case they were perfectly willing to enlist under the banners of the highest bidder.

The hopes of the latter were soon set at rest; Leopold, the second son, assuming the government of Swabia, Alsatia, and Switzerland, as Duke of Austria; while Frederick took possession, by mutual agreement, of the Italian provinces.

Rewards of great amount were offered for the apprehension of the assassins, who, hitherto, had escaped from the hands of justice; the most dreadful severities were committed upon their relatives, and even upon their vassals, and more than a thousand lives sacrificed to avenge the death of Albert.

The events we have just related, delayed the march of the Austrian army, but made no alteration in the hostile intentions of the new duke, who was more than ever determined to follow out his father's plan for subjugating the Swiss, his determination being supported by the belief that the principal murderer, John of Hapsburg, had taken refuge, and received protection in the Swiss mountains.

Under all these circumstances the advance of the forces was ordered, and directing their march towards the road leading to the lake Egeri, the Austrian columns moved on towards the mountains of Schweitz.

CHAPTER XXVII.

MEETING OF THE CONFEDERATES.

Oh! think what anxious moments pass between
The birth of plots, and their last fatal periods:
Oh! 'tis a dreadful interval of time,
Filled up with horror all, and big with death.

Overcome by terror at the dreadful sight he had witnessed, Walter Tell left the scene of death to return home. Firm and daring as his foot usually was, when upon his native hills, the terrified boy trembled as he walked, and felt as if relieved from a load of anxiety, when he reached a safer part of the road, and came within sight of his native home.

When he entered, he found his father seated in the cottage, pale and dispirited, and as unlike the hardy hunter of other days as could be well imagined.

"Well, Walter," said Tell, "what news from Erni? when is the meeting held?"

"At Werner's house to-morrow night," returned Walter. "But, father, I have been so frightened on the glacier."—

"What happened there?"

"A poor traveller was dashed to pieces down that dreadful chasm where Gaspard fell."

"What! near the Alderstein?"

"The same, father; I tried to save him, but I was too late. Oh! had you seen his look, when he let go his hold; I never shall forget it."

"What brought him to that dangerous spot? was he a hunter?"

"He was dressed like an Austrian, an Austrian peasant; he said he hated Gesler."

"He said so, did he? what made him tell you that?"

"He came, he said, from Lady Gertrude's friends, and had a letter for Arnold Attinghausen."

"Did you ever before see this man, Walter?"

"No, father, he came from Austria on Lady Gertrude's business. He said he was a peasant; but, now that I remember, he must have been in battle: he had the scar of a deep wound upon his right cheek, quite from the eye to the mouth."

"'Tis as I thought; it was Friesshardt, boy, who sought young Arnold's life. He said he had a letter?"

"Yes, but he gave it me; I promised to take it on to Rossberg."

"Where is it?—let me see it—I must hasten to the castle without delay; there is some plot I cannot yet unravel."

So saying, Tell rose from his seat, and seizing his cross-bow, his constant companion, again betook himself to the hills.

On reaching Rossberg, and relating the circumstances connected with Friesshardt's death to Arnold, the latter at once agreed with Tell that the letter, which appointed a meeting at a lonely spot in the mountains, was intended to have decoyed him away from his friends, and then sacrificed him to the vengeance of Gessler.

Arnold, through the agency of Benedict, had been made aware of the impending fate of Hans, and was at present employing every means within his power to save the life of the faithful herdsman. On this account, it was impossible for him to attend the meeting of the confederates at the house of Erni; Tell, therefore, was about to depart alone, bearing with him the good wishes of Arnold and his friends to the good cause in which they were all engaged.

Faithful to their appointment, William Tell and his three coadjutors were assembled at the house of Werner, to mature their plans for the liberation of their country, and determine upon the time when the decisive blow should be struck.

14

"Friends," exclaimed Werner, "again we are assembled in secret, and still the proud oppressor lords it over us. At our next meeting, should Heaven's good will permit it, the mid-day sun shall shine upon our councils, and the proud Austrian's yoke be shattered."

"It is decided, then, on the Lord's feast to strike the blow—say, how is it ordered?"

Young Arnold will attack the towers of Rossberg; Tell, heading the workmen employed at Altdorf, will level to the ground the tyrant's dungeons; the walls of Sarnen never can resist the mountain tribes of Underwalden—Walter Furst will lead them on; while this is acting, it shall be our task, Erni's and mine, to seize on every Austrian we can find, and drive them o'er the borders."

"It were well," said Tell, "could it be done without the loss of life; all but the bailiffs would I spare. The miserable wretches who serve the tyrants have no will of their own; they dare not act against their masters' orders,—but they must not remain within the land."

"It is so determined—but how is this?" exclaimed Werner; "you are wrong in thus intruding."

The last words of Stauffacher were addressed to his wife, who at that moment opened the door of the chamber.

"Dear Werner, I should not have thus intruded, but a man has just arrived, who says that he must see you instantly on matters of importance."

"Who is he—do you know?"

"I know not; he is not from this part of the country, I am sure;—but yet he is not an Austrian."

"Well, lead me to him, and let me learn the purport of his visit."

"Think you it is safe to go alone," said Tell; "it may be some plot of the bailiff's, Werner."

"Tush, man, there is no fear; come on, Matilda."

During the absence of Werner, which, however, was not of long duration, the time was spent in various surmises as to the business of the new-comer, for they had all made up their minds to the certainty of its being connected with the purpose they had in hand.

On his return, Werner introduced Bernard, the innkeeper of whom we have already spoken; he was aware of the interest the former took in the contemplated outbreak, and accordingly, as soon as he had obtained the papers from Gessler's messenger, he hastened with them to the house of Stauffacher.

The contents of these papers plainly showed the necessity of urging forward their proceedings with all the haste they could; and as the messenger to the Austrian court would most likely return by the same road, it was determined to watch closely the path through the mountains at Morgarten, and, if possible, intercept him on his route, and thus prevent any communication between the Emperor and his agents: the superintendance of this duty was imposed upon Bernard, who undertook to place his two sons upon the watch.

"The country, Bernard," said Werner, "owe you a debt of gratitude for your vigilance in this instance, and will be doubly indebted to you and your sons if you succeed in your present undertaking; meanwhile farewell, and hold yourself in readiness to act at an hour's notice."

"My best energies shall be devoted to the cause, countrymen, and those of my two boys, than whom there are not two hardier or braver in the whole canton. Farewell."

As soon as Bernard had departed, the letters of Gessler were more carefully perused, and, accustomed as the confederates were to the cruelties of the bailiff, they could not contemplate without horror the bloodthirsty strain in which these communications of his to his imperial master were written. In them he recommended the destruction of all the most prominent men in the country, either by open violence, or secret assassination.

"And shall this fiend in human form pollute our native hills with his foul presence? He has escaped my arrow once," said Tell, soliloquizing, "but shall not so again."

"Why, Tell, thus moody when the scene of action is at hand? Give me your hand—yours, friends, and with me swear never to sheath the sword again until our native hills are free."

In answer to this demand of Werner, the deliverers of Switzerland locked together their hands in token of amity, and shaking their weapons in the air, with one voice exclaimed—

"Never will we sheathe the sword again till Switzerland is free!"

"And now," cried Werner, the long account of tyranny is nearly closed, and the great day of its discharge is close at hand. Remember, friends, the cause in which we are engaged; let no private wrong stand in our way and turn us from the path that leads to the redress of public grievances. But see, Bernard returns; how wild he looks—what ails you, man?"

"I had not ridden two miles from your house, ere I met my youngest boy, riding with breathless speed—"

"Well, say on—fresh cruelties of Gessler?"

"No, neighbour! no! The shaft of vengeance has fallen upon his master—the Austrian despot's dead!"

"Dead, by the hand of heaven?"

"Murdered by his own kin—by Duke John of Hapsburg and his friends."

"Merciful heaven! And the murderers?"

"They have escaped; but whither they have fled, none know. Duke John himself, they say, has reached the mountains. An envoy from the Empress is close at hand; the bearer of a proclamation, it is said.

"Friends," said Werner, "let us repair to the market-place of the village, and hear the communication of the Empress."

The band of patriots at once betook themselves to the open space in front of the village church, where they found the greater part of the inhabitants assembled to listen to the messenger, just arrived from the Austrian Court.

The bearer of the letter from the widow of the late Emperor, having ascended the steps at the summit of which the crucifix that adorned the market-place was erected, motioned his hearers to silence, and addressed them as follows :—

"The Queen Elizabeth greets the men of Uri, Schwietz, and Underwalden."

" The Queen Elizabeth !" muttered Tell ; " her empire is concluded ; she is no more than Duchess."

" In the midst of the deep grief in which she is plunged, she still remembers the ancient faith and love of Switzerland.———"

" Mark how adversity humbles even the proudest," said Werner.

" Relying upon their faith, and on their hatred of the cruel deed, she calls upon them to refuse protection to the wandering murderers; and if they fall within their power, to give them up to the just vengeance of the Empress.—She begs them to remember the ancient favours they have received at the hands of Rodolphe's house.———"

" We disallow not," said Tell, " the favours we received from the Emperor Rodolph; but what have we to boast of from the son ? Have not our messengers been rudely driven back ? ourselves oppressed ? Have we not endured the cruelties of his bailiffs ? What have we to thank him for ?"

" Let us not," observed Furst, " triumph over his fall, nor at a time like this, remember his evil deeds. Friends, we never will screen a murderer; although his deed has ridden us of a tyrant.—So tell the Empress Austrian."

" This news," cried Werner, " will paralyse the efforts of the enemy for a time only ; we must pursue our plans as if the Emperor lived. We know our duties ; farewell, till next we meet."

CHAPTER XXVIII.

THE OUTCAST.

....May his dreams be of his victim!
His waking a continual dread of death!
May the clear rivers turn to blood as he
Stoops down to stain them with his raging lips!
May every element shun or change to him!
May he live in the pangs which others die with!

Notwithstanding the pacific message of the Empress Dowager, which had indeed been despatched without the privity of her sons, the intentions of the House of Austria against the liberties of the Swiss Cantons remained unaltered, and the army moved forward to its destination, under the command of Leopold.

Grisach, the Austrian messenger, directed his course towards the Castle of Rossberg, to reach which, instead of travelling by the banks of the lake to the pass of Morgarten, he pursued the mountainous road which led him directly to the borders of the Canton of Schwietz.

The difficulties of the route became more insurmountable as he proceeded, and at length he had no alternative, if he prosecuted his journey in that direction, than to advance on foot, and leave his horse behind. Unwilling to retrace his steps, and yet dreading the laborious journey which lay before him, Grisach was some time before he could determine upon the course he ought to pursue. At length he determined to leave his horse in the care of the tenant of a lonely cottage, which was visible a short distance in advance of the spot on which he stood while deliberating upon his future proceedings.

When he arrived at the cabin, he was welcomed by its hardy tenant, and regaled with such frugal fare as the place afforded.

Rubli, the tenant of this lonely dwelling, followed the occupation of a chamois-hunter, and supported his wife and two young children by the labours of the chase. The mountain paths were well known to him, and he had followed their dangerous tracks from his earliest boyhood.

When Grisach mentioned his intention of proceeding on foot through the mountains, to reach the Castle of Rossberg, he endeavoured to dissuade him from the attempt, and pointed out the impracticable nature of the road.

The messenger of Leopold, however, declared his determination to make the attempt, notwithstanding all the representations of Rubli; and the latter, finding persuasion useless, pointed out to him the road he ought to follow with the greatest chance of success, and having provided him with a store of simple food to meet his necessities on the journey, he wished him "God speed," and retired into his humble dwelling.

Guided by the directions of the hunter, he gradually overcame the difficulties of the path, and although somewhat oppressed by fatigue, felt confident of reaching the Castle before nightfall, as soon as he perceived a large grey stone of a peculiar form, to which his attention had been directed by the hunter, for he was aware that, as soon as he reached it, one half his labour would be performed.

Seating himself on the foot of the rock, to rest awhile, he opened his humble scrip, and was about to refresh himself with its contents, when his attention was suddenly arrested by a hoarse voice commanding him to refrain.

"Stay, as you value your life," said the intruder.

Grisach gazed with wonder upon the form of the man who interrupted him. He was evidently young in years, but misery and distress had stamped the appearance of age upon his care-worn countenance. The garb in which he was dressed was that of an ecclesiastic; it was dark and flowing, but injured by exposure to the weather, and in many places torn or ragged.

"Four days," exclaimed the stranger, "I have wandered amid these mountains, and never tasted food. I have drank the cold stream of the melted snow, and chewed the bitter lichen, to silence my gnawing hunger. —Give me that food."

"Who are you? what do you here in this strange garb?"

"I cannot parley—give me that food, I say."

"When you have said who and what you are."

"I'll pay you for it; see, I have money, soldier, money—hark how it chinks;" and he shook a well-filled purse before the eyes of the Austrian.

The latter, surprised at his actions, and gazing intently upon the purse, at once recognised the symbol of the house of Austria in the embroidery with which it was ornamented. He looked with a searching eye into the face of the monk, and by degrees becoming satisfied the suspicion which arose in his mind was correct, he sprang forward to seize the stranger, exclaiming loudly, " Murderer ! I know thee well—thou art Duke John of Hapsburgh."

The pretended monk, perceiving he was recognised, turned suddenly, and eluding the grasp of his pursuer, sprung forward along the rugged path with the speed and boldness, which, in his present exhausted state, despair alone could have supplied.

Although possessed of greater strength than the fugitive, his pursuer was unable to keep pace with his intended prisoner, much less to overtake him, now he had gained the start. Still, however, the Austrian pressed forward in the chase, in the hope of wearying out the little remaining strength of the fratricide. Success seemed about to crown his perseverance, and he was fast gaining ground upon the outlawed Duke.

Before them lay an extensive thicket or low wood, towards which the path they were pursuing seemed to lead and become suddenly lost among its umbrageous shadows. Towards this the fugitive directed his steps, and plunged fearlessly into the midst of its leafy covert, as if well acquainted with the locality.

Staggered at the sudden disappearance of his victim, Leopold's messenger arrested himself in the midst of his career, gazing vacantly around, for the action of the outlawed Duke was so quick and unexpected, it completely deceived his powers of vision. He did not, however, remain long in this state of incertitude, but advancing to the thicket, he also plunged into its deep recesses.

Long and earnestly did Grisach search, as he thought, through every cranny of the wood, but still without success ; nowhere could he find the fugitive. At length, wearied by his vain endeavours, he again sought the open road, and was just issuing from the leafy screen, when the sound of rustling leaves caused him to turn, and before him stood the man of whom he was in search.

With haggard looks and brandished dagger he faced the messenger, and before the latter could recover from his surprise, he felt the dagger of the outlaw in his bosom. The blow was mortal; he staggered a few paces, and fell lifeless on the ground.

With looks more akin to madness than sanity, the wretched being stared vacantly upon his second victim, or watched with senseless eye the drops of blood as they fell from the dagger he still held in his hand.

" Blood is once more shed. The stream, when once begun, flows on with ceaseless tide ; one crime committed begets a dozen others, which follow in its train, and drive us on to madness. What have I gained—revenge ? Ah, no ! if he looks down and sees what passes here, sure his revenge is ample. The blow I aimed at him recoils upon myself. Poor wretch, I pity thee. Why didst thou come between me and my madness ? I'll drag thee to the thicket, and heap the leafiest branches on thy corpse."

With this, the wretched man succeeded at length in removing the body of the soldier to the wood, where he covered it over with branches of trees, on which he heaped such stones as lay in the neighbourhood, to protect it from the wolves ; again rushing forward, like another Cain, he seemed as if he felt the burning brand upon his guilty front.

In vain did the sons of Bernard wait patiently in the gorge of the mountains near the pass of Morgarten, in anxious expectation of the return of Grisach. Little could they suspect the fate of the unhappy man, whose corpse was now rotting in the woods near Rossberg.

Wearied at length with continual watching, the youngest of the two, having obtained the assistance of a friend to relieve him of his duty, descended the hills into the plains of Zug, to endeavour, if possible, to ascertain if their intended captive had passed through the villages that lay in his route towards Morgarten.

He pursued his course without meeting with any circumstance to interest him, until he reached the little village of Ob, on the banks of the lake Egeri. Here he was astonished to find the inhabitants of this peaceful hamlet in a state of violent agitation and bustle: every boat that could be obtained was in requisition, to convey the women and children, and the most valuable and portable effects of the villagers, to the opposite side of the lake.

Brienz, for such was the name of Bernard's youngest boy, astonished at the unusual appearance of the village, inquired the cause. He was informed that a messenger had just arrived, and warned the inhabitants of the rapid approach of the Austrian army. The whole body had crossed the Reuss, and it was expected had by this time reached the town of Baar.

The behaviour of the soldiers was described as brutal in the extreme, and their rage was further excited by the presence of Agnes, the Queen of Hungary, and daughter of the deceased Emperor, who, suspecting the murderers of her father had taken refuge in Switzerland, breathed vengeance against the whole race of mountaineers.

From all the inquiries he had made, he was enabled to suppose that the sudden advance of Leopold and his army had rendered it unnecessary to send back the soldier Grisach.

Unable to obtain further information, he hastened back to inform his friends of the state of affairs, that they might adopt such measures as might be considered best in the approaching emergency. Accordingly, on his arrival at his father's dwelling and finding he was absent, he hastened after him with all the speed he could.

CHAPTER XXIX.

THE MURDERER'S LOT.

.... Twenty thousand years, perchance,
Hereafter (or even here in moments which
Might date for years, did Anguish make the dial)
May not obliterate or expiate
The madness and dishonour of an instant.

Goaded to madness by his guilty conscience, and the pangs of unsatisfied nature, the exiled murderer wandered onwards, unconscious of all that was passing around him.   The half-roused wolf glared at him as he went by, unnoticed; the nimble chamois crossed his path unseen, and he strode along the extremest verge of the precipice, heedless of the danger incurred.

Insensibly he wandered into a more beaten track, as if intending to direct his steps towards a neighbouring village; at length, the excited state of his mind, and the restless energy with which his body was endued, gradually gave way to his increasing exhaustion, and sinking beneath an utter prostration of strength, he sank down upon a bank of earth by the road-side, in a state of insensibility.

How long he remained in this condition is unknown, but on recovering his senses he found a Swiss peasant bending over him, and employing the best means that occurred to him to restore sensibility.—As soon as he opened his eyes, his rude nurse offered him food and drink from his humble store.

"Here, friend," he exclaimed, "drink this: it is none of your sparkling Rhenish, I am aware, but it will cheer you.   You seem exhausted quite;—is it from want of food or fatigue? here's bread and good goat's cheese—it's new, and pleasant eating."

So saying, the peasant placed the various viands in his hands, and the wanderer ate voraciously.   Having sufficiently refreshed himself, he returned thanks to his entertainer, and endeavoured to rise from his seat; but his stiffened limbs refused to perform their office, and with a look of despair he sank back upon the bank.

"You have travelled far to-day, father, and are weary; shall I support you on your way to Rossberg, or will you partake of the shelter of my cottage—it's close at hand?"

While thus engaged, the well-known form of Tell approached the pair; he had repaired to Rossberg to convey information of the decision of the confederates to Arnold.   As soon as he reached the place where the monk was seated, he demanded of the peasant the name of the wearied man.

"I know not," returned the other, I found him resting almost lifeless here—see, he revives again.

The monk slowly raised himself on the seat, and stared wildly round on Tell and the peasant.

"Whence come you, brother?" said Tell. "Say, who are you—speak—"

"Who is it asks the question? thy name."

"My name is Tell."

"Thou art the man whom Gessler hates."

"The same, but what of that?"

"Would you not take revenge upon his head if opportunity should offer?"

"'Tis a strange question, friend, and plainly asked; I'll answer you as plain:—I would, for my dear country's sake, the Land of God would take the tyrant's life."

"You would slay the Bailiff who has injured you—I have slain an enemy who refused me justice; he was your enemy as well as mine; and I have rid the land of him."

"Of whom?—who are you?—gracious heavens—oh horrible!—you are the Duke of Austria, and have slain the Emperor—your liege lord —your father's brother—"

"He wronged me of my rights, as Gessler you."

"Unhappy man! do you confound the crime of fierce ambition with the stern duty of a father and lover of his country. After the deed you say I would commit, I should but have avenged that holy nature which you have shamed—thine has been murder—mine would be but defence of those most dear to me."

"And must I wander still a houseless outcast—will no roof yield me shelter?"

"Away—pursue thy fearful path, and leave unpolluted this land of innocence."

"Alas! no longer can I live—my doom is sealed."

"And yet I pity thee," cried Tell, "great heaven! so young. The branch of such a noble stem—grandson of Rodolph—an outlawed murderer!"

"Alas! you weep—oh, let my fate excite your pity. How happy might I have been could I but have controlled my fierce impatience. I saw my cousin Leopold, though so young, possessed of land, and crowned with glory, while I his equal in age was doomed to pine in slavish pupilage."

"Thy uncle, wretched man, knew well thy temper when he denied

15   Q

thee power. Thy recent deed has justified his wise precaution. But where are those who in thy acts supported thee?"

" Never since that bloody day have I set eyes upon them.—They fly, like me, where the avenging spirit drives them. Oh, if you feel humanity and pity!"

" How can I aid you—yet, horrible as is thy crime, you are a man."

" Oh, save me from despair!" cried the exile, seizing the hand of Tell.

" Nay, do not touch me—here you cannot rest, at least undiscovered; and, if known, you could not hope protection.—But whither can you fly?"

" Alas! I know not."

" 'Tis heaven suggests the thought," cried Tell; " away to Italy; there seek the holy city, fall at the Pontiff's feet, confess your crime, and purify your soul."

" Will he not yield me up to the avenger's hand?"

" Receive as heaven's decree whate'er he wills. I will describe the way to thee; follow the track beside that mountain stream—it is the Reuss that rushes through that chasm."

" It was near the Reuss the bloody deed was done."

" You trace the glacier's verge until you reach a rustic bridge that crosses a huge chasm, that passed, a cheerful valley lies before you; the road again ascends until you reach the great St. Gothard; there you take leave of German land, and a gentle stream conducts you into Italy. Meantime you can take the rest you so much require within this shepherd's cottage—you may rely upon his faith—but leave this land with all the speed you can, and heaven forgive you."

Assisted by the shepherd, the conscience-stricken man directed his feeble steps towards the cottage, to partake of that repose his exhausted strength so much required.

The murderer's act of fell revenge, soliloquized Tell, thus yields them no advantage, while we with stainless hands may freely reap the happy fruits of this most bloody deed. The sceptre of the empire now will pass into another house, and Austria's cruel duke shall have his glory shorn.

See there the murderer's doom.—Alas! what is the deed I now contemplate—is it not murder?—'tis shedding human blood. Ah, no! call it rather, mercy; once was I foiled, but this time he cannot 'scape me. The woods that shroud the side of Rossberg's hill will screen me well from view, and as he crosses over the dangerous bridge I can command him well, and the wild torrent shall receive his corpse.

Returning to the village, he rejoined the party assembled at the house of Ulrich, and recounted his meeting with the exiled duke. The alarming accounts received from Altdorf imperatively demanded the return of Gessler, and on the morrow he intended to take his departure. The execution of Hans had been delayed, in the hopes of obtaining some information, through his means, of the plots of Arnold and his associates, which he still believed were known to Gertrude and the herdsman; and, in the bustle of preparation, the fate of their prisoner had been forgotten.

The information respecting these movements of the bailiff had been obtained through the agency of Benedict, assisted now by Romont, who had been induced to take part against his master by the respect he bore to Gertrude, and the expectation of a large reward as soon as a decisive blow had been struck.

Matters were in this condition when the arrival of Tell brought the news of the death of the Emperor, and the advance of his successor's troops, with which the reader is already acquainted.

The preliminaries for wresting Rossberg from the hands of the bailiff had been partially discussed by the little band of conspirators, but still much remained to do before the plan could be put in execution. Among other matters necessary to be done, was the means of releasing Hans as soon as all was ready, or rather of enabling him to release himself.

Leuthold, on whom they believed they could now depend—for his cupidity had been excited by the receipt of considerable sums of money, and the promise of more—appeared to be the agent most likely to succeed in this part of the undertaking.

In following out their design, they were obliged to have recourse again to stratagem; Leuthold was to proceed to the castle, and seek an interview with the bailiff; he was to frame the best excuse he could to account for his lengthened absence from his post, and to make Gessler acquainted with the death of Friesshardt, which he had heard, he said, at Burglen, from those acquainted with the bowman Tell.

The plot so far succeeded, that he was reinstated in his post, and again entered upon his duties. He was to endeavour to obtain admission to the prison of Hans, and arrange some plan by which the doors of his dungeon could be readily opened, when the proper time had arrived.

As Gessler was still anxious to obtain information from his prisoner, he appointed Leuthold to act as his goaler, and endeavour to wheedle himself into his confidence, a task he was well fitted for, and it was not the first occasion on which he had been employed in a similar manner.

Leuthold entered upon the execution of this scheme with pleased alacrity, for he contemplated the possibility of turning it to advantage in more ways than one; at present, however, the bias of his mind was in favour of fulfilling his promise to Arnold, to assist Hans in devising some means of escaping at will; reserving to himself, by a tacit agreement to which none but himself was privy, the liberty of turning his acquired knowledge to good account if an opportunity should occur.

Actuated by these laudable motives, he entered upon the performance of his new duties. On first visiting the prisoner, he found him seated in his dungeon in moody silence, with his arms and eyes fixed upon the ground. The entrance of his new goaler did not appear to attract his attention, for he remained unmoved.

Leuthold first broke silence by exclaiming, "Is this the way you greet an ambassador from your friends?'

"My friends," said Hans, glancing at the uniform of the Austrian, "are not dressed in the manner you are."

"Why, man, what is there in dress? Could I have passed the guards— could I have persuaded the bailiff to take me into his service—nay, more, to appoint me your goaler, if I had shown myself dressed like one of your friends?

"For what purpose have you come?"

" To find the readiest means of releasing you from prison."

" Humph !" returned Hans, " there is no very ready way for that, I think."

" Stay," continued Leuthold, who had been examining the fastenings of the door with a light, " I shall want your help in this. I must undo your fetters for a time ; but let us be cautious."

The bonds of Hans being loosened, his attention was directed to the stone in which the bolt of the lock shot when the door was locked.

" Do you see," observed the Austrian, " this upright stone, which forms the door-post ? It does not reach quite to the ground, and the cement is loosened through age ; but it is deeply imbedded in the massy wall. Do you think it could be moved with a strong lever ?"

" I don't know," said Hans, " but I'll try. Have you the lever ready ?"

" Aye, here it is : now place it in the hole here in the masonry, so. Now, are you ready ?—now pull."

" It does not move," said Hans.

" I felt it tremble," continued Leuthold ; " now place it in this cranny, lower down."

Hans did as he was directed, and in a few minutes the stone was loosened ; the task now became more easy of execution, and after half an hour's labour, it was detached from the masonry ; it was then carefully replaced, and kept in its original situation in such a manner as to enable a man of moderate strength to remove it at pleasure.

The loose mortar was carefully removed, and with it all outward appearance of interference with the fastenings of the dungeon.

" Now," said Leuthold, " whenever the proper time for your escape arrives, you can easily force open the door, by removing the stone we have just replaced ; but be sure you do not attempt it until you have received sufficient notice."

Having given this direction to his prisoner, Leuthold closed the door, and left him to his meditations.

CHAPTER XXX.

THE EASTERN TOWER.

Beneath these battlements, within these walls,
  Power dwelt amidst her passions : in proud state
Each robber chief upheld his armed halls,
  Doing his evil will, nor less elate
Than mightier heroes of a longer date.

Gertrude and her faithful attendant had been almost closely confined to their chambers since the visit of Gessler, and seldom obtained the liberty of wandering in their favourite garden, except under the surveillance of their gaoler, Romont ; from him, however, they received every mark of respect and lenity he dared to exhibit, without incurring the risk of being removed from the situation he held in their neighbourhood, and Gertrude and Hildegard willingly submitted to the necessary restraint, for fear their friendly gaoler should be superseded by one of Gessler's more brutal followers.

On the morning previous to his intended departure for Altdorf, the bailiff again made his appearance in the presence of the Baroness and her attendant, and again wearied them with questions as to their supposed knowledge of the machinations carried on against his authority.

Gertrude succeeded in answering satisfactorily the queries of her tormentor, although the knowledge she had obtained of Arnold's movements, through the means of Benedict and Romont, prevented her from being so positive in her replies as she would have been had she been entirely ignorant of his proceedings. The suspicious mind of Gessler detected her hesitation, and caused him to be more searching in his inquisitorial demands.

Failing in all his efforts to obtain information from his prisoners, his rage overcame his respect for their sex, and he addressed them in more uncourteous and violent language than usual.

"Gertrude Walstein," he exclaimed, "this conduct of yours is past all bearing. I would have treated you with that respect a scion of your father's house should merit, but in you I see that most disgraceful and most dangerous character—a plotting woman. As such you must be treated. The duties of my office call me hence: during my absence, the eastern tower must be your abode. If there your lover finds you, I can well forgive him."

"You dare not so far wrong me and yourself, as to commit this act of base injustice."

"I dare do that, and more, 'gainst those who plot my ruin."

"Beware! Lord Governor. The time will come when Heaven's just vengeance shall fall upon thy head."

"Why, let it come; but my just vengeance, first, shall fall upon the heads of those who injure me. What, Fritz, come hither."

At this summons, a tall, weather-beaten trooper made his appearance, and stood submissively before his master, waiting for further orders.

"You know the chamber in the eastern tower?" said the bailiff.

"I do, my Lord."

"Has it been dwelt in since Eric was imprisoned?"

"It has been lately used as a watch-tower, my Lord: it overlooks the country to a great distance."

"Well, let that watch be discontinued, and see it furnished in the same manner as in Eric's time. Be quick, and then return."

"The place is airy, lady, and lofty, like yourself; the prospect is delightful. As for the apartments, they are the best we can afford. You will have ample time to reflect well on all I have said to you, ere I return."

"It may so please the Almighty, Gessler, that you may ne'er return; though slow in pace, the punishment of crime is always sure."

"It is so, Gertrude Walstein: in your own person you shall find the truth. Well, is all ready?"

The last words were addressed to Fritz, who at that moment entered.
" I have obeyed your orders, my Lord."

" Now, mark me, Fritz. I have found you ever faithful to my commands. The ladies you now see are your prisoners. That chamber is their prison. See no one knows who you have under your charge. Maintain the secret, your reward is certain—divulge it, and your punishment will surely follow. Whatever food is wanted, deliver it with your own hand—I'll see it is forthcoming."

" Ladies," he continued, with a sneer, " behold your chamberlain. Fritz, see to your charge."

The trooper beckoned to his prisoners, who, satisfied that opposition to the orders of Gessler was useless, bent their desponding steps towards the eastern tower, and the next information obtained from the Castle, by means of the monk Benedict, alarmed Arnold and his companions beyond measure. Gertrude and her companion had disappeared from their usual quarters, and no account of the cause of their absence could be obtained either from Romont or Leuthold.

The most cruel surmises passed through the minds of the assembled friends. Had they been removed to some other place of confinement? or was it possible that the bailiff had resorted to more desperate acts of violence? How were they to act in this juncture?

These and a hundred other questions passed through the confused brains of the group, as they contemplated this sudden change in the aspect of affairs. Arnold and Ernest, who felt more keenly than any the uncertainty of the fate of their affianced, felt certain that they had not been removed from the precincts of the fortress, and, desperate as the attempt would be, calculated upon the possibility of entering the Castle, in spite of the vigilance of Gessler's myrmidoms ; but this intention was decidedly overruled by the rest of the party, and they were obliged, for the present, at least, to be satisfied with their usual opportunities of obtaining information, and trust to the chapter of chances for the solution of the riddle.

Within the fortress, all was now preparation for the departure of the Bailiff. Leuthold still remained true to his trust, and at the same time that he conveyed such information as he could obtain to Hans, used all his influence over the less acute mind of his captive, to restrain his impetuosity ; but when he heard of the mysterious disappearance of Gertrude and his inamorata, his cautious gaoler began to lament the insecurity of the prison door, and wish from his heart he had the means of more securely confining his charge.

The shadows of evening at length shut out the garish light of day, and now the night had far advanced in her course, when the imprisoned inmates of the eastern tower of Rossberg were seated at the narrow window of their chamber, looking out with resigned, yet pensive countenances, upon the moon-lit landscape.

Each, engaged in her own thoughts, had remained silent for nearly half an hour ; at length, before the time had quite expired which would have compelled the vilest despiser of the loquacity of the fairest part of the creation to allow the possibility of woman being a denizen of Heaven, when Gertrude, turning to her attendant, observed—

"How little effect have the circumstances in which we are placed upon the resources of the mind. I was thinking of other times, Hildegard, and the pleasures of the days of my childhood arose so vividly to my imagination, that our present situation, melancholy as it is, was utterly forgotten."

"And I, my Lady," returned her companion, "fancied I could discover a resemblance between that distant hill and my native place. See, there is a white speck close to that tuft of trees—I took it for my mother's cottage, and I almost thought I heard the bleat of my mountain goat, and the welcome bark of Ernest's dog."

"How beautifully ordered it is," said her mistress, "that the heaviest inflictions of human oppression can be thus rendered harmless by the aspirations of an innocent mind. But yet, in spite of all my philosophy, I feel our present situation irksome enough; I care not so much for myself, as for the anxiety under which Arnold must labour, while he is uncertain as to our fate."

"Hark, Madam! Did you hear that sound?"

"It is the guard going his usual round;—but stay, I thought I heard a voice; listen, Hildegard—your hearing is more acute than mine."

"'Tis some one speaking, my Lady—Iv'e heard that voice before—It cannot be—yet, again he speaks—it is Hans, I'm sure. How has he gained his liberty? what does he here?—he will surely be discovered, the madman!"

"Are you sure it is him, Hildegard? Listen again."

But now both the prisoners were enabled to hear distinctly the name of Hildegard pronounced in a shrill voice; for Hans well knew the necessity of pitching his voice in a high key, to enable himself to be heard at the distance at which he stood.

Hildegard, being certain it was her rustic admirer, demanded, in the same tone of voice, the reason of his appearance so near their prison at that hour of the night. From his answers to her questions—for Gertrude, unused to these distant colloquies, was unable to modulate her voice so as to be heard by their midnight visitors, she ascertained the state of affairs.

Hans, it seems, unable to repress his desire to discover the situation of Hildegard and her mistress, had broken through the restriction imposed upon him by Leuthold, and forced his prison door. He had wandered for some time through the least frequented parts of the Castle, and at length discovered the light shining in the casement of the eastern tower.

With a kind of instinctive feeling, which is at any rate quicker, and at times, surer than reason, and without in any manner calculating the probabilities, Hans at once jumped to the conclusion, that he had discovered the place of confinement of those concerning whom he was so anxious. As it happened, he was right in his conjecture; but, although he had found their place of concealment, it did not appear clear in what manner he could render them any service.

Gertrude was anxious to let Arnold know their condition, and this might be effected if Leuthold was made acquainted with their prison-house; but, if Hans were to inform him of his discovery, his absence from toe dungeon would be known, and means taken to prevent his escape on any future occasion.

Under these circumstances, it was suggested that Hans should, in conversation with his gaoler, draw his attention to the eastern tower, as a place likely to contain the missing prisoners, and if he could be induced to visit its neighbourhood, Hildegard or the Baroness were to be on the alert to inform him of their presence.

As nothing further could be done at present, Hans, following the advice of Hildegard, returned to his prison, and with some difficulty replaced the stone in its original position.

While these events were taking place within the Castle walls, the anxiety of Arnold and his friends, for the safety of the imprisoned maidens, induced them to remain in consultation until a late hour of the night, and when they retired to rest, the same feeling drove sleep from their pillows.

Tell, contemplating his intended deed, to dissipate his nervous excitement, left his bed and strode forth into the open air.

The moon was shining brightly in the sky, and silvered the grey battlements of Rossberg's towers as the clouds flitted past; shrouding her beauty with their dark mantles, and as suddenly unveiling her silvery form. Tell, who had been regarding intently these changes, uttered his thoughts aloud.

"Alas! how like the varying scenes in the life of man is yonder sky: like the bright moon, our prospects for a time are brilliant, and our own happiness spreads pleasure all around; but when we least expect it, misfortune, like yon dark and envious cloud, throws its deep shade around us.

"The good man yields to sorrow, and feels its chilling influence; but when the tyrant, checked in his wild career, is hurled from his high place, the anguish of his tortured breast no tongue can tell. Bailiff, thy days are numbered! To-morrow's rising sun shall shine upon thee, glittering in gold and jewels, and gazing round, in thy fierce pride, upon thy abject followers. But ere his setting, how will the scene be changed! A pallid corpse will be the sole memorial of Austria's haughty Bailiff.

"But see, the gray light of the morning brightens the eastern sky, and the moon soon will fade before the coming day. I must unto my post, and wait in patience until proud Gessler passes. The time, I fear, will pass but heavily; but then I watch for noble game. The poor hunter who seeks but to ensnare a silly chamois, will climb the glassy walls of the steep glacier, and watch for days together in winter's piercing cold.—I seek to win a richer prize by far—the heart of him—my deadly enemy who would destroy me. But I must not delay. The first blush of the rising sun, drawn like a streak of blood along she sky, points out my errand, and warns me of the time."

With this the deliverer of Switzerland began to climb the hill, and was soon hidden within the leafy screen we have already noticed.

CHAPTER XXXI.

THE TYRANT'S FATE.

....Now does he feel
His secret murders sticking on his hands;
Those he commands move only in command,
Nothing in love: now does he feel his title
Hangs loose about him, like a giant's robe
Upon a dwarfish thief.

THE day was not far advanced when Gessler prepared for his return to Altdorf; mounted upon his richly caparisoned steed, with knitted brow and haughty look, the tyrant rode forth in the midst of his adherents. As they passed along, he maintained a conversation with one of his immediate attendants, who, it appears, had been expostulating with him on account of his severity.

"Still, Stussi, I am the Emperor'sservant, and must do his bidding. I was not sent to flatter and caress—obedience to his power is what I seek."

"Yet, there are certain rights," said Stussi.

"This is no time to weigh them. The house of Austria would stretch its power and influence.—And these Swiss hinds must be subdued: they are our stumbling-blocks, and by fair means or foul must be removed."

At this moment a horseman arrived at full speed, and addressing Gessler, demanded a private audience.

16

" From Altdorf?" demanded the Bailiff.

" From Altdorf, last," replied the messenger. I sought you, there, my Lord; the people of the town are almost in open rebellion; the news I bring from Austria had reached them before my arrival."

" What news?   My messenger from the court should have arrived ere now."

" Has not Grisach then returned?" said the new comer in amaze. " The Emperor Albert is assassinated."

The countenance of the Bailiff turned pale on the instant, and had he not firmly grasped his saddle-bow, he would have fallen to the ground. Recovering himself, however, quickly, he demanded the particulars of the occurrence.

" And this," he muttered to himself, after hearing the messenger, " has been concealed from me till now."   Then suddenly turning towards the horseman, he exclaimed,

" Leopold, you say, is marching on with the same intent as the last Emperor; my task remains the same—to quell these stubborn mountaineers."

Turning then to his followers, he again placed himself at their head, and directed their march towards the road to Altdorf.

The window of the room in which the Baroness and her attendant were confined, overlooked the route Gessler and his party took.   They had witnessed the departure of the cavalcade from the Castle, and the subsequent occurrences, but were only able to conjecture the meaning of what was passing.

" Yon messenger," said Gertrude, " has brought hasty tidings;— but see, a woman forces her way through the crowd; she has two children with her; what can she mean?"

" See, they repulse her;" said Hildegard.   " Oh, God! the horses trample on the child!—have they no mercy?—they pass on, and heed not its cries—will no one rescue it?—the monsters! have they no pity?"

" But, Hildegard, what is that upon the hill by the road-side? there, almost hidden in wood; surely it is a man, armed with some weapon."

" It is William Tell," said Hildegard.   " I know him well; he always bears his cross-bow in his hand; see, he prepares to shoot."

" He directs his arrow towards the Bailiff!"

" See, the Bailiff falls.   They draw the arrow from his breast; they cannot staunch his blood; oh, heavens! how he writhes in anguish. I cannot bear the sight, my Lady; oh, let us leave the window."

" Bad as he is, this awful death is shocking."

" Is he dead, Madam?"

" He surely must be; they bear him in their arms back to the Castle."

" I cannot see the bowman," said Hildegard, who had been carefully examining the spot from whence the arrow came.   " Some of the soldiers climb the mountain side—they'll surely overtake him."

" They must be fleet of foot, to do it, damsel; for see, yonder in the far distance, the bowman's form stands out against the sky."

" I see him, on the brow of yonder hill; now he is hid from view."

The confusion which arose among the followers of Gessler at this sudden consummation of his fate, can be better conceived than described. They returned with panic-stricken countenances to the Castle, bearing with them the bleeding form of their leader.

The wound of Gessler, when examined, was pronounced mortal; but when his system was recovered from the shock it had received, the suffering tyrant so far mastered his agony as to motion one of his officers to draw near. Raising his trembling hand, he placed it on that of his follower, and in slow and broken sentences addressed him.

"Pursue my assassin until death. I know him well; no hand but William Tell's could strike so surely. I saw him climb the mountain as I fell—Altdorf—hasten—the people are in arms—"

Here a pang of intense pain arrested his speech, and every muscle quivered with agony; drops of cold and clammy sweat stood upon his brow, and his countenance assumed a mingled expression of horror, pain, and rage.

"Curse on that peasant's arrow—to fall ignobly thus—Tell—revenge—Altdorf—" he muttered, and sank back upon his couch a lifeless corpse.

The officer who now assumed the command, directed one half the garrison to prepare themselves again to resume their march to Altdorf.

The unruly spirits of which the followers of Gessler were composed, no sooner perceived the breath had departed from the body of their commander, than they broke out into all manner of violent excesses, and the halls of Rossberg Castle rung with the sounds of ribaldry and drunkenness.

Although in a secluded part of the building, Gertrude and her companion could well understand, from the confused sounds that reached their ears, the riotous state of the inmates; and believing themselves to be the only females within the precincts of the Castle, they felt not a little uneasy with respect to their own fate, in the midst of so licentious a crew as those by whom they were surrounded.

Again, however, the belief that their place of confinement was known to a few only, caused them to assume more confidence. Still they considered, it would be but a proper precaution, to secure themselves within their apartment as well as they could.

In pursuance of this resolution, they barricadoed the door to the best of their ability; and had not long completed their task, before a rude and violent knocking for entrance, satisfied them of the propriety of their precaution.

Clinging to each other, as if for greater security, the affrighted girls made no answer, although the knocking was repeated with greater violence than in the first instance.

At length a hoarse voice was heard demanding admission, and they recognised in the speaker their gaoler Fritz.

"It's Fritz, my Lady; I have brought your provisions. Never were such times since the old Castle was first built—such glorious Rhenish—ladies, will you open the door?—what would our old dragon say, if he were living?—Hildegard, you're a sweet girl; undo the door, or I shall drop the meat—it's as hot as—as—the hand that welcomes the Bailiff, now—nay, I can hold it no longer—mercy on us, there's a crash—you may cook the next yourself, I tell you that."

From the incoherence of his speech, it was clear that Fritz had been partaking too largely of the produce of the Bailiff's cellar, and the prisoners, aware he had been selected from the rest of his comrades on account of his uncompromising rudeness of disposition, were still further alarmed when they found him in a state of intoxication.

They trembled, therefore, as they listened for the continuance of his demands for admission, which they hardly dared to grant, and knew not how to refuse, when they were delighted to find that, overcome by the effects of the liquor, he had sunk into an unquiet slumber, declaring his presence only by the loud melody of his nasal organ.

Relieved from their present cause of anxiety, they prayed inwardly that his slumber might not be disturbed until reason had re-assumed her sway.

While matters were proceeding in this manner in the eastern tower, the Castle hall rung loudly with the noise of the revellers; the ribald song, the blasphemous jest, and the slanderous tale went round, until, excited by liquor, the rude joke became savage earnest, and from words the swaggerers came to blows.

The vessels out of which they had been drinking were ready weapons in their hands, and blood began to flow in all directions in liberal streams, as if in mockery of the wine so lately poured.

The captain of the guard vainly strove to quell the disturbance, and finding all his authority useless, was fain to call in the assistance of the soldiers on guard; who, after much exertion, and some bloodshed, succeeded in quelling the riot, and placing the most violent of the party in confinement; and thus concluded the day which witnessed the downfall of the tyrannical Bailiff, the wild uproar of riot and debauchery sounding a funeral knell appropriate to the character whose death it announced.

In the morning, when the fumes of the wine had passed away, Fritz began to remember the events of the previous day. The death of Gessler, it was easy to understand, would produce great changes in the Castle, and it was not unlikely that the star of his prisoners might soon be in the ascendant, for the bailiff's successor would hardly dare to continue their incarceration.

Actuated by these feelings, his first object was, as soon as his senses were sufficiently restored, to endeavour, by his conduct, to obtain the good graces of Gertrude. Having, in pursuance of this design, obtained admission to her presence, he endeavoured to excuse his former rudeness by referring to the control under which he was held by Gessler, whose orders he dared not disobey; and in confirmation of the truth of his assertion, he referred to his drunken condition on the previous evening, which he assured his listeners merely arose from joy at the fate of the tyrant.

Whatever opinion Gertrude might hold as to the former conduct of her gaoler, she deemed it advisable to grant him her full pardon; and he, in return, promised to assist her in any way that might be of service to herself or companion.

CHAPTER XXXII.

THE NEW GOVERNOR.

......Let us presently go sit in council,
How covert matters may be brought to light
And open perils surest answered.
Let us do so : for we are at the stake,
And bay'd about with many enemies.

The news of Gessler's death spread through the land like wildfire, and alarmed the fears of the bailiffs Landenberger and Wolfhausen ; the latter, whose power extended over the canton of Sweitz, on the confines of which the Castle of Rossberg stood, undertook the task of attending to the interests of his master in Uri, now left without a governor by Tell's act of vengeance.

Accordingly he repaired without delay to Rossberg castle, to take measures for the interment of the bailiff, and endeavour to trace the Swiss patriot and punish him for his deed of blood.

On his arrival at the castle, he found matters in a state of great confusion, for the soldiery, accustomed to the iron sway of Gessler, refused to submit to the uncertain power of their present chief.

Upon the arrival of Wolfhausen, who stood second only to the late bailiff for his cruelties, the less audacious spirits among them began to quail, and submitted at once to his authority, but it was not until several severe examples had been made, that the more violent of the troops acknowledged the new comer as their master.

The confinement of Hans and of the two prisoners in the eastern tower was intimated to Wolfhausen, who ordered matters to remain in their present state until he had given the subject the consideration it deserved. The imprisonment of Gertrude was, however, made less strict, and she and her companion were allowed to walk in the garden at stated times under certain restrictions.

The aspect of affairs at Altdorf next demanded his attention, and after ordering things at Rossberg to the best of his judgment, he determined to proceed thither in person.

Accordingly he immediately commenced his journey, accompanied by all the force he could spare. The cavalcade passed without interruption on their road, the latter part of which was along the beautiful banks of the Lake of the Three Cantons.

Before them now lay the mountain regions that form the northern portion of Uri, and they were soon at the foot of the lofty Axenberg, whose vast shadows stretched out for miles along the plain. The road soon became more difficult, winding along the sides of the mountain, on the verge of a steep precipice.

Wolfhausen at the head of his party was in deep conversation with one of his followers, when their attention was arrested by a loud and shrill voice which seemed to come from the rocks above ; on looking up, he saw a band of peasants among whom were many women, perched upon the projecting portions of the crag, and armed with huge masses of stone, which they appeared about to hurl down upon the heads of the advancing party.

At length one of the peasants stepped forth from the group, and raising his hand, addressed Wolfhausen :—

"Austrian, if you advance another step the lives of all your followers and your own are sacrificed; retreat in time, and avoid your fate."

The Austrian looked up, and saw the impending danger; nevertheless he spoke in terms of defiance to the peasants.

"Rebels, are you from Altdorf?"

"We are, and its towers will soon become our own—retreat, I say."

"Retreat, and Altdorf's towers in danger? never! soldiers, dismount, move on, keep close to the mountain's side, they cannot hurt us."

The men obeyed the orders of their commander, and each leading his shore, defiled along the mountain road, keeping as far as possible from the edge of the cliff. Before this manœuvre could be executed, an arrow, evidently aimed at the bailiff, grazed his plume and entered the breast of the soldier who followed him; the man, who was in the act of dismounting, fell from his horse, and rolling over the edge of the precipice fell into the gulph below.

"Bailiff, that arrow was meant for thee, the next shall come with surer aim."

Another arrow was discharged, but a projecting fragment of rock intercepted it in its passage."

"You are a poor marksman, peasant—soldiers, move on."

By this time the troopers, under the shelter of the overhanging crags, were moving stealthily along. As they passed those spots where the smooth face of the rock offered no projecting masses, the peasants above hurled down upon their heads the pieces of rock with which they were armed, and many a hapless man shared the fate of their late comrade.

Still, however, the Austrians pushed on, and at length reached a more open part of the road, less exposed to the projectiles of the mountaineers; but ere this time, one half their number had fallen victims to the enraged Swiss.

Wolfhausen and his little band still continued to advance, harrassed during the whole of their route by the peasants. At length they came in sight of the little village of Fluelen, on the banks of the lake, and as the night was close at hand, the bailiff determined to rest, to allow his jaded followers time to recruit their strength, intending on the following morning to proceed by times to Altdorf.

At Rossberg, in the meantime, Arnold and his little band of patriots were preparing to take advantage of the altered aspect of affairs; their intercourse with the inhabitants of the fortress was more frequent than it had formerly been. Their new allies within the walls had hitherto proved trustworthy, and as the Austrian power in the land was evidently on the wane, there was every chance of their remaining so.

At the same time, their anxiety for the fate of Gertrude being somewhat relieved, they saw no reason to hasten their attack upon the castle, or proceed to extremities before the appointed time.

Tell, after the death of Gessler, had proceeded in the direction of Altdorf, with the excited state of whose inhabitants we are already acquainted.

While this was the state of affairs in the mountain Cantons, the Duke of Austria still advanced with his overwhelming force. But the progress he made was slow on several accounts, the chief obstacle to his rapid advance being the impoverished state of the country, for the inhabitants fled at his approach, driving their cattle and flocks into the mountains, or crossing to the opposite shore of the lake. On this account he had to convey the greater part of the provisions for his army, from the more fertile provinces on the other side of the Reuss.

As yet he was unacquainted with the death of Gessler, but as soon as information of that event reached him, he suffered a paroxysm of rage which rendered it dangerous for his attendants to approach his person. While under the influence of this accession of passion, he issued orders for the instant and rapid advance of his columns. It was in vain to represent to him the difficulties of the road, or the condition of the army with respect to provisions; the Swiss nation must be crushed, and he would suffer no delay.

The soldiers murmured at the excessive fatigue they had to undergo, and the privations they had to endure, and in this unsatisfactory condition the Austrian army continued its march.

The difficulties of the road increased every hour, and at length, when the foot of the mountains was attained, the Duke himself perceived the necessity of commanding a halt, until the means of proceeding in a more satisfactory manner had been devised; accordingly, the whole army encamped at the base of the mountains, with the lake Egeri in their rear, and the famous pass of Morgarten in front of their advance columns.

In the dead of the night the anxious mind of Leopold banished sleep from his pillow, and he wandered forth through the camp, a prey to many a bitter thought. It was not until that moment that the difficulty of his undertaking appeared before him in its true colours. He pictured to himself the hardy and valiant nature of the mountaineers, and the nature of the country in which the battle must be waged.

Before him he saw the ice-crowned mountains through which his army had to pass, and he eyed with distrust the mighty precipices with which the only practicable pass was flanked, and his heart sunk within him at the sight.

The chill air of the morning at length compelled him to seek his couch, upon which he tossed restlessly, troubled with uneasy sleep until the morning rose. At daybreak he began to take measures to ensure the safety of his troops in their passage through the mountain passes; bands of men were sent out in every direction to reconnoitre the passage; all the *materiel* necessary for the conveyance of the heavier implements of warfare ordered to be prepared, and every precaution taken which the necessities of the case required.

CHAPTER XXXIII.

THE DAYBREAK OF LIBERTY.

Come, go we in procession to the village :
And be it death proclaimed through our host,
To boast of this, or take that praise from God,
Which is his only.

WHEN the sun rose above the summit of the huge St. Gothard, dark clouds obscured its disk, and the fitful gusts of wind that rose and fell, as if they were the violent expirations of some monstrous living creature, swept over the landscape.

The darkness of twilight fell on every object, and cast a melancholy gloom on all. In the midst of the darkened sky, at length, a bright spot appeared; it gradually became brighter, and suddenly, as if torn asunder by some violent effort, the clouds opened for an instant, and a flood of light was poured forth upon the castellated turrets of Altdorf, rendering the rest of the landscape still darker by the contrast. It was but for an instant—the dark screen again became impervious to the sun's rays.

On the field to the right of the ancient building, a new structure was in the course of erection. It had been intended by Gessler as a prison, and the forced labour of the men of Uri was doubly irksome when they contemplated the nature of the building on which it was bestowed. The death of Gessler had caused them to suspend their labours, and the partial gleam of sunshine that fell upon the spot, exhibited groups of discontented workmen in anxious consultation.

The bright light of the lamp of day seemed like a ray of hope, and encouragement sent from Heaven to cheer their drooping spirits.

"Why should we wait for further information?" said one of the masons. "Is not the tyrant dead?"

"If we are men, shall we allow this stronghold of the tyrant to remain?"

"We helped to rear the structure—let us o'erthrow the accursed labour of our hands."

"Quick, spring the arches, tear down the scaffold, comrades."

These and a hundred other exclamations arose on every side, and the workmen, assisted by the boys and women, began with eagerness the work of destruction.

At this instant, Tell approached the spot, and cried aloud—

"It is a holy action you perform, my friends; complete the task this good bow has begun."

The sight of their deliverer from the tyrant's power, increased the enthusiasm of the populace, and in spite of the opposition of the Austrian troopers, the work of destruction was soon completed.

"The horn," cried Tell, "the horn of Uri, where is it?"

"'Tis here," was repeated by a hundred voices; "quick, hand it to Tell."

Having received the rude instrument of music, Tell raised himself upon the ruins so as to gain a considerable elevation, and placing the point of the horn to his lips, blew a blast, so long, so loud and shrill, that the mountains' echoes repeated it on all sides,

Osmond Castle

"Prepare yourselves," at length cried Tell; "look to the mountain road."

"By Heavens!" exclaimed the bystanders, "it is Wolfhausen; I know him well; he comes to take revenge for Gessler's death."

"Listen!" rejoined Tell; "that blast was not in vain; the men of Uri are no sleepers, friends; twice in two distant parts I heard the sound repeated; hark!—again,—again!—fear not the Austrians, our mountain warriors will soon be here.—See, yonder they come from Burglen.— The men of Attinghausen, too, are here; run, friends, and meet them.

The troopers of Wolfhausen were gradually approaching the village, but ere they arrived sufficiently near to perceive clearly the position of affairs, the men of the neighbouring villages had joined themselves to the inhabitants of Altdorf, and entrenching themselves behind the ruins, they offered so formidable an appearance, that the Bailiff refrained from making an immediate attack.

At length, as fresh assistance was continually arriving, and swelling the numbers of the mountaineers, he deemed it most prudent not to delay his attack.

In following up his intention, however, he met with a most determined resistance: his men were hurled to the ground as fast as they advanced, by fragments of the ruins, which showered around them as thick as hail. The most active resistance appeared to proceed from a part of the ruins on which a man with a crossbow stood encouraging the others, and at times levelling his arrow at some unfortunate trooper, who, in advance of his comrades, appeared by his near approach to his

17

entrenchment, to displease our bowman. His aim was unerring; but he was observed never to direct a shaft against any but those who pressed forward before the rest.

The mischief they sustained from this man attracted the attention of Wolfhausen, who determined to drive him from his stronghold by leading the attack in person. Accordingly, after selecting the most determined among his followers for the assault, he advanced towards the bowman.

Tell—for the bowman could be no one but him, on perceiving his intention, made a signal to his own party to cease their hostilities. This was immediately done by all, with the exception of two or three boys, who, unused to discipline, could not resist the temptation of having a sly fling at some Austrian, who offered at the moment a fair mark for his missile.

The Austrians also held back from the attack, and Tell addressed their leader—

"Bailiff, we seek not your life; all we aim at is our liberty; draw off your men, and you may pass unhurt; but you must leave these States. In Austria there is ample room for you and all your followers, but we have sworn no Austrian here shall rule."

"What, fear the threats of a poor chamois-hunter; on to the attack, and drive them from their hiding places."

With that, they again advanced, and the Swiss recommenced hostilities. Wolfhausen, at the head of the attacking party, passed the limit which Tell, in his own mind, had assigned for his opponents, and on the instant received an arrow in his arm, and fell wounded.

Again, at the signal of Tell, hostilities ceased, and again he made the offer to his opponent of retiring into Germany; but, in spite of his wounds, he obstinately refused to accept of the terms. The Swiss, in their turn, now acted on the offensive, and leaving their entrenchments, soon drove back the dispirited followers of the Bailiff;—the latter was taken prisoner, and his wound being dressed, he was committed to the charge of a small party, who were enjoined to conduct him across the frontier, and liberate him in some place where he might easily rejoin the Duke Leopold.

His followers, seeing the fate of their chief, dispersed in all directions. Some fled to Unterwalden, to place themselves under the protection of Landenberger; a few found their way back to Rossberg; but the greater number escaped into Germany, as no opposition was made to their departure.

The men of Altdorf having thus heroically ridden themselves of their tyrants, proceeded to destroy every evidence of their former power; they razed the walls of the castle to the ground, despatched messengers in every direction to spread the news, and at night beacons were lighted on all the hills to raise the country.

The insurrection thus prematurely begun spread through the land on every side. Landenberger, alarmed, had shut himself up in his stronghold at Sarnen, after despatching messengers to Leopold, reporting the alarming aspect affairs had assumed.

As soon as Erni became acquainted with the fate of Altdorf, he directed his attention towards the Castle of Sarnen. Prepared as it had been to resist an attack, by the fears of Landenberger, the task appeared to be difficult, and if it were not for the necessity of crushing the Austrian power within the limits of the three cantons, the attempt would have been little short of madness.

The fortress of Sarnen was equally, strong, from natural causes, with that of Rossberg, and was much more indebted to art for an addition to its natural strength. It was situated at the northern extremity of a small lake which communicated with the lake Lucerne by means of a narrow stream.

The castle itself rested upon the summit of an isolated rock, which stood in the midst of a fertile alpine plain. The mountains, lofty as they are in that part of the country, were too far removed from Sarnen to cast their shadows upon its site, or deprive it of the influence of the cheering beams of the sun.

The access to this stronghold was by a winding path, which made three revolutions of the rock before it reached the castle-gate; from this it is evident a small body of men could defend it from an army, so long as their provisions lasted; and before the application of gunpowder to its present destructive purposes, it must have been perfectly impregnable.

To the reduction of this important and well-defended place, Erni addressed himself. Tell, whose influence was from recent occurrences perhaps greater than that of any other man in the country, was taken into his councils, but when they regarded the means at their disposal, the task seemed almost hopeless. One point in their favour was, that on account of the short time he had for preparation, the bailiff had been able to collect but a small quantity of provisions, and the number of his retainers who had taken refuge with him, rendered this small supply of less avail.

If it had been possible to scale the rock, which seemed extremely doubtful, it could not be done without alarming the inmates, supposing proper watch were kept; and besides, a few men would be of no avail against the numbers of the garrison, should they even succeed in effecting an entrance.

Yet, with all these disadvantages, thefirst idea that occurred to them was, that of scaling the rock; and while their attention was directed to this business, they took up their abode in the small hamlet which stood at the foot of the rock inhabited by a few fishermen, who gained their livelihood by selling the fish they captured in the neighbouring lake, to the inmates of the castle.

A second object also attracted their notice,—namely, the keeping a strict watch at the base of the rock, to prevent the ingress or egress of the garrison; to gain this end, twelve of their party were always on the alert.

It so happened, that one of the peasants, while performing this monotonous duty near the foot of the winding path we have described, overcome by sleep, was dozing at his post. He was roused from his lethargy by a smart blow from a falling stone, and suddenly rising, was astonished to see several men descending the rock. He cautiously gave the alarm to the nearest sentinel, who also passed the word to the next, and in this manner the whole were roused and soon assembled on the spot from whence the alarm was given.

The men who descended the winding path, were evidently the followers of the bailiff, a fact which was at once known by noticing their dark forms against the sky. Although they must have been aware of the neighbourhood of the sentinels, the tone of their conversation was incautiously loud, and appeared to be filled with complaints.

As they drew close to the base of the rock, however, they became more cautious in their behaviour, and peered carefully around. As fast as they reached the level of the ground, the troopers were singly taken prisoners by the assembled peasants: six men had already fallen into their hands, and from all they could discover by careful examination of the rock, no others were following.

After disarming and securely binding their captives, six of the peasants bore them off at once to the village, to deliver them into the hands of Erni and Tell.

CHAPTER XXXIV.

THE SECRET PASSAGE.

In this place is to be seene a verie singular caverne; which, in olden tymes, is supposed to have beene the hiding.place of a desperate gang of ruffians.—The openinge is facing to the north, and in the very front of the precipice itself.

On the first news of the capture of the Austrians, Erni and Tell, and many [of their attendants, rose from their rest, for the purpose of questioning the prisoners. From the answers they obtained to their questions, it appeared they were much dissatisfied with the Bailiff, who, on account of the shortness of provisions in the fortress, had compelled them to leave, with directions to make the best of their way to Rossberg; and they expected that others would soon share the same fate, owing to the crowded state of the garrison.

Erni, aware that in their present discontented state they would be likely to make disclosures, which, in a cooler frame of mind, they would withhold, ordered refreshments to be provided, and withdrawing the most communicative of the party from his comrades, questioned him closely as to the possibility of effecting an entrance into the Castle.

"Why, as for that matter," replied the prisoner, "there is a means of entrance, which, I believe, is unknown to all within. It was by chance that I discovered it."

"Indeed! Could many enter by the way you mention?"

"Not at once; two at a time, perhaps; but they must be good cragsmen."

"There are some among us could do such duty well."

"What if I pointed out the secret way?"

"The safety of yourself and comrades would be gained; shall it be so, Tell?"

"Yes; if he makes a full disclosure."

"I'll tell you first, how I discovered it," said the Austrian. "The water to supply the Castle is drawn from a deep well, whose surface is some forty feet below the summit of the rock."

"I know it well," said Tell; "it is near the square tower; but how can this assist us?"

"You shall hear. One day I and my comrades, for want of better sport, were flinging stones, pieces of wood, and other trifles, into the well, to hear the sounds they made, as they bounded from side to side, or fell into the water. Some time after—you know the waterfall that streams down the rock's face, and afterwards flows in a small stream, right through the village?"

"I have often watched its fall."

"Do you think that you could climb the rock to the place from whence it issues?"

"Climb it! well; why there are stepping-stones at frequent intervals."

Two days after the sport I told you of, I passed the waterfall, and on the ground I saw the objects we had thrown into the well. I scaled the rock, and reached the opening whence the water issues. The rock above formed a low arch, some five feet high; I crept along, and came at length to the surface of the water in the well. When looking round, on either side I saw a spacious cavern, or rather chamber, for the rock was hewn—there many might assemble."

"But the deep well—how can its sides be climbed?"

"If one man scaled its sides, and the task is not difficult—two knotted ropes, secured above, would give the means for all the rest to follow.

"I like the plan," said Erni. "You are safe here, Austrian, and shall be conducted where you will, you and your companions; but first, let us ascertain the truth of what you say."

As soon as the morning yielded sufficient light for the purpose, Tell and Erni repaired to the waterfall; they found it better adapted for their purpose than they anticipated, for the upper part of the rock at this spot, so completely overshadowed its base, as to render them perfectly secure from the observation of the castle's inmates. The ascent also, although it might appear impracticable, to one unused to the hills, offered no peculiar obstacles to an experienced cragsman. Such being the case, Tell and his companion were not long in reaching the opening from whence the waterfall issued, and without much difficulty, advanced until they came to the chambers noticed by the Austrian. These were of sufficient capacity to hold from twenty to thirty people each, and admirably adapted for the carrying out of their plot.

It was evident that, at some distant period, they had been inhabited, from the mouldering remains which were left, of several articles of furniture. While thus engaged in examining the chambers, a rumbling sound was heard in the shaft of the well, and a water bucket let down into the water.

The men engaged in this office were talking to each other sufficiently loud to be heard by Tell and his companion.

"This carrying of water, Hamel, will be hard labour soon, if we continue upon short allowance."

"You say right," returned his comrade," and there are but three sheep left; plague take the Bailiff, for hurrying as he did; I thought he had more courage; besides, he need not fear these Swiss so much as Gessler or Wolfhausen; he oppressed them less."

"If two hours' time had been allowed, I could have added a score of sheep, besides the carcase of a good fat ox. I almost wish he would take offence, and send me off like Schneider and his friends. But, come, we must not stand loitering here."

Upon this, the bucket began to rise, and when it reached the summit, the voices of the speakers ceased.

Tell and Erni now retraced their steps, and on their return, their prisoners, at their own request, were conducted with safety across the lake to Kussnacht, and thence to the canton of Zug, to enable them to join their countrymen, now following the Duke Leopold.

Sarnen now appeared delivered into their hands, and it only remained for the confederates to appoint a time to carry the place by assault. In order to render success more certain, the following night, when the moon would be at full, was unanimously agreed upon.

The sky was cloudless, and a brilliant moon illuminated the landscape when Tell and twenty selected men, well accustomed to the dangers of the glacier and the precipice, left the little hamlet to proceed towards the rock of Sarnen.

The point from which they started was buried in the gloom of the shadow cast by the vast pile of granite upon which the fortress stood. Taking advantage of this friendly shade, they directed their steps at once to the base of the rock, keeping close to which they, by a circuitous path, soon reached the waterfall, and prepared for their ascent.

Tell, flinging his cross-bow across his shoulders, and bearing an unlighted torch in his hand, was the first to reach the mouth of the cavern; here, having lighted his torch, he thrust it into a crevice in the rock, as a guide to those who were to follow, and stood ready to assist them to enter the rude arch.

At least two hours were occupied in the ascent, and when they reached the excavated chambers, they found a short rest necessary before they proceeded to execute the remainder of their task.

Unconscious of the nature, or of the near approach of the danger which threatened him, Landenberger, and a few of his more intimate associates, were enjoying themselves with potent draughts of wine, although the night was then "at odds with morning." The fumes of the liquor they had drank rendered their voices thick, and their thoughts incoherent, and with loud oaths and vehement execrations, they were cursing the rebellious Swiss.

To cool their burning foreheads, they sallied forth into the open air to enjoy the refreshing breeze, and gaze with vacant stare upon the full orb of the moon, as she rode like a silver globe through the pale gray sky. In this manner, with swaggering but unsteady gait, they roamed through the different parts of the castle, conversing loudly.

"By St. George," exclaimed Klaus, a raw-boned follower of the bailiff, "the air seems fresher here than in the plain; we are nearer heaven, my lord; the moon, too, seems larger to my eye,—but see—stand back, do you see that blaze?"

"Where?" cried Landenberger, staring round, but directing his attention more directly towards the heavens, "I see no blaze."

"It is no heavenly fire I am speaking of," returned Klaus, "it more nearly resembles that of—hush—what's that? that of the infer——— Zounds! governor, flames are rising from the well, and yonder's the archfiend himself!"

As he said this, Tell sprung upon the level ground, and stooping down, busied himself in attaching a rope to the wood-work which supported the rope by which the bucket was lowered; immediately afterwrds, Erni, bearing a torch, also leaped from the well. Suddenly he was aware of the presence of Klaus and the bailiff, and by a sign made Tell acquainted with the fact.

No sooner had our hero turned round to face the men he so little expected to see, than he perceived Landenberger rushing forward, and striking him with his sword, Tell struck down his arm with the butt end of his bow, and springing to an elevated spot, so as to gain a vantage ground, levelled his arrow at the bailiff.

The latter seeing him thus armed, and in this attitude, at once recognized the avenger of Switzerland; he cowered before him, and yet inwardly rejoiced in his anticipated capture. But how it was possible he could have thus appeared among them he could not possibly comprehend.

In the meantime, Erni and Klauss were engaged in combat, while Tell, with his eye upon Landenberger, still kept his arrow pointed against his foe, who, well aware of the skill of his opponent, dared not move from the spot on which he stood.

The noise occasioned by the engagement between Erni and Klauss had roused several of the sleeping soldiers, who were rushing forwards to the assistance of their leader and his friend, when they were suddenly transfixed with fear at the spectacle exhibited at the well's mouth, for the followers of Tell, many bearing lighted torches were rapidly emerging from its cavity, the strong glare of the torches casting a ruddy glow over their countenances.

Their first feeling was that of surprise, their second, fear: and under the impulse of the last, they fled from the sight they witnessed.

His followers gone, the bailiff endeavoured in the confusion to escape, but the quick eye of Tell was not to be decieved, and the arrow flew from his bow.

At that moment, in the heat of the conflict, the gigantic form of Klauss was interposed, and the arrow, with a crashing sound, passed through the bone of his skull and entered his brain; he fell to the ground a corpse, and Landenberger in the confusion succeeded in making his escape.

His object was to collect his panic-stricken forces, and endeavour to lead them on against the mountaineers, but so overwhelmed were they with the fear inspired by the apparently supernatural sight they had witnessed, that it was long before he could muster even a small part of the band, so as to enable him again to face his opponents.

Tell and his party taking advantage of this state of affairs, had posted themselves in the most advantageous positions, and when at length the bailiff was enabled to appear again upon the scene, he found his little party exposed to the unerring aim of more than a score of stout bowmen.

Reduced to this dilemma, more than half his forces unwilling to act, and the remainder apparently at the mercy of his opponents, it is easy to anticipate the result: Landenberger, after some further parley, agreed to surrender to the patriots, who, on their part, promised to save their lives, and conduct them safely out of the country.

Thus was the last of the Austrian bailiffs expelled, and nothing was left for the confederates to effect previous to the coming struggle with the Austrian Duke himself, except the reduction of the Castle of Rossberg.

In pursuance to the promises made to their prisoners, Erni and Tell caused the bailiff and his followers to be conducted in safety across the boundaries of the three Cantons, and there set at liberty, with the threat of summary punishment if found again in any part of the Waldstetten.

Their next efforts were directed to the destruction of the fortress, for although, in case the war should be brought to their own firesides, the stronghold might be of service to keep their enemies In check, they rather chose to rely upon their own valour and the nature of the country, which enabled them to convert every rock into a castle, than allow the least vestige of Austrian tyranny to remain.

They resisted even the temptation of appropriating to their own use the valuables found in the building, which they allowed the Austrians to carry with them. Every part of the structure which was capable of yielding to the agency of fire was consumed. The masonry was overturned, and hurled over the precipice, not a stone left resting upon another; and in a few days the site on which the famous castle of Sarnen stood, offered to view the bare rock alone, blackened by the action of fire, as if heaven, indignant at the crimes of its possessors, had wreaked its vengeance upon the seat of their crimes.

CHAPTER XXXV.

THE ENVOY.

The dangers of the days but newly gone,
(Whose memory is written on the earth
With yet appearing blood), and the examples
Of every minutes instance, (present now),
Have put us in these ill-beseeming arms.

The last of the hated bailiffs of Austria expelled the country, and the remaining adherents of the duke shut up in Rossberg Castle, the oppressed Swiss began to breathe more freely, and in spite of the threatened invasion of their country, already calculated on the blessings they were likely to derive from the late assertion of their rights.

Tell and his companions proceeded now to the general rendezvous of the patriots at the little village of Rossberg, travelling on foot until they reached the town of Alpnac, on the banks of the eastern branch of the lake Lucerne, when they embarked upon its beautiful waters to reach the opposite shore.

How delightful did their present situation appear—urged gently along the placid waves by a pleasant breeze, aided by the exertions of the rowers, who kept time to their oars, and lightened their labours by a cheerful song.

BOATMAN'S SONG.

Sound, brothers, sound, the wild Uri's horn,
 Let the standard of Schwietz be displayed in the air;
To the earth, in disgrace, the oppressors are borne,
 And the pride of the Austrian eclipsed by despair.

Pull, brothers, pull, Unterwalden is free;
 Shout! let the wild fowl our liberty share;
Strain every nerve—see, the boats dance with glee;
 There's a smile on the waves, and a laugh in the air.

Hark! brothers, hark! 'tis the Waldstetten's cry,
 'Our green fields are blessed, and our wild hills are free;'
Our forefathers' shadows look down from the sky,
 And smile through the mist upon liberty's tree.

"It is true, countrymen," said Tell, "that the tree of our liberty is planted and firmly rooted in the rocks of our native land, but although we have driven out the Austrian bailiffs, we have yet another storm to abide; which, if I am well informed, will require all our energy to resist.

18   T

The Austrian army, under the son of the late tyrant, is composed of not less than twenty thousand men, inured to war, and practised in all its arts.   Nature, it is true, is on our side, and a hundred hardy men, in one of our mountain passes, can hold in check a thousand men at arms."

"The country once our own," returned Erni, "we can defy the powers of Austria; without their chief, the followers of Gessler pent up in Rossberg walls will offer but little resistance; these once dispersed, the three mountain Cantons, directing all their forces against the Austrian, will, with Heaven's help, maintain their freedom inviolate."

Cheered by their recent successes, and elated by the anticipation of ultimate victory, the rowers laboured with so much good will and vigour, that long ere night they reached the town of Kussnacht, and disembarking, crossed the narrow neck of land by which the lake of Zug was separated from that of the four Cantons.

Again they took water, and in a short time the lofty towers of Rossberg appeared in view, and before sunset Arnold and his companions were made acquainted with the success of the late attempt upon Sarnen.

"And we," said Arnold, "are the last to strike a blow in defence of our country."

"All in good time," exclaimed Tell; "the walls of Rossberg are not so easily won, and if we fail in our first attempt, we know not the fate that may await our prisoners."

"It is true," observed Ernest; "and our numbers at present are not sufficient to make the attack."

At this instant Father Benedict entered, and from him they learned that the Austrians within the Castle were about to despatch a messenger to the patriots, but the purport of his errand he knew not.

He had scarcely concluded his communication, when an Austrian soldier made his appearance.

"I speak," he said, "I believe, to those who lead the discontented people to rebel against their rulers?"

"If you mean to resist those who strive to impose a foreign yoke, you are right."

"I am no casuist," returned the soldier; "my duty is to obey the Duke of Austria's orders, whate'er they be. The death of my superior officer has placed me in command within the walls of Rossberg, and I must hold it for the Duke."

"Aye," muttered Tell, "hold it until it is wrested from you."

"I am aware," continued the Austrian, without noticing this interruption, "it is your intention to make the useless attempt to storm its walls, and rescue the prisoners we hold."

"Austrian, you are right; we are pledged to that event."

"It's boldly spoken. Now hear what I propose: disarm your people through the entire land, and we'll restore our prisoners to you unhurt, untouched."

"Disarm the people! now the day's our own; why, Austrian, all but yonder paltry fortress has fallen into our hands; our states are free; your Bailiffs dead or banished, and we disarm while danger still may threaten us!"

"Nay, hear me out; not only shall our prisoners be set free, but all my interest shall be exerted to appease the wrath of Leopold, and cause him to accept of your submission, and grant you easy terms."

"Austrian, we will have none of Leopold, and none of you; to the Emperor of Germany do we owe allegiance, but not to Austria's house."

"Let then your private interests, young Arnold Attinghausen, have their weight: the Lady Gertrude is prisoner behind yon walls. Amid the crowd of wild unruly spirits there assembled, are men, who, when their passions are once aroused, defy authority. Think then, I pray you, on what might be her fate, amid the wild uproar of a besieged castle.

"What! man; dare you threaten in such unmanly mode? For Lady Gertrude, let not a hair upon her innocent head be touched, or vengeance such as yet was never wreaked on mortal head, shall be the lot of all within those walls. Austrian, the mountaineer is slow to move to acts of violence, but when once roused, his vengeance need be feared."

"Lord Attinghausen, in honour of the place which you once held in Gessler's favour, I made you this offer; you have rejected it; let the consequences fall on your head. Farewell!"

The emergency in which they were now placed, appeared in its true colours as soon as the Austrian had departed, and the necessity for immediate exertion was apparent. The hint of the messenger respecting the danger of Gertrude among the rude inmates of the Castle arose also before his mind in the most distressing characters.

The question was, how the evils now so apparent were to be warded off. It was clear, in their present state of preparation, they were not capable of attacking Rossberg with certainty of success, and to make an unsuccessful attack would but endanger the safety of those in whose welfare they were so much interested.

The sudden outbreak at Altdorf, although successful in that instance, and although it had been the means of driving Landenberger from the country, had somewhat disjointed their plans as to the simultaneous rising of the people on the Lord's Feast.

It appeared, therefore, clear, that the inhabitants of the three Cantons should be warned of the necessity of assembling at one point, on the shortest notice that their assistance was required; this spot, we need not say, was Rossberg, and who so active and efficient an agent for this purpose as William Tell.

The task he had to perform was now comparatively easy, for the country was open in every direction, and a few hours would suffice to convey the requisite information to the most distant parts of the Waldstetten.

With his soul bound up in the duty he had to perform, and full of that cheerful feeling which recent success will impart to the bosom of the least ardent of the human race, did our hero proceed on his mission.

The lighted brand of the Scottish Highlander, as it flew from house to house, at the gathering of the clans, was tame in its effects upon the bosoms of the hardy Caledonians, compared with the enthusiastic ardour aroused among the Swiss mountaineers when William Tell held his bow aloft, and cried out to the assembled groups, "See, countrymen, this is the bow by which the first blow of our freedom was struck."

The men, at the sight, flung aside their instruments of husbandry, and sought for warlike weapons. The women gazed upon it as if it were some holy relic, and lifted up their children in their arms that they might touch the hallowed weapon.

At every place at which he raised this banner of liberty, the fleetest of foot prepared to carry the tidings he bore in every direction.

The success of his rapid progress through the country was beyond his most ardent expectations. The men in the most distant parts of the Cantons were first to rise, and march towards the towers of Rossberg. Their arrival was to be notified to those nearer to the place of action, by beacons composed of huge piles of blazing wood, on the top of the most conspicuous hills, whose smoke by day, and flames by night, should intimate their near approach.

His duty to his country thus far performed, Tell began to feel his heart yearn towards Charlotte and his children. The little village of Burglen was visible in the distance, and there were sheltered those in whose affections he delighted, and who equally doated upon his.

He saw the distant spire of the village chapel, he thought he heard the cheerful sound of bells, and his excited imagination almost told him he could hear the sound of the voices of those he most loved, offering up prayers for his safety at the shrine of the blessed Virgin.

Can the lover, can the father, can the patriot, blame him? For what? He turned away from his direct road to the Castle of Rossberg, to pay one short visit to his anxious family; the duties due to his country performed, he thought of home.

As he approached the cottage, he saw the children playing near the door, as unconscious of the scenes in which life and death were at odds, and which were occurring around them, as the sportive kids, whose activity they smiled at, and vainly strove to rival.

Walter Tell, on whom, during his father's absence, the manly duties of the family devolved, had just flung from his weary shoulders the carcase of a chamois, which he threw with exultation upon the green sward.

He looked round to meet the approving smile of his mother, but, instead of her fond yet timid glance, he saw his father stand before him, resting upon his cross-bow, and gazing with delighted looks upon his boy, and the fruits of his prowess.

"Ha! father," cried Walter, "how glad I am to see you; how glad mother will be. See, father, is it not a fine chamois? Two days I've followed it; I thought of mother, and would have left the chase, but then again I thought how glorious it would be to take a chamois; it is the first I ever shot, father."

" 'Tis a fine buck, my boy, and many a youth thy elder by some years, would never have succeeded in the chase. But where's your mother?"

"Where is she, Eugene?" said Walter, addressing one of the younger children.

"She's gone to drive the goats in from the hill.—See, here she comes."

Tell looked up, and Charlotte, too busy in her occupation to notice what was going on at the cottage door, continued her attention to the vagrant charge, until a shout from the children attracted her attention, when, looking towards the cottage, she saw her beloved William standing near the door. As swiftly as the fleetest of her charge, she rushed down the declivity, and was soon locked in the arms of her husband.

CHAPTER XXXVI.

THE GATHERING.

The fisherman forsook the strand,
The swarthy smith took dirk and brand;
With changed cheer, the mower blithe,
Left in the half cut swathe his scythe;
The herds without a keeper strayed,
The plough was in mid furrow stay'd;
Prompt at the signal of alarms,
Each son of Alpine rushed to arms.

The interview of Tell with his wife was but of short duration, for in the midst of his affection for his family, he did not forget the duty he owed his country, and long before his return was expected, he presented himself again before the confederates at Rossberg.

"Comrades," he exclaimed, "before to-morrow's dawn our friends will muster in sufficient force to storm this last stronghold of the Austrian. But whither are you bound, Ernest?"

Arnold responded, "Ernest is determined to enter the Castle to-night; he thinks, if once within the walls, himself and Hans, and Leuthold, if he be true, may aid us much during the assault, and may find an opportunity to open the Castle gates."

"It is a desperate venture; but where do you propose to make the attempt? The rock is inaccessible, and the gate is too well guarded."

"A little to the right hand of the gate, some ten yards or so, the wall is broken in several places, and will afford sufficient foot-hold to reach its summit; once there, this knotted rope will help me to descend, and Benedict has pointed out to me the road I ought to take, to reach the dungeon where Hans is in confinement."

"I will not dissuade you from the attempt," said Tell, "for your judgment, combined with the strength of Hans, must needs be of great service to our cause; without some one to direct his movements, I fear he would but lead himself into danger.—When do you proceed upon your errand?"

"Within an hour; they close the gates at sunset."

"Well, I'll accompany you," said Tell; "I may assist you to scale the wall."

With the assistance of Tell, Ernest succeeded in reaching the summit of the castle wall, and fastening the rope in the interstice between two of the stones, proceeded to lower himself cautiously; he had nearly succeeded in his enterprise, and his feet were but a short distance from the ground, when he felt the stones to which his rope was attached, tremble ; they were evidently giving way; he released the rope from his grasp, and alighted on the ground, but his caution came too late—the loosened stones fell, and in their descent struck him so violent a blow on the forehead, as to level him with the ground, and for a time to deprive him of his senses.

As soon as his senses returned, he was conscious of the glare of torches, and perceived several grim faces leaning over his prostrate form, and talking rapidly.

"Ha! ha! ha! Here is another bird taken in our trap," said one of the soldiers; "why, we might take all the wild spirits of the Canton with the bait we have. These Swiss lovers are rather venturous. Hallo! stranger, which of the ladies have you come after, the mistress or the maid?"

"I thought," cried another, "this fellow had saved us trouble, by breaking his neck of his own accord, but it seems he still lives; what shall we do, comrades, dispatch him on the instant, or leave him till the morning, when the Captain can decide his fate? But here comes our valiant leader."

The soldiers made way for their commander, who instantly ordered Ernest to be bound, and placed in confinement.

"Where shall we take him, Captain? To the eastern tower, to console the ladies? He seems a likely spark."

"Confine him with his comrade in the dungeon. Here, Leuthold, he is your prisoner."

The decision of the commander of the garrison relieved the mind of Ernest, for now he would be able to concert with Hans upon the best mode of effecting their purpose.

As soon as Leuthold had conveyed his prisoner beyond the hearing of the soldiers, he spoke in a low voice—

"By the mass, comrade, if you continue to enter the Castle in this manner, we shall soon have enough to master the garrison."

"I have gained my purpose, friend; I wished to join Hans, and my wish is gratified."

"Few men would participate in your gratification, in a case like this. I heard it whispered, your fellow prisoner is in the morning to meet his death. As you have arrived, you will no doubt be included in the ceremony."

"So soon! At what time in the morning?"

"Oh! early, early; before breakfast, to give a zest to the morning repast of the captain."

"And early in the morning will the fort be stormed."

"Indeed! Are you ready for the effort?"

"We shall be, I have no doubt."

"If you are certain it will be so soon," said Leuthold, "I'll venture a plan will save your lives."

"But will it aid our cause?"

"Aye, both; look, this is it: I will remove Hans from the dungeon, and conceal both him and you; for myself, I must be hidden also. Now, if your friends assail the Castle early, there will be enough to do within its walls, to keep them well employed, without seeking for you or I; but if those without should not be ready for the attack, we cannot long escape their search,—and then all hopes are lost. I trust, huntsman, if we succeed, you'll represent the danger I have run on your account, and place that in the list of services I have rendered to your cause. I am not mercenary, but like to have my due."

Tell, when Ernest disappeared, marked the fall of the stone, and calculated on its probable consequences, but being unable to render any assistance, he hastened back to his friends and communicated his fears.

All that could be done, under the circumstances, was to hasten their preparations for the attack, and with great anxiety did they await the arrival of the expected reinforcements.

Tell, whose anxiety was equal to that of even Arnold himself, was the first to call the attention of his comrades to a faint light in the horizon, which appeared to come and go, like the feeble flickering of an expiring candle.

Suddenly, the light became brighter, and it was visible in various parts around. At length, fires could be plainly distinguished on the distant hills; they increased in number, and were lighted on hills nearer to the intended scene of action. Soon the Castle of Rossberg appeared as it were encircled with a zone of flame, which still continued to narrow its circumference as it increased in brilliancy.

Joyfully did the assembled group of patriots mark these tokens of the approach of their friends, and with still more lively joy did Tell first distinguish the sounds of the horn of Uri, as its shrill notes were heard in the distance. The hum of voices was heard, small bands continued to arrive from every point of the compass, and at length the little army assumed a most imposing appearance.

Arnold, on whom the task of directing the operations of his countrymen had been imposed, viewed with pride the sinewy forms and athletic appearance of his mountain warriors, and busied himself with all the ardour of a youthful commander in his first campaign, in preparing for the approaching conflict. By the time these preparations were completed, day had begun to break, and as soon as it was sufficiently light to distinguish objects, the walls of Rossberg Castle, on the side nearest to the hills, which, as we have already seen, was the only vulnerable part of the romantic pile, was seen lined with soldiers.

It is natural to suppose that the beacon fires of the mountaineers had not been unnoticed by the inmates of the castle;—with increasing rage did the commander of the garrison perceive their numbers and magnitude, which clearly demonstrated the magnitude of the rising.

Enclosed within his rock-girt fortress, he considered himself capable of resisting all their attacks; but how long he might have to remain thus isolated from the world he knew not, and the castle was but ill provided with provisions. But he contemplated with complacency the prisoners he held in his possession—and in the case of extremity, calculated on making their captivity subservient to his purposes.

Great was his rage when, on ordering Ernest and his companion into his presence, it was reported they were missing. Leuthold also, their gaoler, was absent; this was the greatest blow of all—for when he believed treachery existed among his immediate followers, he felt more strongly the insecurity of his position.

Prompted by fear, he despatched a messenger to ascertain the safe custody of his female prisoners. Fritz, he found, had been true to his duty—his charge was safe. To forward an object he had in view, he caused Gertrude and her attendant to be placed on the roof of the eastern tower, a situation in which they could be easily seen by the besiegers, and from which they could be witnesses of the conflict.

The next act, by which he increased the impregnable nature of the fortress, was the destruction of the rude bridge which led to the castle gates. Thus completely isolated, he considered himself secure—and having manned the walls with his troops, awaited the approach of the besieging party.

Gertrude and Hildegard were soon recognized by their friends without, who vainly endeavoured to unriddle the intentions of the Austrian in placing them in that situation.

CHAPTER XXXVII.

THE ASSAULT.

In peace there's nothing so becomes a man,
As modest stillness and humility:
But when the blast of war blows in our ears,
Then imitate the actions of the tiger;
Stiffen the sinews, summon up the blood,
Disguise fair nature with hard-favoured rage.

Before hostilities commenced, Arnold Attinghausen, accompanied by several others, approached that part of the castle where the commander of the garrison was seen giving directions to his soldiers, and having, by signs, made him understand he wished to address him, thus spoke—

"Austrian! we seek not the blood of any man—release your prisoners—surrender up the castle—and depart in peace."

"Lord Attinghausen, I gave you credit for more wisdom than your demand exhibits. Our castle is impregnable against any force, much less a rude undisciplined band like that you lead."

"Rude as it is, it has driven from the face of our country your boasted bailiffs; all, all are gone, and we are free once more."

"Rebel! we hold a hostage for thy good behaviour: withdraw your forces, or that lady's life"—

"Villain! you do not dare, in the broad face of day, utter that threat!"

"Not dare!—you see I do proclaim it."

At this instant an arrow from the castle glanced slightly by Arnold,

grazing the feather in his cap. Behind him stood Ulrich the smith, who raising his brawny arm, while he uttered a shout of defiance, received the weapon in the fleshy part.

Tell witnessed the occurrence, and instantly levelling, with deadly aim, at the Austrian bowman, who was exulting in his deed, buried the shaft in his bosom, This was the signal to commence hostilities—and both sides began to discharge their missiles at their opponents.

According to a preconcerted plan, the Swiss leader directed all his means of annoyance towards a part of the walls at some distance from the gateway : this was done for the purpose of drawing off the attention of the Austrians from the efforts of their party within to open the castle gates.

This manœuvre had been persevered in for some time, causing considerable loss to the Austrians, whose men fatally found out the unerring aim of the mountaineers, whenever they ventured to show themselves above the walls. The Swiss, on the other hand, being more exposed than their opponents, suffered considerably.

No appearance of the assistance they looked for from within was exhibited, and they began to fear that Ernest and his friend Hans had been detected by the inmates of the castle and placed in durance : suddenly the sound of clashing swords, the rattling of chains, and clanking of bars of iron, announced the progress of some deadly struggle behind the massive portals. Then there was a swaying and heaving of the gates—they were suddenly thrown open, and Ernest was about to step forth, when, perceiving the bridge was gone, he started back in dismay.

Great now was the peril of the Swiss within the walls, as they stood in a little phalanx opposed to overwhelming numbers, and in spite of their bravery they must infallibly have perished, if it had not been for the arrows of their friends without. Headed by Tell, the archers remained perfectly at rest until they saw an Austrian weapon raised against their countrymen. In an instant a bow was levelled, and as instantly the arrow was buried in the bosom of the daring man.

This result of an endeavour to harm their late prisoners was so frequently brought about, that at length, no one dared to raise his weapon against them, and they seemed, as it were, to bear a charmed life, defying all the attempts of their opponents.

This state of things could not, however, continue long—nor were the views of either party forwarded: if the Austrians could not subdue the small band of patriots—neither, on the other hand, could the Swiss enter the castle. But while Tell and his archers were engaged as we have seen, Arnold Attinghausen had been contriving some means of repairing the injured bridge.

He had observed a large tree at no great distance, which appeared admirably adapted for his intended purpose: thither he repaired with a party of men who, applying themselves with great vigour to the task, succeeded in felling it. They then lopped off the unnecessary branches, and with great labour succeeded in dragging it to the place where the former bridge had stood.

Here the greatest difficulty occurred :—how were they to succeed in laying it across the chasm ? They raised it upon the thickest part of the stem near to the brink of the precipice, and suddenly allowed it to fall : down it came with a crashing sound, and nearly spanned the opening, the extreme end resting upon a projecting mass of rock about four feet from the base of the gates.

The trunks of smaller trees were soon procured, and at length a practicable bridge was formed, and both parties prepared for the decisive struggle.

A party of selected men, under the guidance of Arnold, armed with the huge two-handed sword of the country, advanced first, their advance being covered by the bowmen under the directions of Tell, whose harrassing flights of arrows succeeded in checking the onset of the Austrians. Still, however, a brave resistance was made, and it was not until after much severe fighting that the Swiss succeeded in making good their entry into the castle.

It was now the strife in reality began—those who fought with swords let fall their ponderous weapons with such deadly effect upon the crests of their opponents, that the Austrians were fain to give way, while Tell and his bowmen, having scattered themselves over the more elevated parts of the building, galled them desperately with their arrows, which they plied incessantly.

The battle now was evidently becoming more and more favourable to the patriots, when suddenly a cry of alarm was raised that the eastern tower was in flames—a scream of horror burst forth from the lips of the Swiss, while shouts of exultation and scorn were heard from the Austrian leader.

" Rebels!" he exclaimed, " you need a memorial of your victory— you have it there—let your poets sing, ' we gained the Castle of Rossburg, and Gertrude of Waldstein perished in the flames—resist them, men, until the fire has done its duty."

The Austrians now collected all their forces to resist the attempt of the besiegers to reach the eastern tower;—vain were their efforts— they could not break through the serried mass—and, raving in the agony of despair, Arnold flew from point to point.

Tell, who had heard the deriding shout of the Austrian, had kept his eye steadily fixed upon him;—at length he again raised himself above the heads of his followers, and was preparing to utter another shout of derision, when an arrow from Tell's bow passed through his body, and he fell to the ground a bleeding corpse, the smile of scorn still resting on his distorted lips, while the anguish of his death-wound was shown by the painful contraction of his knitted brow.

By this incident the Austrians were thrown into partial confusion, and a vigorous effort now, on the part of the Swiss swordsmen, succeeded in breaking through their ranks; they fled in dismay—and, unopposed by the mountaineers, whose attention was now attracted to the means of saving Gertrude from the flames, they passed through the castle gates and escaped into the country.

Suddenly a human form, which in the midst of the smoke appeared magnified to a superhuman size, was seen bearing in his arms the senseless body of a female; with hurried steps he passed through the suffocating fumes, and as soon as he entered the pure air, gently laid his burden upon the grass, and sunk down exhausted by her side. The female was Lady Gertrude, and her gigantic deliverer Hans Winkelreid.

Arnold raised her tenderly from the ground, and after throwing back her dishevelled hair, and resorting to such simple means of restoration as occurred to him on the moment, was delighted to perceive symptoms of returning consciousness. She gazed wildly round her, and seemed bewildered at the sight of so many anxious faces; at length her eyes rested upon that of Arnold. A gleam of pleasure passed across her countenance, and, as if doubting the reality of the vision, she raised her hand for the purpose of satisfying her doubts.

Arnold seized the proffered hand, and imprinting an ardent kiss upon it, completely restored the maiden to her senses; she blushed and smiled, and raising herself in his arms, inquired anxiously for her preserver.

Hans was pointed out to her, seated upon the ground, and swallowing with great avidity a draught of some restorative, administered to him by his late gaoler Leuthold. Blackened with smoke,-the sable colour of which was only relieved by the crimson streams of blood which flowed from his lacerated hands and limbs, Hans could have been scarcely recognised as a human being, so ghastly and so grim did he appear.

Gertrude related to Arnold the dangers which Hans had undergone to rescue her, and expressed her gratitude in unmeasured terms of approbation.

But where was Hildegard? was the question asked by all; her lady could not tell, she had left the apartment to seek some means of escape and had not returned when Hans rescued herself from the flames. Thus in an instant the joy experienced at the safety of the Baroness was damped by the uncertain fate of her faithful attendant.

Ernest made another effort to enter the blazing fabric, but unsuccessfully, when the attention of all was attracted by the appearance of the maiden herself, on the frame of one of the gothic windows of the building; she called for help, for the flames were close upon her, and was about to spring to the ground from the dangerous height, when her rashness was checked by the sings made by Ernest.

Accustomed from his youth upwards to the dangers of the chase, Ernest was in the habit of climbing the most precipitous rocks; his light and graceful form possessed all the advantages of strength and activity; the slightest foot-hold on the face of the crag was sufficient to enable him to scale the most dangerous and inaccessible places. He had carefully examined the walls of the tower, and noted many a jutting frieze, and many a crevice in the ruined wall, snfficient for his purpose, and he immediately began his daring ascent.

With anxious eyes did the assembled multitude watch the progress of the adventurous youth, as taking advantage of every projecting piece of the masonry, he slowly, but surely, drew nearer to the object of his affection, until at length his hand was placed upon the spot on which she stood. Another effort, and he was at her side.

No time was to be lost, for the heat of the burning ruins was becoming unbearable; to descend the way he ascended, burdened with the weight of Hildegard, was manifestly impossible. He had carefully provided himself with a stout rope, and having tied a portion of her dress firmly round the affrighted maiden, he attached the cord to the belt it formed, and carefully lowered her down the face of the wall until within the reach of those below.

As soon as she was in safety, the preservation of his own life became his object. To descend by the way he came seemed utterly hopeless, for the flames were bursting forth from the lower windows of the building, but the distance at which he was placed from the ground would render it too dangerous an attempt to leap; no time, however, was to be lost.

About one-third the distance from the spot on which he stood, a wide projecting ledge or moulding ran round the tower; if he could rest his foot on that but for an instant, the remaining distance could be accomplished by one so active as himself without much danger; if he failed in alighting upon the moulding, destruction seemed inevitable.

Carefully lowering himself down, and holding on by the framework of the window for an instant, he relaxed his hold, and alighted with more firmness upon his first resting-place than he anticipated, and a friendly projection in the stone-work enabled him to cling for a few seconds to the wall, before he leaped to the ground. This circumstance was of vast service to him, and taking his leap with more confidence, he alighted safely in the midst of his friends.

CHAPTER XXXVIII.

THE ARMAMENT.

This offer comes from mercy, not from fear :
  For lo ! within a ken, our army lies ;
  Upon mine honour, all too confident
  To give admittance to a thought of fear.

The last stronghold of the Austrians had now fallen into the hands of the confederates, and the liberty of Switzerland was so far accomplished, but already were they well acquainted with the presence of Leopold in the Canton of Zug, and fully sensible of the necessity of taking measures to oppose his progress.

Rossberg Castle, although strong in its natural and artificial resources, was too near the scene of the operations of the Duke of Austria to render it safe to allow it to remain in its present condition ; it was therefore determined it should not only be dismantled, but levelled to the ground, like the other seats of Austrian tyranny which had already fallen into the hands of the mountaineers.

The dead were buried—the wounded on either side removed to the village of Rossberg—and Ulrich's house became, for the time, the head-quarters of the leaders of the patriots ;—there, also, until other arrangements were made, Gertrude and Hildegard took up their abode, but were subsequently removed to the town of Altdorff on account of its greater distance from the expected scene of action.

Delightful as the company of the lovers were to each other, after their late painful separation, it was a pleasure they were necessarily enabled to enjoy but for a short time.

At a solemn meeting of the principals of the confederation, the plan of their future operations was decided on ; a party of the most active of their young men and those best acquainted with the mountain passes, were to undertake the duty of scouts, and watch and report the movements of the enemy. The conduct of this party was entrusted to Ernest, assisted by the experience of Bernard and his two sons.

The most experienced bowmen of the three cantons were to obey the orders of Tell, and as this party would be of the most essential service for the purpose of annoying the enemy in the mountain passes, it was to be rendered as efficient and numerous as possible.

Young Arnold Attinghausen, to whom, under the directions of the confederates, the chief conduct of the campaign was entrusted, was placed at the head of all the heavier armed troops, those who wielded the two-handed sword, the lance, and the battle-axe.

In addition to these principal divisions of the Swiss forces, the army was to be followed and assisted by as numerous a body of peasants, not even excluding women and children, as could be brought to bear with advantage upon any point of defence, and, as the sequel will show, these irregular forces rendered great assistance during the ensuing war of independence.

These preparations being made, and the means of resistance thus prepared, it was agreed, that messengers should be sent to Leopold, to endeavour to avert the threatened conflict, by pointing out to him the great wrongs they had suffered, and at the same time warning him of the dangerous task he had undertaken to subdue a band of daring men, protected from outward danger by the inaccessible nature of the country, prepared for the conflict, and flushed with victory.

Stauffacher and Erni, accompanied by Melctor, the victim of Gesler's cruelty, were to proceed on the embassy, protected by a small escort of armed men, until within a short distance of Leopold's camp. It was expected the sight of the grey-haired victim of the bailiff might plead with Leopold in defence of the conduct of the Swiss, in their violent expulsion of the Austrians from their country. While Stauffacher, as the representative of the more wealthy class of inhabitants, would be able to explain more fully the feelings and resources of the three Cantons.

According to these arrangements the deputation set forward on the almost hopeless task of softening the heart, or changing the determination of the Austrian despot.

As the nearest road to the probable position of the Austrian army was that by which the hapless messenger of the Duke had travelled, they determined to pursue the same course, and as the way was well known to several of the party, it was decided that they should proceed at once and obtain shelter for the night at the cottage of Rubli, the chamois hunter; towards that part of the mountains they therefore directed their course, the steps of Melctor guided by his son Erni.

As they passed the wood in which the body of Grisach had been deposited, the well-known marks of the recent presence of a pack of wolves was visible, and on searching further, the mangled remains of the trooper were found; his apparel was scattered in various directions, and among other remains of his garments was seen a leathern case, evidently intended to hold letters or other written documents; it was much gnawed by the wolves, but still the contents remained uninjured.

This case was carefully opened, and found to contain a letter from the late Emperor Albert, addressed to Gessler, in which he declared himself pleased at the violent measures to which he had resorted, promised assistance, and declared his intention to subjugate the Swiss, at any expense of blood and treasure.

"The monster!" exclaimed Werner, after he had perused the writing, "Hear what he says—'Spare neither age nor sex;' and here again, 'Construct more castles, we must o'erawe the country; impose more taxes, we must impoverish it.' These were his intentions. Did we not well, friends, when we asserted our rights?'

"Leopold, they say," observed Erni, "declares the same intentions."

"Aye, so it is said; but then, remember, he is burning to revenge his father's death, and has strong grounds to believe the murderer has found shelter in our mountains. But see, yonder is Rubli's hut."

The chamois hunter, perceiving the party approaching his dwelling, came out to receive them; his wife and children also appeared at the door of the cottage, for the sight of so large a party was to them a perfect novelty.

When the wife of the hunter ascertained it was the intention of the party to remain during the night, she began to consider what means she had at her disposal to accommodate so many guests, and in perfect bewilderment as to the disproportion between her necessity and her ability to meet the occasion, she sat down in despair.

From this dilemma she was soon relieved, by the display on the part of her visitors of an abundance of provisions, while others of the party were busy in constructing a rude hut or shed, the materials for which they found among the pile of firewood which had been prudently stored up for winter use, in the neighbourhood of the cottage.

The accommodation thus obtained was of the rudest kind, but it formed a sufficient shelter for the hardy men who took refuge beneath its artless roof.

In the morning early, after taking leave of the host and his family, they began to descend the mountainous road which led to the Canton of Zug, and as they approached the level country, they fell in with several peasants, from whom they learned that the army of Leopold was encamped at the southern extremity of the lake Egeri. Thither they directed their course, meeting, in their progress, with numerous bands of peasants, accompanied by their families and flocks, who had left their homes on the approach of the Austrian army.

From these people they understood that every effort was being made by Leopold to procure provisions and instruments of war; that his army was daily increasing in number, and that he had expressed his intention of subduing or exterminating the natives of the three Cantons.

The information thus obtained, argued ill for the success of their mission, and they pursued their course with diminished hopes of an amicable termination of their differences with Austria, but cheered up by the knowledge of the efficient means they had already prepared for their defenc

Towards evening, two of their party who, having procured horses from the inhabitants of the valley, had ridden forward to discover the proximity of the army, returned with the information, that from the summit of a hillock, about two miles in advance, they were able to distinguish a part of the Austrian camp.

On receiving this information, it was determined to halt until the morning, and then proceed at once to lay before the Duke the object of their mission.

CHAPTER XXXIX.

THE AUSTRIAN CAMP.

Had I thy brethren here, their lives and thine
Were not revenge sufficient for me :
No, if I digged up thy forefathers' graves,
And hung their rotten coffins up in chains,
It could not slake mine ire, nor ease my heart.

The morning sun had scarcely risen when Erni and Werner, accompanied by their blind charge, left the cottage at which they had rested for the night. As they proceeded along the road, the resposibility imposed upon them by the task they had undertaken, forcibly impressed itself upon their minds.

Could they persuade the haughty Austrian to relinquish his attempt against their liberties, how many innocent lives would be saved. But of this there appeared little hope, if the reports they had heard of the mood of the despot were true.—Already had they witnessed the distress occasioned by war, even when waged on a limited scale. What evils would it not bring with it, when two nations brought forth all their resources, and strove together in mortal fight.

No common cause of quarrel was theirs—on the issue of the combat the liberties of one party depended, while the pride of the other, combined with the military fame they had gained as a nation, forbade their yielding to a foe they had so frequently despised. All this was well understood by the Swiss deputies, and they saw how hopeless their task would be.

As they came in sight of the Austrian camp, their hearts, for the moment, sunk within them. There it lay, stretched out before them as far as the eye could reach, the plains whitened by long rows of tents, which rose in perspective one above the other in endless lines.

In the centre of this mass of canvass a group of tents, more splendid in their decoration than any by which they were surrounded, were seen, and in the midst the broad standard of Austria displayed its ample folds to the morning breeze, while all around pennons of every hue, bearing the devices of their different owners, streamed abroad in undulating lines.

The bustle of the day had already begun, and as the bands of lancers moved through the different alleys formed by the rows of tents, they seemed in the morning sun like living streams of silver.

We say, the heart of the Swiss sunk within them at the sight. But when they looked up and saw the vast amphitheatre of eternal rocks that rose in awful majesty behind the scene of the despot's splendour, their minds were re-assured.

" Those are our native mountains, Erni," observed Werner. " What will the Austrian's force avail against these barriers, which nature has thrown up to guard our land. If he were not blinded with pride he would not dare to pass over the belt of rocks with which we are girded."

Their attention was now arrested by the advance of a group of horsemen, who, surrounding the little party on all sides, demanded their business so near the Austrian camp.

"We come," said Werner, "to seek an interview with the Duke of Austria."

"From Switzerland?" demanded the leader of the horsemen.

"From the confederates of the mountain Cantons, to seek an audience of the Duke."

"The Duke shall hear of your demand," returned the Austrian; "meantime, dismiss your escort, and come with us."

The small band of armed men which had accompanied the deputation were accordingly dismissed, and returned to the nearest village, while Werner and his companions, guarded by the soldiers, approached the camp. They entered its spacious confines, and passing through the bustling crowds, assailed by the coarse jokes of the soldiery, they soon came in sight of the Ducal tent.

For more than an hour the Swiss deputies were kept in anxious expectation, without the tent, without receiving the smallest attention which their condition, as representatives of the mountain Cantons, justly entitled them to, their simple bearing and homely garb provoking the rude remarks of the passers by.

At length it was announced to them that the Duke was ready to hear their mission, and the three envoys entered the tent. The bold and unaltered bearing of the two younger of the party, and the venerable appearance of the aged Melctor, rendered still more affecting by his blindness, attracted the attention of all.

After a few minutes' silence, the Duke broke silence, speaking in the haughty and uncourteous manner for which his father had been so much noted.

"Men of Uri, or whatever other desert you belong to, the desire of obtaining some knowledge of the movements of the murderer of my parent, has alone induced me to admit you into my presence.—Say, know you aught of John of Hapsburg?"

"The Swiss, my Lord, never yet strove to shield a murderer. If the assassin had been within our power, we should not have hesitated to have given him up to your authority."

"Say it is true," returned the Duke, "what submission have you to make for your outrageous assault upon our bailiffs and strongholds? Have you aught to say to ward off my punishment, or induce my clemency?"

"We came not here, my Lord, to compromise our honour, or the dignity of our country, by pleading guilty to deeds which we consider not only innocent, but praiseworthy. You call us rebels : do you remember the contracts made by Austria, when Rodolph was the Emperor? Look back to your records, my Lord; you will find that even Rodolph, the founder of your house, could not subdue us. While Austria was just, the Waldstetten served her with their lives; when she oppressed us, we asserted our independence. As defenceless men, now within your power, we can offer no resistance ; but we know how to die, and our brethren how to avenge us."

Irritated beyond measure at this bold address, the Duke was about to order the deputies into custody, when his attention was arrested by Melctor stepping forward ; raising his hands to command attention, his venerable and melancholy look checked the fury of the Duke, who again was silent, that he might hear what he had to urge.

"My Lord Duke," said the old man, "in me behold one of the victims of the cruelty of your bailiff. Look on me, my Lord, and say, had you a father suffering like me, would you not be instigated to revenge? But, my Lord, I am but a single sufferer ; the three Cantons abound with instances of gross oppression. You, call us stubborn—but here, with all my wrongs about me, do I bend my knee to thee, which never yet bent except to Heaven.—No foolish pride of mine, my Lord, shall break that peace, so blessed, so invaluable to man."

"Arise, old man," said the Duke, in as mild a voice as he could assume ; "we are ready to hear you."

"My Lord," said Melctor, rising, "this paper contains a full account of all our wrongs, of the oppressions we have suffered from your bailiff. Still, my Lord, we endured them all, thinking, as we hope now, they were unsanctioned by the Emperor himself. But when our messenger was sent back in disgrace, how could we act? We saw our crops destroyed, our herds driven off, our wives and daughters imprisoned and ill used, and to save ourselves, we turned against our oppressors, and drove them from the land."

"This, my Lord, an act of self-defence, is the extent of our offence.

All that is due to Austria we are willing to yield, and live in peace. If war should once begin, as long as one of us can wield a broad-sword or lift a halberd, the strife would still continue. Behold those rocks, my Lord; with barriers such as those, given us by nature, our country is covered—a land of rock and ice—a wilderness, as you have truly called it, yet dear to us as the most fertile plains of Italy. If you should conquer these wastes, of what avail would it be? What could you gain by such a strife? The jewels on the harness of your war-horse are more in number, and far exceed in value, all you could find within the three Cantons."

"If you seek for glory, can your ambition be gratified by conquering a horde of poor mountaineers? If you should fail, and Heaven will sometimes aid the weakest side, great would be your disgrace. Oh! weigh the difference well, and grant us peace."

"Silence, for more than five minutes, pervaded the assembly; at length, Leopold again addressed the deputies :—

"Think you, old man, we seek for profit in our conquests? There is a duty imposed upon our station, which compels us to root out from their dens a horde of savage brutes like your wild mountaineers."

"Again, my Lord," said Erni, who now took up the word, "let me warn you of the danger of the attempt.—As conquered enemies, we can be of little service to you; as friends, we may assist you greatly. Look at the former wars of your grandfather, Rodolph—who, among all his troops, were of more service than his faithful band of Swiss, when they accompanied him through the fields of Italy, and saw him crowned King of the Romans?"

"We have heard you fairly," said Leopold: "return to your mountains, and be thankful you are allowed to escape with your lives. Tell your friends who sent you we shall soon be upon your frontiers, and if you wish for peace, you must come in humbler guise than now."

"Leopold of Austria," observed Melctor, in a warning voice, "the miseries of war and all its crimes be upon your head. On our sides, a war began can never end, unless in victory or extermination. Farewell! and Heaven yet turn your mind."

The Swiss deputation departed from the tent of the proud Duke, and with all the haste the nature of the road would permit, returned to Rossberg, and related to the confederates the result of their embassy.

"It is as I expected," said Arnold; "the proud blood of the Austrian can never brook opposition; well, brethren, we must bide the brunt of the storm as best we may. Tell, how many bowmen have you in your ranks?"

"Three hundred, my Lord; and all well practised men."

"Your party, Ernest, amounts, I think, to two hundred; no more?"

"Two hundred cragsmen, well acquainted with all the mountain passes; you shall hear good report of them in the ensuing strike."

"And the main body of our little army," continued Arnold, "does not reach a thousand men. What do the Austrians muster, as you have heard."

"There is no doubt," said Werner, "they can muster full twenty thousand men; their numbers will impede their action; of what service can their numerous horses be in a mountain district?"

"That's true again; still these are fearful odds."

"Why, man," cried Tell, "have you forgot our boys and women, to say nothing of the active part they can take; why, every man in their presence will do the work of three. Still heaven is on our side." "We need some other hand to help us," observed Arnold, "than our own feeble strength; but come, ours is a righteous cause, and heaven's help is certain."

War being now certain, the Swiss leaders put their little army in motion; they had ascertained from their scouts, that the first object of Leopold's attack was intended to be the town of Swietz; but as the only road by which they could reach that capital of the province was through the pass of Morgarten, they determined to concentrate their little force in its neighbourhood.

Ernest and his followers scattered themselves through the mountains to watch the motions of the enemy as they prepared themselves to cross the mountains. Matters being thus disposed, the mountaineers with patient courage awaited the coming events by which their fate as a nation was to be decided.

CHAPTER XL.

THE MURDERER'S FATE.

> Away with me !
> The clouds grow thicker—there—now lean on me;
> Place your foot here—here take this staff, and cling
> A moment to that shrub—now give me your hand.
> The chalet will be gained in half an hour.

WHEN John of Hapsburgh had taken that needful rest at the shepherd's cottage which his exhausted nature required, he rose from his humble couch, and although day had not yet broke, began his dreary journey. To avoid contact with every human being, he followed the least frequented roads, and if a solitary traveller came in sight, concealed himself until he had passed, and again began his melancholy journey.

Travelling in this manner, he passed the base of the lofty Myttenstein, and, as night approached, began to ascend the broken sides of the Axenburg; the sinking sun, as it threw back its parting rays from the surface of the lake, had no charm in his eyes, although he regretted its fading light, which would soon again leave him in darkness.

Plodding thus on his weary way, faint from hunger as well as fatigue—for, fearful of encountering the glance of any human being, he had avoided the cottages that lay on the roadside, and had only refreshed himself during the day by one draught of milk, which had been offered to him by a child—the outlaw now pursued his journey.

The darkness of the evening now began to fall more thickly upon the landscape, the road was more intricate, and the danger increased at every step; moving on with trembling and cautious steps, he was not aware of the proximity of a man dressed as a hunter, who, it seems, had been watching him for some time.

The stranger, seeing him about to take a step which would endanger his safety, stepped up to the wanderer, and placed his hands upon his shoulder.

The gentle touch of the hunter acted like an electric shock upon the conscience-stricken man, and he turned his ghastly look upon him. The peasant who was about to address him, started back at the sight of his haggard countenance; at length recovering his self-possession, he spoke.

"Father! you are wandering late upon the hills, and you seem weary; go you to Altdorf?"

"No! not to Altdorf, but in that direction: I wish to reach the valley through which the river flows."

"What, the valley of the Reuss; it lies before you, but the descent is difficult by this dim light? Seek you no shelter to-night?"

"I am in haste, my friend, and must not rest me on my journey."

"Surely, you'd better rest and take some food. I know by your sunken cheek and your dull eye, that you are hungry. If you will enter no where—and, by the mass! I know no place of shelter near at hand—sit you down awhile and partake of what I have here in my scrip: I'll show you then the safest way to descend, and the moon will soon be up."

So saying, the hunter opened his wallet and offered his scanty store to the exile. Impelled by hunger, which overcame every fear of personal danger, the famished man greedily partook of the offered food.

The efforts of his entertainer to induce him to enter into conversation were useless, and after a reasonable time had elapsed, he offered to point out to him the road he had to pursue.

Having performed his promise, and received the thanks of the monk for his assistance, the hunter left his unsociable guest, much wondering at his morose and silent behaviour.

The moon had now risen, and the outcast reached without accident the level ground, and began to pursue his journey along the banks of the Reuss.

The sight of the river near which his crime was committed, added fresh anguish to his mind, and he wandered on in a state bordering on insanity; the very violence of his feelings accellerated his steps, and he soon left the town of Altdorf in the rear, and saw before him the lofty Alps, with the peak of the St. Gothard mountain standing conspicuously in the midst.

Still he moved onward, directing his steps towards that spot, which, if he passed, he would be comparatively safe. As he approached the pass in the mountains through which his road lay, his personal fears becoming gradually less, his mind had more leisure to reflect upon former events, and the memory of his act, which had been awakened recently by the sight of the river, arose with all the vividness of reality. Before him he saw his uncle staggering from the effects of the fatal blow he had dealt, and he again beheld him wreathing with torture, as Walter Eschenbach tore the spear from the body of his victim.

His overwrought mind no longer allowed reason to maintain her throne, and with horrid imprecations he began to apostrophize the fancied scene of blood.

"Monster," he cried, "give me my heritage—hah! that blow avenged me—what have I done?—sure it's my father's brother—my uncle.—Oh! villain! who urged you on to this? 'twas you—'twas you—tempters, avaunt!"

While uttering these last words, he plunged forward as if to strike some imaginary being, and stumbling over a piece of broken granite, fell into the waters of the Reuss.

As soon as he recovered his senses, he found himself stretched upon a pallet bed, in a small and dark chamber, into which the light only entered through a long and narrow perforation in the massive walls of the building, placed at some distance from the ground; through this opening a stream of light passed, which fell directly upon a small crucifix placed at the foot of the bed.

The light thus thrown upon the sacred emblem so powerfully illuminated the image, that when contrasted with the darkness of the other parts of the chamber, the spectator might almost imagine its luminous appearance arose from some supernatural cause inherent in the crucifix itself.

To the astonished eye and perturbed imagination of the wretched man now resting upon the humble pallet, the figure appeared not only as if shedding a holy light around, but magnified to the size of life.

Clasping his hands and bowing his head in token of veneration, for his enfeebled frame was incapable of raising itself in the bed, the conscience-stricken man appeared overcome with grief and remorse, and sobbed aloud, while he appeared to utter some inarticulate prayers.

He had not remained long in this condition, when he felt a gentle pressure upon his shoulder, and starting at the touch, looked up and beheld a venerable man dressed in a priest's garment, leaning over him.

"What cheer, brother?" he said in a gentle voice; "come, raise your head—look on that holy emblem."

"I dare not, it frowns upon me;—oh, take it from me, it sears my eye-sight,—I strive to pray, but cannot."

"Peace, brother, peace."

"Father, you have passed your days in peace and holiness, without a crime or care, save those ills we are all heirs to—such has been thy lot from youth to age."

"Such may be the lot of all who seek for peace."

"I sought for peace—for joy—friends I had, and revelled in the luxuries of life—but then came long days of weariness and pain. Ambition rose in my soul—by it I fell.—Ask me not, father, what my crimes have been, I dare not look on them myself—I dare not seek forgiveness e'en from heaven."

"Thy mind is troubled yet, thy body weak, and a clear head requires a healthy body;—another time we'll talk these matters over."

"True, 'twere better, for my mind wanders—but say, how came I here? The last I can remember was a roaring sound of confused noises—a painful feeling in my brain, and a bright flash of light before my eyes."

"We'll talk of that anon."

"Nay, now—how came I here?"

"One of the brethren of our order, brother, saved thee from the waters of the Reuss."

"The Reuss, said you, the Reuss? That dreadful name will ever rise before me."

The good monk, perceiving his patient's mind was becoming excited, succeeded in changing the subject, and directed his care for the restoration of his bodily health.

Days, weeks, and months passed on, but although the bodily health of the outcast was restored, the canker of his mind still preyed upon his soul, and depressed his spirits. At length he expressed his desire to the friendly monk to proceed on his journey, and bidding adieu to the peaceful community, he directed his course towards Italy, and after a weary pilgrimage, rested in the city of Pisa, where he entered a monastery of Augustin monks, and passed the rest of his days in the infliction of the severest penance, in the vain hope of quieting the pangs of his conscience.

But what became of his companions in crime? The castles of De Wart and De Balm were levelled with the ground, and all their inmates, although unconscious of any crime, put to the sword. De Wart himself was broken on the wheel, and while suffering under the agony of his punishment, he still maintained his self-possession, and declaring himself innocent of the actual crime, still justified the act for which he died: "a wretch, not an Emperor, had been destroyed, who murdered his liege lord the Emperor Adolphus."

The lady of De Wart remained in prayer upon the scaffold on which her husband suffered, until she perished for want of food, which she persisted in refusing. Walter, the last of the conspirators, died in exile, pursuing the occupation of a simple shepherd, and maintained his disguise until the hour of his death.

The chief agents, as we have already said, in the sanguinary scenes which occurred in revenging the death of Albert, were his widow Elizabeth, and her daughter Agnes, who, after having caused more than a thousand innocent persons to be sacrificed, founded a monastery in the place where the murder was committed, and had the grand altar placed upon the very spot where her husband fell.

CHAPTER XLI.

THE STANDARD OF LIBERTY.

But these are deeds which must not pass away,
And names which must not wither, though the earth
Forgets her empires with a just decay,
The enslavers and enslaved, their death and birth:
The high, the mountain majesty of worth
Should be, and shall, survivor of its woe.

THE troops of the Swiss in the neighbourhood of the pass of Morgarten were in hourly expectation of receiving news of the advance of the Austrians, but the preparations of their enemy appeared as yet not to be completed, and they remained unmolested in their cantonments.

In the mean time, a day was set apart to be spent in appeals to Heaven for the success of their enterprise, and the blessing of the standard of the new confederation. A plain between Rothenthurm and Sattel was chosen as the scene of their religious exercises.

The day was propitious to their wishes, and the whole army, in conjunction with the women and boys that followed it, were assembled on the plain a little after daybreak. The standard of the confederacy, attached to the summit of the stem of a mountain pine, was carried to the place on which it was to be reared by Tell and Erni, assisted by the strength of Hans.

It was a small hillock in the middle of the plain where this symbol of Swiss independence was placed; as soon as the united strength of the bearers had reared the lofty pole, and the sound of the hammer by which the wedges that supported it had been driven, had ceased, a breeze of wind sprung up, and its ample folds were displayed to the air. At once the shouts of the assembled multitudes arose, and reverberated from the hills; instead of appearing to proceed from the voices of not two thousand persons, they seemed like the united cry of an immense army. The whole assembly, as if by one impulse, paused, and looked suddenly round, as if in expectation of seeing armed hosts spring up around them.

The venerable priest of Schweitz now arose, and extending his hands towards the standard, poured forth his benediction upon it.

"As proudly and freely as you now wave over the heads of freemen, may the God of armies grant you may continue to wave over the heads of our descendants, for ages yet to come; may the sight of thee cause the Austrian despot to tremble in the midst of his armed hosts; and let not a deed of cruelty or cowardice be witnessed among those who now surround thee."

A loud shout again rose from the crowd, and a hymn was sung by the confederated army. All then addressed themselves to prayer; and after receiving the blessings of the priest, they separated for their respective quarters.

Tell and the rest of the leaders now repaired to the town of Schwietz; on their road thither they remarked upon the enthusiasm of their little army, which seemed to augur success to their daring enterprise,

"Reding de Bilberek," said Arnold, "will be able to assist us by his advice, you say, as to our mode of proceeding."

"He will," replied Erni; "although he has lived far beyond the age of man, his mind is still as youthful as in his fresher days. He remembers well the tyranny of the grandfather of the great Rodolph of Hapsburg, and the first connexion of the Waldstetten with the empire. There is not a passage in the mountain but he knows."

At Reding's house they saw that venerable man: his great age had rendered him incapable of bodily exertion, but his mental powers were as vigorous as ever. From him the young leaders obtained all the information they required, and returned to the camp for the purpose of putting their plans into execution.

The different passes into the country were reconnoitered, and small rude towers erected in their gorges, in which bodies of bowmen were placed to annoy the enemy, if they attempted to force their passage. Across the ravines which led to these passes, great stakes of wood were driven into the ground, wattled together so as to form strong pallisades.

The perfecting of these works occupied some time, and it is not to be supposed the enemies were inactive spectators of what their scouts had discovered was going on. The consequence was many conflicts, in which much personal skill was exhibited on both sides.

Hans Winklereid, whose spirits and intelligence seemed to rise with the necessity for their exertion, had been entrusted to superintend the construction of one of these wooden defences.

The width of the pass it was intended to defend, was greater than usual, and a strong beam of timber was requisite in the centre, to give sufficient stability to the structure. Among all the trees growing in the immediate neighbourhood, there were none of sufficient strength for the purpose, but far below, and almost on a level with the country occupied by the Austrians, there grew a young pine which appeared to the longing eyes of Hans to be admirably adapted to his wants.

This tree, therefore, our sturdy Swiss determined to obtain; at first thought of performing the exploit alone, and if his object had been merely to fell it, he would certainly have proceeded without a companion, but his late experience in his new trade of wood-cutting had taught him that its carriage to the required spot was beyond even his bodily strength.

Accordingly, he associated with him in his enterprise the two sons of Bernard, and together at the first peep of day they descended the ravine, and began their labour. They had nearly completed the object they had in view, and two of the party were guiding the ropes by which they meant to direct its fall, while the third was completing the work with his hatchet, when they saw three of the Austrian troopers approaching at a hard trot; they no sooner perceived they were riding towards the spot on which they were, than they placed themselves in an attitude of defence, and stood awaiting the onset.

The only rampart they could interpose between themselves and the horsemen, was the trunk of the tree they were in the act of felling, for they were at too great a distance from the refuge the ravine had to offer, to be enabled to gain it in sufficient time.

Onwards the horsemen came, sword in hand, and with loud imprecations threatening vengeance. Hans and his companions awaited them with the apparent determination of withstanding the shock, each wielding the axe he had lately used. But the wily mountaineers were too well aware of their inability to stand against the rush of the powerful horses of the Austrians, to keep their ground; they waited until the troopers were close upon them, and then suddenly springing on one side, the horsemen passed on without injuring them.

The speed with which the Austrians were riding was so great, that they were unable to arrest the course of their steeds, until they had passed several hundred yards beyond the tree; this gave time to the three Swiss to make some defensive preparations; two more blows of the axe brought the tree to the ground, and its thick branches formed an admirable rampart against their enemy.

The horsemen seeing them thus entrenched, rode round to the opposite side to take them in the rear; but the nimble mountaineers, before they could ride upon them, had passed through the leafy branches, and were again entrenched on the opposite side of the tree. Irritated beyond measure at being thus foiled, they were at length fain to dismount.

Seeing their enemies thus more on an equality with themselves, the Swiss left their woody screen, and appeared ready to act on the offensive or defensive, as the case might require. It was not long the impetuosity of the Austrians would allow them to wait, they rushed forward upon Hans and his companions as if ready to bring them to the ground by the first blow; but the cool determined demeanour of their opponents, each stalwart arm holding a well-sharpened axe, which glittered in the morning rays, caused them to pause, and they withdrew cautiously a few paces, confused at the sight of so unusual a weapon.

Again, however, the combatants came to close quarters, and many a deadly blow was dealt by either side, but with little advantage. The long sword of the Austrians, and their practice in the art of self-defence, would have materially tended to give them a superiority over the mountaineers, had not the length of their scabbards, which were more adapted for encounters on horseback than on foot, materially impeded their movements.

As it was, the activity and strength of the Swiss were evidently getting the better of their opponents' skill; at length, a well-dealt blow from the hand of Hans wounded the sword arm of the Austrian, with whom he was engaged, and who, falling to the ground thus desperately wounded, was placed *hors de combat*.

One of their enemies thus disabled, the odds were now materially in favour of the mountaineers; and the Austrians, finding themselves overmatched, succeeded in leaping into their saddles, and making their escape, leaving their wounded comrade and his charger at the mercy of Hans and his two companions.

The Austrians having departed, our little party perceived there was no time to be lost; they quickly lopped the unnecessary branches from the tree they had felled, and taking advantage of the services of the horse of the wounded man, eased their own labour by obliging it to drag their burden as far up the ravine as the nature of the road would permit.

They had just time to remove the trunk of the tree beyond the reach of the Austrians, even if they had been inclined to follow, when they perceived a troop of horsemen riding from the camp.

They had no sooner arrived at the spot, than they reconnoitred the road taken by the Swiss; but after duly examining the locality, deemed it most advisable to relinquish the pursuit; upon this they lifted up their wounded companion, and returned to the camp to report their mischance.

The tree thus obtained by the powers of Winkelreid and his comrades, was long after known, and pointed out to strangers, as the Palisado of Hans.

These labours of the confederates in every quarter of the mountains were eminently successful; and before many days had elapsed, the whole of the mountain passes, which it was thought advisable to fortify, were sealed against the approach of any foe, let them be ever so numerous.

These precautionary measures taken, and the frontier strengthened from the Red Tower, on the road to the Abbey of Einsidlen, as far as the Tower of Scholen, the confederated bands felt themselves in readiness to meet the enemy, let him appear in what quarter he might.

The ardent desire for liberty, thus aroused in the breasts of the nation generally was shared by a number of individuals, who, on account of some infringement of the laws of the various Cantons, had been banished their country. As soon as these men heard of the jeopardy in which their native land was placed, they advanced to the frontiers, to obtain permission to show themselves worthy of their origin, by fighting for the public weal.

The confederates, however, much as they stood in need of reinforcements, were unwilling to bend the law, on account of the altered course of events, and refused to admit them within the boundary of the Canton; but this refusal did not discourage their patriotic zeal ;—they took up their position beyond the frontier, in a position overlooking the pass of Morgarten, resolved to hazard their lives for a country that would not acknowledge them.

CHAPTER XLII.

THE NOTE OF PREPARATION.

By heaven it is a gallant sight to see,
(For one who has no friend, no brother there),
Their rival scarfs of mixed embroidery ;
Their various arms that glitter in the air !
What gallant war-hounds rouse them from their lair,
And gnash their fangs, loud yelling for the prey.
All join the chase, but few the triumph share ;
The grave shall bear the cheerful prize away,
And havock scarce for joy can number their array.

LET us now turn to the Austrian array ; not less inspired by a feeling of courage were the breasts of the numerous hosts that assembled under the shadow of the eagle of Austria.

The army itself was comprised under the head of two divisions. The heavy horse might be considered as the principal part of its force, and in any other situation almost, would have proved itself worthy of the character it bore. The ancient nobility of Hapsbourg, Lenzbourg, and Kibourg, had hastened from the borders of the Thur and the Aar, to join the banners of the Duke.

There might have been seen the Mareschal of Halwyll—always true to the House of Austria—bold in arms, but depressed by a deep-rooted melancholy, in consequence of having accidentally slain a noble adversary at a tournament.

Landenberger was there, breathing vengeance—the sons of the bailiff Gessler—Count Henry de Montfort de Tettang, the pride of whose race rendered him the implacable enemy of the Waldstetten—the youthful Counts of Thun and Lauffenberg, eager to dip their maiden lances in the blood of an adversary—with a hundred others of note, all anxious for the contest, and certain of victory.

But in the midst of the gay and glittering crowds by which they are surrounded, who are those, whose simple vestments of white and blue bespeak them of another country to those who fill the ranks of the army among which they are found ?

Those are fifty citizens of Zurich, doomed by treaty to swell the army of the usurper—yet anxiously yearning for their well-filled coffers, and their smiling families, left at home.

Such and so numerous were the enemies now assembled to overthrow the liberties of the simple Swiss, and again fill her vallies and cover her mountain sides with the victims of despotism.

The scouts of the Duke had been out in all directions, and returned to head-quarters with the same uniform report, that all the passes, with the exception of that of Morgarten, were so completely closed, as to render any attempt to force them useless.

Towards this one point, therefore, it was necessary he should direct all his energies. In order the more perfectly to be prepared for the passage of this only road into the country of the Swiss, it was necessary he should be well acquainted with the locality; and to this end, he determined, before active operations commenced, to explore all the intricacies of the route.

A small band of selected men were appointed to this service, sufficient in number to enable them to resist successfully any small detachments of the enemy that might endeavour to intercept them in their route, and yet not of sufficient force to alarm the suspicions of the main body of the Swiss.

These men proceeded to the performance of their task at an early hour in the morning. The sun shone brightly, as if ominous of the successful conclusion of their labour. But unused to the task of climbing the steep sides of mountains like those they now had to encounter, they soon began to find the duty imposed upon them more difficult than they had imagined.

It is true, a band of hardy men like themselves might have succeeded in passing, without any extraordinary effort, into the plains of Schwietz, if unopposed; but would the paths by which they were enabled to proceed be sufficiently accessible to a large army, loaded with baggage, armed to the teeth, and exposed to the harrassing attacks of a race of hardy warriors, whose liberty or life was staked upon the issue of the contest?

This question, if fairly answered, must have been answered in the negative. The path, as they proceeded, became more intricate and steep, and the rocks, which, until now, slanted slopingly upwards on either hand, began now to present their precipitous sides, and soon the overhanging cliffs threatened to overwhelm them with their frowning masses of rock.

As yet they had not reached that part of the mountains which, by common consent, was considered the boundary line between Zug and the Canton of Schwietz.

They were proceeding on their upward course, taking notice, as they moved on, of the intricacies of the route, and wondering, in their own minds, that hitherto they had been unmolested in their course, when suddenly a shout, which rung through all the surrounding hills, caused the whole party to stop; and, stout though their hearts might be, and capable as they were of meeting, without flinching, almost any danger, the loneliness of the spot, and the sudden nature of the interruption, caused every heart to beat more loudly, and every brain to reel.

The Austrians stopped, and the shout was repeated; they looked upwards, and a band of men, dressed in the garb of Switzerland, peered over the edge of the precipice on their right.

"What ho! you gaily tinselled men, what ho! what seek you here?" said the foremost of those above—"whence come you, are you Austrian? by your gay feathers I should think you were."

"Captain," exclaimed one of the Austrians to his leader; "I know the face of him who spoke. I have often seen him at the town of Zug."

"Well, and what then? he is a mountaineer?"

"He is one of those, who having broken through the laws of the Canton, has lived in exile; the place where he and his companions are posted now, is not in Schweitz."

"Ha! say you so? are they all exiles, think you?"

"I think they are,—they differ from the Schwietzers in their dress."

"Ho! countryman," exclaimed the Captain, addressing the mountaineer; "you are one of those oppressed by the laws of the state."

"Austrian? I am a Schwietzer."

"Aye, but an exile; exiled by those you call your countrymen."

"Well, and what then?"

"We come to overthrow their petty tyranny."

"And substitute a greater. No, Austrian! we have erred against the laws of Schwietz—true, we thought them harsh—but they were the laws; and, as they stood, they were administered; what would you more?"

"Persuade you that we come as your deliverers."

"You would protect us as the wolf would the sheep; we are about as well assorted."

"Rebellious cur! know ye to whom ye speak? The Duke of Austria, with twenty thousand men, is close at hand, and soon will sweep through all resistance; for yourselves, perched there, like vultures snuffing the air for carrion, an earlier fate awaits you."

With that, he addressed himself to one of the soldiers, and whispering his orders to him, the whole of the Austrian party filed off behind a huge mass of rock which shrouded them from the band of the mountaineers. The intention of the Austrian leader was to move forward, by what appeared to be a practicable path, so as to come upon the band of exiles in the rear, and attacking them thus at advantage, drive them over the precipice.

The patriots kept their position—the Austrians began to ascend the rocks—and, by dint of great exertion, attained their desired position. They found themselves upon the same platform of rock as the Swiss, but not so advantageously situated as they expected. Still they were evidently in a better condition than when below; and marvelled at the apathy of the mountaineers in allowing them to gain their present position.

Doubtful of the issue of the conflict if he attacked the exiles, and well aware of the importance of performing his task of exploring the pass without delay, the leader of the Austrians again attempted to bring the Swiss to terms.

" See," he exclaimed, " how easily we might drive your ill-appointed bands over yon precipice ; but still I hold out to you the hand of fellowship, and offer to avenge you all on your oppressors."

" We fear you not," replied the mountaineer ; " if you are willing to try our metal, come on."

Defied in this manner by a band of almost unarmed peasants, the pride of the Austrian leader would not allow him to restrain any longer the impatience of his men for the attack : but fighting upon level ground, and upon the dizzy verge of a precipice, were far different matters.

The Swiss, accustomed to their perilous situation, had merely to repel the attacks of their adversaries in the best manner they could, or act, when opportunity offered, upon the offensive. The Austrians, on the other hand, unaccustomed to the insecure ground upon which they trod, had their attention continually distracted by the care they were obliged to bestow upon their personal safety.

This diversion of the mind from the principal object in view, was productive of the worst consequences : it exposed them to the attacks of their half-armed foe, who, taking advantage of the inattention of an adversary thus off his guard, would seize upon him unawares, and hurl him down the steep sides of the mountain. In this inglorious manner many a man at arms of the Austrian party fell, dashed to pieces, upon the craggy sides of the mountain.

The ranks of the Austrians were thus thinned ; and as they became thus more equal in number to their opponents, they found more room for their exertions, and forming themselves into close order, they prepared to make a deadly rush upon the Swiss. The latter feeling themselves unequal to withstand the shock of the encounter, climbed the adjacent rocks and dispersed themselves in all directions as quickly as if they had been a flock of goats ; and before the wondering Austrians could well understand what had become of their enemy, their loud laugh of derision was heard from the summit of a rock above their heads.

Boiling with rage, the leader of the men-at-arms began to climb, what appeared to him to be the place of easiest ascent, and beckoned to his men to follow ; before, however, they were able to pay obedience to his commands, a fragment of rock, hurled downwards, by one of the mountaineers, struck him on the forehead, and he fell senseless over the precipice.

" Austrians !" exclaimed the man who first spoke among the mountaineers, " return to your proud Duke—tell him how well the exiled men of Schwietz can meet his efforts—tell him to dread the power of our congregated nation ;—we seek no more blood—return at once."

Struck with awe at the fate of their comrades and leader, the soldiers made no remarks in answer to the boasting threats of the Swiss, but returned as speedily upon their steps as the nature of the road would allow.

When they again reached the camp, and related the opposition they had met with from the small band of exiles, the rage of the Duke knew no bounds ; he cursed the cowardice of his men—invoked the wrath of heaven upon his adversaries—and swore that not a soul of those who fell into his hands, should escape with life; so great, indeed, was his rage, that the councils of those around him could scarcely induce him to refrain from putting his army in motion at once.

CHAPTER XLII.

THE ADVANCE.

Some say, he is mad; others, that lesser hate him,
Do call it valiant fury: but, for certain,
He cannot buckle his distempered cause
Within the belt of rule.

The behaviour of the Swiss exiles had not been unnoted by their countrymen: for the two sons of Bernard, and their companion Hans, had overlooked the strife, and were hardly restrained by their sense of duty, to abstain from a participation in the fray. Hans, indeed, was obliged to be kept back by main force; for no reasoning could persuade him of the propriety of looking on, while so stirring a scene was being enacted.

Although a sense of what was due to the law had prevented their allowing their exiled brethren to enter the territory, they could not help admiring the manner in which they had acted, and felt gratified at the idea of their soon being enabled to make out a case which should warrant their re-admission into their native land.

While the confederates were thus assembled, a hasty messenger arrived to inform them that the Austrian army was about to be put in motion; the messenger, on being questioned, stated, that as he was on duty, watching the movements of the enemy, and in their close neighbourhood, he heard a conversation between two of the soldiers. The purport of it was, that the late reverse of the Austrians, in the pass of Morgarten, had so worked upon his mind, that he was more like a maniac than the leader of a mighty army; although his preparations for attacking the Swiss were not yet completed, he insisted upon immediately commencing operations.

Once he had been persuaded to refrain for a time, but during his next paroxysm of rage, he had given positive orders for the cavalry to advance.

"The cavalry!" exclaimed Arnold. "The madman. Where are they now encamped?"

"Near to the lake—not far from the defile that leads to Morgarten."

"Who leads these troops?"

"Montfort de Tettnang."

"Ha! that proud young Lord; I know him well; there is not one who bears such hatred to the mountain tribes."

Tell at this moment entered, and joined the rest. As soon as he appeared, Arnold addressed him:—

"Tell, the madman Leopold begins the atack by offering up the

flower of his army to our just vengeance; would you think it—his cavalry, we are told, have orders to move on along that narrow defile by
the lake side, that leads to Morgarten."

"Why!" exclaimed Tell, in surprise, "there is scarcely room for
four abreast, and we can occupy the heights above without the slightest
danger—who brought this news? it is almost too fortunate to be true."

"Here stands the messenger; he heard it from the mouths of two
Austrian soldiers, who, more wise than their master, augured but ill
success, and shook their heads in doubt.—But see, here come's another—
'tis Hans Winklereid."

"Well, Hans, what news with you? Are the Austrians come?"

"No! but they soon will move; there is great bustle in the camp,
and all the horses are being caparisoned."

"Then there's no time to lose; let's all unto our posts; our plans are
fixed; they fall into the snare more easily than we anticipated. All
those with heavy arms will follow me," said Arnold.

Great was the joy of the little army of patriots when they heard they
were about to enter upon action, for they had already began to grow
weary of the inactive state in which they had lately rested.

Proudly did young Arnold look upon his little army as it passed in
review before him : first went a band of athletic men, with the ponderous two-handed sword swung at their backs—that weapon which,
wielded by the hands of the mountaineer, the gay and ardent
Austrian often afterwards had cause to dread, as it clove their glit-

tering arms in twain, and hurled to the ground the bravest of their chivalry.

Then followed those who bore the deadly halbert, somewhat resembling the Lochabar axe, which could be used equally as spear and battle-axe. The remainder of his small force were armed in various ways, many bearing huge clubs shod with iron, others swords, or any rude instrument of war circumstances enabled them to procure.

At the head of this small armament Arnold Attinghausen placed himself, and, according to a pre-concerted plan, proceeded towards the north, for the purpose of descending upon the Austrian by the pass defended by the palisado of Hans. Tell and his bowmen took up their position on the rocks which overlooked the narrow defile, by the side of the lake we have already noticed, as it was there expected the chief scene of strife would be.

While the fatal conflict, on which the future liberty of Switzerland depended, was thus on the eve of being waged, Gertrude and Hildegard remained at Altdorf, in anxious expectation of news from their lovers. The latter were so engaged in the necessary preparations for the fray, that even their pure love was placed in abeyance, to make room for the ardour of patriotism, which at that moment filled their bosoms.

The anxiety of the maidens increased daily, for even Hans, who, hitherto, in all their previous calamities, succeeded in conveying intelligence to them, had not made his appearance. Unable any longer to bear the state of incertitude in which they were placed, Gertrude determined to proceed at once to the scene of action.

" 'Twere unworthy," she said, " a descendant of the ancient nobility of Switzerland to remain here, sheltered, at a distance from those whose life's blood, perhaps, even at this moment, is being shed in our defence. We cannot help our friends, Hildegard, with our arms in the battle, but we may solace the wounded, and smooth the pillow pressed by many an aching head."

" I did not like, my lady, to express my own feelings," said Hildegard, " but I am delighted to hear we are to leave this place, and be nearer to those who risk so much for our welfare."

" Well, Hildegard, I am glad we so well agree on this subject, for I should have been sorry to have led you into any danger against your own feelings or judgment."

" When do you propose we should leave this place, my lady ?"

" Early in the morning ; and if we make good use of our time, we shall reach the town of Schwietz before the sun has set, and from thence 'tis but five miles to where the army rests."

In accordance with this determination, the Baroness and her attendant left Altdorf on the ensuing morning, and as the last rays of the setting sun still lingered on the snowy summit of the Myttenstein, they entered the town of Schwietz. The deserted appearance of this capital of the Canton, in which none but the aged and the young were to be seen, contrasted so strongly with its usual bustling state, that Gertrude and her companion felt their spirits subdued by the air of sadness which seemed to pervade the remnant of its population.

At the door-ways of the principal buildings might be seen aged men and women, surrounded by groups of children, greedily listening to the tales of the early exploits of the Swiss, and the cruelties perpetrated by the late agents of Austria.

Beneath the shade of a venerable lime, a party of aged men were seen, listening to the discourse of one yet older than themselves—it was Reding de Bilberek, the patriarch of the Canton, whose name we have already mentioned; towards this group the Baroness and her companion directed their steps. The party rose to receive them, all but Reding, whose great age rendered him incapable of paying that mark of respect to the descendant of the ancient nobles of the land.

"We are honoured, Lady Gertrude," said the venerable man, "by the presence among us of one so highly respected, at the sight of whom I almost fancy my youthful days have returned—when the ancestors of the house of Waldstein were regarded with filial affection by all the inhabitants of the Canton, who lived happily beneath their mild and parental sway."

"That such days should again return, or others as happy, is the constant prayer of the last feeble remnant of that house. You, no doubt, wonder, father, to see two females, thus unattended, wandering abroad in these troublesome times."

"I thought, indeed," returned Reding, "you were safely lodged at Altdorf; but if the Swiss swords are true to their owners, I doubt not you are as safe here, lady, as you could be in the most distant part of the Canton."

"I doubt it not; but even at this distance from the scene of action I cannot rest, and I seek your counsel, Reding, as to the safest plan I can pursue to reach the army."

"I fear, my lady, you could render but little service to our cause."

"Render no service, father? I cannot fight, its true, but I can help the wounded; and brave as our Swiss mountaineers may be, they are not invulnerable."

"I shall not combat your intentions, my lady, which are well worthy of the race you spring from. At Sattel was the army lately posted, near to the pass of Morgarten, but I expect to hear each hour of their advance to meet the Austrian, and see, here come's a messenger."

As he spoke, a mounted horseman dashed at full speed into the street, and reining up his steed, as he reached the spot where Reding and his companions were seated, dismounted, and gave a paper into the hands of the old man.

Reding, after he had perused the paper, turning to Gertrude, said, "It is as I expected, Lady; the armies soon must meet: young Arnold, with the chief part of the force, has moved towards Rothenthurm, to watch the Austrian's movements. Wait till the morning, lady: by that time some well-digested plan may be laid down; there is more news in this paper requiring consideration. We have ample room in Schwietz; and if you would deign to accept the shelter of my humble roof, it would be honoured."

Gertrude willingly agreed to this arrangement, and in company wit Hildegard she took possession of the apartment allotted to her.

As soon as the Baroness had retired, Reding, turning to his companions, exclaimed, "Here is wild news, brethren, from Einsidlen; hear what they write:—'Two men from Schwietz, accompanied by their families, before they joined the army, performed a pilgrimage to Our Lady at Einsidien. When they had concluded their devotions, four titled canons of the monastery accosted them, and taxed the Schwietzers with insolence and injustice, with regard to the late distribution of lands in the Canton. The men replied, 'they asked for nothing but what was equitable; that although they were noble, a Baron had not more right than a freeman.'

"'Upon this these reverend men drew their knives and wounded the two pilgrims. The women screamed—a large crowd collected—and in the midst of the turmoil our conntrymen escaped.'

"This, friends, is what they write, and ask advice how they had best proceed.—How say you?"

"These men of Einsidlen acknowledge for their head the house of Austria?"

"They do."

"Is it not plain this has been done to aid the Austrian cause?"

"I think as you do," said Reding; "and it were better, without more delay, to punish these rude monks, before they shall receive aid from the Duke."

"This counsel was agreed to, and the messenger was to be despatched in the morning, with instructions to Arnold, recommending an assault upon the monastery.

On the ensuing morning Reding made his guests acquainted with the state of affairs, and recommended them to remain in Schwietz until the issue of the attack on the monastery was known; but the Baroness would listen to no recommendation to delay her departure, and Reding, finding her resolved upon her course, forbore to press her further on the subject. Accordingly, under the escort of Arnold's messenger, Gertrude and her attendant proceeded towards Rothenthurm, where they expected to meet their lovers.

Great was Arnold's surprise at the sight of Gertrude; but the gladness which pervaded his heart was somewhat clouded when he thought of the probable danger she might incur when hostilities commenced.

Hildegard in vain looked round to catch a glimpse of Ernest, and her mistress, perceiving her distress, and unwillingness to ask a direct question concerning him, made inquiry herself for the young chamois-hunter, and learned that he was absent on duty.

CHAPTER XLIV.

THE MONASTERY.

.........................When the fight began,
Roused on a sudden from their drowsy beds,
They did, amongst the troops of armed men,
Leap o'er the walls for refuge in the field.

ARNOLD ATTINGHAUSEN having divided his small force into two battalions, proceeded with one half of his troops towards the monastery of Einsidlen.

It was not until the dusk of the evening had rendered the surrounding objects obscure, that he put his little army in motion; slowly and silently they moved along the road, until the lofty walls of the monastery showed their dark outline against the sky. Our little band of patriots now halted, and while the men remained hidden from view in the vicinity, Arnold himself, accompanied by two others, proceeded to reconnoitre the walls, to select the best place for the attack.

As they paced its boundaries, the stillness of death seemed to hang around; the gates were closed, and not a single sentinel was seen upon the walls.

"It seems," said Arnold, in a whisper to his companions, "an act of cruelty to attack them sleeping thus; but our own safety demands the sacrifice. We must prevent the Austrian gaining possession of this place, and bringing aid from Zurich. But here appears a place well fitted for our purpose; see, the walls are broken, and here is good foothold; you wait below, I'll try if I can reach the summit."

So saying, our young leader began to climb the wall; the ravages of time had so destroyed the masonry in many places, that he experienced little difficulty in the attempt; when he looked down into the deserted courts of the monastery, he could see no living being within its precincts; all the inmates had evidently retired to rest. Here and there, in different parts of the building, a glimmering light was visible in a casement window, but with the exception of this sign that it was inhabited, it had all the appearance of a deserted house.

"It were easy," observed Arnold, as he again reached the ground, "to find our way to the gates: think you we could open them? You Michael, have often been here: do you know the mode in which they are fastened?"

"If we could obtain the keys, my lord, it were easily accomplished; and they are in possession of the porter, who sleeps in a small building close within the gates; we could take them from him without causing an alarm, the task would be by no means difficult."

"In two hours," observed his leader, "their sleep will be profound: by that time our little army can be close beside the gates, and if us three could open them from within, the place would soon be ours, without, I trust, much blood being shed. Having thus ascertained the practicability of entering the monastery, Arnold and his followers returned to the little army."

Darkness now rested upon the face of the earth, and the friendly moon, as if to favour the enterprise of the patriots, shed no ray of light upon the scene of their operations; the stars themselves were only visible at intervals in the dark blue zenith, as with noiseless steps the armed band approached the devoted building. Having posted the soldiers close to the wall, and on either side of the lofty portals, Arnold and six chosen companions proceeded to the execution of the more dangerous part of their enterprise.

The wall offered but little obstacle to their progress, and they soon found themselves within the building. Cautiously creeping along the narrow passage which intervened between the buildings and the wall, they soon arrived at the little room, in which the porter who had charge of the keys, slept.

On looking through the window of the apartment, they perceived this functionary resting upon his pallet, and by his side, affixed to his girdle, hung the prize at which they aimed. The door was cautiously tried, but being locked within, it refused to yield to their efforts; they soon directed their attention to the window, which they found they could open with ease; but its dimensions were so narrow, that one man alone could pass at a time, and the distance at which it was placed from the ground, rendered the task still more difficult.

However, as there was no other method of effecting an entrance, except by forcing the door, the noise of which would be sure to alarm the inmates of the monastery, they determined to make the attempt by the window. Arnold undertook the task of entering first; but in springing to the ground, his foot slipped, and he fell; the noise occasioned by his descent awoke the sleeper, who, springing to his feet, seized a battle-axe which hung up in the apartment, and aimed a deadly blow at Arnold. Before, however, it fell, Michael, who had followed close to the heels of his leader, had reached the window; he was about to spring into the chamber, but seeing the dangerous situation in which Arnold was placed, he raised a huge club with which he was armed, and directing it with unerring aim against the forehead of the porter, felled him to the ground, just in time to save the life of Arnold.

All now had entered the room, and the keys were removed from the girdle of the prostrate man. Their next task was to open the door of the room, and effect their exit; but its keys were no where to be found; they searched the dress of the porter in vain. An attempt was made to return by the window, but the smooth face of the wall within the room rendered all their efforts useless; in this dilemma, the only plan they could adopt, was to break open the door at all risks.

This was soon effected, but not without considerable noise; they flew now to the outer gates of the building, and with the assistance of Michael's knowledge, unbarred and unlocked the fastening, and had just time to fling them open to admit their comrades, when the inmates of the monastery, roused by the noise occasioned by the bursting of the door, rushed from their places of repose, and gazed with fear and astonishment upon the group of armed men, which as torch after torch was lighted, seemed to increase in number, and grow before their astonished eyes.

The terror of the assembled ecclesiastics knew no bounds; the religious character of the place, they expected, would have protected them from so daring an attack; they fled before the confederates into the chapel of our Lady; but the miraculous character which was attached to the place, failed to alarm the infuriated men; in the canons of Ensidlen, they beheld no longer the ministers of religion—they merely regarded them as men, Austrians in heart, and joined in secret with their enemy, for the purpose of subjugating them.

The sacred vestments and the relics were overthrown, the registry and the rent roll burned, and the provisions carried away. No blood, however, was spilled, but the whole of the community were taken prisoners, and carried off to the head quarters of the army.

Having thus crushed in the birth the mischief that was plotting against them by the lordly canons, Arnold again collected all his forces into one body, and directed his course towards the mountains, by which the lake was overlooked.

It was with difficulty, Arnold could persuade Gertrude to remain behind at Rothenthurm, so urgent was her desire to be at hand during the battle.

"My dear Gertrude," he said, "your presence would impede my actions; I pray you rest at Rothenthurm; doubt not I bring good tidings ere it's long."

"I doubt it not; and therefore, Arnold, there is the less danger."

"It would be scarcely possible for you to follow the rugged ways we have to travel—nay, rest here in peace—there, God bless you, it shall not be long before you hear from me."

So saying, Arnold Attinghausen, with less real equanimity of feeling than he assumed, placed himself at the head of his troops; but often during his march did he look back, as long as the red tower of Rothenthurm was visible in the distance, to her its walls enclosed.

The pass of Morgarten, or the garden of the marsh, so called on account of the soil, was, at the time we are speaking of, much more difficult to traverse than at the present; at least, so much of it as formed the defile we have already noticed between the lake and the mountains. In some places, the sides of the hills slope gently into the lake; but in general, precipitous masses of rock rise almost from the margin of the waters.

The heights of Morgarten form a long piece of table land of rocks, which overlook the pass we have already noticed; and on these heights, the exiles, the women, and the boys had ranged themselves. The bowmen, headed by Tell, had scattered themselves over various parts of the rocks, and all overlooked the scene of action.

The Austrian despot was aware of the preparations made by the Swiss for their defence, and when his rage allowed him a moment's time for reflection, he plainly saw the hazard he ran in attacking the foe, thus protected by their natural fortification.

The Mareschal of Halwyll, on whose advice Leopold was wont to rely, when the violent passions of his nature were not in the ascendant, had almost induced him to postpone his attack upon the confederates until circumstances became more favourable. But again the youthful leaders of the cavalry, inspired with ardour, and enraged at the resistance of a small body of mountaineers, to the legions of the Austrian army, urged upon him the necessity of making head against the Swiss, and crushing them in the outset.

Following the advice of these evil counsellors, and of his own blind rage, Leopold determined on the mode of attack we have already noticed; and accordingly it was arranged that the cavalry, the flower of his army, should first move on to the assault.

Elated by pride and confidence, the Duke of Austria contemplated with pleasure the troops of well-appointed horsemen as they passed in review before him, and his swelling heart told him no force could surely withstand the powers of his long-famed legions, led on as they were by all the youth of the nobility, eager to distinguish themselves in the field of honour.

Many a youthful noble aspired to the honour of leading into the battle this division of the army, on which it seems all considered the fate of the day would depend; but the choice of the Duke fell upon Henry de Montford de Jetnang, whose ardent disposition, well known bravery, and the hatred of the mountaineers, seemed to point him out as the best fitted for task.

The day on which the fate of the Waldstetten was to be decided at length arose, and the first rays of the morning sun fell brightly on the helmets and cuirasses of the knights, and nobles who led the Austrian host. As far as the eye could reach, pikes and lances glittered in the morning light, and disclosed to the spectators the numerous hosts of which the army consisted; the first army which according to ancient, tradition, ever attempted to penetrate into the fastnesses of the Waldstetten.

As soon as the cavalry had put itself in motion, a shout arose from the assembled Swiss, as shrill as the wildest cry of the female eagle, when she discovers the loss of her callow brood. It ran along the mountain ridges, and was heard from every defile; innumerable echoes repeated the cry; and the wild birds of the rocks, startled at the sound, hovered over the heads of the armed hosts, and added their wailing notes to swell the discord.

The Austrians looked up in amazement for an instant, the horsemen reined in their steeds, as if unwilling to proceed, until the voice of their leader recalled them to a sense of their duty.

As the road they were taking became narrower, their army, instead of moving onwards in mass, were obliged to attempt the defile three or four abreast, according to the nature of the road. Then it was the danger into which they were running became apparent, and they moved on with palpitating hearts, and with the feelings of men who were walking above a hidden volcano.

The advance of the cavalry had continued for some time unmolested, and the leading horsemen had reached the extremity of the lake, where the pass assumed a more practicable appearance; the more experienced officers of the ducal army, looking in the mean time ominously at the rocks above, as if dreading the impending storm.

CHAPTER XLV.

THE BATTLE OF MORGARTEN.

Come, go we in procession to the village,
And be it death proclaimed through our host,
To boast of this, or take that praise from God
Which is his only.

It was not long before their expectations were realized: a sudden shout from the rocky platform we have already noticed was heard, and in an instant huge masses of detached rock were hurled over the edge of the precipice, and descending upon the Austrian soldiers, felled horse and man to the earth.

Their young leader, perceiving the snare into which they had fallen, urged his men to ride on with all their speed, so as to reach the extremity of the defile, where there would be more room for their numbers to act; but alas! he had discovered his error too late, and while raising his arm for the purpose of attracting the notice of his troops to the orders he was giving, an arrow, guided by some skilful bowman, entered his side, and falling from his saddle, for the wound was fatal, the haughty de Montfort became the first victim on that fatal day.

The fall of their leader tended materially to increase the confusion of the troops: and although some of his faithful followers attempted to raise his body from the earth, the task was useless, and trampled upon

23   B A

by the horses, who could scarcely maintain their footing in the marshy soil, the remains of the youthful chief soon became so much disfigured, as scarcely to be recognised as a human form.

Meantime the wild uproar of the women and boys, as they witnessed the effects of their missiles, increased the dismay of the troops, who, unable to offer any resistance to those who assailed them, struck from the backs of their horses, were either trodden down under foot, or suffocated in the waters and mud of the lake.

Tell and his bowmen performed their duty well, and the leaders of the army fell quickly by their unerring arrows, which thick as hail were flying in all directions; and many who escaped the missiles of the Swiss, were borne into the lake by their horses, now perfectly unmanageable, and there drowned.

The rout appeared now to be complete, their numbers impeding their motions, preventing the possibility of rallying, unless they could gain a more open space; to this end they still pressed onwards, and were assembling in considerable numbers at the extremity of the defile; but ere they could form into anything like order, the Swiss, under the command of Arnold, were seen in good order descending the sides of the mountain.

As soon as they reached the level ground, they formed themselves into a body, and rushing with impetuosity upon the distracted Austrians, put them to the sword, or felled them to the earth with their clubs. The nature of the ground prevented the Austrians offering much resistance, and in spite of many single acts of valour performed on their part, they fell easy victims to the enraged Swiss.

Armed with a heavy club, Hans Winklereid distinguished himself in the action, crushing, by the exertion of his herculean strength, the armour of the enemy, and levelling many a hardy trooper with the earth; in the heat of the fray, he had thrown himself into the midst of the enemy's ranks, and found himself suddenly cut off from his companions.

For a time he maintained the unequal combat, and maintained himself sturdily against the fearful odds he now had to encounter; but hemmed in by the horsemen, and weakened by his violent exertions, he was about to sink before the swords of his enemies, when a sudden rush from part of the Swiss opened the ranks of the enemy, and rescued him from impending destruction.

Ernest, whose duty on the hills had enabled him to overlook the scene of action, had witnessed the victorious career of Hans and his subsequent danger, and assembling a small number of his party, he rushed to the rescue of his sturdy rival; together now they fought side by side, and the annals of that day relate the acts of powers they each performed.

In the hottest part of the battle were seen the men of Zurich, who, for certain mean advantages in commerce granted to them by the Austrians, had arrayed themselves against their countrymen. Not one escaped to tell the tale of their defeat to their townsmen, but all fell beneath the swords of the Waldstetten.

Leopold, the haughty leader of the army, who looked upon his assembled forces in the morning as invincable, with difficulty escaped from the field, guided by a peasant through the most intricate ways to the small town of Winterthurm where he arrived with the pallor of death on his countenance and sadness in his soul. The remains of the army fell into the greatest confusion; and in less than an hour and a half, the Swiss, by the courage and ability with which they took advantage of the errors of the Austrians, without any considerable loss, obtained a complete victory.

Need we say with what feelings of joy and pride the confederated bands withdrew from the scene of conflict. The defeat of the enemy had been so complete, that pursuit was considered needless, and merely leaving a few men at the different passes, the whole of the forces repaired to Rothenthurm, and from thence to Schwietz.

When Arnold and his companions appeared in the presence of their venerable countryman Reding, they told him of the success which had resulted from following his advice.

"It is well," said Reding, "the blow was struck so quickly: the men of Lucerne unmindful of their interests have joined the Duke, and aided by the Count de Strasburg, are advancing now on Unterwalden with four thousand men.

"Comrades," exclaimed Arnold, "our task is not complete : the madness of the Austrian has no bound; we must to Brunnen instantly; there we shall find sufficient boats to carry us across the lake."

Without farther delay, the force of the confederates embarked at Brunnen, the wind was favourable, and heaven seemed to smile upon their efforts; so rapidly did their little fleet cleave the waters, that the sun had scarcely performed one half his course, before the little village of Buchs appeared in sight.

Directing their prows towards the landing-place, they soon disembarked, and ascending the high land by which the town is overlooked, perceived, in the hollow beneath their feet, the forces of the men of Lucerne. Without a moment's hesitation, the confederates attacked the Lucernois, who, unprepared for the encounter, (they were on the way to join the troops and the Count de Strasberg at the time) gave way at the first onset, and fled in all directions.

They now proceeded towards the town of Alpnac, where Strasberg and his troops were posted; the Austrian partisan no sooner heard the triumphant shouts of the Swiss as they advanced, and saw the standard of the confederation which he knew had so recently been spread in Schwietz, than the truth of the reports he had lately heard of the total defeat of the Austrians rushed upon his mind; he believed defence would be useless, and although the men under his command far exceeded those of his opponents, the sight of their confident looks and warlike bearing struck a panic into his soul, which he could not overcome.

Accordingly he ordered his troops to make good their retreat, while he himself, with a small body of picked men, endeavoured to stem the advance of the confederates,

The place he had chosen was admirably adapted by nature for this purpose; it was a narrow gorge in the hills, through which the Swiss must pass, if they pursued the main body of his troops. Here he posted himself and his determined followers, resolving to resist until the last, so as to enable the rest of his forces to escape.

With this determination De Strasberg distributed his little force to the best advantage, and his position seemed to be impregnable.

As soon as Arnold advanced to the spot, he summoned the Count to surrender.

"We have shed Austrian blood enough," he said, "and long for no further strife. We have shown your countrymen what the men of Switzerland can perform when fighting for their homes and liberty. The proud Duke himself fled before our forces, though backed by all his army.

"Switzer," returned the Count, "it was your native hills that conquered Leopold, not your men; look where I am placed; with this small band I can arrest your progress, retire at once, and when my men are once in safety, I'll leave this passage open; till then, not all your boasted courage can unseat me."

Confident in their prowess, and elated by their recent success, the confederates prepared to mount the pass, but active as they were, they found the Austrians too strongly posted to be easily dislodged. Several of the foremost had been already wounded by the Count or his men, and the issue of the contest seemed uncertain, when Hans, whose mode of action was generally independent, having parted from his comrades, had scrambled up the rock until he reached a spot above the Austrians. The latter, although their ranks had been thinned by the arrows of Tell, still maintained their ground, and still refused to yield.

Hans, who had not forgotten the havoc committed by the showers of stones poured down upon the Austrians at Morgarten, had evidently some plan of the same kind in his mind, at the present moment, to over-whelm his adversaries.

After reaching the spot he had gained, and carefully examining the rock, he retired for a short time, and then returned, bringing with him a strong wooden stake which he had torn from a tree growing in the neighbourhood; he introduced this into a fissure in the rock, evidently for the purpose of detaching a portion, and hurling it upon the heads of the Count and his party. His efforts, however, seemed to be ineffectual, for he was obliged to desist from his attempt.

He appeared vexed at the result of his efforts, and approaching the edge of the crag stood up in the act of casting down upon the Austrians the wooden stake he had lately used. At that instant his companions below perceived the rock on which he stood tremble; he endeavoured to retreat from his dangerous position, but in vain. The stone had been loosened by his former exertions, though not detached, but the addition of his weight proved sufficient to cause it to separate from its parent rock. The huge mass thus detached, fell down the face of the cliff with a crashing sound, tearing up by the roots the shrubs it met with in its course. On the heads of the devoted Austrians it fell, and buried the leader and three of his men under its enormous weight.

Hans Winkelreid at the same time fell with it, and almost by a miracle he rested on its surface, when it reached the ground, unhurt, but the moment after, a fragment which had been loosened in the fall, rattled down the face of the cliff, and striking Hans on the forehead, laid him prostrate. The Austrians who were unhurt, had fled from the pass, and the Swiss rushed forward in a body, to render what assistance they could to their countryman ;—but, alas! their aid was useless; whether the effects of the blow from the stone, or the concussion of the fall, life had become extinct.

CHAPTER XLVI.

THE PATRIOT'S GRAVE.

Here in the sultriest season let him rest,—
Fresh is the green beneath those trees ;
Here winds of gentlest wing will fan his breast,
From heaven itself he may inhale the breeze.

With heavy hearts for the loss of their comrade, did the confederates recross the lake, and again repair to Schwietz, bringing with them the corpse of Hans, that it might be interred with those that fell at Morgarten, in the field of Rutli.

Deep and unaffected was the grief of Hildegard at the death of her rustic lover, whose goodness of heart and devoted attachment to herself she could not overlook; for, although her love for another prevented her returning his affection, her heart beat warmly for his welfare when living, and bled with grief at his unhappy fate.

The last blow now given to the power of Austria, it was determined to pay such honour to those who fell in their country's cause as should best bespeak the gratitude of the survivors, and hand down to posterity a record of the glorious day.

To effect this, the bodies of those who fell in the battle were conveyed to the field where the confederates first met to confer on the liberty of the Waldstetten. A vast pile of stones was reared on the spot, to point out the place where their ashes were deposited, and a day appointed to celebrate their obsequies in the most imposing manner they were able.

On the morning of the appointed day, those who had to take a share in the ceremonial proceeded to Brunnen, where a vessel lay to convey the mourners by water to Rutli. The Sacristan of our lady's chapel at Schwietz was present, attended by the priests and choristers of the chapel. In the same boat were seated Tell, Arnold, Werner, and the other leaders of the confederation. In another vessel followed Gertrude of Waldstein and her attendant, the wife and children of Tell, and the families of some of the principal men of the Waldstetten.

As they rowed gently along the surface of the waters, a low and mournful ditty was sung, the burden of which was taken up by those who followed in the numerous boats with which the surface of the lake was dotted. The scene, the occasion, and the tone of tenderness in which the hymn was sung, affected all who heard it, and by the time they had reached the main land, and the field of Rutli was before them, there was not a dry eye in the crowd.

Here they all landed, and the ecclesiastics and their assistants advanced to the heap of stones round which they ranged themselves; the chiefs of the confederates and their friends sat apart, and the assembled multitudes clung to the rocks which enclosed the meadow like a swarm of bees.

The Sacristan raised the crucifix he held in his hand, and the whole assembly bent before the sacred emblem.

"Under this sign, countrymen," said the ecclesiastic, "was our battle waged : the God of mercy crippled the energies of the proud Austrian, and strengthened the mountaineer ; to Him is the honour due.   Nevertheless, countrymen, we have assembled to do honour to the memory of those who fell in the holy strife.   Their names shall be handed down from father to son, and inscribed on the records of Swietz, of Uri, and of Unterwalden."

"Whenever this day returns, these names shall be repeated in the hearing of the assembled multitudes ; listen."

In a loud voice the priest repeated the names of those who fell, and as each name was mentioned, the whole multitude exclaimed, "A grateful country prays Heaven rest his soul."

At each repetition of this sentence the crucifix was raised, and the people bent before it.

Erni, Werner, and Walter Furst stepped forward in front of the rude tomb, and raising their hands to Heaven, exclaimed with one voice, "By the ashes of those who rest beneath these stones, we swear to preserve our union inviolate.   Never to submit to a foreign yoke, or aid a despot to shackle liberty.   We swear this for ourselves and for our children—say, brethren, is it so ?"

And the whole multitude exclaimed, "We swear."

"Who, then," cried Werner, "shall ever enter the boundaries of the Waldstetten, or cross our rocky girdle, with hostile intent ?"

"No one."

Two boats were now seen to approach the strand, loaded with men attired in the native dress of the Swiss.   When the boats touched the shore, the Sacristan approached the margin of the lake, and having assisted the first of the men to descend, the others immediately followed, and stood upon the bank.

The priest, then gaining the centre of the meadow, raised his voice, and said,

"Countrymen—as the minister of the religion of mercy, let me be the means of restoring these exiled men to their homes.   At Morgarten they did good service—forgot what they considered to be their wrongs, and helped their country in its exigency.   Say, are they pardoned ?"

"As we expect pardon, so we pardon them," exclaimed the whole assembly, as with one voice.

"Friends," cried the priest, addressing the new comers, "your resistance to the laws is now forgotten ; receive the hand of fellowship from your countrymen."

The leaders of the confederacy then advanced, and grasped the hand of the foremost of their exiled countrymen, who, thus accosted, took their seats among the multitude, in the midst of the congratulations of the whole assembly.

Due honour having been thus paid to the memory of the departed patriots, a solemn requiem was sung by the choristers of the chapel.

REQUIEM.

With hasty step death presses on,
 Nor grants to man a moment's stay;
He falls ere half his race is run,
 In manhood's pride is swept away:
Prepared or unprepared to die,
He stands before his judge on high.

But sure that power who rules supreme,
 And guides the ways of man for aye,
Will list to gentle mercy's theme,
 And pave with heavenly joys the way
Of those in manhood's pride who fall,
Shedding their blood at freedom's call.

The music ceased, and after a parting benediction from the sacristan, the assembled crowds began to bend their steps homewards, each party taking with them such of their restored countrymen as had formerly resided in their immediate neighbourhood.

The boats with the confederates and their fair charge returned to Brunnen, and by the time they reached the shore, evening had closed in; but such an evening! the moon rode high amid the clouds, and the dark forms of the numerous boats that floated on the lake, were reflected in her silvery light. The war had passed away, and their native hills were free; sounds of merriment were heard in all directions, and happiness beamed from every countenance, cheerful fires were blazing in every house, and unwonted luxuries were placed on every board.

The Lady Gertrude had distributed with a liberal hand all that was necessary to enable the inhabitants of the village to celebrate the joyful occasion, and all looked up with eyes bright with gratitude to the highborn dame, as she passed the streets of the village after her disembarkation.

The war had passed away, and its dreadful clangour was no longer heard, amid the peaceful hills of Schwietz; the shrill horn of Uri was no longer uttering its piercing notes, except when sounded from the hill top to collect the roving cattle. Arnold Von Attinghausen, seated in the hall of his ancestors, was surrounded by the elect of the land, and the chief of his retainers. Gertrude, the delight of every eye, was seated near him, but although she endeavoured to maintain her dignity, she could not repress her looks of delight.

"At length, countrymen," said Arnold, "we are free from the yoke of the Austrian; shame would it be, if, after driving the oppression of the foreigner from out the land, we cherished it among ourselves; by the ancient laws of the country I hold a power over all my vassals, unfit to be held in a free land. I trust we have used this power with moderation, but it should not exist. Countrymen, let it be proclaimed throughout my lands, that all my serfs are free. How say you, Lady Gertrude, does my decision gain a smile from you?"

"With all my heart I thank you, Arnold."

"I well remember the words my uncle Attinghausen used, when chiding me for my attachment to the pomp of Gessler's court. Alas! his words had little influence on me, until thy gentle voice, dear Gertrude, urged the same arguments in more persuasive terms. I well remember how he reasoned: "Cast not thyself away," he said, "for tinsel and vain pomp. Thy nobility should be to boast thyself a chief among a free people; by love devoted to thee, these, in the hour of danger and of death, will still be true. These will resist the shock when tempests rage, and serve thee better in the hour of need than all the favours of the Austrian court.'—So spoke my uncle, and well I acknowledge the truth of all he said."

"The good old man," responded Gertrude; "he thought me faithless to my country's cause, and you too, Arnold,—he little knew the bonds in which the monster Gessler held me."

"Would he were here to witness the triumph we have now achieved! Oh! had he heard the sound that fell upon our ears at Rutli, it would have smoothed the pillow of his death-bed."

"Such as he was," said Tell, "our ancient nobles ever were, until the gold of Austria and its luxuriant tables altered their simple manners. Could they have known the pleasure that we taste sharing our frugal meal at home, amid the freedom of the rock and meadow, they would never seek the false glare of a court, where all is hollow, deceitful, and uncertain."

"Spoke like an ancient Schwietzer. Say, countrymen, how shall we best express our thanks to Tell, for it is to him we must attribute the mighty movement that crushed the Austrian power."

"His crossbow," said Stauffacher, "we will place within Our Lady's shrine at Schwietz, and all due honour pay the hardy bowman."

"Never more shall that weapon, which avenged a country's wrongs, be used to serve the hunter's purpose. When shall the ceremony of its consecration take place?" demanded Werner.

"This holy father, here, can name the day," observed Arnold, referring to the Sacristan.

"How say you, friends? There are two ceremonies to be performed in our holy chapel, in which two youthful couple are concerned; by their good leave, the day that sees them wed may be the day when the brave bowman's weapon is placed at the high altar, there to rest, a monument, for ages yet to come, of Unterwalden's hero."

"Does Gertrude give consent?" said Arnold.

"If my consent is needed, Arnold, even so; but surely, father, it will not be showing honour to the occasion, to let our simple bridal interfere with the more glorious purpose of the day?"

"Fear not, daughter: a holy contract between two of our ancient nobles now leagued with us, and bound to maintain their country's liberty, could not be celebrated on a day more auspicious, than that in which we pay due honour to a peasant's skill."

"Then be it so, good father; and yonder pair of youthful lovers shall share our joy; say, Ernest, is it so?"

"We should be highly honoured, my lord, but Hildegard declares it would be deemed unkind to Hans' memory to wed so soon after his sudden death, for he was faithful to the last, poor fellow; and though he was my rival, I would not do one act to slight his memory."

"I think," observed Arnold, "the fear of Hildegard is surely unnecessary: Hans Winkleried died in his country's cause, and all that could be done to honour his remains, has taken place. Come, let the same day suffice for all our purposes."

Thus, then, the acts that were to take place on the eventful day were arranged, and before the night had far advanced the guests of Arnold separated, and all retired to their respective places of rest.

CHAPTER XLVII.

> Have mercy, heaven!
> Nay, soft,'—twas but a dream,
> But then so dreadful, it shakes my very soul.

LET us once more turn to the Duke of Austria: overwhelmed with grief, despair, and rage, on account of his late defeat, he fled, as we have already said, and rested at length at the town of Winterthurn. His wearied body required rest after the fatigues of the day, but his agitated mind refused to allow that rest his exhausted nature needed.

In vain he rolled upon his uneasy couch and sought for sleep; his wearied frame would sometimes sink into a broken slumber, but no rest did it afford to him. The events of the preceding day, decked out in all the imaginative colours of a diseased mind, flitted before him in all their horror. He saw the flower of his chivalry crushed beneath the fall of huge rocks, while figures resembling what he might imagine to be the avenging ministers of heaven, seemed rending the mountains themselves asunder, to arrest his progress.

Suddenly the dream changed, and the bleeding form of Gessler beckoned him, and pointing to his wound, called upon him for vengeance; he called for help, and fancied himself in the midst of the waves, struggling for life—he clutched at an object that lay near to save himself—it was the disfigured corpse of Montfort de Tetthang, the pride of his youthful nobility; he looked around, and there lay the rest of his nobles, all bleeding and covered with blood.

The cries of the distracted man, while his mind was thus dreadfully agitated, were fearful in the extreme, and ere the morning light he was in a state of high delirium. For weeks did the fit remain upon him, and when at last intervals of reason occurred, his state of nervous excitement was so great, and evinced itself by the exhibition of such violent gusts of passion, that none of his councillors dared to approach the subject that had caused his malady.

And yet the necessity of taking some decisive plan with regard to the Waldstetten became every day more apparent; the Swiss still kept their passes closed, and a complete stop was put to the commerce of Zurich and Argau, for the greater part of their traffic with Italy had to pass through the united Cantons to reach the pass of Mount St. Gothard.

Under these circumstances, it was at length decided, at all hazards, to open the question to the Duke. The Waldstetten, although they still continued on the alert, had made no aggressive movement, and the Austrians were assured that so, long as their own independence was acknowledged, they were willing, as heretofore, to assist the duke in any wars he might undertake, if his efforts were not directed towards the country of the Swiss.

This forbearance on the part of the victors produced so favourable an effect upon the minds of the Austrian leaders, that they were anxious to conclude, at the least, a truce with the Waldstetten, until a more definite arrangement could be made. By degrees the subject was laid before the Duke, and although, at first, he could not be induced to relinquish his intention of making another effort to be revenged on the mountaineers, yet by degrees his feelings on the subject became more cool, or rather, they were directed into another channel.

Louis of Bavaria, between whom and the House of Austria the most mortal enmity existed at the present moment, overjoyed at the defeat of Leopold, had collected a large army, and entered the territories of Austria, laying the country waste in all directions; in vain had he been opposed by Frederic, the brother of Leopold, who, after a decisive victory on the part of the Bavarians at Muhldorf, was taken prisoner. As soon as this news reached the ears of the Duke of Austria, he took advantage of the forbearance of the Swiss, and concluded a truce with them until their differences were more perfectly settled.

The trade of the country again revived. Each man sought his own home, and enjoyed with unadulterated pleasure the liberty which had been achieved by his own prowess. Still, however, the precautionary measure resorted to by the Swiss of securing their passes against surprise, was continued, and persisted in for many years after these events. The morning after the renewed pledge of the confederates at Rutli witnessed none but smiling faces, and as it shed its cheering influence over the little port of Brunnen, all was bustle and activity, mirth and joy; all were preparing themselves for the ceremony of consecrating the weapon of the patriot Tell, by which the liberties of the country had been achieved; nor were those actors in the scene less interested in the approaching festivities whose individual happiness was to be at the same time ratified by the authority of the church.

Gertrude and her companion Hildegard, bound in the strictest bonds of affection by the dangers they had undergone in each other's company, appeared to have forgotten their relative stations in life, and confided their joys and sorrows to each other with all the familiarity of affectionate sisters. Free from the restraint of company, they each expatiated upon the valour and accomplishments of their respective swains—and many a friendly quarrel arose as to some particular perfection in which each conceived the man of her own choice excelled.

Then arose the momentous business of selecting proper attire for the occasion. The simple habits of the country prevented any approach to extravagance in dress, but did not forbid the exercise of the taste of the wearer. The upper vest of the Baroness was a tunic of a lively colour, nearly closed at the throat, and confined at the waist by a silken sash interlaced with threads of gold. This tunic, which reached to about the middle of the leg, covered an under garment of a different hue, and of the same length as the tunic itself.

Her feet were defended by sandals, secured by strings of silk bound in a symmetrical manner round her well-proportioned ankle, and ornamented at the points where they crossed each other with golden studs. Her hair, which fell in ringlets on her shoulders, was enclosed in the upper part of her head by a small cap or bonnet, of a form defying description, but ornamented with a slender golden chain and a heron's feather.

The dress of Hildegard partook of the character of that of her mistress, but was, of course, of less expensive materials, and more in accordance with her figure, less delicate in its proportions than that of the Baroness. She had substituted, however, the broad straw hat of the country for the more fanciful head gear of Gertrude; and thus attired, the mountain maidens proceeded to the apartment where their impatient lovers were awaiting them.

CHAPTER XLVIII.

THE CONCLUSION.

> Blest in kind love, my years shall pass away,
> Content with just hereditary sway;
> There, deaf for ever to the martial strife,
> Enjoy the dear prerogative of life.

ALL the taste of the population of Schwietz had been exerted in preparing the town for the occasion, when due honour was to be awarded to the saviour of their country. Their little gardens for miles round had been laid under contribution, and robbed of stores; a series of triumphal arches had been constructed along the road leading to the chapel of Our Lady, covered with flowers and green leaves.

The inhabitants were in their best attire, and garlands of flowers hung from every house; the interior of the chapel was in like manner decorated, and all the imposing ornaments of the Catholic church the little community could muster, were displayed to the best advantage.

At the entrance to the town, the priests of the chapel accompanied by the elders of the place, at the head of whom was the venerable Reding, awaited the arrival of Tell and the chiefs of the confederates. The populace stood aloof, occupying the most elevated spots they could attain, to have a better view of the proceedings. At length the cavalcade was seen to approach in the distance, and all eyes were engaged in watching its movements.

In the front, on foot, came Tell, holding his young son Walter in his hand, and carrying his cross-bow across his shoulder. Arnold, Werner, Furst and Erni, next followed on horseback, escorting in the midst of their party the lady Gertrude. Amid the group that followed, was seen the wife and family of Tell, and the blushing Hildegard attended by her faithful lover.

As soon as the procession reached the place were the elders stood, it stopped, and Reding approaching Tell, received from him his far famed bow. For a while, before he relinquished the grasp of his favourite weapon, he gazed fondly upon it, and appeared as if apostrophizing the object of his affection.

At length he yielded it into the care of Reding, who again placing it in the hands of the priest, observed—

"Holy Father, in all the people's presence I deliver into your charge this famous bow—an arrow from this weapon struck that blow which roused our country to enforce its liberties! let it be preserved, father, that after-generations may be taught by how weak an instrument the power of a tyrant may be overthrown."

The Sacristan received the bow, and raising it above his head, proceeded towards the chapel amid the acclamations of the people, who bowed their heads as he passed, as if before a sacred emblem. At length he reached the door of the edifice, and immediately he entered the choristers burst forth in a loud and solemn strain, which did not cease until he reached the altar, on which he placed the bow.

The music had ceased, and the Sacristan addressed himself to the assembly. "Brethren, the hand of God was visible when Tell directed the arrow against the head of his child, aad again was manifest when Gessler fell. To whom, then, can we consecrate this holy weapon but to him. See, brethren, above the altar do I hang the bow, that it may still remain in your remembrance, and that you may still give honour due to heaven, and not forget its agent, Tell, to whom our liberty is due."

The Sacristan advanced towards our hero, who stood in advance of the rest; and, motioning to him to kneel, placed a chaplet of oak upon his head.

"The honours," he said, "we bestow on those to whom the country is indebted, are emblematic of our native land and thy deeds. May thy race flourish, until the tree from which these leaves were plucked sinks to the ground from age, and may thy name be heard by nations yet unborn, and fill the breasts of other daring men with thoughts of liberty, if tyrants ever dare to oppress the tree—'Long life to Tell, the Swiss deliverer."

The whole assembly repeated the words, and Tell rising from the ground, confused, on account of the conspicuous situation in which he stood, was about to speak, when the attention of all was attracted to the door of the chapel. The crowd drew on one side, to discover what was going on, when a troop of girls, decorated with garlands, were seen headed, by the wife of Tell, bearing in their hands a broken pole, which supported the hat of Gessler.

With timid looks Charlotte advanced, and having received permission to speak from the Sacristan, she said:—

"Holy father, forgive the boldness which I show by this intrusion; but we have brought this emblem of the tyranny of the Austrian under which my poor boy's life was placed in jeopardy."

"Walter, bring forward that hat and pole," said the Sacristan; "let us preserve it: the instrument of tyranny it has been, henceforward it shall be the badge of freedom. But now, my brethren, another duty has to be performed."

The crowd drew back, and the two couple were left standing by themselves, and overcome by confusion, at a sign from the Sacristan they advanced to the altar, and the holy ceremony having been performed, Arnold taking Gertrude in his hand, turned towards the assembled groups, and addressed them. "Countrymen, the struggle is now over, and all within the states are free. I and my fair bride, among the ancient nobles of the land, now stand before you as simple citizens: we ask not other privileges;—the brand of slavery has been removed from all our serfs,—they all are free, and you have witnessed now the union of the free Swiss maiden to the free Swiss man."

The little chapel rang with acclamations, which the sacred nature of the edifice could not suppress at this acknowledged union between all classes of the Walstetten, when the noise had somewhat subsided, Gertrude appeared as if she would address the assembly. Blushing deeply as she was about to speak, but supported by her native dignity, she smiled as she said—

"Confederates, countrymen, will you then take me into your league? The happiest of you all, in your brave hands I place myself, and all my fortunes; will you protect me?"

"With our lives we will," exclaimed the whole.

We need not follow out the story, nor say how day by day the affection of Arnold and his fair seemed to grow with the growth of time; how the love of their dependants increased, as they became better acquainted with each other, until at length it knew no bounds, and willingly would they have sacrificed their lives for the protection of these remaining scions of their ancient line of Swiss nobles.

For the patriot Tell, he again found himself seated under his own roof, and again beheld with pleasure his frugal board surrounded by his smiling family. Again also did he betake himself to the chase, and breathe the free air of his native hills, in spite of all the remonstrances of his wife; and in his dangerous excursions he was still followed by Walter.

Of Ernest and Hildegard, and their numerous progeny, I need say no more, than that they were as happy as they deserved to be, and to the gentle readers who have accompanied me through this little volume, I shall address the words of the Scottish Bard, and:

> ....bid the gentles speed,
> Who long have listed to my rede.

> A garland for the Hero's crest,
> And twined by her he loves the best;
> To every lovely lady bright,
> What can I wish, but faithful Knight?
> To every faithful lover, too,
> What can I wish but lady true?
> And knowledge to the studious sage;
> And pillow to the head of age,
> To the dear school boy, who this day
> I've cheated of thy hour of play,
> Light task and merry holiday!
> To all, to each, a fair good night,
> And pleasing dreams and slumbers light!

THE END